CHARLOTTE VALE ALLEN

SOMEBODY'S BABY

MIRA BOOKS

MIRA

ISBN 1-55166-124-1

SOMEBODY'S BABY

Printed in U.S.A.

For Susan Baldaro

One

"I'm sorry I can't stay."

"It's all right."

"I love you."

"I love you, too."

"I'll call you tomorrow."

"Okay."

"I'd better run or I'll miss my train. I really am sorry."

"It's all right."

He grabbed his briefcase and made for the door. She followed.

"Call you tomorrow. Okay?"

"*Okay,* Mark."

He gave her a quick kiss, got the door open and hurried away.

She waited until the elevator door slid shut, then stepped back inside and closed and locked her door. Depressed and angry, she looked around the loft wondering—as she did every time this happened—why she didn't/wouldn't/couldn't put an end to the affair. It wasn't what she wanted or needed. And even though she obediently parroted the words each time he said I love you, she not only didn't love him, she actively wished either that there was someone she *did* love, or that she didn't give a damn about men at all.

In the shower, washing away the evidence of lovemaking only her body had enjoyed, she considered how she might spend her unexpectedly free evening. There were friends she could call to go to dinner or to take in a movie, even grab last-minute tickets to a Broadway show. But the idea of sitting down to go through her address book and phoning people only added to her depression. Toweling dry, she decided to work. She'd develop today's film and do the contact sheets. That would give her extra time tomorrow to do the printing of the Dunfield and Rubenstein sittings from the week before. With the finished prints ready for collection, she could go ahead and prepare the billings. Good idea. Work was always an answer. Her mood was improving already.

Dressed in a T-shirt and jeans, socks and sneakers, she went into the studio area of the loft to retrieve the three rolls of film from Katie's to-be-done basket. After taking a minute or two to put the first disc of *La Bohème* on the CD player, she headed for the darkroom.

With the glorious Puccini music filling the loft, she had just inserted the three exposed films into developing canisters when the telephone rang. The film now safe from the minimal light exposure that would result from opening and closing the darkroom door, she ran to turn down the volume on the stereo before picking up the receiver.

"That you, Snow?" asked an elderly male voice.

"It's me, Rudy," she said, simultaneously recognizing her mother's next-door neighbor and undergoing a spasm of alarm. There was only one reason Rudy Howell could be calling: Something had happened to her mother.

"I think you'd better come on up here, Snow," he said apologetically. "Your mother's had a heart attack, and it doesn't look good."

"My God! When? Where is she?"

"Happened a few hours ago. Lucky thing I was out working on the garden, and saw. Thought she just took a spill, but when I went over to give her a hand, I knew right off what it was. Called the 911 people, then gave her the mouth-to-mouth before the ambulance came. She's in the intensive care thing over at the hospital, and she's asking for you."

"God! I'll leave right away." She glanced at the time: coming up for seven. "Depending on the traffic, I should be there by ten, ten-thirty. Thanks for letting me know. I'm on my way."

"I'll tell her. It'll ease her to know you're coming."

"Thanks, Rudy."

Shaky and agitated, she turned off the stereo, then ran to the living area of the loft to grab a jacket, her bag and keys. Uncoordinated, she fumbled the keys into the two pickproof locks of the metal-reinforced front door, then bolted down the four flights of stairs rather than waste time waiting for the elevator. Once on the street, she took off at a run toward the garage three blocks away where she kept her car.

Stomach lurching, hands trembling, she paced back and forth while she waited for Mario, the young, ever-friendly attendant, to get the Volvo.

"What's up?" he asked, studying her face as he slid out of the driver's seat and held the door open for her.

"My mother's had a heart attack," she explained, and thought how odd that sounded. An attack of the heart, the heart attacked. She was desperate to be on her way.

"Hey, too bad." He bent to look in at her as she settled behind the wheel. "Listen, Snow, don't go drivin' too fast. You'll have an accident. Take it easy, you'll get there in one piece. Where you goin' to, anyhow?"

"Rhode Island."

"She'll be okay. You'll see. Go easy now," he cautioned, backing away as she belted herself in, pushed the stick into Drive and pulled out into the street.

He's right, she told herself, hands damp on the wheel as she headed for FDR Drive. I've got to calm down. Stopped for a red light at an intersection, she pulled half a dozen cassettes from the pocket in the driver's door, got one open and pushed it into the player. In the fifteen or so seconds of silence before the music began, she took several deep breaths, trying to steady herself. The lights changed, Pavarotti began singing "Che gelida manina," and she drove on, the exquisite voice filling the interior of the nine-year-old car. Rather than soothing her, the man's emotionally loaded intonation brought tears to her eyes and created a frantic clutching in her chest.

By the time she reached I-95, the inner quaking had abated and dread had taken over. Her mother was only sixty-three, too young to die. God knows, they'd never been as close as her mother would have wished. But if Anne Cooke had been less obsessively attentive, less vigilantly overprotective, they might have had a better, easier relationship. She'd never been able to make her mother understand this, particularly during Snow's teenage years when she'd felt stifled, suffocated, and had taken to answering her mother's ceaseless intrusions, interruptions, interrogations with, "Yes-mother." Privately, ruefully, she'd smiled to herself over this mild rebelliousness because what she was actually thinking and saying was, "Yes, smother." It was how she'd felt all her life: smothered, overwhelmed, deprived of sufficient air and space in which to grow. And that was why, periodically, she'd gulped down furtive mouthfuls of scotch or gin or vodka from bottles that remained otherwise untouched from one year to the next in the liquor cabinet; it was why she'd sneaked cigarettes down on the beach, getting dizzy and nauseated initially, and eventually hooked; it was why, at the age of sixteen, she'd gone to a motel in Providence with a local married man and spent that afternoon and quite a few subsequent ones indulging in sexual acts that were pleasurable primarily because of the distress they would have caused her mother, had she ever found out; and it was why, finally, immediately after graduating from high school, she'd left Rhode Island for the School of Visual Arts in New York.

They'd done battle over it, but in the end Snow had won out, threatening to work her way through school if necessary. Her mother at last conceded, but not before getting Snow's solemn promise that she'd phone home at least three times a week. A small price to pay for such a large victory. She'd kept her promise and, even now, at the age of thirty-one, was still in the habit of making those calls—just less often.

At a distance, she'd acquired an amused tolerance of her mother's eccentricities. However, within minutes of arriving home for a visit, she'd find herself becoming angry and defensive. It was an effort every time to maintain her equanimity when presented with incessant cautionary advice. "I hope you don't go out alone after dark." "Be sure to keep your car doors locked." "Are you remembering to put the chain on the door when you're home?" "Don't ever open your door to a stranger." On and on, endlessly, as if Snow's safety were the only aspect of her existence that was of any importance. Only incidentally did her mother ask about her work. Of far greater interest, and second only to her physical well-being, was the question of whether or not Snow had yet managed to find herself a decent man.

Her mother's face took on a glow at the thought of grandchildren, but Snow had as yet no interest in being a mother. She was the first to admit she hadn't managed to recover from the long-term effects of being her mother's child. And while she loved children, revered them, cherished their energy, their self-absorption, their completeness, she knew she had a way still to travel before she could even begin to contemplate parenthood. It was all she could do to restrain herself from surrendering to her ongoing exasperation, to stop herself from throwing the facts about her married lovers in her mother's face. There were moments when, as her mother rhapsodized about babies, Snow wanted to leap to her feet and scream that she'd never subject a child of hers to the kind of obsessive attentiveness that had wound up turning her into a soft-spoken anarchist prone to acts primarily self-punishing.

As well, given that her mother had been married only briefly— having been widowed when Snow was just a few months old—and given that in the intervening years she'd had almost nothing to say about her late husband—nor had she had so much as a single date— her abiding fear that Snow might wind up an "old maid" seemed not only disproportionate but also out of character. But fear it she did, vocally, and often. It was why, Snow reasoned, she had from the start of her sexual life taken up either with men who were set fairly permanently in their single ways, or who were married.

Mark was her fifth married lover. Unfortunately, he had from the outset embarked upon the gratuitous fiction that he would leave his wife for Snow. He seemed to feel it was what she expected, despite all her declarations to the contrary. It appeared to be beyond his comprehension that she liked him primarily because he was safely wed to someone else. He refused to accept this, even though it was to her mind fundamentally simple.

Being married, he couldn't leave sundry items of clothing in the loft, nor could he drop by unannounced at inconvenient times. He wasn't free to stake any claims on her, and she had no wish to be claimed like some prize yearling at a horse auction. Granted, she had to accommodate him on occasional weekday afternoons and evenings, but never without warning and never for more than a few hours. And, in view of the stringent limitation on time, their involvement was almost entirely sexual. Which was perfect, because the majority of his values and viewpoints were diametrically opposed to her own. He was good in bed and didn't, couldn't, take up too much of her time. She was repelled by the idea of having someone around constantly, crowding her and diminishing the available oxygen supply in her home. She'd had more than enough of that growing up.

It was well after dark by the time she crossed the Connecticut state line, but I-95 was lit for a good long stretch and she was able to relax a bit, concentrating less fiercely on the road. But the instant the tension in her neck and shoulders eased, she was gripped by the fearful thought that her mother might be dead by the time she reached the hospital. It revived the lurching in her stomach and, seeing the signs for a rest area ahead, she decided to stop briefly.

After gassing up the car, she parked and went into the Mc-Donald's to use the john before grabbing a coffee to go. As she was leaving with her coffee, she paused to glance at a "Have you seen these children?" poster. Three small smiling faces; family snapshots taken in happy times. God, she thought, heading back to the car. Where are you? What monster snatched you from the heart of everything happily secure? The posters, the milk cartons, the brown supermarket bags all emblazoned with those photographs were wrenching. Throughout the country there were grieving, terrified parents praying for the safety of their children. All Snow's life her mother had been ready, at a moment's notice, to join their ranks. She'd been so cautious that Snow had turned secretly reckless simply to balance things out. She was sometimes amazed to think of how lucky she'd been in escaping any real harm.

Before switching on the engine she organized the cassettes she wanted to hear: highlights of *The Marriage of Figaro,* duets by Montserrat Caballé and Shirley Verrett, Puccini and Bellini arias by Maria Callas, and *The Best of Play Bach* by Jacques Loussier. She felt a pang, aware that she'd inherited her love of opera and classical music from her mother, along with a passion for reading, and for visual images, particularly those of young children. Which was why she'd decided to focus on photography, eventually specializing in children's portraiture.

Rejoining the flow of traffic, she considered her work and the enormous pleasure it gave her. Those meticulously lit black-and-white studies literally thrilled her. She spent most of her time during a sitting arranging the lights and positioning the child or children if it was a group sitting. Because of the flawless purity of the faces she could use strong direct and indirect light to enhance the qualities she perceived. She especially loved the three- and four-year-olds—the rounded sweetness of their emerging features, their vitality and profound self-interest, as well as their tremendous curiosity. It was always difficult to get them to sit still while she and Katie kept up a stream of banter, encouraged them to listen to the bouncy music they played, and tried to get their clothes properly draped, the light and shadow balance perfectly attuned. In the six years they'd been working together, she and Katie had honed their techniques, moving quickly to complete the shoot before the children became bored and fidgety and their faces lost that wonderful inner light, shutting down with stubborn finality.

With a jolt, she realized she'd have to call Katie, let her know what was happening. And, damn it! She'd left those films in the darkroom. She'd ask Katie to finish the developing, print up the contact sheets, cancel the bookings for at least a week and reschedule them.

As she approached New Haven, she wished, as she had so many times, that she had a father, brothers and sisters, cousins, aunts and uncles, family members who'd rally around at a time of crisis. But there was no one. And it was why, she knew, her mother had made her the sole focus of her life. Anne didn't even have any close friends really, just the group of local women with whom she played bridge on Thursday evenings. Anne Cooke was an odd and solitary woman who had always claimed she had no particular need of other people. She was independent and self-reliant, financially secure, she'd explained early on to Snow, as a result of a carefully managed inheritance she'd come into in her late twenties.

One thing Snow had to concede: Her mother had been an emancipated female long before the majority of other women. She'd resumed her maiden name after her husband's death—hence their different surnames. "If you choose to be rid of your father's name," she'd told a ten-year-old Snow, "you may do so once you turn eighteen. I certainly won't object."

Because she felt it connected her in some nebulous way to the father she'd never known, she'd elected to keep the surname Devane. Besides, she'd always thought Snow Cooke didn't sound right. Bad enough to be called something as absurd as Snow—a name baby boomers automatically assumed had been chosen by stoned hippy parents. In any event, Snow Devane was becoming a well-respected name; she'd worked hard to establish herself, and couldn't see the sense of muddying the waters by changing her identity so late in the day.

Her thoughts returning to her mother, she felt guilty. She didn't visit often enough: It had been more than a month since she'd been home. When was she going to develop some genuine tolerance and stop responding so negatively to her mother's well-intentioned concern? Aside from the endless admonishments, Anne was a good person, well-read and generous, with a passion for movies. She'd acquired her first VCR in the late seventies and rented two or three films a week. She was one of the few people who could actually figure out how to program a VCR.

Anne Cooke was, Snow thought, forgivably vain. She took pride in her appearance and had a standing Wednesday morning appointment with Lillian, the Stony Point hairdresser. On her annual visits to New York, when she insisted on staying at a hotel rather than at the loft with Snow ("We both need privacy, dear."), she took at least two entire days each time to shop for clothes at Bergdorf Goodman and Henri Bendel. Unlike her daughter who was five-seven, rail thin, brown-eyed, with a mass of wildly curling carroty hair and pale freckled skin, Anne was a rounded five-two, blue-eyed, with permed short blond hair and tiny size-five feet. Mother and daughter bore no resemblance to one another, and Anne had assured her that Snow strongly took after her father who had been a very good-looking man.

Anne had rarely spoken to Snow of Aidan Devane. She'd rarely spoken of him at all. "It was a painful time, and I'm sure you understand that I prefer not to discuss it."

The only father figure in Snow's life was Rudy Howell, the rather diffident but innately kind man who'd lived in the house next door since the year Snow turned eight. His wife had died the year before he moved in and, he quietly told her in the course of a back garden visit that first summer, since they'd never been fortunate enough to have children and had concentrated instead on each other, he'd had to get away from the life they'd lived together in Boston. "Too many memories," he'd said. So he'd sold his home and his business, and bought the cottage and a sailboat—"Something I'd always wanted," he'd admitted shyly, as if confessing to a character flaw—and embarked upon a determined course of small daily pleasures: sailing on Narragansett Bay, walking the half mile into town to buy the morning paper to read over his breakfast at the Stony Point Café. He'd chat with Lucy LeGallienne, the jolly and rotund, middle-aged owner who proudly claimed Acadian heritage, and who knew all the comings and goings of the three hundred-odd Stony Point residents and loved good gossip as much as she did cooking. After this leisurely meal, he'd stroll over to the market to buy the day's food before walking home. He'd work on his garden for the remainder of the morning, or sit reading a library book at the kitchen table in the winter; on mild afternoons he'd take the Bull's-Eye out for a sail. Later in the day, he'd cook himself a simple meal before settling in the BarcaLounger to watch a few hours of baseball or hockey or football on TV. Two or three times a month, he'd change out of the khaki pants, sports shirts and deck shoes he routinely wore, put on a suit, tie and well-polished oxfords, and come next door to have dinner with Snow and her mother. And after dinner, they'd play Chinese checkers or dominoes or Monopoly. Snow had loved those evenings when Rudy Howell came to visit; it felt, for as long as it lasted, as if they were a family.

Rudy had been allowed to take Snow sailing on the bay that first summer after specially purchasing a bright orange Mae West for her, and after vowing to guard the child with his life. Until leaving home, she had spent the majority of her summer afternoons on the water with Rudy. They'd shared hundreds of hours of companionable silence on the boat.

Once a week every summer for twenty-three years, Rudy had come to their back door with an offering of fresh flowers cut from his garden. And each Saturday, year-round, her mother made a trip next door to give Rudy some of the rather dry cake, or crumbling, overbaked cookies she'd just made. If Anne had one real friend— in the sense of someone who cared, quietly and unobtrusively, but who cared, nonetheless—it was Rudy Howell. And Snow could picture him pacing the hospital corridors, waiting anxiously until she arrived. For some reason, the image of the lanky, seventy-one-year-old pacing back and forth made her throat ache and brought tears to her eyes. She really didn't want her mother to die. Despite having fought long and hard for the right to her own life, unencumbered and free of her mother's oppressive concern, she couldn't bear the idea of losing the one person who had always loved her unreservedly. Resisting the impulse to press her foot down harder on the accelerator, she drove on, fearful of what she might find upon arrival.

Two

As she ran from the parking lot toward the hospital entrance, the interior trembling started up again. Her lungs were so constricted she could scarcely make herself heard when she asked at the information desk for directions to the Intensive Care Unit.

This late at night the corridors were all but deserted. Finding everything surreal, nightmare-like, she hurried along the gleaming linoleum floors, daunted by the smell of the place, by glimpses through open doorways of ghostly white-gowned figures spotlit by overhead reading lamps, by an empty wheelchair parked by a nurses' station, by the sight of a man seated, head in hands, in an attitude of profound despair, alone in a row of orange molded-plastic chairs.

From moment to moment she had the feeling that came so often in dreams of being simultaneously a participant in and an observer of the unfolding scenario; she couldn't seem to get centered. Her mind craved an alternate reality, one less alarming, less threatening. Irrationally, she tried to keep her breathing shallow, hating the idea of ingesting the tainted hospital air that smelled of disinfectant and, underneath, the sweetish reek of decay.

As she'd imagined, Rudy Howell was pacing the floor of the waiting room next to the ICU. Eased simply by the sight of him—why had she never realized until that moment that she loved this dear modest man?—she embraced him, and stood for a few seconds drawing comfort from his lean, solid body and his perennial scent of the garden and the sea; rich earth and salt air subtly commingling.

"How is she?" she asked at last, her voice still thin as she took a step away to scan Rudy's face for clues as to what to expect.

"Holding on," he said soberly. "You'd better go right on in and see her. I'll wait."

There it was! Not in his face but in his words. She turned and rushed to the nurses' station.

The duty nurse directed her to the door of the unit, and in a hushed voice said, "It's good you managed to get here. She's been asking for you."

"How is she?" Snow asked for the second time as she tried now to read this woman's face, but couldn't. The pleasant features were carefully controlled, revealing only what was likely an habitual, generalized concern.

"I'll page Dr. Wu. He's attending tonight. It may take a while, so go ahead in and see your mother."

Obliquely the message was being transmitted by everyone: Hurry, there's not much time left. Snow was having trouble breathing, denial and innate optimism warring with her ripening sense of loss. Apprehension had her feeling as if she were approaching the brink of a chasm, or the scene of a terrible accident.

Standing in the doorway of the unit she saw there were three beds, only one of them occupied. Heart jolted, she approached this bed, eyes on the diminutive figure there. This couldn't be her mother; this person wasn't big enough. How ridiculous! Anne Cooke was petite. She'd always taken a certain inverse pride in her size, and Snow assumed it was a generational and cultural thing: Her mother had grown up at a time when females were encouraged to believe that tiny women were more sought after by men by dint of appearing to be in need of their superior height and strength for protection. From what, precisely, remained unstated. It was simply understood that women required protecting. Ironically, Anne had not only managed well without a male partner, she'd also taken on the role of protector traditionally expected to be assumed by men.

Snow tried to absorb the fact that the small, so-pale person hooked up to various monitors and machines that beeped and chirped, showing graphs and flashing numbers, was actually her mother. Fear was doing odd things to her perceptions. She truly couldn't recognize the woman in the bed, and she stared at the face on the pillows, trying to force familiarity to click in. Her mother's eyes were closed; a plastic contraption fed oxygen into her nostrils; lead wires ran from monitors up her arm and disappeared beneath the voluminous sleeve of the hospital gown; others emerged from the neckline, snaked across the sheet and out of sight. It was a scene from a science-fiction movie. Everything that particularized the woman was missing: her clothes and makeup, her jewelry. She'd been neutralized, depersonalized, rendered unspecial. Anne Cooke had always been a harsh critic of the medical system, insisting that the majority of doctors concerned themselves solely with symptoms, neglecting to consider patients as complete people. Now, seeing her stripped of all that had contributed to her external uniqueness, Snow thought perhaps she'd been right. Patients were packages of problems, not individuals, and now Anne had become a patient. Her healthy heart had misbehaved and the penalty for that was a loss of status.

Gripped by a need to restore to this woman some measure of what had been taken away, she found a sense of purpose. "Mother?" Moving closer, sorrow welling, she touched her mother's hand. She'd never seen her in a vulnerable state, never witnessed her suffering anything more serious than a cold. Anne Cooke had a history of exceptionally good health, and had viewed Snow's sundry childhood illnesses with skepticism and impatience, even fear; going so far now and then as to suggest that Snow was malingering. Oh, she'd done all the proper motherly things—cosseting and comforting, providing glasses of juice and ginger ale, allowing the ailing child to spend the day in her mother's bed—but even through the miasmic haze of a fever Snow had been aware of the displeasure she'd caused by falling victim to chicken pox, to measles, to bronchitis and influenza. Anne had little tolerance for weakness, of any kind. As a result of a lifetime's well-being, she failed to comprehend or to sympathize with those less hardy than herself.

Snow's favorite portrait of her was one she'd done during a visit home some eight years earlier when she'd posed her mother on the beach. Dressed impeccably as ever, in a crisp pale blue shirtwaist dress and smart navy-and-white spectator pumps, the breeze heightening her color and flattening the bodice against her full breasts, emphasizing her narrow waist, she'd looked like a Victorian matron, hale and proper. Seeing her now in this otherworldly place was bizarre, jarring. "Mother?"

As if drawn from somewhere distant by the sound of Snow's voice, her mother's eyes opened. Snow forced a smile. The eyes remained vague, unfocused for a long, bleary moment. Then they fixed on Snow and leapt to life. With features firmed by sudden urgent energy, her mother clutched at her hand, saying, "I was so afraid you wouldn't get here in time. I have to talk to you. There are things I must tell you."

"It's okay. We've got plenty of time. Take it easy. I'm here now, and I'll stay." Snow's smile became less forced. She knew this woman after all, knew the smooth rounded forehead, the wide-set blue eyes and elegant little nose, the deeply bowed full upper lip, the dimpled chin, the pampered perfect complexion; this was her mother. She pulled a chair close to the bed and sat down, again taking hold of her mother's hand. How childish and silly she'd been, overdramatizing the situation. Things would be fine.

"Listen! There's no time to waste. I'm not going to get out of here. I thought I'd have longer...years.... Stupid to assume anything, ever. I should've known that." Anne spoke in breathy bursts, visibly chafing at her lack of strength.

"There's all kinds of time," Snow disagreed. The hand inside her own was as delicate as a child's. Through the flesh of her fingers and palm she absorbed, fascinated, its dainty architecture and silky texture, the smooth length of the manicured nails. "I know this is scary, but you'll be home before you know it." It seemed right to acknowledge how scary it was, for both of them. "You'll see." Snow kept smiling.

The small hand turned and closed fiercely around Snow's; the face was transformed now by urgency and her entire being appeared to be straining toward Snow. She took a deep, raspy breath and said, "I have to tell you. I'm not your mother."

Snow automatically laughed. "Don't disown me yet. I know I haven't been too great about getting home for visits but..."

The grip on her hand tightened insistently, silencing her. *"Listen to me!* I've debated so long over whether to tell you. I...never mind. That's not important now. *I am not your mother."*

"What? Are you saying I'm adopted...?" Vistas of possibilities all at once spread before her; questions began slotting into place. In a kind of mental cul-de-sac, she latched on to the logic of the concept: If she'd been adopted it would explain the tremendous physical and temperamental differences between them; it would explain why she had no father and why she'd suffered such an egregiously overprotected childhood.

Anne Cooke was shaking her head again. "Not adopted," she said in a lowered but no less emphatic voice. "Understand this, it wasn't a spur-of-the-moment thing. I planned so carefully...not you specifically...just a baby. I had to have one. For months I'd been ready. It was so simple...a trip to the cemetery on Long Island, studying the headstones, finding the right one.... It only took a few hours. Then a visit to the town hall to get the birth certificate. Once I had it, all I had to do was find a baby to fit.''

''What are you saying?'' Was the woman delusional? Had they put her on some kind of hallucinogenic drugs?

''Just *listen!* I scouted...in department stores first, but that was no good, too many plainclothes detectives.'' Her free hand gave a brief dismissing wave; her eyes left Snow and fastened on some point in space. ''It had to be the supermarket, early in the morning when the young mothers did their shopping. They were everywhere...'' Her tone was rich with envy and resentment. '' ...the babies in infant seats propped in the shopping carts. They'd run to another aisle for a minute to get something they'd forgotten, or they'd step away looking at the shelves. I watched them all.'' Again, that deeply envious, resentful tone. ''...weeks on end of watching, deciding which one it would be. It had to be a girl, and the right age. The first time I nearly took a boy by mistake. Luckily, I realized, and left him. It couldn't be a boy. Not that I'd have loved him any less, but the birth certificate was for Snow Devane, a female infant. So I went on watching, waiting. Then one morning, I did it...went to the market knowing this was the day she always came.... I was prepared, had a big canvas carryall...took a cart, pushed it slowly along the aisles, keeping her in sight, waiting. The moment came. She looked at her list, laughed and shook her head, then went for something she'd forgotten. So easy. Luck on my side...the baby was sleeping...a few steps, one quick move, that's all. The baby was in the bag and I was on my way out of the store. Not too fast, just casually heading out. Into the car. Half an hour later we were on the highway, leaving New York behind.''

''What are you *saying?*'' Stomach knotted, Snow was having terrible difficulty assimilating what she was hearing; not wanting to believe, she was trying but failing to reject this tale as the drug-induced ramblings of a critically ill woman.

''September twenty-first, 1963. That's the day I became your mother. My will's in the desk. There's a letter explaining. I couldn't tell you...I thought after I was dead you'd find the letter.... I'm sorry, but I'm also not sorry.'' The dimpled chin lifted defiantly. ''You've meant everything to me. I loved you more than life itself. I know you'll never forgive me. It's why I couldn't tell you, even though I considered it...many times.''

"This doesn't make sense. It's the medications. Of course you're my mother. When you're back home and I repeat this story, you'll laugh...."

"You'll find out," Anne said enigmatically, gasping for air, eyes again on Snow, her expression one of naked pleading as the machines began beeping and chirping more loudly, faster. "I *love* you. Remember that."

"I love you, too, and everything's going to be all right."

"You have to leave!" a voice ordered, as a hand on Snow's arm urged her up out of the chair.

"But wait..." Snow protested.

"Leave now!"

A young Oriental doctor and two nurses came crowding around the bed. The nurse who'd escorted Snow to the unit now had a firm, almost painful grip on her upper arm and was propelling her from the room.

"Wait a minute! We haven't finished talking."

"Not now!" Snow was pushed from the unit and the door was shut in her face.

"What's going on?" Rudy asked, coming to stand beside Snow. Both of them watched through the window as the doctor and three nurses positioned a crash cart next to the bed. Inside the unit everything was frantic motion. "Aaah," he sighed, knowing. "Better come on with me, Snow. You don't want to see this." A gentle arm around her shoulders, he directed her back to the waiting room.

"She said she wasn't my mother, Rudy, told me this crazy story about kidnapping me from a supermarket." Her laugh had an hysterical edge to it. *Was* this real? Would she wake up to find it had been nothing more than a monstrous dream? But no. She could feel the floor, very solid beneath her feet; could feel her clothes, clinging in spots to her sweat-dampened skin. And Rudy Howell was gazing at her in bewilderment. "It's what she said," she told him, in the grip of near panic. Her body wanted to go in a dozen different directions at the same time. Her brain felt hot, swollen. She touched the top of her head, expecting to feel heat radiating from her skull, but it was cool. "What the *hell?*" she cried, profoundly distressed. "Rudy, why would she tell me something like that?" She wanted him to confirm that it was a form of chemically induced, temporary madness.

"Must be the drugs," he said thoughtfully. "They probably have her on all kinds of stuff."

"That's what *I* think!" she pounced, yet derived no comfort from this confirmation. Mentally she was scrambling backward over everything her mother had said, wanting badly to write it down so she wouldn't forget any of it. God above! What if it was true? Could that incredible story conceivably be true? Supposedly there was a letter that would verify it. No, no. A grotesque fantasy. And yet the longing in her mother's eyes and voice, the all but palpable envy and resentment she'd displayed when speaking of those unworthy women with their babies in the supermarket. That had been real. She wanted only to get back into the unit and hear more.

Rudy sank into a chair and sat studying his hands. Snow paced, arms folded tightly across her chest, chewing on her lower lip, wanting to scream. Her grip on reality had been drastically loosened. If that story was true, who was she? It *couldn't* be true. But if it was, if by some aberrant twist of fate circumstances had provided her with facts she wasn't meant to learn, perhaps for decades, it meant that somewhere there was a family who in all probability believed she was long dead. No, no. It was the drugs. That was the only rational explanation. Inconceivable that her conservative, cautious, zealously vigilant mother was a criminal, a heartless felon who'd stolen another woman's baby. Ridiculous, impossible.

Rudy was looking over at her, his brow furrowed.

"I don't believe it!" she insisted. "Whatever they gave her has affected her thinking, that's all. What's *happening* in there?" She walked to the door to look in at the ICU. The curtains had been drawn over the windows. Did that signify something? Such arcane goings-on in hospitals. You never knew what anything meant. No one bothered to explain what was happening. Not just patients were depersonalized, their families were, too. The rights you'd enjoyed throughout a lifetime ceased to exist inside a hospital. You became entirely subject to the dictates of the medical hierarchy. Either you obeyed or you were forcibly removed.

Rudy had risen and was standing by her side when the ICU door opened and the nurses emerged pushing the crash cart. Snow interpreted this as a good sign. They'd managed to subdue those wildly overactive machines. She'd be able to go back in and talk more with her mother, refute that implausible tale.

Dr. Wu stepped into the doorway, paused, then started toward them. "I'm very sorry," he said, and Snow's body finally gave in to its conflicting instincts and tried to go both backward and forward. She was steadied, held in place, by Rudy's encircling arm. "We couldn't save her."

"I want to see her!" Snow declared aggressively, as if anticipating an argument.

"Of course," said the doctor. "Please accept my condolences."

Snow couldn't speak, couldn't respond. The doctor nodded apologetically, his eyes liquid and gentle, then went to the nurses' station and began making notations on the clipboard he carried.

Snow stepped out of the circle of Rudy's arm and walked stiffly into the unit. She was hyperaware of her body, awed by its continuing ability to function. Her eyes felt stripped, as if of a previously unknown membrane that had diffused her vision. Every last thing had a razor-edged clarity.

Her mother hadn't been covered over with a sheet. Maybe they only did that in movies or on television. Irrelevant, irrelevant. The oxygen tube and the wires had been removed, the machines all shut down. Anne Cooke might have been sleeping, looking once again recognizably herself. Snow approached the bed and stood gazing at the motionless figure, suffering a kind of emotional seizure—grief, massive confusion, uncertainty. I'm the only one left. But maybe not, maybe not. If you're not my mother, who are you? Who am I? Do I in fact belong to someone else, some other family? Why did you do this to me? In spite of our differences, I loved you. You were my *mother.* You were all I had, and you took that away. What's left?

Wiping her eyes on her jacket sleeve, she studied the face of death, unable to accept the too-swift transition. She put a hand on her mother's arm; still warm. Warm. She turned toward the door thinking to call them back. They'd made a mistake. But no. Nothing pulsed beneath the flesh, no silent steady flow of blood fueled the stilled heart. Utterly inanimate. The warmth was merely residual. She turned back. Here, then gone; alive, then dead. So quickly. There was no magic to reverse it. The machine had shut down, ceased to perform.

All at once she was afraid and pulled back her hand, yet she was unable to look away from the lifeless face. Maybe it wasn't lifeless; maybe they *had* made a mistake. Anne Cooke would open her eyes and say, "Make sure you look underneath the car before you get in. I've read that rapists have taken to hiding under women's cars. And always, *always,* lock your car doors."

Were you overprotective because you were guarding secrets? Did you preach caution because of your own necessary overabundance, because you'd committed the crime yourself and so knew how very easy it was to steal a child? Did you steal me? Unstrung, panic raging against her ribs, Snow flew from the room into the corridor where Rudy was waiting, hands jammed into his pockets, head downcast.

"I've got to get *out* of here!" she told him, barely able to stand still, but keeping a lid on her emotions out of love and respect for him. He was no longer young; he'd had a traumatic day, lost a friend. She had no right to upset him further with wild speculations. "You should go home, Rudy, get some sleep. Tomorrow I'll make arrangements . . . the funeral, whatever."

"I'll help you with that," he offered.

"I'd appreciate it. I really don't know what to do." It was true. She'd never had to arrange a funeral; she'd never doubted her identity. She needed air and room to think. And she needed to find that letter. She saw in Rudy's eyes how much he'd cared for her mother and how much he'd miss her. For a second time he'd lost a woman who'd played a central role in his life. She wanted to commiserate with him but it would have to wait. "I've *really* got to get out of this place," she said regretfully, gulping down the sadness that was like some living thing trying to crawl up her throat. She had a hand on his arm, the worn cotton of his shirt reassuring to her touch, while everything inside her was violently churning. Like a small child needing to go to the bathroom she could barely keep from jiggling, all but dancing with the need to find some wide-open space where she could release some of the demented energy holding her in its grip.

"You go on, Snow. We'll talk in the morning."

"I'll meet you at the café for breakfast. Okay?"

"Sure. That'll be fine. I'm awful sorry about this."

"I know." She hugged him hard, kissed his cheek, then tore away and began running for the exit, more frightened than she'd ever been in her life.

Three

Snow parked in the driveway behind her mother's Buick, turned off the ignition and sat for a time looking at the house where she'd lived for the first seventeen years of her life. It was a very well kept, spacious white two-story clapboard colonial with the shutters and front door painted glossy black. A light was shining in the living room; it was on a timer and would turn itself off at 2:00 a.m. The house was programmed almost to run itself: timers on the lights, a thermostat that adjusted automatically to send heat or cool air through the rooms, self-defrosting refrigerator, self-cleaning stove, a coffee maker that, at a preset time, would grind the beans and then brew a pot of a predetermined number of cups. Over the years Anne Cooke had spent a lot of money modernizing the place, making it, by her standards, the essence of efficiency and comfort. Right then, sitting in the dark, the sight of it was reviving the claustrophobia Snow had experienced at the hospital.

Leaving the car, she crossed the road and walked down to the beach. The May night was chill with a gusty wind whipping up whitecaps on the waves. In the light of the half-moon she began to walk, but in moments—propelled by violently conflicting emotions—she was running, the sand hard packed and damp beneath her Reeboks, each step jarring her spine. She howled like something wild, head thrown back, cries erupting from her throat until, at last, she felt hollow. Her ribs seemed to want to collapse inward; her lungs heaved, as if laboring to fill her newly emptied interior. She wished briefly, fiercely, that she could just climb into the car and run away, flee from the need to deal with the countless details attending the death of her mother—or whoever she'd been. Funeral arrangements, legal arrangements, matters of fact still to be determined, all stood like squalling children demanding her attention. And she hadn't had a chance yet to call Katie.

She ran until she was out of breath and had a stitch in her side. Panting, she collapsed on the sand, wound her arms around her knees and looked out at the bay. Instead of helping clear her mind, the rising wind was giving her a headache. The flow of tears burned. She bent her head, blotting her eyes on the knees of her jeans, then gazed again at the water. The wind kept whipping the hair into her eyes and mouth, but she couldn't be bothered brushing it aside. She sat and listened to the crash of the breaking waves, trying to summon the energy to go home and find that letter in her mother's desk. There was no question of putting it off: She had to know the truth. Her mother, who claimed not to be her mother, was dead. The image of her, newly deceased in that hospital bed, sent a stabbing pain through her midriff. Snow wanted that final view of Anne Cooke, smaller than in life and in so many ways unrecognizable, erased from her memory. She shouldn't have insisted on seeing the body. But if she hadn't seen for herself, she wouldn't have believed there'd been a death. She'd always been pragmatically graphic—had to see and touch things in order to make them real. Still, if she hadn't been home to receive Rudy's call, she wouldn't have had to hear that deathbed confession....

Stupid. At some point she'd have got a message and come hurrying here in the middle of the night, too late to see her mother before she died. And then, in due course, she'd have found the letter. Her mother would be no less dead; and she herself would be no less shattered. No, she was not sorry she'd managed to get there in time. Regardless of what the future might reveal, there was a certain rightness in having been with her mother at the end, in having confronted death for the first time. She had seen it, touched it; it was real.

Suddenly she was in the center of a circle of light and, startled, raised one arm to shield her eyes.

"Oh, it's you, Snow." The light went off.

She lowered her arm as the police chief, Pete Briggs, dropped to his haunches in front of her. A no-nonsense, powerfully built man in his early fifties, he knew every last person in Stony Point and was universally well liked. She'd known him all her life, had gone to school with his son, Rod.

"Had a call from old Mrs. Hoover." He waved his flashlight in the direction of the road some hundred yards behind Snow. "Said someone was down here screaming blue murder. Not one of her typical calls, you know, with her complaining of raccoons on the back porch, or kids partying on the beach, but really feeling in need of a little company. So I came on down to check it out. That was you, huh?''

She nodded, embarrassed, having completely forgotten about dear old Mrs. Hoover and her peculiar hours, her tendency to start baking cakes at two in the morning.

"I guess I'd want to let off a few screams myself," he said. "I'm really sorry about your mother. It's a damned shame, young woman like her."

"Word travels fast," she said, surprised. Even for Stony Point this was some kind of record.

"We've been checking in with the hospital every hour since Rudy put in that 911 call," he explained.

"That was decent of you."

"Folks around here liked her."

"Did they?" Genuinely curious, she asked, "Why?"

"You're upset," he said softly, not in the least dismayed by her question. "It's only natural. You ought maybe to think about heading on home now. You'll catch a chill out here."

"I'll be going in a minute or two. Tell Mrs. Hoover I'm sorry."

"Sure. You want me to run you home? Or you could maybe come on back with me. We could put you up for a night or two if you don't want to stay on your own."

She looked down the beach, then back at him, touched by the offer. "Thanks, but I'll be okay, Pete."

Rising, he said gently, "Go on home now, Snow. You need to get some rest. Next couple of days're gonna be kind of rough. There's anything you need, don't hesitate. Okay?"

"I won't. Thanks."

"Go easy," he said, and walked away. A minute or so later she heard the cruiser start up, then drive off.

Groping in her pocket, she found a tissue, blotted her eyes again, blew her nose, and with a ragged sigh got to her feet.

When she returned home, dazed from hunger and fatigue, she got a glass of orange juice and some crackers and carried them to the living room. The house was, as ever, immaculate. The surface of the desk was polished and bare, the cubbyholes containing embossed stationery and envelopes; a gleaming silver tray held several fountain pens and a sterling letter opener. A fearful fluttering in her chest, she sat down to go through the drawers.

It was right there waiting: a legal-size manila envelope. On the outside in block letters was printed, Will. Inside was the will, a letter with her name penned on the envelope, and a piece of paper listing what she assumed were bank account numbers.

Afraid to open the letter, she got up just as the timer turned off the light. Frightened, she darted back to the desk to turn on the lamp there, then stood, heart racing, searching the darkened perimeters of the room. Not once had she ever felt afraid inside this house. But she did now. To hold off the shadows, she ran from room to room, upstairs and down, turning on all the lights. Then, back in the living room, she drank some of the juice and ate a cracker, all the while eyeing the letter. Heavy bond her mother ordered through Tiffany's, the handwriting as familiar as her own. She looked over at the hallway fully expecting her mother to call down the stairs to her to come up to bed—it was late, what was she doing down there? Nothing. The only sounds were those generated by the house itself—the refrigerator motor, the faint creaks of walls and wood floors as the dwelling settled, forever, endlessly, realigning itself with the earth—and those that entered through one or two slightly opened windows—the nearly inaudible susurrous lift of the curtains in the breeze, the rhythmic approach and retreat of the surf. Hands palsied, she picked up the sterling silver letter opener and slit the envelope.

My dearest Snow,

There's no easy or polite way to do this, so I'll come directly to the point. I am not your natural mother. I always wanted a child, but for reasons too numerous to list here, it wasn't possible. None of that is relevant now.

On Tuesday September 21, 1963 I abducted you from a supermarket in New York and brought you directly to this house. I'd made all the arrangements well in advance, including purchasing this property, and obtaining a false birth certificate for you.

I know this will come as a terrible shock to you, and I am sorry for that. You've given me more than thirty years of joy, and I did my very best to be a good mother to you. I hope you won't judge me too harshly. I did what I had to, and gave you everything, within reason, I believed it was your right to expect.

I won't ask you to forgive me. I'm not so foolish as to believe that's possible. But it's my sincere wish that you'll try to understand. Since you are reading this, it means I am no longer with you. If you find this letter in time for my wishes to be considered, I would like a nonreligious service with no eulogizing, just something short and simple. Then I'd like to be cremated and have my ashes scattered in the bay.

It was always my dream as a child to live by the sea. Being your mother allowed me to fulfill that dream. I've been happy here, and I think you were, too.

With all my love,
Anne Cooke.

It was true. True. Not the mother, not the daughter. Queasy now, she carefully laid aside the letter and picked up the will, but was too exhausted to make sense of the blocks of type. It wasn't important, could wait until morning. Somebody's baby, but not hers. Whose? And who was the dead woman in the Intensive Care Unit?

Leaving all the lights burning, she went leadenly up the stairs to her room, set the alarm for seven, turned off the light, and crawled beneath the bedclothes in her underwear. Her nerve endings were buzzing just below the surface of her skin, and the Volvo's engine seemed to be idling inside her, making her body vibrate. Through the open window she could hear the muted rush of the waves washing in to shore a short distance away, a sound that had always been comforting but that now served only to underscore her dread. Her entire life had been an illusion. The dead woman was a stranger. Who were you? she wondered, closing her eyes tightly. God! Who am I? Around and around, a mental carousel: Who are you, who am I, who *am* I?

The instant she'd silenced the alarm it all rushed back to her. The woman of the house was dead. Snow was entirely alone, and had no idea who she was. That deathbed image of Anne Cooke filled her mind, and she shuddered, pushing it away. She was bound to remember the woman; it was inevitable. But she was determined to remember her as she'd been in life. She would do that.

On her way to the bathroom she realized that, for the benefit of the townspeople, she was going to have to handle this as if she were, in fact, the grieving daughter. There was nothing to be gained from making public what she'd learned and upsetting the small community. But she'd tell Rudy; he'd help her. He always had. Once he'd moved into the cottage next door, it was Rudy, not her mother, who'd dealt with the sundry scrapes and gashes of her childhood, applying ointments and Band-Aids with a matter-of-factness that was beyond Anne's abilities. Until Rudy came, Anne had rushed Snow to the doctor for everything from slivers to bruises. No matter how minor the injury, Anne had reacted as if to a major disaster. Mortified, Snow had tended to dismiss the scrapes and bumps in order not to have to see the nurse roll her eyes at the sight of Mrs. Cooke dragging that poor kid in to see the doctor yet again.

Rudy had put a stop to that, his quiet competence soothing the mother and comforting the child. Eventually, Anne came to expect Snow to present herself to Rudy if she'd fallen off her bike, or slipped with the paring knife, or bumped into an open cabinet door in the kitchen. Rudy would help. Anne couldn't cope, got too upset. "It's because I love you so much," she'd explained. "I just can't *bear* seeing you hurt your poor self." Oh, is that right? the child thought. Okay, then. Imagine how *this* feels! she said silently, gulping down a mouthful of rye whiskey, then going reeling down the beach, laughing like crazy before she suddenly, violently vomited. Imagine how this feels! she intoned mutely, fingernails digging into the palms of her clenched fists as her twenty-nine-year-old married lover pushed himself inside her for the first time in a seedy Providence motel room. What d'ya think of *this?* she demanded, boldly walking the 3:00 a.m. Manhattan streets, seventeen and alone, daring danger to take its best shot at Anne Cooke's precious baby. God, the stupidity of it all! It was sheer luck nothing really bad had ever happened to her while she was busy taking risks only because knowledge of these acts would give her mother pain. Pointless and stupid. At least she didn't do things like that anymore. Mark, notwithstanding.

Dressed, hair still damp, she went to stand in the doorway of the master bedroom. Overcome by horrendous ambivalence, she felt sorrow on the one hand at the loss of the only family she'd ever known, and rage on the other at having been deprived of her real mother. Much as she wanted to from one moment to the next, she couldn't set aside the love she'd had for the woman who'd played out the role of her mother. "I loved you," she whispered to the thoroughly feminine room with its flounced bedspread and matching swagged curtains over pristine sheers. "I really loved you. Maybe you shouldn't have told me. Why the *hell* did you have to tell me? I'd never have known and I'd've been able to deal. How the hell'm I supposed to *deal?*''

She turned away and ran down the stairs, grabbed the letter from the desk, then left the house, heading up the road to walk the half mile to the Stony Point Café.

It was a clear sunny morning, still cool, but by noon it would be warm. Tricked by light and memory, she was a child again, skipping along on her way to meet the school bus at the crossroads. If she looked back over her shoulder she'd see her mother waving from the front door. Unlike her friends' mothers who came to the door in their bathrobes, holding a coffee cup, Anne Cooke would be dressed and made-up, with, perhaps, a written list in hand of errands to do that day. Until she was about ten, Snow hadn't known whether to be proud of or embarrassed by a mother who was so different. After the age of ten, she decided to be proud of her. That lasted for about two years before she changed her mind and was embarrassed, prompted then to engage in secret acts of defiance. Years and years of private conflict.

Passing Rudy's house, she was stricken by the sight of the half-dozen huge azalea bushes in full bloom in vibrant pinks and oranges and reds. The lilac tree at the far end of his front garden was heavy with fragrant flowers, and around its base was a tidy circle of lilies of the valley. The beauty of his garden was almost unbearable. She increased her pace, embarrassed anew as she went past Mrs. Hoover's house. In all likelihood the old dear had loved the drama of having a legitimate reason to call Pete Briggs. Snow smiled automatically, promising herself to stop by to see the eighty-four-year-old. Unlike the other kids in town who'd pretended Mrs. Hoover was a witch, Snow had grown up fascinated both by the woman and by her wonderful old house. She'd never objected to accompanying Anne on her regular visits when Mrs. Hoover allowed her to roam through the attic, searching for treasures. That was the thing about having a mother who was different: At a certain point, you had to accept that you were different, too, and go with it. And it wasn't so bad at all. Especially Mrs. Hoover's attic, with trunks and boxes full of mothbally old clothes and even a spinning wheel. Then, too, there were the fantastic cakes and cookies and pies Mrs. Hoover baked at two or three in the morning.

Once past the three houses on the point—her own, Rudy's and Mrs. Hoover's—the land on either side of the road afforded uninterrupted views of the sand beach on her right, and of the deep but narrow inlet to the left where most of the town's residents kept their boats moored. Rudy's little boat was there, and the sight of it affected her just as strongly as his garden had. I'm an emotional ruin, she thought. Got to get a grip on. But it was so hard. Raging one moment, sorrowing the next. Back and forth, dizzyingly. Her head was feeling hot again, as if her brain was boiling.

Lucy came out from behind the counter and held Snow to her mammoth bosom. "I'm just so sorry," she crooned, stroking Snow's hair. "It's a hard thing to lose your mama."

The café's patrons were all nodding sympathetically, looking on. Wishing she could stay safely swallowed in the woman's warm cushiony embrace, Snow managed to thank her as Lucy took her by the hand to lead her to the back booth where Rudy was waiting. Along the way half a dozen people offered their condolences, reaching out to touch her arm or her shoulder. Snow gave them watery smiles, fearful of the potency of her roiling emotions.

"You sit yourself down," Lucy told her, "and I'll get you a nice breakfast. Need to get a little meat on you, Red. You're lookin' way too thin."

"Get any sleep, Snow?" Rudy asked as she slid into the booth.

"A few hours. How about you?"

"About the same."

Keeping her voice low, she handed him the letter. "I think you'd better read this."

He glanced at the letter then at her. "So it's true, huh?"

"Evidently."

"I'll be damned." Reaching for his glasses, he read the letter once, then once more. Finished, he folded it carefully back into the envelope and passed it over to her, asking, "What're you going to do?"

"I don't know. Maybe get in touch with her lawyer...I don't know. Get organized, take care of the funeral arrangements. Then I'll start trying to unravel this thing, find out the truth. It's just so... I can't *believe* it!" Beneath the table she held her clenched fists on her knees, and chewed on her lower lip, swallowing down the angry sorrow.

"Hell of a thing. Can't understand it, to be honest." He took a sip of his coffee as Lucy brought over a cup for Snow.

"Food'll be up in just a tick," Lucy said, and went off to make the rounds of the breakfast crowd, refilling coffee cups along the way.

"Last person on earth I'd've thought could do a terrible thing like that," Rudy said in an undertone after Lucy had passed out of earshot. "I'm genuinely shocked. Here I thought I'd seen and heard just about everything. Goes to show you. How're you feeling?"

"Crazed," she whispered. "I can't believe she's dead, I can't believe she wasn't my mother. I don't *want* to believe any of it. I feel like screaming until my lungs explode. I'm so goddamned *angry*, Rudy!"

Lucy came bustling over to slide two heaping plates of food in front of them. Giving Snow's shoulder a reassuring squeeze, she said, "You eat all of that now. You're going to need your strength."

Snow looked down at the pair of eggs over easy, the four strips of bacon, the mound of home fries, the four triangles of whole wheat toast, and was surprised to find she was hungry.

"Looks good, huh?" Rudy chanced a smile.

She returned it. "It really does." You can't vent on him, she cautioned herself. Somehow you're going to have to keep the lid on tight.

"Don't worry, Snow. One way or another, we'll get you through it, find out what's what."

Eyes filling, she croaked out, "Thank you, Rudy."

"No need to go thanking me. Eat up now. Then we'll start getting things arranged."

Traveling from grief, to rage, to grief again in the time it took to pick up her knife and fork, she began dutifully to eat, the food forcing its way past the clotted emotions stuck in her throat.

"How's about if I get on to the funeral home, take care of that?" Rudy suggested as they headed back along the road to the point.

"You wouldn't mind?"

"Nope. I saw in the letter where she wants to be cremated, so there's no sense to running up a big bill for embalming and a fancy casket. We'll keep it nice and simple, the way she wanted. I was thinking, once it's done, you and me we'll take the ashes out in the bay."

Reaching for his hand, she said, "That'd be good. Thank you."

"Don't keep on thanking me, Snow. Whatever I'm doing, it's as much for my sake as yours. I spent a lot of time over the years with your mother. Now all of a sudden I find out I don't know who it was I was talking to. It's upsetting, and it's got to be a hundred times worse for you. So now—" he cleared his throat and firmed up his grip on her hand "—why don't you go make your phone calls and I'll make mine. Then we'll get together, look through her papers, see if we can't make heads or tails of this thing."

He left her in front of his house, promising to come over when he'd made some preliminary arrangements for the funeral.

She went directly to the kitchen extension to call Katie.

"Hey! Where are you? I tried you half an hour ago and got the machine."

"I'm up in Stony Point. Katie—" her voice went wobbly and high "—my mother died last night." Another emotional seizure was waiting to take hold of her and she had to take a deep breath, fighting it off.

"Oh, no! My God! That's awful. I'm so sorry. What was it, a heart attack or something? God! What a shock!"

"A heart attack, right." Snow blinked away the death image. "Listen, I don't know how long I'm going to be up here. Could you do some things for me?"

"Of course. What?"

"The film from the other day's shoot is in canisters in the darkroom, all ready to go. Could you go ahead, finish, print up the contacts?"

"Sure. What else?"

"Let me think. Phone and cancel all the appointments for the next week at least, see if you can reschedule for, say, after the twenty-second."

"Yup. Anything else?"

"I can't think. The billings for those shoots. Could you get them ready to go with the contacts?"

"No problem."

"You're great. I really appreciate it."

"You sound awful, babe. Listen, why don't I clear up this stuff, then get on the train and come up?"

"*Would* you?"

"Hey! I just offered, didn't I?"

"Katie, I can't tell you over the phone, but there's something very weird going down. I keep feeling like I'm about to lose it. Let me find the train schedule. Hold on." She put down the receiver and went to the utility drawer where her mother had always kept the schedule. "Okay. There's one out of Penn Station at 2:05 this afternoon that'll get you into Providence at 6:12. How does that work for you?"

"Fine. I'll be on it."

"Katie, could you maybe stay for a while?"

"Definitely."

"God, thank you." Snow exhaled tremulously. "Could you do me one more favor and pack up some clothes and gear, the Nikon body with the 50 millimeter, the medium wide-angle, the zoom, the small tripod, and maybe half a dozen rolls of black and white?"

"You're going to *work?*"

"No, I just want my stuff. Am I sounding crazy?"

"A little, but it's allowed under the circumstances. You want me to pick up your mail, dump stuff from the fridge, any of that?"

"Please. I'd forgotten. I'll have to check the machine, change the outgoing message. There's so goddamned much to think of!" she said angrily.

"I know it's rough, but take it easy, stay cool. I'll be there, and we'll get everything taken care of."

After the call to Katie, Snow dialed her studio number. She touched in her code, waited while the tape rewound, then listened to her messages.

"Hi, sweetheart." It was Mark. She felt something twist unpleasantly inside her. "Sorry, but I'm going to have to cancel tomorrow. I've got an emergency client conference. I'll call you later to reschedule."

The prick. "Call to reschedule," she repeated, disgusted.

The tone, then a hang-up followed by three beeps indicating the end of the tape. She recorded a new outgoing message, saying she'd be unavailable until after May twenty-second, and hung up, steamed by Mark's pomposity. "Reschedule," she repeated several times, making a face. What was she doing, involved with someone like him?

She had to disconnect the timer mechanism and refer to the instruction manual—twice throwing it across the room in frustration—before she was able to reprogram the coffee machine and get a pot brewing. Furious, she stormed into the living room and began emptying every cubbyhole and drawer of the desk. Dumping everything she'd found on the dining table, she got a cup of coffee and sat down to begin sorting through the papers but was so distraught she couldn't. She gulped down the coffee, got up to get more, stood in the kitchen glaring at the microwave, the top-of-the-line toaster oven, listening for footsteps overhead. Just silence. Her mother was dead, and she hated being in this house alone.

Four

By ten-thirty Rudy had completed most of the funeral arrangements, and he and Snow were seated at the dining table with cups of coffee, both of them gazing, mystified, at the stack of papers sitting between them—bank statements with account numbers that matched the ones on the list Anne had left, monthly statements from her stockbroker, utility bills and subscription renewal notices.

"Granted," Snow was saying, "I haven't *really* searched. I mean, torn things apart. But I can't believe that's all there is. Not a single personal thing."

"What about a safe deposit box?"

"If she had one, I don't know where she put the key."

"She must've had one," he said. "Stands to reason. Even someone keeping secrets big as hers has to have documents of one kind and another. Title to the car, the house, insurance policies, that kind of thing."

"Then where's the key?"

They looked blankly at each other.

"Guess you'll have to tear things apart," he said with a small shrug.

She was thinking, not for the first time, how handsome he must have been in his prime. He was still a good-looking man, with a full head of silver, side-parted hair, appealing laugh lines around clear blue eyes, a long thin nose, wide mouth and a strong, slanting jawline. His cheeks were rosy from hours spent sailing, and he had, overall, an aura of good health and quiet wisdom. She'd photographed him dozens of times. Her favorite shot was one taken on the Bull's-Eye—in profile, eyes on the water, his expression concentrated, serene.

"It feels sneaky," she said at last, looking over at the doorway, "as if she's going to come in any minute and catch me going through her things."

He nodded and ran his forefinger around the rim of his mug, saying, "I know how that is. But sooner or later it's got to be done. You'll find yourself some detachment one way or another, and box up her clothes and what-have-you, call the Goodwill folks to cart them off."

"Katie's coming later. I'll get her to help."

"Katie's coming, huh?" His features brightened. "That one'll turn this place upside down no doubt."

For some reason his fondness for her friend brought her to tears. She drank the coffee to ease her aching throat. "Katie loves a mystery," she said after a moment or two. "The only shows on TV she'll watch are things like *Unsolved Mysteries,* or *America's Most Wanted.* All she reads are mysteries and true-crime nonfiction. You know what she's working on now?"

"What?"

"She's actually doing a series of paintings inspired by *Unsolved Mysteries.* It's wild. There's one of an injured alien, this tiny pale creature being spirited away by shadowy figures in military uniforms—very powerful, believe it or not. Another is this family reunion, half a dozen seniors who were separated as children. It's very moving. She's bound to get a show soon. Bound to."

"It's good she's coming. You need friends by you at a time like this."

"I had the creeps being alone here last night," she admitted. "I kept thinking I heard strange noises." Managing a smile, she said, "I felt kind of like Mrs. Hoover."

He nodded, smiling. He'd responded often enough to late-night calls asking if he wouldn't mind coming over to take a look, she thought she'd heard someone creeping around outside. A good old soul, just lonely. "A house'll do that when it's been home to a strong personality. It's why I had to sell up and get out of Boston after Martha died. Wasn't any place I turned that I didn't expect to see her. You think you might sell up, Snow? No. Don't try answering that. I shouldn't've asked. It's too soon for you to know, and pure selfishness my asking."

"No, it isn't. I've been thinking about it. I don't know if I could sell this house. It's the only home I've ever had. You know? I mean, yes, I've got the loft. But that's a place I rent to live and work in. I've never thought of it as home." She took in the sunny room, reflected slabs of light partitioning the far wall. "I love Stony Point.

In high school, I used to listen to the other kids saying how they couldn't wait to get away, move to Providence or Boston, wherever, and I couldn't understand why they were so anxious to go. I mean, sure, I took off for New York but I had to get away. You know,'' she said, referring to the many conversations that had taken place in the secure privacy of the boat out on the open bay waters when she'd given voice to her need to escape, and Rudy had listened nonjudgmentally. "I love every last thing about this place—the beaches, the marina, Lucy's café, Mr. Willard's drugstore, Mrs. Hoover, all of it, everyone. Sometimes, it seems to me Manhattan's like this war zone. Dangerous, exciting in a scary way. It's as if I'm on assignment there, war correspondent or something. I don't know.''

"Big cities are like that. It's sometimes hard for me to believe I lived more than forty years in Boston. Well, now. You look worn out, Snow. Maybe you should try to take a nap. I told the funeral-home folks we'd be by this afternoon so you could sign the papers, make the deposit and so on. They're fetching the body from the hospital this morning. I said I thought you'd probably just have one day of what they call 'visitation,' that being tomorrow, and the funeral service Thursday afternoon. Didn't know how you felt about open or closed caskets, so I said we'd take care of that this afternoon, too.''

"Not an open casket!'' For some reason the idea alarmed her.

"Don't care for it myself,'' he agreed. "Find it kind of barbaric, but lots of folks I know wouldn't agree. Anyhow, Lucy's organizing some of the women, so there'll be food and what have you after the service. She'll let people know to come back to the café.''

"I hadn't thought about afterward,'' she said, daunted by the multiplicity of details a death entailed.

"Can't think of everything, especially when you're upset. The thing is people *want* to help. And you pretty much have to let them. It's their way of honoring the dead, showing they care. Sometimes, the only way you can show you're sorry is by doing practical things. Anyhow, Lucy's got it all in hand. So, what say we head on out about one-thirty? That'll give you time for a nap, if you want to take one, and something to eat. I'll heat up some soup and expect you, say, a quarter to one. Okay?''

Tears dripped off the end of her nose, and she wiped her face on her sleeve. "Sure. Rudy, you've been wonderful....''

"None of that. I'm happy to help. As I said, it's a way of paying last respects. And it takes my mind off other matters, questions I've got that don't have answers. It troubles me to think you've got family somewhere who don't know what became of you. Troubles me a lot." His jaw went tight and for a moment he looked as angry as she felt. Then his features relaxed, and he got up to carry his cup to the sink. "Try to rest," he told her as he opened the back door. "You've got a rough couple of days to get through."

She told him she would, then stood at the door and watched him step easily over the low fence between the properties, heading for his own back door. He paused a moment to wave before he went inside.

After switching off the coffee maker she stood looking at the array of papers on the dining table for a time, then turned at last and went upstairs. Funny, but in daylight the house was simply her childhood home, nothing the least sinister about it. At the top of the stairs she stopped, listening, expecting to hear Rudy's and her mother's voices in the garden below. She's dead, she reminded herself, stunned by the repeated impact of the words, and feeling a retroactive guilt for her failure to be properly sympathetic to those she'd known who'd sustained losses and whose prolonged grief had seemed to her at the time to be tiresome and self-indulgent. She'd been unknowingly callous. But then she'd never suffered any losses—at least none she'd been aware of. Now, stricken, she thought of the mother somewhere who had to have agonized for years, not knowing if her child was alive or dead.

"I don't even know my name," she said aloud, eyes on the window at the end of the hall where the curtains belled inward on the breeze.

How could the mother she'd known have done such a thing? It was a crime so frightful it didn't seem possible that dainty little Anne Cooke could have committed it. But she had. Without any evidence of conscience, she had confessed to creating unspeakable misery for another woman somewhere out there. And now, with her death, she'd created a new and different misery for that woman's child. A goddamned horror story, no less awful for being viewed in sunlight.

Suddenly, more than anything else, she wanted to know her name. As well, she wanted to know how the woman she'd loved, that woman who'd soothed Snow's childhood fears in cradling arms, and who'd wept at the sight of a skinned knee, could have been so absolutely, positively heartless.

Selecting a coffin and an urn to contain the ashes was grotesque, as was signing the sundry papers Ms. Brickman, the young mortician, passed over to her. The funeral home would, for additional fees, arrange for a casket-top spray of flowers, for an organist to play at the service, for an obituary notice in the newspaper. They would, in fact, take care of almost everything. Amazing. All Snow had to do was be present for the "visitation" the following day between 4:00 and 7:00 p.m. and for the service at two o'clock on Thursday. After the service, the coffin would be removed to the crematorium and she'd be free to collect the "cremains" on Monday.

At the mention of "cremains" Snow had to stifle a laugh, then at once apologized. The last thing she wanted was to give the impression she didn't care, that she took any of this lightly.

With a surprisingly sweet smile, Ms. Brickman said, "It's okay. I laughed myself the first time I heard the expression. Nobody expects you to give up your sense of humor because there's been a death in the family. You need it now more than ever. So, please, don't apologize."

"What made you choose this as a career?" Snow asked. She'd imagined she'd have to deal with some lugubrious, Uriah Heapish, middle-aged man. But this woman, who looked to be Snow's age, had been so helpful and pleasant she'd managed to make a disagreeable task relatively painless.

"A lot of people find it hard to believe, but I like it. I mean, I like being able to help at a difficult time."

"I appreciate it."

"Thank you. Here's my card. If you need anything, just call. I'll have the organist stop by tomorrow during the visitation to consult you on the musical selections for the service."

Pocketing the card, Snow shook the woman's hand, waited while Rudy followed suit, then they left and went out to the Volvo.

"It wasn't as awful as I thought it'd be," she said, holding open the passenger door for him.

"Yup. Nice young gal. Fella I had to deal with for Martha was straight out of a Charles Addams cartoon."

Surprised, Snow laughed and went around to the driver's side.

"What?" His eyebrows lifted. "You think I don't know about things like that?"

"That's exactly the kind of guy I was expecting," she said, fastening her seat belt. "I think maybe I'll adopt you."

"Fine by me," he said equably. "The one great sadness for Martha and me was that we couldn't have children. Tried for years before they told us it wasn't ever going to happen. For a time there, long ways back, I wished I had some kind of romantic feeling for your mother. But she always struck me as a tad too persnickety."

"Persnickety?"

"You know. Fussy, finicky."

"You thought that? How come you never once said so?"

"Come on, Snow. No one with any sense goes criticizing a parent to the child."

"I guess not."

"But since we're getting down to brass tacks, I might as well tell you I thought you were right to go off to New York. She kept you on too tight a rein. A few times over the years I tried to tell her she'd do well to try remembering what it was like to be young."

"I can't believe this! I'll bet she told you to blow it out your ear."

"Words to that effect. Impression I got was she had no idea what I was talking about, as if she'd never *been* young. But I'll give her credit, she wasn't one to hold a grudge. Some people, you go giving them advice on child rearing, especially when you've got no kids of your own, that'll be the last time you see them. Not your mo... not Anne. She just shrugged it off, as if to say, that's only your opinion. Then in the next breath she'd ask was I coming for dinner as usual Friday night."

Thinking about it, she said, "You're right. She wasn't someone you could imagine being young. She was so set in her ways, so straitlaced. She never really liked my friends, either, although she pretended she did. I knew she hated it when I had kids over, worrying we'd make a mess. So I stopped inviting them and went to their houses instead. It was as if she didn't want to share me with anyone. Now, I guess we know why."

"Don't forget her good points, Snow. I know that's hard right now, but she was generous, helped out a lot of folks in town. And she was never one to go throwing in people's faces what she'd done for them. She just did what needed doing."

"Really? How?" This was surprising news.

"Oh, she gave Lucy a second mortgage on the café back in '83 when times were tight. Wasn't for that, Lucy would've gone under. Helped Jane Fergus get that boutique of hers started, and loaned Rod Briggs his college tuition. Helped Matt and Dominic finance the marina. Never charged any interest, either. There's no question that what she did to you was evil, but maybe in her own way she was trying to make amends. Leastwise, I'd kind of like to think so. It paints a nicer picture of her."

"It's great she helped them, but I can't be objective about her right now, Rudy. I'm too upset, too angry and scared."

"Only reasonable you would be. How about a lime Coke at the café?" he suggested—something they'd done several times a week when Snow was growing up. He'd be waiting to meet the school bus at the crossroads, and they'd sit in one of the booths at the café, drinking lime Cokes while he helped with her math or science homework.

"I'd love it. Like old times, huh?"

He smiled, and she was assaulted by love for him, realizing in that moment how much he'd contributed to her childhood, how much she'd trusted and relied on him. Wasn't that what a father provided?

Since the day they'd met, some three weeks into their first semester at the School of Visual Arts, she and Katie had been the closest of friends. Never, before or since, had either of them met anyone who instinctively understood them so well. Katie was intelligent and funny and gifted; she was also angry about the status of women, somewhat alienated as a result, and generally dismissive of the symbols of status. While Snow had always been quiet and fairly subtle in her acts of rebellion, Katie had at once seen through to her anger. "I grew up with lots of divorced kids just like you," she told Snow. "So you didn't have a father. Get over it! It's nothing."

Katie's realism put things into perspective for Snow, and she was able to revert to being proud again of her mother—especially when Katie came to visit the first time and not only charmed her mother, but liked her, too. Of course, it was difficult not to be charmed by Katie. She was good-natured, witty and startlingly beautiful: olive skin, long glossy black hair, enormous melting brown eyes, a heart-shaped face and spectacular smile—the adored daughter of a Jewish mother and Japanese father.

"She's so lovely," Anne had murmured to Snow. "A lovely girl."

"She's decent, kiddo, and she loves the ground you stand on. Enjoy her," was Katie's advice during the train ride back to Manhattan after that first weekend trip home to Rhode Island. Remarkable what a difference an outside opinion could make. Once Katie came into her life, Snow's relationship with her mother became less effortful, more pleasant, and Snow was deeply grateful.

After leaving school, Katie had had a number of part-time jobs—taken to support her painting—and any number of lovers. Men were constantly pursuing her, finding her almost unbearably exotic. The majority lasted only a short while. Until Robbie, who was, Katie claimed, the only man she'd ever met who wasn't secretly scared to death of women and who also didn't subscribe to racial stereotyping. Periodically she fretted aloud over the discrepancy in their ages—she was almost six years older—but they'd been together more than three years now, and seemed content, despite her intermittent complaints about his impossible hours as a medical intern.

Where her career was concerned, it had been a long, difficult struggle. And finally, when she'd reached the point of considering asking her parents for a loan to tide her over, Snow had come up with the idea of hiring her to help in the studio. It was one of the best ideas Snow had ever had. Katie made things infinitely easier. The children enjoyed her, and she worked quickly and efficiently in the darkroom. While Snow did all the actual printing, Katie saved her a lot of time by developing the film and doing the contact sheets.

In the past year, Katie's paintings had at last begun to sell, and Snow knew she'd be losing her in the not-too-distant future. Given Katie's inescapable talent, it was only a matter of a short time now before one of the galleries gave her more than a place in a group show and let her have a show of her own. Then, she'd be on her way. She deserved it. She'd worked damned hard.

She came off the train lugging Snow's camera bag and a backpack. Snow ran along the platform. Katie saw her coming, put down her bags, and opened her arms. Snow wrapped herself around her dearest friend, gulping down sobs, while Katie held her, murmuring, "It's okay, it's okay."

When she could speak, still holding Katie tightly, she said, "God, Katie. Things are so fucked! I'm so glad you're here."

"I'm really sorry, babe. She was young. It's hard to believe."

Snow pulled away, wiped a hand impatiently over her face as she took in Katie's sympathetic expression, and tried to smile. Failing, she picked up the camera case, saying, "I thought we'd have dinner before we head back to Stony Point. Hungry?"

"When am I ever not hungry?" Katie countered, retrieving the backpack and trying not to let her shock show. Snow seemed to have lost ten pounds overnight and aged ten years.

Looping her arm through Katie's, Snow said, "I'm just so glad to see you. The past twenty-four hours have been a complete nightmare."

"I'm sure," Katie sympathized, slinging the backpack into the trunk of the Volvo. "When's the funeral?"

"Day after tomorrow. Italian okay?"

"Sure."

On the way to the restaurant Snow told her everything.

Katie listened wide-eyed, stunned. "That's the wildest thing I've ever heard! No wonder you look shell-shocked."

"Believe it! It's how I feel. Everybody's been so kind, sympathizing with the grieving daughter. And that's what I am, her grieving daughter. But, God, Katie! I don't know who the hell I *really* am, or who she was. I've never been so scared." She thought of her seventeen-year-old self walking the middle-of-the-night city streets, glancing into darkened doorways with low-level fear whispering along her nerve endings, and it was nothing, nothing. This was terror. This was finding out there really was a monster in the closet, and another one under the bed: every child's worst fears come true.

"I can imagine." Katie stared at the traffic ahead, trying to absorb the implications. Suddenly all kinds of things made sense, particularly Anne Cooke's visibly obsessive love for Snow. Initially, Katie had found it touching. But on subsequent visits, she came to understand why Snow had felt such a tremendous need to get away. The woman's love had been like an overheated room, stifling and oppressive, and Katie had been moved by the deference Snow had shown her, by the effort she'd made to reciprocate an emotion that was like an avalanche.

"If I could just find her papers. I've looked in all the obvious places, but so far, nothing."

"Leave it to me," Katie said confidently. "I'll find them."

Having hoped this would be Katie's response, Snow was reassured, and said teasingly, "All that true-crime nonfiction and those TV shows are going to pay off, is that it?"

"Are you kidding? Absolutely! You can learn a hell of a lot from them. I admit the shows are tacky, invasive, and represent journalism at its lowest level, but they're very informative. If there's anything in that house, I'll find it."

"I hope so. Otherwise, I don't know how I'll ever find out the truth. She claimed she took me from a New York supermarket back in 1963. Jesus! I'm listening to the words come out of my mouth, and it sounds so *bizarre!* Anyway, she said something about going to a cemetery on Long Island, checking headstones."

"Oh sure," Katie said knowingly. "It used to be a cinch to get new IDs that way. You'd scout around until you found the headstone of someone born around the same time you were, then you'd go to the city hall and ask for a copy of your birth certificate. Once you had that, you were set. With it you could get a social security number, driver's license, everything. They wised up, though, and you can't do that anymore. But thirty years ago? Definitely. I know this is horrendous for you, but it's going to be very interesting, Snow. Man! That's probably not even your name." Reaching over, she gave Snow's arm a squeeze. "That was insensitive. Sorry. I'm having a little trouble wrapping my mind around this. You must be going nuts."

"Feels that way."

"Don't worry, babe. We'll get to the bottom of it."

Snow got Katie installed in the guest room, then said, "I'm wiped. You won't mind if I head off to bed now, will you?"

"Course not. I'm kind of wiped myself from the train ride."

"I thought maybe we could start looking for her papers and whatever in the morning. The visitation isn't until four, and the only thing I have to do is run over to Janey's Boutique at some point to buy something to wear." She shook her head. "I'm standing here talking about buying black to wear to my mother's funeral." Starting to quake, she wrapped her arms around herself and looked over at the window. "Is it possible she just worked up this whole lunatic story to punish me or something for leaving her to go away to school and never coming back to live here again?"

"I really doubt that," Katie said, sitting cross-legged on the end of the bed. "Granted I didn't know her the way you did, but I've been coming here to visit for years now, and she always struck me as pretty tightly woven. I've got an awful feeling the whole thing's true. Partly because the two of you couldn't have looked less alike, or been more different, and partly because there's not one single, solitary relative. If you'd had a father who'd died all those years ago, like she claimed, somebody from his family would've turned up somewhere along the line. Don't you think?''

"I don't know. I used to wonder about that, but her explanations were so plausible. He was the only child of only children.''

"What about her? Did you ever even meet one relative of hers?''

Snow shook her head. "She disliked her relatives, she said, and had no interest in seeing them, and her parents had died long ago.''

"She had it all covered, but I think Rudy's right. She had to have titles and deeds, papers. They're somewhere, and we'll find them.'' Getting up from the bed, she went over to Snow and lifted the hair back from her face. "Go to bed, sweetie. You're falling on your face. We'll get answers for you. It just might take some time, but we'll get them. I love you.''

"I love you.'' Snow kissed Katie's satiny cheek, then, feeling drugged, turned and went to her room.

Comforted by Katie's perennial common sense, and by her presence in the house, Snow curled up on her side in her childhood bed, closed her eyes, and allowed herself to be lulled to sleep by the night breeze wafting through the open window and the sound of the in-rushing waves.

Five

Katie awakened her with a cup of coffee, complaining, "It took me a good twenty minutes to figure out the instructions for that idiotic space-age coffee maker."

Snow laughed. "I know. Me, too." She sat up and took a sip of the coffee.

"You look better," Katie said, perching on the side of the bed. Her glossy hair was plaited into a long braid and she was wearing an oversize bright red T-shirt. Across its front in large black letters was printed Never Book A Judge By Its Color. "I had a look around while I was waiting for the machine to do its magic and, you know, this is a really nice house. I mean, the basic structure. The furnishings are a bit too *House and Garden,* but not totally terrible. You could do a lot with this place, if you wanted to."

Snow heard the question, and said, "I'm going to keep it. But that's all I know."

"Yeah. I kind of thought you might. Okay." Katie climbed off the bed. "I'm going to throw some breakfast together. There's enough food in that kitchen to feed a family of five for six months. Did she always stock up like that?"

"Always."

"Maybe she was one of those Depression kids, although she struck me as someone who came from money. Still, you never can tell. So, we'll eat, then start searching. Okay?"

"Fine. I'll brush my teeth and be right down."

Halfway to the door, Katie stopped. "Does it bother you, people referring to her as your mother?"

"It's who I thought she was. I have to admit 'mother' doesn't mean quite what it used to, but don't worry about it."

"I just don't want to go blithely tromping on your emotions. The thing is, you're not wrong. This really is weird. I mean, if I hadn't read that letter... Okay. I'll go cook. You do definitely look better."

Snow padded into the bathroom where she examined her reflection briefly, never comfortable with the sight of herself. She turned abruptly away from the mirror as that deathbed image flashed again in her mind, resurrecting the grief. Then anger mixed with anxiety edged in beside it, the combination threatening to immobilize her. The white ceramic tiles cold under her bare feet, a new image took shape, that of a young woman confronting with horror an empty infant seat in a supermarket shopping cart. Too terrible. Grabbing a barrette, she clipped her hair back, then reached for her toothbrush. She wound up sobbing, swallowing half a mouthful of minty foam and, like a high school coach before a football game, pep-talked herself out of being overwhelmed by the fear and confusion and wrenching sadness. She gave herself a shake, put more toothpaste on the brush and started again.

Over eggs scrambled with scallions and cheddar cheese, crisp bacon and toast, Katie said, "After some serious thought on the subject, it's my opinion the lady of the house had a hidey-hole, and she had it close to her. She wouldn't have taken the chance of having you, as a little kid, happening on to it."

Snow pictured herself peeking in her mother's dresser drawers, in her closet, and could see Katie's point. "Okay. So?"

"Therefore, it's got to be somewhere in the master suite. And that's where I think we should start. We'll empty every drawer, take everything out of the closet, go through the clothes and stuff, then start checking the walls and floor, inch by inch. Why're you looking like that?"

"Like what?"

"Like it's visiting day at the bughouse and you can't believe what you're seeing through the safety glass."

"The walls and floors?"

"Definitely. More coffee?" Katie lifted the carafe.

"Okay, thanks. Good breakfast."

"Yeah," Katie said absently, refilling both their cups before putting down the carafe. She was relieved to see Snow visibly less fraught, less aged, back to looking remarkably like Rossetti's portrait of Fanny Cornforth, *Bocca Baciata.* Years before, Katie had been admiring a book of Pre-Raphaelite women and was jolted to turn a page and see her best friend in a full-color reproduction. The woman in the painting, with a mass of center-parted red curls decorated with flowers and ribbons and jewelry, even had the same distant gaze and rather sad set to her mouth in repose as her friend. She'd studied the portrait for a long time, using it as a tool to clarify why, despite the assertiveness of Snow's stride—she always scissored along the city streets as if late for an appointment—and the clipped, tightly controlled New England precision of her speaking voice even when angry (which she was, back then, often), the impression Katie had from the outset was one of melancholy vulnerability. She'd been drawn to Snow because, despite Snow's determined self-reliance and her refusal initially to admit to it, Katie had sensed the loneliness of a fellow outsider. In Katie's case, she'd been relegated to the outside as a result of an interracial marriage that had produced four children who'd banded tightly together to protect themselves from the varying levels of racism and bigotry they'd encountered growing up. Snow was on the outside both because her instincts were those of an observer rather than a participant, and also because her mother's overpowering love had sent her running to the uncharted territory of the disenfranchised in order to be left alone.

In getting to know Snow, Katie had been dismayed to learn that too much love could be as damaging as too little. It was a revelation. But after years of watching Snow veer automatically toward involvements with men who were free only for furtive, infrequent encounters, while at the same time longingly, lovingly, spending most of her days with other people's children, Katie had realized just how much damage Anne Cooke's superfluous love had done to her daughter. Once her trust had been gained, Snow was gentle and giving and kind, but self-protecting above all—as if she'd learned very early on that the only way to keep her identity intact was by stringently limiting access to her private thoughts and emotions, and by hiding behind her cameras.

Now, as a result of Anne's dying disclosures, Katie was watching the walls around Snow start to crumble, and there were, she thought, two things that could happen: Either Snow would finally emerge and begin revealing herself to the world at large, or she'd erect new, even thicker walls to keep everyone out forever. Katie intended to do everything in her power to see her friend step out at last from behind the walls and begin connecting more directly with others.

"Here's a significant question," Katie said now. "You've mentioned that your mother had a lot of work done on this house. Was the contractor local?"

"Uh-hunh. Wally Schaefer."

"He still around?"

"Yup."

"Good. Because if we don't find her hiding place, we might have to go ask him if he happened to build one in. Which reminds me. Have you looked behind all the pictures, in case she had a wall safe installed?"

Snow shook her head. "How do you think of these things?"

"Knowledge is power, babe. All that reading and those shows are going to come in very handy here. Are you almost finished? I want to get started."

After they'd emptied the two dressers and removed the clothes from the closet, piling everything on the bed, Katie said, "Okay, now we examine the drawers. I doubt she would've—it's kind of a lame number scriptwriters love but actual people with stuff to hide rarely ever do—but it's possible she taped an envelope to the side, back or bottom of one of them. While I'm doing that, why don't you run down and get some garbage bags and pack up these clothes? Unless that's a problem and you're not up to it."

"No. It's okay." Snow went down to the kitchen, glad of Katie's take-charge attitude. She was making matters much easier.

Returning, she saw Katie had the drawers from the first dresser stacked atop one another on the floor and was on her hands and knees peering at the inside of the dresser frame.

"Nothing here," Katie announced, getting to her feet and noticing the open jewelry box on the dresser top. "I must say she had good taste when it came to expensive goodies. What're you going to do with all this?"

"I don't know. I don't think I could wear anything of hers." She was all at once repelled by the idea of wearing any of Anne Cooke's clothes or jewelry. Astonishing how her feelings toward the woman had changed. One day there was someone she'd known and loved as her mother. The next day that person's identity was a complete unknown and so were her feelings. "It's funny," she said, standing next to Katie, both of them looking down into the compartmented Florentine-leather box. "I used to play dress-up with her things as a kid. She actually let me. Imagine letting a kid play with gold and diamonds." There was a soft note of wonder in her voice.

"Maybe," Katie said quietly, "it's what she thought real mothers let their kids do."

"God, that's sad!" The never-distant tears started up, and Snow wiped her face with the back of her hand, wishing her self-control would return.

Putting a consoling arm around her shoulders, Katie said, "Yeah, it is. I just want you to remember one thing. No matter what your name turns out to be, you'll still be you."

"But I'll never know who I *might* have been."

"Wrong. You already are that person. Sure, the influences would've been different, but the genes would've stayed the same. She took you away from your family but she couldn't alter the genetic imprint. And let me say this. She tried to give you a normal life. I mean, all things considered, she was basically a regular person. A little on the doting side, granted. But she never harmed you. She never whacked you around or deprived you, never did any sick sexual stuff to you. Most kids that're abducted turn up dead, or never turn up at all. You were lucky."

"I guess."

"You *were!*" Katie insisted. "I know you can't see your way clear to that point of view at the moment, but I hope you'll try hard to be fair."

"I'm trying. It's a little too soon, Katie." Snow looked at her watch. "We'd better get on with it. I've still got to buy a dress, and I want to get to the funeral home a bit early so I'm there when people start arriving."

"You sure you're up to this? I mean, it could wait until after the funeral."

"I'm not sure about anything. Let's just do it."

"Okay. Why don't you put on some music? And please, anything but *Turandot*. I mean, I know the music's divine, but I have a problem with an opera about a bunch of Chinese people, written by an Italian, and sung by performers from half a dozen different countries. And I especially have trouble with the simplistic notion that love will suppress a woman's rage and turn her into a lollipop."

"Gee!" Snow said sarcastically. "I guess I won't put on *Turandot*."

"Play anything. I forgot for a minute what's happening here. I didn't mean to give you a hard time." Katie was already dumping the contents of the second dresser, and looked over to see that Snow had, for perhaps the tenth time since she'd arrived the previous evening, slid without warning into a distracted state. "You okay?" Katie asked, prepared to go to her.

Snow's eyes clicked back into focus. "Sorry. Yeah. I'll just go put on the music." She turned and went off.

Thinking to spare her at least one difficult task, Katie grabbed a garbage bag and dumped Anne Cooke's lingerie into it, then knotted the top and set it to one side.

Downstairs, just as Snow was about to turn on the stereo, the telephone rang.

"I heard about your mother, and I thought you probably wouldn't want me coming in to clean today."

"Oh, Irma. I completely forgot." The woman had been coming to clean the house twice a week for more than twenty years. "I'm really sorry. Could we leave it until next week?"

"Course," Irma said. "I'll come Monday like always."

"That'd be great. And don't worry, we'll pay you for this week anyway."

"You don't have to go doing that," Irma said, nevertheless sounding pleased.

"No, we will." Snow knew the woman relied on the hundred dollars a week Anne Cooke paid her.

"That's decent of you, Red. Hope I didn't catch you at a bad time."

"No, it's okay."

"Well, I guess I'll be seeing you at the funeral, then. I'm, uhm, real sorry about your mom."

Snow hung up and tried to remember why she'd come downstairs. Music. She scanned the cassettes, pulled out a recording of Mozart's Piano Concertos 21 and 17, popped the cassette into the machine, then returned upstairs to see that Katie was halfway through the contents of the second dresser. The pile of things on the bed was enormous.

"Nothing yet," Katie said, opening another drawer and quickly examining its contents. "Wow! These are Hermès scarves. You sure you want to give these to the Sally Ann or whatever? They're really beautiful."

"They are, but I'll never wear them."

"Would it be ghoulish of me to ask for them? My mother and Grandma Bloom would love to have these."

"Please take them," Snow invited, shoving blouses into a garbage bag. "And anything else you want, too. I promise you there's nothing of hers I want."

"Are you hating her now?" Katie asked, concerned.

"No, not really. It just feels like, I don't know, a sacrilege or something, to be going through her things. I felt the same way yesterday when Rudy and I were looking through the stuff from her desk. I keep expecting her to walk in and frown in that disappointed way she had that was worse than if she'd shouted or hit me."

"It was pretty potent, all right," Katie agreed, remembering clearly many occasions when she'd seen the expression attach itself like a mask to Anne Cooke's face.

"So, please, take whatever you want. There's plenty of room in the car."

"You're not heading right back to the city, are you?"

"After the weekend probably." Snow began returning the empty drawers to the dresser.

"But what if we haven't found anything by then?"

"Then I'll just have to come back and keep on looking when I've got the time. I can't stop working. I don't want to. It's pretty much all I've got now."

Katie held back her response to this. It wasn't the right time to go into the flaws in Snow's view of herself.

Twenty minutes later, Katie had finished inspecting the second dresser. "Nothing," she said. "Next, the upper part of the closet. Got a stepladder?"

"Down in the cellar, at the bottom of the stairs."

"Okay. Be right back."

Snow went on filling garbage bags. By the time Katie had cleared the closet shelves and examined the contents of every box, bag and suitcase, Snow had eight large lawn-and-leaf bags lined up on the landing. The bed was fairly well cleared and she was feeling less timid about handling her mother's things.

Katie had moved to the bedside table and upended each of the half dozen books from the lower shelf, giving them a shake before setting them aside. "The woman had strange taste in reading matter. An eight-hundred-page tome on the oil industry, a cookbook, *The Stand,* a biography of Dickens I personally found relentlessly boring, and Dick Francis."

"She had some oil stocks, I think," Snow said, leaning against the footboard. "And that copy of *The Stand* is mine. I loved it and wanted her to read it. It's been there for at least five years. The Dickens bio was a Christmas gift from one of the women in the bridge club. My mother said she couldn't get into it. But she loved Dick Francis, read every book he ever wrote."

"My Grandma Shimura likes him, too," Katie said, sorting through the contents of the drawer. "He's not bad. So what've we got? Emery boards, a nail file, hairpins, Kleenex, a ChapStick, couple of pens, a notepad and a large bottle of Tums." She removed the drawer, flipped it over, set it aside, and got down on her hands and knees to scan the interior. "Nothing. Time for a coffee break. You want to wrestle with that machine, or shall I?"

"I'll do it. You keep looking. I want to flip the tape anyway."

"Okay, fine." Katie tipped the bedside table to one side to look at the bottom, then the back. Straightening, she let her eyes run slowly over the room. The bathroom was out. No one in her right mind would hide important documents where water could damage them. That left the bedroom itself, and the closet.

She lifted the several watercolor paintings to peer behind them, and checked each of the electrical outlets, unscrewing the switch-plate covers with the nail file she'd found in the bedside table. Just wires, no disguised mini-safe. She felt along the entire perimeter of the wall-to-wall carpeting, testing for loose edges. There were none.

By the time Snow returned with two mugs of coffee, Katie was sitting cross-legged in the closet doorway, playing with her braid and looking carefully around the small enclosure. She accepted the mug from Snow, asking, "What's wrong with this picture?"

"I don't know. What?"

"Look!"

"What? It looks okay to me."

"Probably would to ninety-nine percent of the population," Katie said, taking a swallow of the coffee. "But when did you ever see baseboards complete with quarter-round moldings in a closet?"

"Don't they all have them?"

"They do not. Having an architect for a father, I happen to be aware of tiny niceties. The thing is, builders don't waste money on expensive frills like that. Unless the closet's been added on to an existing room, you never see baseboards. Hold this." She handed her mug to Snow and knee-walked into the closet where she began in the left-hand corner, feeling along the molding, pushing here and there.

Bemused, Snow watched. "She was the kind of woman who'd have had Wally put baseboards in her closet, Katie."

"Yes, but is Wally the kind of guy who'd have suggested it?"

"No, probably not."

"I rest my case. She had it installed because *this* is where the hidey-hole is. I know it!" She worked her way around to the back wall, rapping her knuckles on the baseboard, feeling along the top and bottom. At the point where the right-hand wall joined the rear one, Katie exclaimed aloud.

"What?" Snow asked, startled.

"This is it! I've just got to figure it out."

Caught up in Katie's excitement, Snow put the mugs on the bed-side table, then returned to watch her friend prodding experimentally at the baseboard.

"I *know* it opens! But how? Come on." Katie laid both hands flat on the four-foot-long board and tried to move it. "No. Slow down," she told herself. "It's hollow," she explained over her shoulder, knocking on the piece with her knuckles to illustrate.

"Doesn't sound any different to me."

"Well, it *is!*" she insisted, playing now with the molding strip, emitting a shriek as it lifted upward. "Gotcha! It just slides in there. See? It's not nailed or glued down. The walls hold it in place. Now, open up," she said, pulling at the top of the baseboard. "Open *up! Why* won't it *open?*"

"Maybe if you try pushing instead of pulling," Snow suggested.

"Sure. What the hell!" Katie gave the white-painted piece a push and the board popped free of its moorings and fell into her hands. "Holy shit, Snow! We found it!"

"What's in there?" Snow wanted to know.

"Find out in a tick." Katie reached into the opening and came out with a flat metal box. Her expression triumphant, she crowed, "Didn't I *tell* you?"

"It's locked."

"So, we'll unlock it." Katie handed Snow the box. "Where are the tools? Kitchen, cellar? Where?" she asked, already racing down the stairs.

"Bottom drawer in the kitchen, beside the refrigerator."

"Come on!" Katie yelled.

The box in hand, Snow hurried after her. Maybe all the answers were right here, she thought, heart pumping wildly as she flew toward the kitchen.

Six

The topmost item in the box was a wide brown envelope containing a thick stack of hundred-dollar bills.

"My God! Let me see that!" Katie picked up the envelope, sat down beside Snow at the kitchen table and, muttering to herself in disbelieving tones, began to count the money.

Snow continued to examine the other items in the box: six long-term certificates of deposit, which she set aside to study later; the title for the Buick; sundry papers pertaining to the purchase of the house; two life insurance policies of which she was the named beneficiary; several promissory notes, which would have been surprising had Rudy not already told her about the loans her mother had made to a number of people in town.

A sudden roaring in her ears and a leaping hope that she'd taken a large step toward learning Anne Cooke's true identity, she looked in turn at three different social security cards: one in the name of Anne Alicia Cooke, the second for Margot Chapman, and the third for Elizabeth Garvey. Was it possible either of these last two might be her real name? Snow found she was trembling as she examined the next items: passports, out-of-date for better than twenty-five years, in all three names and bearing her mother's photograph, as did a pair of long-since expired driver's licenses in the names of Chapman and Garvey issued by the states of New York and Rhode Island. Her brief surge of excitement ebbing, puzzled now by these three sets of ID, she moved on.

A fourth passport, issued on November 19, 1963 and expiring in 1968, was in the name of Snow Devane and contained a photograph of herself as a baby. The only logical explanation for this additional document had to be that Anne Cooke had, at some point, planned to take her out of the country. Perhaps the search for the kidnapped child had been getting too close, and she'd become nervous, preparing contingency plans.

The final item in the box was a yellow-jacketed document with CERTIFIED COPY printed on it. Typed beneath were the words:

BIRTH
SNOW DEVANE
BORN
MARCH 2, 1962

"Here's my birth certificate," Snow announced somewhat breathlessly, folding open the document and quickly scanning the information it contained. Under Mother of Child, Full Maiden Name, it read: Anne Alicia Cooke. "She *was* my mother," she said in a thick voice, feeling foolish and sickened. "Look. Here it is."

"Let's see." Katie studied the document and after a few moments said, "No way, Snow. Check out item 17, age at time of this birth. Twenty-two. Your mother or Anne Cooke, whoever, would've had to be *thirty*-two. Plus, sweetie, look at the birthplace. *Leeds, England.* Whatever she was, the woman you knew was definitely North American. Maybe Canadian. But English? Never. No way she could've disguised an accent like that. Ever heard a North Country English accent?"

Snow shook her head, feeling even more foolish now.

"Trust me," Katie said kindly. "Your Anne Cooke wasn't *this* Anne Cooke."

"I'd like to see it again," Snow said, bothered by something about the document but unable to pin it down. Aloud, she read out the relevant lines. "'Place of birth, Nassau County, Town of Bellmore. Father of child, full name, Aidan Devane; residence, Bellmore, New York; race, Caucasian; age at time of this birth, twenty-four; birthplace, Dublin, Ireland; usual occupation, hospital orderly; Industry or Business, Long Island Hospital.'" She stopped and said, "You're right. This couldn't possibly be mine. Which means the story's true. But how could she have the same name as this woman? I don't get it." That certain something kept nudging at the edge of her brain, like someone grown impatient in a long lineup at a bank, jostling the person ahead.

"Didn't she say she went looking in cemeteries until she found a headstone? Obviously, once she found a dead baby who fit her agenda, she had her name changed legally, so everything would match up. If anybody got suspicious and started asking questions, she could pull out your birth certificate and her brand-new ID and say, See? There's her name on a driver's license and a social security card, proving she's Anne Cooke, mother of baby Snow. And who'd argue with a woman about her age? Plus, thirty years ago, she could probably have passed as being in her twenties. Look at you, for example. You don't look more than twenty-two or -three. Nobody ever takes *me* for thirty-two. No, she had all the bases pretty well covered. Anything else in there that might give us any clues?''

"These, maybe." Snow indicated the three sets of ID. "How can we figure out which one she is, or even if she was any of them?''

Katie studied the passports and licenses, then stacked them in a tidy pile on the table. "The thing you have to understand is, she couldn't go after the real Anne Cooke's ID for lots of reasons, not the least of which was that Anne Cooke was probably still alive, and also wasn't born in this country. The only way your mother could take on the name was by having her own legally changed. Oh, wow, Snow!'' she said excitedly. "Follow this! If she changed her name legally, she had to have notified the Social Security people because, unless she'd spent her entire life from birth living in a cave somewhere, she had to have been paying taxes. You can do a lot of things, but you can't fool around with the IRS, especially not when the last thing you'd want to do is draw attention to yourself. So, logically, she'd have changed her name, then notified all the pertinent bureaucracies to keep everything kosher.'' She paused to take a swallow of coffee.

"People change their names every day," she went on. "You get certified copies of the court document and send them in to the Department of Motor Vehicles, the IRS, Social Security, et cetera. The point is, there'd be records somewhere. I think these others, for Margot Chapman and Elizabeth Garvey, are just spares, in case things turned sour and she had to get away in a hurry. Without the baby, of course. Otherwise there'd be a couple more birth certificates in there showing Chapman and Garvey as mothers of a female infant. But she didn't get caught, so Anne Cooke was the name she stuck with, and that's the one we'll concentrate on. If we don't get anywhere with it, we can always backtrack and work on the other two names.''

"That makes sense," Snow said thoughtfully.

"I've got no idea how you'd access the Social Security records, or even if you could, but it shouldn't be hard to find out. We'll check all the angles. I mean, her money came from somewhere. It wasn't just sitting in Rhode Island for thirty-odd years, waiting for her. It was most likely transferred here from somewhere else.''

"Why d'you think that?"

"Simple. She came to a place where nobody knew her."

"Oh! Right." Snow frowned, trying to catch hold of that elusive fragment that, like a bothersome hangnail, kept drawing her attention.

"Anyway," Katie continued, "the same applies to her investments. It may go back thirty years, but she left a paper trail."

"How are we ever going to get to the bottom of this?" Snow wondered aloud, distressed by the logistics of trying to gather thirty-year-old information.

"We will," Katie assured her. "The first thing is for you to call up the police chief and ask him to take your mother's fingerprints before she's cremated. They might be useful. No point bothering with her dental work. She's bound to have had fillings and what-have-you, which means that, even if by some miracle we were able to track down her one-time dentist, he'd never be able to identify her by her teeth. The fingerprints, though, might be a lead. Maybe she was bonded at one time, or held a high-security job, although that's pretty doubtful. Anyway, it's definitely worth a shot. It's a way to cover at least one area."

"I can't just call him up and ask him to fingerprint her. He'd want to know why."

"So you'll tell him. Snow, you're acting as if *you've* done something wrong. None of this is your fault. You're the injured party here. And your real parents. So, we'll stop by the cop shop while we're out getting you a dress, show him the letter and these IDs, and ask him to do her prints. Why wouldn't he want to help?"

"This is so unbelievable," Snow declared, shaking her head. "Even if we do find out who she really was, we still won't have a clue as to who *I* am. I mean, she took me from a *supermarket*. It's not as if she actually knew my parents and decided one day she'd make a better mother than mine would. This wasn't personal. The woman wanted a baby so she went stalking other, unsuspecting women in supermarkets, until she found what she wanted. Then she helped herself."

"It is unbelievable," Katie concurred. "But she did give you one major piece of information—the date she did it. Plus, she said it was New York. Right? It was a *crime*, Snow. There'll be police or

FBI records. And it had to have been written up in the papers. As soon as we get back to the city, we'll hit the library and start checking back issues of the newspapers. They're all on microfilm. It won't be hard."

Snow silently pulled her own passport from the pile. Opening it, she looked again at the photograph of her infant self. Then she checked the date of birth. "Look at this, Katie," she said, the pieces finally pulling together. "How old would you think this baby is?"

"I don't know. A year tops, maybe less."

"But according to the birth certificate I was born on March 2, 1962. The passport was issued in November of '63. That would mean I'd've been closer to two when it was issued."

"You're right! I can't believe I missed that. Good call, babe! Passport photos have to be recent. And another thing. Why a separate passport? Babies are usually listed on the mother's, unless the mother and child have different nationalities. It just proves that one of these is a fake—either yours or hers."

Deflated, Snow said, "All it proves is there's one more thing I don't know. I don't know my name, or my age, or where I was born. I don't know one goddamned thing."

"Don't go all defeated. We've hardly started. Let's be practical, deal with one thing at a time, like this money. There's ten thousand dollars in this envelope, and these CDs are all in your name. It adds up to three hundred thousand dollars, none of which is subject to probate. The insurance policies are worth a million. You're going to have to get in touch with her lawyer, her accountant and her stockbroker, and start liquidating her assets. She had a bunch of money, Snow, and she left it all to you."

"Where did she get it?" Snow wondered, unmoved just then by the prospect of possessing such wealth. Nothing felt real except her expanding sense of loss, and her anger. In her head a voice kept asking, "How could she *do* that? How *could* she? What kind of person did a thing like that?" The questions ran in a repeating cycle.

"Good question. The accountant and stockbroker might be of some help there. Plus, she may have left other documents on file with the lawyer. Jeez, babe! You're going to be a rich woman."

"A rich woman who doesn't even know her goddamned name."

"Hey! We'll find out," Katie promised. "Right now, we'd better get cleaned up and head into town. We can swing by the local bank and get this cash transferred into your account before we buy your dress and go see the police chief.''

"Doesn't it have to go through probate or whatever?''

"Nope. Cash is cash. You put two or three of these nice hundred-dollar bills into your wallet and have the rest wired to your account in New York. If it's under ten thousand in cash the bank doesn't have to report it to the IRS. It's free money, my darling. You don't have to declare it as income, because as far as everybody's concerned, it doesn't exist. You might just as well take it. And while we're at it, we should bring along the will to show the bank manager so he can go ahead and set up an estate account to cover the funeral expenses.''

"This is insane!'' Snow said despairingly.

"No kidding! She was pretty smart, I'll admit it, but so'm I. Somewhere, somehow, we'll uncover someone from her old life, and find out who she was. In the meantime, we're going to be working on finding out who *you* are so we can put you back together with your family. I know you're scared. I'm kind of scared myself. But we'll get to the bottom of all this.''

Mr. Innes, the bank manager, expressed his sympathy, and said her mother had been much respected and admired in the town, and would be missed. Snow listened politely. She was quickly learning that her silence was usually interpreted as a natural response to the shock of her loss. People accepted it and, once they'd declared their own sadness, were willing to proceed with the matters at hand.

Innes was no exception. He said he'd be happy to wire the cash to her New York account, and assured her he'd assist in whatever way possible. "We'll make the change to an estate account right away. I'll just copy this page in the will citing you as executor, and get you to sign a couple of signature cards so that, once the estate's cleared probate, you'll have access. And of course the bank will pay any funeral expenses directly out of your mother's funds. Just have the funeral home send the bills here to my attention. This'll only take a minute or two,'' he said, leaving the office to get the signature cards and use the copier.

Fifteen minutes later, Snow was shaking the man's hand, saying thank you and good-bye, and she and Katie were on their way to Janey's Boutique.

Bothered, Snow said, "I just put almost ten thousand dollars of that woman's money in my checking account. It doesn't feel right.''

"Don't make it sound like stealing. It's *your* money."

"We don't know that it's my money. Maybe she's got a family somewhere, too."

"Didn't you tell me she said she couldn't have children?"

"No. She said she had to have a baby. I don't think she said she couldn't have one."

"I hope I'm not out of line, but my impression was that she didn't care much for men. In spite of the way she dressed and the trouble she took with her appearance, I always thought she was kind of sexless. It was as if she didn't give off pheromones, at least not the hetero kind."

"You think she was gay?" Snow asked, intrigued by Katie's assessment. "Is that what you're saying?"

"No, I think she was kind of neuter."

"I know what you mean." Snow thought back. "I used to think it was strange that she never dated. But I figured it was because of being a widow, left with a baby. You know, her story of why I didn't have a father. I never really questioned it. Kids don't tend to dig too deeply into the stuff their parents tell them, at least I didn't. Did you?"

Katie considered the question for a second or two, then said, "Not really, no."

"The thing is, you wouldn't, I don't think, unless you had a reason. Something about your mother or father that was wrong, out of whack. Then, you might start looking into their histories, trying to see what went wrong. Since she died, I've been looking for holes, but haven't spotted a thing I might have missed at the time. I do remember wondering when I was sixteen or so if she and Rudy were doing the deed and just maintaining a cool front so I wouldn't find out. But I knew in my bones they weren't. Not because Rudy wasn't attractive but because I just couldn't picture her getting naked with him, or any man, and doing the kinds of things I'd been sneaking off to Providence to do. So I wrote off the idea. But maybe you've got a point, maybe she wasn't into men. She didn't seem to have any interest. And the times when I was a kid and asked her how come she never went out with anyone, she laughed it off and said our life was perfect the way it was and she hated the idea of messing it up by bringing some man into the equation. She didn't show any more interest in women than she did in men, though. So who knows? The whole thing gives me a headache."

"Maybe she was a closet case."

"It's possible," Snow allowed. "It'd certainly explain a lot."

"It sure would. Here you are, this good-looking woman who secretly finds men repellent, but you want a baby. So what do you do? It's the early sixties, artificial insemination's out of the question for some reason. You've got plenty of money and resources and you've done enough homework to know how to get your hands on fake IDs, so you start planning to abduct a baby. It works for me."

"Maybe," was all Snow was willing to say.

Wisely, Katie let the matter drop.

Pete Briggs listened closely to everything Snow had to say. Then he examined the letters and the various forged documents, a furrow gradually forming between his brows.

"This is one hell of a story," he said, his expression troubled.

"Is there anything you can do?" she asked, wanting him to say it'd be easy as pie: He'd just punch into the nationwide computer hookup and in a matter of minutes come up with everything she needed to know.

"I'll get over there in a little while and do the fingerprinting, for openers," he said, leaning back in his chair and touching the steepled fingers of both hands to the tip of his nose. "This is a tricky situation, Snow. All we have by way of confirmation of this purported kidnapping is her letter." He held up a hand to stop her from protesting. "Hear me out, please. Try to grasp this from the law enforcement point of view. Let's say for the sake of argument the story's true, that the woman claiming to be Anne Cooke kidnapped you from a supermarket in New York back in 1963. You've got absolutely nothing, aside from this letter, to substantiate your claim. Even if you and your resourceful friend here manage to unearth the details and find newspaper reports of the event, you have no way of proving you're actually the child who was taken."

"Blood testing would verify her parentage," Katie put in.

Pete Briggs gave her a surprised, approving nod. "True," he said. "It would. But the point I'm making is that, in my opinion, no professional law enforcement body is going to open their files to you, or assist you in tracking down either your parents or determining Anne Cooke's identity. You could be anyone, Snow. You could be some crackpot who decided, for reasons all your own, to be the long-lost child of a couple whose baby was kidnapped more than thirty years ago. You could be some certifiable head-case who goes around doing this kind of thing all the time. You wouldn't believe some of the things people come up with, even in a small town like this.''

"But how would I even have *known* about it?" Snow argued, realizing in that moment that she no longer doubted the truth of what she'd been told. She now believed she was in no way related to the woman she'd known as her mother. And having made that transition, she was committed to uncovering the truth, regardless of the cost or how long it took. If she had to spend the rest of her life doing it, she was going to find her family.

He leaned forward on his desk and in a low voice said, "Snow, I'm not saying it isn't true. I know you're not some crackpot. But that does not apply to police in other jurisdictions, especially someplace like Manhattan. You're on shaky ground with this story for the simple reason that you can't prove one single fact. I'm willing to do whatever I can to help, but it's probably not going to be a hell of a lot. I can definitely run her prints through the computer. That I will do. And I can make a few calls, see if I can get some idea what direction to point you in. I suspect, though, that after all these years, the files on that case are buried away in some precinct basement, or lost, or have even accidentally been thrown away. *But.* I don't know much when it comes to the missing persons area, and I could be completely wrong. I think you should do what Katie's suggesting. Check the newspapers and see if you can come up with more details. Then my advice is hire yourself a good, reputable private investigator and see if he can't track down your folks and maybe get a line on Anne Cooke. I think that's your best shot.''

"Somehow, I thought you'd be able to do more," Snow said, suffering a sickening sense of disappointment.

"If I could do more, Snow, I would. The truth is, I'm a one-man show in a very small community. My resources are limited. I'm sorry I can't be more positive. Frankly, I'm going to have to have a long, hard think about this. If it's true, and somehow I don't doubt that it is, the woman we all thought was your mother was a cold-hearted criminal who probably left a lot of wreckage behind her. So I'll do whatever I can to help, but I'm telling you up front, it's probably not going to be much.''

As she and Katie were getting up to leave, he asked, "How're you going to handle it? With the folks in town, I mean.''

"I won't, for now. I want to get through the funeral first. Then I'll talk to her lawyer in Providence, and her accountant and stockbroker. After that I'll go back to the city and start trying to get some answers. Whatever you can do," she said, all at once feeling weak in the knees and struggling not to cry, "I'll appreciate it."

Out on the street, Katie draped an arm around Snow's waist and said, "He believed you. That's the important thing for now."

"But he said no one in New York would."

"He also said he's not that up on missing persons. Let's not assume we're defeated before we've even begun."

"It's so hard. I want to know right now, this minute. I want answers, or at least a direction to go in. Can you understand that?" she asked hotly.

"Of course I do. It just might take some time. You've got to be prepared for that."

Snow emitted a brief, broken laugh. "Like I've got a choice. And in the meantime somehow I'm supposed to keep on going. This is such a fucking *nightmare!*"

"It is, it is," Katie agreed. "But hang in. Okay?"

"I have no choice," Snow said again, imagining months and years passing while she hung suspended, without an identity. She was very afraid, and the fear was like ice around her heart.

Seven

While she dressed for the visitation, Snow kept looking at herself in the mirror. Despite the discomfort it gave her, she had the arbitrary notion that if she looked hard enough, deep enough, she might somehow unlock her mind to retrieve some scrap of memory, some small recollection from those months she'd spent long ago as her actual mother's child. Nothing came. All she felt was an ongoing alienation from the person she'd previously known herself to be, and viewed with rare detachment the woman who gazed back at her from the far side of the glass.

Who, in fact, did she resemble, with her red hair, high cheekbones, short narrow nose and wide mouth? Would she ever know her family? The idea that she might never learn her true identity was like a slow-bleeding injury to her brain. It emitted an acute intermittent pain that at random moments stabbed her like an electric shock, jolting her into remembering that her mother had died, but wasn't really her mother.

There had been many contradictory aspects to Anne Cooke, but her influence overall had been positive. She had applauded Snow's achievements, no matter how minimal, and she had, after the fact, even approved of Snow's insistence on leaving home to go to New York. Viewed as a parent with as much objectivity as Snow could muster, the woman had done a creditable job. Viewed as a woman unrelated to her in any way, Anne Cooke was an enigma, and a felon.

Knowledge of that fact cast Snow's accomplishments into a doubtful light. While before so much of her behavior had been as a direct result of the stringent rules of the household in which she'd spent her formative years, now those reasons had, in large part, been invalidated. She could not determine what influence, if any, her unknown family had had in shaping her. Just as being ill and at the mercy of medical strangers had depersonalized the woman who'd played out the role of her mother, the discovery that she was not Snow Devane had devalued her. It was an altered reality that at unanticipated times she found terrifying. Fear then seemed to shrink her veins and arteries, impeding the blood flow to her heart and brain. The sensation she had was of being in a prolonged free-fall through an endless sky. She came to earth now and again, brought back forcibly by Rudy and Katie. But the rest of the time the rush of air caused her ears to ache, and made it difficult for her to catch her breath. Even though she was determined to get back to the city, she wasn't sure she'd be able to go on with her life, because that life now struck her as fraudulent, having been lived under false pretenses.

Stepping into the simple black dress Katie had helped her buy, she followed her actions in the mirror, bemused by her detachment. There stood a thin, pale, befreckled creature fitting her long arms into the sleeves of a dress that accentuated her thinness and pallor and the fiery hues of her unmanageable hair. Why had no one in town ever questioned the curious aspects of tiny, blond Anne Cooke's having given birth to a tall, sharp-boned redhead to whom she bore not the slightest resemblance?

Of course Anne would've said blithely that the long-dead Aidan Devane had hair just like his daughter's, and everyone would've accepted it. The woman never blinked. She'd concocted her cover story and stuck to it doggedly; cool as can be, and prepared for any contingency with a ton of money that had come from God only knew where. That was Anne Cooke. She'd bought one of the most expensive pieces of property in town, then arrived with a baby in tow, settled in and, eventually, became Stony Point's self-effacing benefactress. *Where did you come from? What drove you to steal another woman's child?*

"How you doing?" Katie asked from the doorway. "It looks good. Have I ever seen you in a dress?"

"It's doubtful." Snow reached for the wide barrette on the dresser. "I think I own maybe one. I've always hated wearing dresses." She remembered herself at thirteen, arguing and pleading with her mother to be allowed to wear jeans to school, like the other kids. "Nobody wears skirts and dresses," she'd argued. "You're turning me into a geek. The kids all think I'm *weird!*" And she saw again her mother's implacable expression as she said, "Don't be absurd, dear. A geek. The things you say. Of course they don't think that."

"Where'd you get the shoes?" Katie asked.

Snow looked down at the black patent flats. "High school, junior year. Rod Briggs asked me to the prom. I had to wear these so I wouldn't be taller than he was. I always wished he could've waited a year to ask me. He had a big growth spurt senior year, and it would've been less embarrassing for both of us. Plus, I was past being obedient by my senior year, and he hit five-ten. You should've seen it, Katie. I looked like Rod's mother in this truly hideous dress. Jane had a fabulous strapless black taffeta number in the shop, but my mother said no way. Black taffeta was absolutely unsuitable for a girl not yet sixteen. I had to get this pale blue little-girl thing, with a full skirt, puffy sleeves and a ribbon sash. God! I felt like such a clown. We had a good time, though. Rod was the best dancer in the school...." Without warning, she burst into racking sobs.

Katie at once moved to take hold of her, again shocked at how little substance there seemed to be to her. Only the slightest layer of skin atop the bones. How could her flesh have dissolved that way in a mere matter of hours? It was scary.

"This is so *hard*, Katie. She was my mother, whoever she was, and from one minute to the next, I think, my God, I'm a thirty-one-year-old orphan, and I miss her. If only she'd been a rotten person, it wouldn't be so bad. But she wasn't. I know she loved me and tried to do her best. It probably sounds crazy, but I keep thinking there are people somewhere who'd want to know she died. I feel as if I should be putting obits in every paper in the country. Unknown woman in photograph, known as mother to Snow Devane, has died. If you knew her could you let me know? Crazy. Okay, okay." She pulled away, grabbed a handful of tissues from the box on the counter and mopped her face. "Sorry about that."

"Hey, it helps to go nuts. I was demento when Grandpa Shimura died. It's so damned final, so utterly irreversible. I kept running into bathrooms so I could freak in private because I knew everybody would think I was out of control and have me committed or something. I was fourteen and feeling generally conspicuous. You know the way you do at that age when you're convinced everybody's watching and judging every single thing you do, and they're clued in to the fact that you're a totally pathetic loser. The fact is, it's how you feel, and whatever way you feel is the right way. So don't give it a thought. Nobody's going to be scoring you on how you handle this, babe."

"You're a good friend, and that helps. Thanks." Snow fixed her hair—a brief, distressing glance at her reflection—then said, "We'd better go down. Rudy'll be here in a minute."

"Why'd you do that?"

"What?"

"Look in the mirror as if you hated the person you saw there?"

"I don't know about hate," Snow said. "You know how much I dislike mirrors."

"I know you do, but why, for God's sake? You're a beautiful woman."

Snow shook her head. "I don't see it."

"What *do* you see?"

Snow made a half turn back to the mirror, as if to refresh her memory. "I see this boring, skinny person with a mouth that's too big, and arms that're too long." Turning back to Katie, she said, as if offering a challenge, "Shall I go on?"

"No, I got it. You're dumb," Katie accused fondly. "Very, very dumb. But I love you anyway. Come on. Let's get this show on the road."

Just before four people began arriving. Snow accepted the consoling hugs and declarations of sympathy, moved by the directness and lack of pretension of these people she'd lived among for so long. She found once more she was required only to receive, and wasn't expected to say much, which was good because she couldn't concentrate. The subtly spotlit coffin at the far end of the room kept drawing her eyes, and she turned often, involuntarily, to stare for long moments at the vivid spray of roses and carnations centered on its lid and at the numerous floral arrangements positioned artfully on the floor and on pedestals. The flowers seemed to glow with an unnatural, eerie brightness that bothered her almost as much as the coffin did.

She wished she'd thought to ask Ms. Brickman if her mother was really in there. Perhaps in cases of cremation the body was kept somewhere else. She needed to know Anne Cooke's precise whereabouts, and the idea that the coffin might be no more than an unoccupied symbol also bothered her, heightening the sense she'd had from the minute she'd arrived at the hospital two nights before that she'd crossed some unseen threshold and was now in a secondary but parallel universe. Things appeared to be the same but there were potent and jarring variations that only she perceived. Nothing and no one looked quite right.

The visitation hall might have been the living room of a very large, quaintly old-fashioned house. Armchairs and settees were casually grouped; there was even a low table with a hardcover art book on it. Below a pair of casement windows was a table with a coffee urn, cups and saucers. The open windows admitted a floral breeze for which Snow was most grateful. It reminded her that once this unnerving interlude had ended, she'd be free to find her way back over the threshold into the primary universe where she could begin in earnest her search into the past.

Without being able to recall any of the details later, in the course of the visitation she discussed the funeral service with the minister and spoke to the organist about the classical selections she wanted played the following day.

People came and went: the three women who comprised Anne's bridge group; Wally Schaefer, the contractor, and his wife; Mr. and Mrs. Willard from the drugstore; Lillian, the hairdresser, and Jane from the boutique; Mr. Innes, the bank manager; Irma, their housekeeper, and a few dozen others. Tiny, eighty-four-year-old Mrs. Hoover got a ride with Pete Briggs in the cruiser. Marching into the room with typical vigor, she gazed up at Snow, blue eyes greatly magnified by thick-lensed glasses, and said, "Your mother used to come visit on Sunday afternoons. If the weather was good, we'd sit out on the back porch and talk. Come visit with me before you go rushing back to New York. Will you do that?"

"Sure I will."

Mrs. Hoover gave her hand a pat. "Don't go forgetting," she said, then turned and made her way over to Katie to ask, "Who are you?"

Visibly amused, Katie said, "I'm Katie, Snow's friend."

"Where are you from?"

"New Jersey originally, but I've lived in New York for a long time." Katie's eyes met Snow's over the top of the woman's head.

"No, no," Mrs. Hoover said impatiently. "I mean, where are you *from?* Are you a native?"

"What, you mean Indian?" Katie gave in to her amusement and smiled. "No, I'm not."

"Oh! Well, you look like an Indian. I had a friend, years back, looked a lot like you. Part French and part Mohawk, she was.

Beautiful girl. You remind me of her. So, if you're not a native, what are you? Never mind," she said abruptly, looking around to see everyone present was following the conversation. With a bark of laughter, she said, "They'll all be jumping down my throat in a minute if I keep on with this."

Katie laughed, too, and offered to get the old woman some coffee.

"I'd like that," Mrs. Hoover said, settling into one of the armchairs, her feet dangling well above the floor. "Black, if you don't mind, Katie dear."

"I love her," Katie whispered to Snow as she got the old woman's coffee. "Lot of interesting characters in this town. Wally Schaefer's a teddy bear. And his wife's such a sweetie."

"I know," Snow said, assaulted again by a surge of emotion. She loved all these people, always had, always would.

"You okay, babe?"

"Uh-hunh."

"You sure?"

"Uh-hunh."

"Rudy says Lucy's got dinner organized for the three of us at the café."

"Okay." Snow smiled vaguely, her eyes sliding back to the coffin as Katie carried the coffee over to Mrs. Hoover, then perched on the arm of the woman's chair to continue talking to her.

No one else seemed to look directly at the coffin, Snow noticed, and she wondered if superstition had anything to do with it. Or was it fear? Her back ached from standing for so long in the unyielding, leather-soled shoes, and her head felt stuffed with too many thoughts. The cloying scent of the carnations overpowered all the other fragrances; she seemed to taste it, and swallowed several times to rid herself of the sweetness.

"Have this," Rudy said, handing her a cup of coffee. "It'll help."

She thanked him and took a swallow, then said, "It feels like such a sham. I keep wanting to tell them she wasn't who they thought, and neither am I."

"It wouldn't serve any purpose," he said quietly, surveying the room.

"No, I know. Mrs. Hoover was telling me my mother used to visit her every Sunday. When did she start doing that?"

"Let's see. Must've been eight, nine years ago, right after the old girl took that spill down her front steps and cracked her elbow. The bridge group decided they'd each take different days of the week, make a point of checking in on her. I usually drop over once or twice a week myself. The woman bakes the best cakes and pies I ever tasted."

"That's true. Rudy, I've been thinking about the trips to New York Anne made every year. You know she always insisted on staying in a hotel because she said we both needed our privacy. But maybe there was another reason. Maybe she didn't want me around when she got in touch with people from her old life. Does that sound farfetched?"

"Nope. Maybe she did. When things settle down, why don't you take a look through all those boxes of papers up in the attic? Might be something there. I know she saved every last piece of paper for tax purposes. She's bound to have saved the hotel bills."

"I'd forgotten all about the stuff in the attic," she said, lifted by the idea of pursuing what Katie called the paper trail. Every minute she spent inactive was a minute longer she remained separated from her family.

"Wouldn't surprise me if you found thirty years' worth of tax papers and so forth up there. She was never one to throw things away."

She reached to take hold of his hand. "I'll definitely check it out," she said, consciously working to keep her eyes on his.

"I've been doing a lot of thinking myself, going back over things she said through the years, trying to recall if there was anything that stood out in my mind at the time. It's not easy. You tend not to pay all that much attention when you think it's just general chitchat."

"I've practically been inverting myself, doing the same, and I haven't come up with a single damned thing. It's maddening."

"You and Katie'll be busy the next little while. If you want, I'll have a go at those tax papers, see if there's anything there."

"Okay," she accepted, knowing he wouldn't offer to undertake such a tedious job just to be polite. As he'd said, people wanted to help, and she had to let them. "That'd be great." Her eyes went again to the coffin and she felt herself helplessly staring.

"Hard to get your mind around it, isn't it?" he said, as if having read her thoughts. "It's like the biggest thing in the universe, a casket. Takes up your whole vision. Everything else seems small by comparison, because so much of your own life's in there with a person you loved. But after tomorrow it'll be gone, Snow, and things'll start getting back to their right size. People'll go back to looking to you the way they should, and you'll stop feeling like you're standing behind a glass wall.''

Dazed, she clung to his hand, struggling not to break down as once again she was assaulted by that image of her mother in the Intensive Care Unit. "I miss her so much, Rudy," she whispered. "How can this be happening?"

His hand gave hers a gentle squeeze. "Drink some more of that coffee," he advised. "This part of it's almost done, and then you'll go on to the next part. Before you know it, it'll be over."

Eight

Late that night, long after Katie had gone to bed, Snow sat in her room, wide awake, angry and restless. Brain racing, she laced and unlaced her fingers; her knees jiggled up and down. Somehow anxiety had turned her into a human conductor, with electrical currents traveling through her body. She was bone weary but couldn't settle. She got up and paced for a time. At last, thinking she might as well put all this energy to productive use, she decided to take a look around the attic.

Trying not to make any noise, she went out onto the landing and pulled the cord that brought the folding staircase down from the ceiling. The mechanism descended with a groan and, wincing, she looked over at the guest room door, not wanting to wake Katie and have to try to explain what she was doing. Logic was currently absent from her life; she had no answers or explanations. Motionless, she listened. Nothing. Katie hadn't heard.

Barefoot, she climbed the staircase and felt on the wall for the light switch. In the hard glare of the dangling naked bulb, she stood blinking at the neatly stacked row of boxes that reached up to the lowest point of the rafters and ran almost the entire length of the right-hand wall. One section was identified by her mother's printing in thick black marker as tax papers; each carton was dated, and, as Rudy had suggested might be the case, went back to the early sixties. Sifting through all those papers would be a monumental job. Nevertheless she was halfway tempted to start there and then, and had to spend a few moments convincing herself she was too tired.

The floor dusty beneath her feet, she took a perfunctory look instead at the other boxes. Quite a number bore her name. Curious, she opened two of the topmost ones to find baby clothes, toys and games from long ago. She backed away, unprepared to see these items. They seemed to constitute additional evidence of Anne Cooke's crime, and of her own innocent complicity. As Katie had pointed out, she did feel guilty, and couldn't understand why. What, after all, had she actually done wrong?

She surveyed the space, thinking distantly what a great studio it would make with its high-peaked roof just begging for the installation of a skylight. At the front was a round ornamental window, and positioned before it was an old rocker she vaguely remembered. Small footprints showed in the dust on the floor around it, and, seeing them, she understood that her mother had spent time up here—obviously sitting in the rocker and looking out the window. It was a picture with distinctly Gothic overtones, something out of one of the books she'd so loved as a child; novels from another era, featuring either children in pairs, or solitary, orphaned girls trapped in menacing circumstances, usually in the environs of crumbling, damp, unheated, castlelike houses. There was invariably a villainous relative or housekeeper, and endless threats to the well-being of the central character who somehow managed to prevail in the end. She'd adored those stories, thrilled both by the danger and also the ingenuity of the resourceful children.

Anne Cooke had been neither young nor imperiled. So why was the image of her sitting alone up here gazing out the window so wrenching? Perhaps because she'd consistently remained apart from the community, preferring, she'd claimed, her own company and Snow's. "I've never been what you'd call a social being," she'd said countless times over the years. "Just because I spend time alone doesn't mean I'm unhappy, dear." Snow had never entirely believed her, primarily because she herself thrived on the company of others, always anxious to see and hear the things people said and did.

Irresistibly drawn, she now moved the length of the attic to slip into the chair. Hands flat on the worn-smooth arms, she turned to take in the view from the window with eyes scratchy from fatigue. She felt impossibly heavy all at once—the strain beginning to catch up to her—and it was a relief to sit down.

The chair rocking gently, she stared out at the nightscape, at the black bay waters lapping the shore on the far side of the road, dappled gold by the May half moon. Inhaling, the breath caught in her lungs as if snagged by many small hooks. Even breathing in this house had become difficult. The place contained too many secrets, and it seemed shameful that she'd lived here in such sheltered ignorance. Irrationally, she felt she should somehow have known, have sensed intuitively that she'd been stolen away from her real family. Absurd. How could she have known anything of the sort?

Oh, sure, as a kid she'd pretended she'd been adopted, that her mother wasn't her real mother. All the kids had played that game, telling each other their *real* parents were famous people. Rod Briggs used to claim he was actually Elvis Presley's kid brother; the family had been so poor they'd had to give Rod away. He'd elaborated on the story with convincing pathos, tears brimming in his eyes when he told them what he remembered about growing up down South with his wonderful big brother. And Lillian's daughter, Maxine, had confided that *her* real mother was a famous actress they'd all heard of, but whose name she'd sworn never to reveal. They'd all known it was only a game but there had been times when Snow couldn't help wondering if maybe it wasn't true. Even in the freedom of the school yard where she was able to race about, playing with an abandon that helped use up some of the welling energy that seemed to simmer inside her at home, threatening to boil over and send her out of control, there was a place in her mind that was always seeking the kernels of truth in the outrageous fabrications. Who knows? she'd thought. Maybe Roddy was Elvis's little brother. He looked a little like Elvis with his pale skin and dark hair. And Maxine was pretty enough to be the child of a movie star. So maybe she'd been left with Anne Cooke by people who already had too many children and couldn't look after any more. Anything was possible.

Eyes fixed unseeing on the night sky, she wondered what her mother had thought about when she'd come to sit up here, rocking slowly and looking out the window. She'd kept the glass clean, Snow saw, aware of the bare bulb's pristine reflection. But, atypically, she hadn't bothered to sweep. Which had to mean she'd cared more about being able to see out than about anyone seeing in. Or maybe the dust had been allowed to accumulate as proof of some strain of rebelliousness—a private declaration (so like the many Snow herself had made through the years) that there were limits to her passion for order and cleanliness, that she'd lived another life in her mind.

Letting her head come to rest against the back of the chair, she thought of how Anne had demonstrated an almost urgent eagerness to comprehend her child's behavior, so that Snow frequently had the impression her mother was studying her, the same way Snow studied her math and history. In retrospect it was apparent that the woman had worked diligently at motherhood, but seemingly without benefit of either a role model or any viable manual. She'd allowed the child to play with her jewelry and to dress up in clothes she herself hadn't yet worn, perhaps imagining other mothers would do the same. And she'd tried to quell Snow's over-abundant energy by insisting she engage in quiet activities: sitting in the living room with a coloring book on her lap and a fistful of crayons, dutifully trying to stay inside the lines, while her mother perched in the chair by the window with a book, and opera played on the stereo. Ever obedient, Snow had crayoned away, all the while wanting to jump up and go jigging around the room, waving her arms and shaking her head. It had been so difficult to sit holding in her need to move, her longing to turn somersaults on the carpet, or to spin around faster and faster to the point that she was so dizzy she fell down laughing. She held everything in until she could get outside and meet up with her friends. Then, in a frenzy of motion, she skipped and raced and tumbled until the bubbling inside had stopped and she'd felt calm, even happy, ready to go home and play quietly indoors, the way her mother wanted.

Hadn't Anne Cooke had a mother of her own? And why had her notions been so outdated—not just about parenting, but about the way a woman dressed and behaved? Her independence notwith-standing, Anne Cooke had managed to get time-locked into the 1950s and hadn't been able to find her way out. Too often her frames of reference had been completely out of synch with the times: her adamant refusal to allow Snow to dress like her peers; her insistence on interviewing every boy Snow dated—"Do come in. How nice to meet you. Tell me, what are your interests, your plans? Are you doing well in school? What subjects do you like best? Have you decided yet what you're going to do after high school?" Snow cringed, recalling her own discomfort and that of the few boys who'd come to pick her up at the house before she'd taken to meet-ing them at the crossroads or the café. And by the time she was six-teen, she was being spirited out of town, crouched low in the front seat of an old Ford station wagon, laughing recklessly once they were safely out of sight and on the way into Providence. She'd loved the danger more than the experience, and had defiantly done all sorts of forbidden things—partly in order to savor the real world that existed beyond her mother's influence, partly to work off some of the energy that, with time, increased rather than diminished, and partly because she knew quite early on that, if she capitulated, her mother would keep her out of the real world forever.

Who was that woman, that monster, with her weekly menu plans and cursory cooking skills? Where had she been and what had she done to arrive at her final years in this gracious house overlooking Narragansett Bay, with few friends and none of them close; with identities in three different names; with large sums of money from undisclosed sources, and an almost complete lack of remorse for what she'd done? Why had she done it? Why?

Beyond the window, on the far side of the road, the surf washed in in a muted rush, and the moon slipped behind the clouds, then out again, turning the view alternately dark, then light—like her thoughts, one moment loving and forgiving, the next outraged and accusing. She thought of Rudy and Katie advising her to be objective, to keep in mind the good things Anne Cooke had done, to bear in mind that the woman had done her no lasting damage, and she felt a bitter laugh rising into her throat. No harm done. A relative concept that had no weight beside the murderous rage that was beginning to build inside her. Her fists were tightly clenched and she willed herself to relax, to unclench, to let the rage carry on past her like a brief tornado blown out to sea before it could do any real damage.

She came awake with a start to find herself still in the rocker, with a blanket draped over her. Stiff, unrested, she looked around stupidly, blinking in the glare of morning light flooding through the decorative window, getting her bearings as she inhaled the aroma of fresh coffee. Hoisting herself out of the chair, she made her way downstairs to the bathroom.

"I thought it'd probably give you a nasty jolt if I tried to wake you, so I just let you sleep," Katie said, pouring Snow some coffee. "Hungry?"

"Uh-hunh."

"Good. Food'll be ready in a minute. That's some load of stuff up there," she said, opening the oven to peer at the bacon spitting under the broiler. "Rudy was telling me he offered to go through the tax papers. It's too much work for one person. Maybe I'll give him a hand, if you have no objection."

"Nope, none." Snow yawned, lifting her cup as the doorbell rang. She jumped, the hot liquid sloshing over her hand.

"I'll go," Katie offered.

"No, it's okay." Blotting her hand with a paper towel, she went to the front door to find Pete Briggs standing there and experi-

enced a brief burst of excitement before a closer look at his face told
her she had no reason to be excited.

"Thought I'd stop by early so we could talk in private," he said.

Snow invited him in, asking, "Had breakfast yet?"

"Hours ago, thanks." He nodded in greeting to Katie.
"Wouldn't say no to a cup of that coffee, though."

Katie opened the cupboard for a mug.

"You two go on and eat," he said.

The three of them settled at the table and Pete drank some of his
coffee, then came right to the point. "I'm afraid nothing turned up.
I was halfway hoping the bells and whistles would go off, and we'd
get a match, but they didn't." Reaching into his uniform pocket, he
brought out an envelope, slid it across the table to Snow. "Those're
the prints, for future reference."

Her appetite gone, Snow looked at the envelope, then at the police chief. "What exactly does the computer check?"

"Pretty much everything available, except for military records.
I'm sorry, Snow. It was a long shot at best. But you've got other
directions to go in."

"Right, sure. Well, thanks for trying anyway."

He looked into her eyes, read the disappointment there and said,
"Finding out who she was isn't something that's going to happen
in one day. I know it's not what you want to hear right now, but it's
better to face the facts squarely. And the fact of this matter is, you
might never find out who she was. She knew what she was doing,
and I'd hazard a guess and say she covered her tracks very carefully. I know you think there's a paper trail, Katie. Maybe there is,
and maybe it just leads to a dead end. It's not a good idea to have
your heart set on knowing, Snow," he cautioned. "That's a hard
line to take, and you probably think I'm being overly pessimistic,
but I've got a feeling about this whole situation, and I'd hate to see
you building up for a big fall."

She nodded to indicate she'd heard.

"In my opinion, I think you've got a far better chance finding
your family. But that's only one person's opinion, and as I told you
in the office, missing persons isn't an area I know much about. So,
I'm sorry I couldn't be more helpful. You two go ahead and eat
before your food gets cold," he said. "I'll see myself out."

"No, I'll walk you to the door."

In silence she accompanied him along the hall to the front of the house, then offered her hand, saying, "Thanks for taking the time to come over, and for being straight with me."

"Take it easy. I'll see you this afternoon."

She stood in the doorway until the cruiser had reversed out of the driveway and driven off, then she returned to the kitchen.

"Too bad," Katie said. "But he's right. It was a long shot."

"I know." Snow pushed away the plate of food and reached for her coffee. "I have a feeling there's going to be a lot of this, and I'm not sure I can handle it."

"You know what's always the first impression people have of you?"

"What?"

"You come across as confident, absolutely in charge of yourself. Never a wasted motion. You move like you're in a hurry and nobody better get in your way. So the impression is, here's a woman who knows what she's doing. Don't waste her time. When it comes to your work it's bang on. But when it comes to your life you get shaky as if different rules and standards apply. Yet you always manage to deal. And you'll handle this, too. You've got some truly peculiar ideas about men and relationships, and you dress funny, but you're not a wimp."

Snow laughed and shook her head. "*I* dress funny? That's very amusing coming from a woman who thinks high fashion is colored laces in her work boots."

"We're not talking about me. And since when are secondhand jeans haute couture?"

Snow reached over to take hold of Katie's hand. "I felt as if I was drowning there for a minute."

"No kidding. I was watching the bubbles come to the surface. Listen, d'you mind if I call Robbie? I'll pay you back."

"Don't be silly. You will not pay me back. Make as many calls as you want. I'm going to grab a shower."

"You ought to check your answering machine."

"Right. I'll do that before we head out." Snow continued to keep hold of Katie's hand, and chewed on her lower lip for a moment, before saying, "My head's very messed up. Part of me feels incredibly lethargic. I listen to you talk about helping Rudy go through those boxes of tax papers and the idea of it wears me out. Then I think about what that woman did and I think it's a goddamned good thing she's dead, because I want to fucking kill her."

Katie studied her friend for a long moment—this too-thin, long-legged woman in ancient jogging shorts and a faded T-shirt, sitting with her knees drawn up, one cold hand clutching Katie's, her eyes stony with anger—and had to say, "We're into territory where I've got no precedents, Snow. I think maybe I'd want to kill her, too, so I can't tell you not to feel that way. I guess it's like this whole grief thing. There's just no right or wrong way. There's only how you feel, and however you feel is legitimate."

"It doesn't feel good," Snow admitted. "It doesn't feel good at all. But you're right. I'll deal. I've never been able to lie down and play dead. Okay. I need a shower." Her features softening, she released Katie's hand, got up and headed upstairs.

Katie sat on at the table for several minutes staring at the remains of her own breakfast and Snow's untouched plate, wishing Pete Briggs had waited and come an hour later; wishing, too, that there was some book she could read, or people she could call to ask how to handle this matter. Just for a moment there, Snow had actually scared her with her ferocity.

"Hi, it's Mark. What's this, you're unavailable until after the twenty-second? Unavailable for what? That can't include me." He gave a breathy, knowing little laugh. "Give me a call. I've got some unexpected free time this afternoon."

"This is Evelyn Miller. I'd like to make an appointment for a sitting for my two children." She recited her number, said, "I'll expect to hear from you after the twenty-second," and hung up.

"Hey, Snow. It's Todd. Me and Josie are downstairs with some great Chinese chow but no you. What's up, and where are you? Call us. Okay? Bye."

"If you're there and you've decided to start screening your calls, I'd like to know why you haven't phoned me back. I blew the entire afternoon yesterday, waiting for you. What's going on? Call me, please. It's Mark, by the way."

A hang-up.

Another hang-up.

"It's Mark. I'm starting to get a tad annoyed here. Why haven't I heard from you? Are we into games now? I really thought we were beyond that kind of nonsense." There was a long pause, then he hung up.

Four tones signaled the end of the messages. She reset the tape, then put the phone down, wishing on the one hand she could be

back in New York, in her bed with Mark, working her way toward
sexual oblivion, and on the other hand that the man would quietly
disappear out of her life. She had no interest in speaking to him, no
intention of calling him back. She was offended right now by everything about him, and by her yearlong involvement with him. It
said something about her she didn't at all like. Yet the truth was if
he'd been anywhere within reach just then, she'd have thrown off
her clothes and dragged him down on top of her purely for the sake
of the release he represented.

Nine

After the service it seemed as if the town's entire population was crammed into the Stony Point Café. The overflow filled the street out front, people standing around in the mild afternoon sunshine with drinks in hand, chatting. A number of small children ran laughing up and down the sidewalk, pushing their way through the adults, slightly wild in the aftermath of nearly an hour's obedient silence in the chapel.

Their giddy noise reached Snow's ears during the conversational lulls, and she couldn't recall ever being quite so affected by the sound of children at play. She would never have been permitted to run about that way, and had to wonder what kind of childhood she might have had with her rightful parents. Hourly, daily, she was becoming more aware of losses that would have remained unknown but for Anne Cooke's sudden death. And the anger she'd managed to control for so long had returned, bigger and more acute than before.

Displays of temper had upset her mother, so from very early on, Snow had stomped off to her room to kick the furniture and pummel her stuffed toys, keeping out of her mother's sight until her emotions had been squashed into a more manageable shape.

Now, as in those childhood days, she kept trying to push the anger down. But she succeeded only in turning the inside of her head into something very like a firing range where recurring rounds of gunfire kept her mentally flinching. Everything was off-key, skewed.

But there was one thing she knew to be a certainty. The townspeople had come to the funeral primarily because they knew and cared about her, not her mother. Anne Cooke had never allowed herself to be known—by anyone, including Snow. She'd remained affably inaccessible, a known unknown in Stony Point. So on this day the woman represented an absence rather than a real loss. The people crowding into the café had come to demonstrate their affection for someone they knew as Anne Cooke's daughter—the person they remembered as a gawky redhead in quaint, smocked dresses and matching hair ribbons, with anachronistically impeccable manners and, once away from her mother, an overt, almost touching enthusiasm for their lives, for the slapdash meals of franks and beans, or leftover meat loaf and home fries, and for the rowdy, sometimes chaotic atmosphere of their homes; the odd girl who never walked if she could run, and who was forever asking people to stay still while she took their pictures.

Looking around now, she could feel the love for her in the eyes that met hers, in the benign smiles. And a corresponding affection for these good people dilated painfully in her chest, because, regardless of where she might have come from, she had a home in their hearts and it would always be there. This understanding brought her an unforeseen comfort. As Katie had been telling her, she *was* someone after all. Her identity was firmly entrenched in the minds and memories of those present. And if she started losing track of it herself, she could always return here to retrieve it.

She took a sip from her glass of rye and ginger. Through the open kitchen door she could see Katie on the telephone, one hand covering her free ear to block out the noise. Lucy was behind the counter with Irma, restocking the platters of sandwiches, the two friends nattering away companionably. Rudy was over by the door, talking to Pete Briggs; both of them sober-faced, intent. She herself was surrounded by members of the bridge group and Miss Morrow, a small, sweet-faced woman in her late sixties who'd taught English at the high school until a few years earlier. Snow looked from face to face, able to see the history written in each, the lifetime of experience in the lines and creases. Anne's face had had few lines; she'd looked far younger than her years, because she'd almost never let anything out past the windows of her eyes. Everything had remained assiduously contained, concealed behind an impenetrable wall of refinement that kept even her own child at a safe distance. No one had known her.

Was it an illusion or did the plastic container feel warm? Illusion, Snow chided herself. It was quite heavy, though. She hadn't expected the weight of it when she'd accepted the "cremains" from the attendant.

It was cool, almost cold, out on the bay, the small boat plowing valiantly through erratic waves. In chinos, an ancient Aran sweater over a red plaid shirt, thick white socks and Top-Siders, Rudy guided the Bull's-Eye through the chop, eyes squinting against the retreating sun. Snow watched a trio of gulls pass overhead, their infant-shrill cries sounding somehow tormented. The plastic container resting heavily on her jeans-clad thighs, she tasted the salt spray on her lips, felt it settling in her hair. Being out on the water was restorative, cleansing, timeless. It could have been last year or twenty years ago. She and Rudy were a harmonious team, long since attuned to the boat's slightest quirk. They sailed together in a mute appreciation and respect for the elements, alert to the weather and to one another. Often in the past, simultaneously, without a word having been spoken, they'd prepared to turn about, having spotted ominous clouds collecting on the horizon, or having felt the bay waters beneath them begin turning rough. To her mind it was utterly appropriate they should be together on this occasion.

"I guess about here," Rudy said, letting the sail slacken, "if you think this'd be good."

"This'll be fine." She turned to gauge how far they were from shore, her eyes automatically going to the end house on the point—Anne's sanctuary, the home she'd created for herself and her expropriated offspring. The anger quivered, like some slumbering beast, threatening to awaken. She moved away, out of its range. "Should we say a prayer or something?" she asked, uncertain of the protocol, if any, for so esoteric a situation.

"Whatever you feel's right, I guess," he said, a hand on the tiller holding the boat's drifting course.

She nodded, and unscrewed the lid of the "cremains." Holding the container upright over the side, she began whispering the Lord's Prayer and tipped out the contents—not just ashes but more solid fragments, too, that sank at once. The ashes sat atop the waves and she watched them as she got through the words, finding them possessed of potent new meaning that had her choking.

Head bowed, Rudy shaped the words along with her. And again, she felt a rush of love for him. He was so direct, so wonderfully uncomplicated. The prayer came to its end; the power and the glory, forever and ever, amen. Good-bye to her mother, to the fragrant warmth and mystery uniquely hers; good-bye to those sudden girlish smiles that revealed a clear picture of the child she'd once been; good-bye to the love she'd given that came with rules attached but that was never less than complete; good-bye to moments of unparalleled sweetness and of maddening rigidity; good-bye stranger.

How could someone simply cease to be? What happened to the energy, the intelligence, the essence of that person? Where did it all go? Was it reformatted and tucked into the brain cells of a new-born who'd one day have unsettling sensations of déjà vu? Or was the truth simply that one survived only so long as one was remembered? If it was a matter of remembering, Anne would stay alive as long as Snow did. She might never come to be any better known than she was during her lifetime, but she would most certainly not be forgotten.

Setting the container down between the boat's ribs, she wiped her face with the back of one hand, then pushed up her sleeve and splashed water over the ashes until the surface was once more clear. Her hand numbed from the cold, she dried it on her jeans as she gazed at the dying sun, feeling the chill seeping into her bones. "I guess that's it," she said at last.

"Guess so," he agreed, and let the air fill the sail. "You take the tiller, Snow, and we'll head on in."

The empty container rolled around the bottom of the boat as the small vessel danced over the waves. It made a light hollow sound that was almost lost to the rising wind and the water noise, the slap of air in the canvas sail. When they were about halfway to shore, she turned back to look, knowing it was silly but unable to stop herself. There was, of course, no trace of the ashes.

"I made appointments for you with the lawyer, the stockbroker and the accountant on Monday. Then I did some checking with Social Security," Katie announced during dinner.

Both Rudy and Snow lifted their heads.

"I called their 800 number," she explained.

Snow put down her knife and fork, not sure she could take anything more in; her head felt as if it was filled with chunks of gravel.

"I halfway expected to get a busy signal but this robot voice came on and said my call would be answered in about a minute, and sure enough it was. I found out a bunch of things, but none of them any good to us." Katie gave Snow an apologetic smile. "According to the guy I talked to, once the Social Security office has been notified of a death, a family member with the proper ID can present herself at the local office and asked for the deceased's history. They'll give you the payment record and names of former employers, but no tax information or previous addresses. They don't even keep those, beyond what's current. Which means they'd be of no help so far as where Anne might have lived before she came here. The one positive note is that if she ever held a job, we'd be able to get the name of her employer, which would be a definite lead.''

"I really don't think she ever worked," Snow said, exhausted just listening to what she'd have to go through to obtain any information.

"You never know. You'll have to notify them of her death in any case, so there'd be no harm in asking, once the notification's in their records. One interesting thing I found out. They've got a letter-forwarding unit. So, if you were adopted and wanted to find your birth parents, you could write to this unit in Baltimore, giving whatever information you have on whoever you're trying to find and your reason for wanting to get in touch, along with your name, address and phone number. You include a letter in a stamped, unsealed, unaddressed envelope, and for a small fee, they'll forward it. Plus, they'll even keep you notified of their progress. Cool, huh?''

Rudy nodded, fascinated. Snow tried to pay attention, but could feel parts of her brain slamming shut, like a series of windows closing.

"The downside is," Katie went on, "it'll only work if the person you're trying to contact is receiving benefits. If your parents aren't disabled or collecting a pension, it's no good. So, now that I've eliminated that area, we'll concentrate on following Anne's paper trail. One of the people we're seeing Monday is bound to have some record of her transfers from New York—either the accountant or the stockbroker, maybe both.''

"What if they don't?" Rudy asked.

Snow watched their interchange like a tennis match, turning from one side to the other, so weary she could scarcely follow what they were saying. It might have been a foreign language they were speaking.

"I guess at that point Snow gets a private investigator to work on finding out about Anne Cooke." She looked over and saw that Snow's eyes were glazed. "Sweetie, why don't you try to eat something, then maybe go grab a nap. You've got that zombie stare you get when you're doing too much and your circuits are overloaded.''

"I can't take anything in," Snow confessed, retrieving her knife and fork. She was hungry, but the chicken casserole Katie had prepared didn't appeal to her. She poked at the mound of rice with her fork, pushed some green beans around on the plate, then gave up. "If the two of you don't mind," she said, "I think I'll go take that nap now."

"Nobody minds, Snow," Rudy said. "You go ahead."

"I'll save this for you," Katie offered. "You'll be hungry when you wake up."

Snow paused to rest her cheek on the top of Katie's head, an arm around her shoulders as she looked over at Rudy. "I appreciate everything you've done. You, too, Rudy. But my brain's shut down. We'll talk later. Okay?"

Katie said, "Sure. Go on."

Down the hall and up the stairs, moving from memory, each step of the way imprinted forever on her consciousness. Snow was asleep the instant her body settled on the bed.

Katie wrapped Snow's plate in foil and popped it into the oven, set the temperature to warm, then returned to the table, saying in a low voice, "I'm worried about her. It's like she's retreating, which is exactly what I was hoping wouldn't happen."

"She'll be okay. Over the years I must've seen her go away inside herself at least a hundred times. She learned early on to hide her true thoughts and feelings from Anne. She was as stubborn in her own quiet way as Anne was in hers, and when things didn't go right, she was like a little turtle, pulling her head inside her shell." He chuckled at the image. "Then, a few hours or a few days later, out she'd pop again, full of spunk and ready to go. Do you know that in all the years I've lived next door I never heard either one of them raise her voice? That's just not natural, Katie. Even me and Martha, close as we were, we had our tiffs. But with the two of them it was like this fierce tug-of-war that never ended until Snow got away to New York."

For a moment he thought of Anne in the immediate aftermath of Snow's departure, the only time he'd ever seen her appear looking anything less than perfect, a distance and disbelief in her gaze as if her daughter had died instead of simply going off to school. For weeks she'd stayed indoors, canceling her weekly hair appointment, keeping all the shades drawn. He'd knocked at the back door every few days, making sure she was all right, handing over bouquets of autumn flowers that she accepted with a vague air. Then one morning she'd reappeared, looking the same as ever, climbed into her car and didn't return until late that night—he'd heard the car and glanced over at the illuminated face of the clock to see it was past midnight. A few days later she'd accepted when asked to make up the fourth at bridge after Loretta Sloan passed on, and that was the end of her upset at Snow's leaving.

"She'll be okay," he repeated, wondering where it was Anne had gone that day. Wherever it might have been, and whoever she might have seen, it had managed to get her back on an even keel.

"It's just that she tends to keep things bottled up." Katie speared a green bean and popped it into her mouth. "Usually, I stay on top of her, dig away until she tells me what's wrong. But at a time like this... It's hard to know how far to push. She's the best friend I've ever had, Rudy. In some ways I'm closer to her than I am to any-one. I have to help her get through this." She paused for a mo-ment, then, as if he'd offered some argument, said, "I know she'd do the same for me."

"I don't need convincing. I know what good friends you are."

"How was it out on the boat?"

"It was okay," he said thoughtfully. "About what you'd ex-pect."

They ate in silence for a minute or two. Then Katie said quietly, "Scary, isn't it?"

"Yup. That's the truth. I've lived seventy-one years, the first forty-odd in Boston where I saw some things I wish I hadn't. But this has me sitting up nights, wondering. You think you know peo-ple but maybe you never really do. Maybe all we ever get to know are other folks' habits.''

Snow had no idea how long she'd been asleep. All of a sudden she was wide awake and simply had to get out of the house. A quick trip to the bathroom, then she pulled on a heavy old sweater and hur-ried downstairs as if pursued. She took a moment to put the front door on the latch, and then stepped outside into the chill, foggy night. Not a sound but the surf, the fog muting even that. Feeling the house at her back—solid, even demanding, like Anne herself— she went down the walk and across the road to the beach.

The fog seemed to open up to enclose her, and rendered every-thing unknown, even treacherous. It was impossible to see more than a few inches ahead. She found her way to the water's edge, jumping back in time to avoid the incoming wash, and, hands clenched at her sides, chewing on her bottom lip, she started up the beach at the tide line. She'd dreamed of her mother and, her heartbeat revving as the details came back, she'd begged to be told the truth. But her mother had just smiled, insisting, "You don't need to know any of that, dear. It's not important."

"But it *is!* Somebody needs to know where I am. It's *very* important."

"Don't get yourself worked up, dear. You know it's not good for you."

"Not knowing isn't good for me. Okay. All right. Just tell me who you are. Please!"

"Don't be silly. I'm your mother, of course. Who else could I possibly be?"

One of their classically maddening, elliptical dialogues in which Snow made no impact, failing consistently to express the scope and depth of her feelings, while her mother tried to shush and soothe her into placid acceptance.

Love for a parent was such a strange thing, she thought abstractedly. It seemed to exist in an inaccessible niche in the heart where almost nothing could alter or erase it, not even the discovery that the parent was in no way related to you. It was the length and depth of the tie, not the blood connection itself, that gave it its power. And no matter who she might turn out to have been, Anne Cooke had been her parent.

Well past Mrs. Hoover's house where, she noted, the lights were on and faint sounds of music drifted out through an open window to be swallowed up in the fog, Snow found a protected little gully and sat on the sand with her knees drawn up, staring into the misty blankness of the night.

It was as if the frustrations of thirty years had coalesced to form a raging indignation that demanded satisfaction. She wanted Anne alive again so she could confront her, strike her if necessary, to get the explanations she needed and deserved. Nothing had ever felt worse than the helplessness that had had her in its grip since the night of that woman's death.

Something far off caught her eye and she turned to her right to see a fuzzy pinpoint of light in the distance. Not Pete again, was it? How could Mrs. Hoover have seen or heard her in this fog? Couldn't have. But the pinpoint was slowly enlarging, moving closer, and she was all at once terrified, knowing it was her mother, coming to find her, to scold her for risking her health out here on a wet beach in the middle of the night. Her dead non-mother was approaching. Couldn't be. But she was paralyzed with fear, and tried to shrink into invisibility in the shallow gully. Was she dreaming? She could wake up if this was only a dream. But how could she be asleep and taste the salt, feel the fog flat against her skin like something alive? What was she afraid of anyway? She was younger and bigger and stronger than her mother; well able to defend herself. But this was more than her mother, nothing against which she had any defense. What was she doing out here? Why couldn't she wake up?

The light drew steadily closer, growing by degrees, and she couldn't look away from it, trying to become smaller and smaller as the diameter of that yellow glow grew. A dream and she could wake up. She could. Concentrate and the ghost would slip back under the water, the ashes drifting down to the bottom of the bay. Her lungs were heaving and she started to cry, wedging her fist in her mouth, as she waited for the figure of Anne to materialize out of the mist.

The light touched upon her briefly then was lowered, a yellow circle moving across the sand. She closed her eyes, felt the air close to her disturbed. Then Katie was sitting beside her, quietly asking, ''What're you doing?''

Relieved laughter gushed out of Snow, and she hugged her friend to her side. No dream, no ghost, just Katie. I'm so ridiculous, she thought, and went on laughing. Infected, Katie joined in. The two of them clung to each other, rocking with hilarity.

It was the thought of old Mrs. Hoover hearing and possibly calling Pete Briggs that finally stopped her. Sitting back, Snow wiped her face with the flat of both hands as her breathing steadied. ''You scared the hell out of me, Katie,'' she said.

''I just wanted to make sure you were okay. You went tearing out of the house like the hounds of hell were after you.''

''It felt as if they were.''

''Why do you do that? Why do you run the minute things turn not nice? Seriously. Avoidance with you is like a major art form.''

''I don't know,'' Snow answered tiredly.

''You can't just run off and hide—even metaphorically. You'll never solve anything unless you confront what bothers you, admit to it, handle it.''

"This bothers me. Okay? How the hell'm I supposed to handle it, Doctor?"

Stung, Katie snapped, "You know what I mean. I'm here to help, and I can do without the sarcasm, thank you."

"Sorry."

They were quiet for a minute or two, the fog drifting around them like an immense, gently billowing veil.

"You're confrontational," Snow said at last. "You're good at it. I'm not. I wasn't supposed to make noise, or argue, or get mad. If I did, I was failing her. No little kid wants to go failing her mother. So I tried to be what she wanted. It wasn't that terrible. I mean, you made the point yourself. She wasn't sick or twisted, none of that. She just had this genteel thing working all the time. You know?"

"I know. I saw that."

"It was quid pro quo. Be a good girl and I'll love you. When I pulled it off, her praise was the best thing in the world. It felt great, on one level, Katie. It really did. At that level my mother was smarter and prettier than anybody else's, and being with her was a treat. She talked so quietly, had such soft hands, such nice clothes. All the dumb stuff you notice when you're a kid. You know? The other women in town wore housedresses and had chipped nail polish. But I liked them, and on another level, sometimes better than my own mother. Because they were easier. You could go to their houses, play with their kids and make noise, and they'd just holler from the kitchen to hold it down." Snow smiled in the dark.

Katie smoothed her friend's tangled hair. "I can just see you," she said, feeling a retrograde fondness for that little girl.

"But when I messed up," Snow continued, "if I fell down again in the school yard, or didn't get a good mark in arithmetic, I was always scared something terrible would happen, that she'd go off and leave me. Pretty goddamned ironic, huh? Every single day when I came home from school I was scared she wouldn't be there, at the same time secretly wishing she'd be gone, and then I'd go live with Rudy. He'd let me play in the dirt, and we'd eat toast and cream of tomato soup and go sailing in the Bull's-Eye all the time, not just on weekends. I'd wear regular clothes and finally be like the other kids. Naturally, thinking that made me feel evil and guilty as sin, so I'd try even harder to be the way she wanted."

"And now she's gone off and left you," Katie said sagely. "The worst thing that could happen, finally has."

"I only *thought* it would be. I've found out otherwise."

Katie slipped an arm around her waist.

Snow drew in a ragged breath and let her head rest on Katie's shoulder. "I know I've been a pain in the ass. I'm sorry."

"Give yourself a break, eh? You've just been through some very heavy shit."

"The thing is, being her child left me with this holdover idea that if you expressed disagreement about anything—to her, or anyone—it was all over. You'd stop loving each other or you couldn't be friends anymore. So instead of saying, 'That's crap! I can't go along with that,' or whatever, I got into the habit of withdrawing."

"Bad habit."

"I know. I *know*. But people don't just change their habits overnight, Katie. Especially not when you've spent the first seventeen years of your life being a Pavlovian puppy."

"We've all been paper trained, babe, one way or another."

Snow smiled. "Yeah?"

"Basically. You bet. Get your nose rubbed in the doo-doo enough times, you learn to hold it in and do it in the street."

Snow laughed, then said, "I'm starving. What time is it anyway?"

"I don't know. About twelve-thirty."

"You're kidding! It feels like the middle of the night."

"C'mon." Katie tugged at Snow's arm. "Let's go back and get you something to eat. It's kind of spooky out here. By the way," she said, as they started off through the fog, "I meant to tell you. I had a very interesting chat with Mrs. Menzies after the funeral."

"Really? What about?"

"We were just shooting the shit. But then when she said she was the librarian, I had this inspiration and asked if she happened to know anything about trying to trace birth parents, and, bam, she started rattling off all this good stuff about where to look and how. Told me I should go to city hall when we get back, and check out the records—marriage, divorce, property, voter registration, motor vehicles. Told me to look at the city directories, court records, employment records, hospital records. On and on. Records, records, records. I just stood there with my mouth open while she went down this list, like she'd had it memorized in case someone should ask. Then she patted me on the arm and said, 'Of course, it'd be easier, if you can afford it, to hire an investigator with a computer to access the information services.' It was amazing.''

"She'd be the one to know, all right. You definitely picked the perfect person."

"How so?"

"All four of the Menzies kids are adopted. When Cheryl, the youngest, was getting ready to go off to college a few years ago, she decided she wanted to find her birth parents. Mrs. Menzies jumped right in and helped. They were at it for months, probably checking all those records she was telling you about. In the end, they hired an investigator. He located the mother in maybe three weeks." Snow paused, swallowing against the sudden dryness in her throat.

"And?"

Vividly she remembered her mother recounting the story with a certain sad relish during one of Snow's weekend visits home. Feeling the cold all at once, she said, "The woman was married, had two other kids, and didn't want anything like a daughter she'd forgotten she ever had messing up her nice, tidy life. She told the investigator to tell Cheryl to stay the hell away from her. Jesus! Poor Cheryl was shattered."

"Not like all those happy reunions on TV shows," Katie observed sadly.

"Maybe I should hire someone, save us the hassle."

Striving to lighten the mood, Katie said, "Personally, I'd love to meet a genuine P.I., see if he's anything like the guys I read about. Probably wouldn't be, and then I'd be totally disillusioned, maybe turned off mystery fiction for life. Ideally, what I have in mind is one of those brooding, ruggedly attractive, intellectual British types; a guy with a divine accent, of a certain age, who writes poetry in his spare time, or who's hooked on Mozart operas, and drives an old Jag in mint condition."

Snow stared at her.

"You're thrilled by the idea. I can tell."

"An investigator who writes poetry?"

"Babe, you've got to give Stephen King a rest and start getting into some decent fiction."

"I read other people besides King."

"Right! I'm forgetting Bradbury. How many times now have you read *The Illustrated Man?* Thirty, forty?"

"I'm pleading the Fifth." Snow tightened her hand around her friend's, directing her to the right. "Ten more steps and you'll be in the water. The house is over this way."

Katie sat sipping a cup of Sleepytime tea and watching Snow eat. "Take your time. Nobody's going to steal your plate," she said, then had to laugh at herself. "I sounded just like my mother, saying that."

"I love your mother," Snow said soberly.

"Hey! So do I. Chill out, woman."

"This is delicious." Snow wolfed down the chicken that hadn't at all appealed to her earlier. "You're such a good cook."

"God knows, you're not."

"I come by my lack of domestic skills honestly," Snow retorted, pausing to drink some water. "She was the worst cook."

"But very clean. Maybe she came out of a religious order."

"What, a nun, you mean?"

"It's possible."

Snow nearly choked on her food, laughing so hard tears came to her eyes.

"It's possible," Katie repeated.

"No way." Snow chewed, swallowed, then said, "She was too fond of expensive things. I always took it for granted she came from a wealthy family, even though she only ever alluded to a 'modest inheritance...'" Suddenly, she thought of all the jewelry upstairs, saw herself tiptoeing down the carpeted hallway toward her mother's room. She dropped her knife and fork, jumped up, and went running out of the room.

"What? What's the matter?" Katie asked, chasing after.

"Something I want to look at," Snow explained, taking the stairs two at a time, heading for the master suite.

"I thought you were choking or something, for God's sake. Don't *do* things like that!"

"Sorry. I had a memory flash." Snow switched on the light, went straight to the dresser, grabbed the jewelry box, and said, "Let's do this downstairs. I'm still hungry."

"You're making me crazy!" Katie grumbled warningly as they headed back down the stairs.

"Sorry," Snow said again, setting the Florentine box on the table and gazing at it with slightly narrowed eyes as she retrieved her knife and fork. "Is there any more of this left?"

"Sure. Want me to nuke some?"

"Yes, please. I can't believe how hungry I am."

"I can. You haven't eaten enough the past couple of days to keep a hamster alive." Katie got the casserole from the fridge while Snow began, between bites, carefully removing everything from the box. "What?" Katie asked, looking over.

"I have a memory about this box, but I'm not sure if it's something I dreamed or actually saw. I was five or six, creeping up on my mother as she was futzing around with this. I went boo, and she jumped a mile. After she landed, she told me it wasn't nice to do things like that. I might have given her a heart attack, and I wouldn't want something like that to happen would I? I wound up feeling guilty as sin, crying my heart out. The thing is, before I jumped into the doorway, I thought I saw a kind of drawer she was putting something into."

"Wow!" Katie said softly. "This could be significant."

Moving her plate aside, Snow studied the tooled leather box for a moment then lifted out the partitioned upper section, set it aside and began removing the sundry items from the bottom. She picked up the box and turned it this way and that while Katie watched.

"I can't figure it out." Snow felt around the inside, examined underneath, then the sides. "It's too shallow on the inside," she explained.

"Maybe the bottom lifts out."

Snow tried. "Nope."

"Let me try." Katie came over and Snow handed her the box. "I'll bet it's like one of those Chinese puzzle boxes. Find one side that moves, then the whole thing comes open."

The timer went off and Snow got up to help herself to more of the chicken, returning to the table while Katie continued her investigation.

Half an hour later, the two of them were sitting staring at the box in frustration. "This is bullshit!" Snow said suddenly. "I know the goddamned thing opens." Grabbing the box, she carried it to the counter, set it down on the chopping block, got a hammer and screwdriver, and proceeded to take the box apart. Ten minutes later, sweating from her efforts, she positioned the box on its side and gave the front panel a mighty whack with the hammer. It dropped open, revealing the concealed drawer she'd seen all those years ago after all. "I was right!" she exclaimed.

"What's in it?" Katie asked, rushing over in time to see Snow remove a small red envelope.

"Safe deposit box key."

"Bingo! Monday, between appointments, we'll hit that bank and check it out."

"I didn't imagine it."

"No, you didn't," Katie confirmed. "Good for you, babe!"

"Yeah," Snow said softly, almost afraid to hope there might be something in the safe deposit box that would lead to some answers.

By Sunday evening, with Rudy helping, they'd managed to get through all of Anne's tax papers. Rudy wanted to hang on to the annual hotel bills, saying, "There's telephone charges every year, sometimes adding up to twenty or thirty dollars. Maybe we could ask the hotel people, see if they kept those records. Be interesting to find out who she was calling."

"For damned sure," Katie agreed.

Aside from those telephone charges, there was nothing of particular interest. She had claimed no unusual expenses. Her deductions had been minimal, the tax bite high. After Rudy went home, Katie and Snow returned the previous five years' worth of documents to the attic, setting the others aside for eventual transporting to the town dump.

Tired and grubby, they headed for bed.

Ten

It was a one-man law office. The secretary, a pretty, middle-aged woman, with short dark hair and a lovely smile, told them Mr. Benson would be with them shortly, and asked if they'd care for coffee. Snow and Katie thanked her, refused the coffee, and sat down to wait.

Less than five minutes later the door to the inner office opened and a rather hefty man, with a crescent of gray hair surrounding a bald dome so shiny it looked polished, came out to meet them. He was wearing a dove gray three-piece suit cut to minimize his girth, a wide welcoming smile, and he sailed across the waiting room with his hand extended. "Bill Benson. Sorry to keep you waiting. I wanted to pull your mother's file before we talked." He looked for a long, admiring moment at Katie, then over at the secretary, then back at them, asking, "Did you want some coffee?"

"No, we didn't, thank you," Snow answered.

"My wife, Ruth," he said proudly. "Sure you won't have coffee? It's a very good blend of Colombian and French roast."

Both Bensons looked expectantly at Snow and Katie who again declined. "We just had a late breakfast," Snow explained.

"Okay, then," said Benson. "Come on in and sit down."

His office was an unexpectedly soothing space, with walls painted pastel peach, and blond modern furniture. The pair of chairs before the desk had clean, rounded lines and on the wall opposite the window hung a beautifully executed marine watercolor.

"Really nice office," Katie complimented him.

"Glad you think so," he said, settling behind the wide desk, one corner of which was occupied by a framed collection of family photos. "Ruth did the decorating."

"She's got good taste," Snow said.

"It's a good thing she does, because, according to her, I could be knee-deep in debris and wouldn't notice. Well now." He swiveled his chair a half turn to the right, keeping his eyes on Snow's. "I was sorry to hear about your mother's death. I saw her just last month and she seemed in the pink.''

"It was very sudden, a heart attack."

"A mixed blessing, I suppose. If I was going to go, I'd want to go fast." He gazed out the window for a moment, smoothing non-existent hair with the palm of one hand. Then he swiveled back to lift open the folder on his desk. "I guess we should get down to business. I take it you're aware of the terms of your mother's will?"

"Basically," Snow replied.

"Okay. Good. We'll get going on the probate right away. It ought to be fairly straightforward."

"I was wondering if my mother might have left any papers with you for safekeeping."

"With me?" He looked puzzled. "No. Aside from the will, there's nothing. Is there something missing you expected to find?"

"Not really." Having discussed it during the ride into Providence this morning, she and Katie had agreed not to muddy the waters by bringing up the issue of Anne's identity with the lawyer. Katie had argued that it could conceivably jeopardize the estate, possibly tie it up indefinitely in legalities. "Let's wait until you've got a lawyer representing your interests," Katie had advised. "This guy, remember, represented hers. He might not be willing or able to help. I think the smart thing is to go ahead just as if you really were her daughter, until somebody advises you otherwise."

"We did find a safe deposit key," Snow told him. "Maybe there'll be documents in the box. We're heading over to the bank after we leave here."

"Oh, I think you'll find you have a problem," Benson said apologetically. "I'm afraid the bank won't open the box for you."

"Why not?" Snow's disappointment was so immediate and so deep it felt as if her heart actually sank lower in her chest.

"They'd agree to a will search, were I to accompany you," he explained. "If it's your opinion that another will might exist, I'd be happy to go with you to investigate the contents of the box. But that's all we'd be permitted to do. Until you can go into the bank with a court-validated certificate of probate, the contents cannot be removed."

"You mean we couldn't look at whatever might be in there, even if we didn't take it away?"

"Sorry, no. Legally, you're allowed to look in the box if it's your belief there's another will that supersedes this one. Otherwise, you can't even look."

"How does all this work?" she asked, wanting to plead with this soft-spoken, teddy-bearish man to throw out the rules and help her get that box opened. "What's the procedure?"

"Give me a minute to review this, would you?" He donned a pair of reading glasses and began scanning his copy of the will.

Katie surreptitiously gave Snow's hand an encouraging squeeze.

"Okay," Benson said after a minute or two, again his eyes dwelling almost lovingly on Katie for a few seconds before focusing on Snow. "I write a lot of wills. Just wanted to refresh my memory. This one's a little on the unique side in that there are no bequests, no unusual conditions. Also because your mother didn't stipulate an alternative executor. You and I are the sole executors. And since there are no other heirs, that does simplify matters. Here's why." Again he swiveled a half turn in the chair, looked over at the window, and ran a hand over his gleaming skull. Then, catching himself mid-gesture, he swiveled back, gripped the edge of the desk with both hands and gazed directly at Snow. "In the normal course of events, we petition the court to admit a will for probate. The court has to give notice to the heirs-at-law and to anyone mentioned as executor or trustee. However, in this instance, because you and I are the only named executors, and because there are no other heirs-at-law, we can sign waivers to the probate court to file with the will and the application for probate. That will move things along and, depending on how busy things are at the courthouse, we could get certification in a matter of days."

"Certification for what?" Katie asked.

"That Snow and I are the named executors," he answered. "A copy will go, for example, to the stockbroker in the event you decide to have him liquidate her holdings. I like to cover all the bases, so as a matter of course the broker and her accountant will receive copies. And you'll have to show a copy to the bank in order to access the contents of the box. If you agree to the waivers, and there's no reason why you shouldn't, since it'll serve to expedite matters, you should, with luck, be able to get into that box in, say, two weeks' time."

"That means I'll have to come back. I live in Manhattan," Snow told him. "I'm planning to go home, probably tomorrow."

"I think I knew you lived out of state. Your mother talked about you constantly. She thought the world of you." He offered Snow a smile of such sweetness she imagined the kids in the desktop photos probably adored him.

Snow smiled back and said nothing. She didn't trust herself to speak at that moment. She was picturing a man very like him spending half a lifetime grieving for the daughter who'd been stolen from him in infancy.

"You'll have to come back anyway, won't you?" he asked. "I imagine there are a number of loose ends to tie up. It's my understanding your mother's estate is substantial."

"I guess I probably will. I'm playing things by ear right now, since I have no idea how long any of this might take."

"Okay, fair enough. Here's how it'll go from my end. First off, I'll prepare the waivers and you can drop by to sign them before you head home. Then I'll get things moving at this end."

"How long will the probate take?"

"Oh, you're looking at anywhere from a year to eighteen months."

Shocked, Snow exclaimed, "That long?"

"Easily. A final accounting of your mother's assets will have to be made. Taxes will have to be paid. Then we sit back and wait for a clearance from the IRS. And, as you'll know if you've ever been waiting for a tax refund, the IRS is anything but speedy. It all takes time. I'll do my very best, but I'd count on at least a year." Returning to the will, he said, "She did make provision to forgive all outstanding loans. Were you aware of that?"

Snow nodded.

"Okay, good. I'll notify the various parties, take care of the nuts and bolts. D'you have any questions? Is there anything you don't understand?"

"No, not really."

"Please feel free to call me if it turns out you do. I'm here to help you in any way I can. In the meantime I'll start the wheels turning." He paused to look at her with sympathy. "I'll try to get you access to that safe deposit box as quickly as possible, since it seems so important to you. But as for the rest of it, I'm afraid you're just going to have to be patient."

With an hour to kill before their appointment with the accountant, Katie and Snow went to a nearby restaurant.

"I can't *believe* we can't get into that damned box," Snow fumed, both hands closed tightly around a cup of tea.

"It's only a couple of weeks."

"It's lost time," Snow argued. "There might be something in there that could help us."

"We've got other leads," Katie reminded her, trying to keep Snow calm.

"I know. I was just hoping..."

"You were hoping it'd be easy."

"You've been encouraging me to think it would be."

"No," Katie said carefully. "I have not. I've been saying there's got to be a paper trail, and that we'll try to follow it. Not once have I suggested this would be easy. I know you're disappointed. So am I."

"I *hate* not knowing who she was, who I am, what the hell the story was. I keep going up and down like a goddamned yo-yo."

"That's understandable. I know how hellish this is for you, babe, but you can't start raging when things don't happen the way you want them to. It's only going to make everything worse."

"I keep thinking this is an insane dream and if I just concentrate I'll be able to wake up. But I can't, and the dream keeps going on and on." Snow sat staring into the steam rising off the tea while Katie busied herself applying strawberry jelly to her English muffin.

"What doesn't kill us makes us stronger," Katie said philosophically.

Snow emitted a brief laugh. "Thank you. I feel so much better now."

Katie looked up sharply, saw that Snow was making an effort to relinquish her anger, and laughed, too. "I have all the aphorisms you could possibly want. Just let me know when you need one."

"Just keep 'em coming. An aphorism a day, you know."

"Of course, I do bill for the service," Katie quipped, biting into the muffin.

"I was so up for seeing what was in that box. I guess I wasn't being very realistic. But then, this whole situation's hardly realistic."

"It could be there's nothing in there but more jewelry, more money. You'll have to be patient, that's all."

"I hate being patient, under the circumstances."

"I know. But, much as I hate to keep having to say it, you don't have a whole lot of choice. We may run into a lot of roadblocks of one kind or another, and there's not much we can do except try to get around them. The thing is, you can't let it make you crazy. Eat your toast. You'll feel better.''

Marty Kauffman was a slight man who had to be well into his fifties but whose boyish air made him appear much younger. He had a good-natured face, with dark eyes behind horn-rimmed glasses, a wide mouth topped by a bushy mustache, and an energetic, efficient manner. Snow had met him many times over the years, and had always found him friendly without being obsequious, the way so many adults were with children.

He greeted her and Katie warmly, asked if either of them cared for coffee or tea, and invited them to make themselves comfortable in his office while he grabbed a Coke from the refrigerator.

"He's so preppy," Katie whispered as she and Snow sat down side by side on the long sofa at the near end of his office. "He's adorable. I love the argyle socks and penny loafers, the bow tie. Half my mom's friends are married to guys just like him. The other half are in interracial marriages—which is something about that group of women that's always intrigued me: how they gravitated toward men with whom they had nothing in common culturally. But none of them in mixed marriages divorced. And what's *really* interesting is that almost all the grandparents—with the exception of mine, on both sides—refused to have anything to do with their kids, until the babies started coming along. Now they're all fiercely devoted to the grandchildren. And none of them remembers disowning anybody. It's very touching, really.''

Marty came back with his Coke and dropped into an armchair facing the sofa, saying, "When I left the old company to start up on my own, your mother was the first of my clients who offered to make the move with me. Her loyalty meant a lot to me. I'd have come to the funeral but it was very short notice, and one of my clients was being audited. It was impossible to seek a postponement." He took a long swallow of the Coke, set the can down on the coffee table and said, "So, aside from preparing for the final tax accounting, what can I do for you, Snow?"

"I have a couple of questions."

He made an expansive gesture with his hands and said, "Fire away.''

"I've written to the insurance company, with a copy of the death certificate. What I want to know is will the money come directly to me, and do I have to pay tax on it?"

"Yes, it'll come direct and, no, you don't have to pay tax on it."

"My God!" Snow said softly.

"A million dollars, tax free," Katie said, awed.

"It's a lot of money," Marty confirmed. "You'll maybe want to think about investing it. I assume you'll be talking to Nick Cameron about the estate."

"He's our next appointment, as a matter of fact."

"We've already spoken," Marty informed her. "He's going to start pulling the figures together for the final return."

Snow glanced at Katie, deciding the moment had come. They'd discussed the day's agenda in great detail, but the timing was at Snow's discretion. Katie gave a go-ahead nod, and Snow said, "I need your help on something, Marty."

"Sure." He took another swallow of Coke.

"I'd like you to read this," she said, and handed him a copy of Anne's letter.

As he read, his mouth dropped open and his eyes went round. "Is this for real?" he asked.

"Afraid so," Snow answered.

"Man oh man oh man," he said in disbelief, looking down at the letter then across at Snow. "If it's true, the woman was one crazy lady. Jesus!" He let the page drop to the coffee table and wiped his hands on his trousers. "What kind of person does something like that?"

"That's what I'd like to know," Snow said, in a small way gratified by his response. It really was as awful as she thought, and each person's appalled reaction was not only confirmation, it was also a certain sanctioning of her inflamed emotions. "Katie and I are going to try to find out who I am, who she was."

"You might just be able to help," Katie put in.

"How? I thought she was a widow named Anne Cooke. She looked like someone who'd be thrown by an ATM but she never seemed to be thrown by anything. I mean, she's the only client I had who read up on the least little change to the reporting laws or tax rates. Boy! I can't get over this!"

"Back in the early sixties, when she first came to you as a client, she must've provided you with at least the previous year's tax return. I know it's a long shot, but Katie and I are hoping maybe you'd still have it on file somewhere.''

"I'd say it's almost a dead certainty that she did, and I do. When I left Bowman & Marks, I was permitted to take my clients' files with me. Knowing how the IRS likes to nitpick, I keep copies of all my clients' returns. You never know when they're going to start twitching, so it's better to be on the safe side. Let me put Judy right on it. Shouldn't take more than ten or fifteen minutes for her.''

"That'd be great!" Snow could scarcely believe their luck.

He got up and went to the outer office where they heard him talking quietly to the secretary. A minute and he was back.

"What we do," he explained, sinking again into the armchair, "is remove old paperwork from the files every five years and put it into transfer files that're stored in the basement. We keep an alphabetized list, with the year and box number, on the computer. So, if we have to, we can locate something in a matter of minutes. Judy'll key in the name, get the box number, then head downstairs, locate the box, and pull the file.''

"Very efficient," Katie congratulated him.

"I'm pleased with it," he said with the satisfied expression of a student who'd just pulled off an A-plus on a term paper. Then, the reality of the situation seemed to strike him and his slight smile evaporated. "What are you hoping the return's going to tell you?''

"Maybe a previous address, or the name of another accountant she worked with, even her real name. Anything," Katie replied.

"Good thinking. Are you as calm as you seem?" he asked Snow.

"At moments, I feel completely demented," she admitted. "In some ways, I wish she'd kept the whole thing a secret.''

"I can imagine. The *idea* that someone could do a thing like that, that *she* could've... It's unbelievable! Your real parents..." He shook his head. "I keep wanting to think it's some kind of perverted joke, but she didn't have much of a sense of humor.'' He looked guilty suddenly, and said, "Sorry.''

"It's okay, Marty. She didn't.''

"How're you planning to track down your family?''

"We'll start with the newspapers and go from there.''

Again he shook his head. "Unbelievable," he repeated. "If you need an investigator, an old college friend of mine handles security for a New York firm and does some moonlighting on private cases. A decent guy. If he can't help you, he'd probably know someone who could. Let me give you his number." He got up and went over to consult his Rolodex, then jotted a name and number on a piece of paper, returning to hand it to Snow just as Judy appeared in the doorway with the file.

"Okay," he said, back in the armchair with the file on his knees. "Let's see what we have here. Yup, here's her return for '63. Let me just run you a copy."

Fifteen minutes later, having thanked Marty profusely and promised to let him know how it all turned out, Katie and Snow were hurrying to the nearest coffee shop with the copy of the last tax return Anne Cooke had filed before her move to Rhode Island.

Eleven

The return had been filed in the name of Anne Cooke.

"Well," said Katie, "I'd say this proves she'd planned everything way ahead of time."

"Unless, of course, her name really was Anne Cooke."

"Come on. We know it wasn't." Reading on, Katie said, "Look at this. Her address back then was in the East Sixties. Not exactly your low-rent neighborhood, plus it tends to confirm that the kidnapping went down in the city."

"After all this time it's unlikely we'll get anywhere with that address," Snow said, trying to be realistic. "The building has probably changed hands half a dozen times, and there'll be no record of former tenants. Still, it's a beginning."

"We'll check it out even though I think you're probably right. But this C.P.A., May Connor, who prepared the return, might still be around, and might even know what Anne was calling herself before the name change. We've got a couple of leads. Not great ones, but definitely leads. We're starting to get somewhere." She looked at her watch. "Should we be leaving?"

"We're okay for time. Nick's office is only a two-minute walk from here."

"How d'you feel?"

"I'm okay." Snow looked around the restaurant, trying to decide if that was the truth. "I was hoping we'd get a little more from the return, but I guess I'm learning to lower my expectations."

"Speaking of expectations, do you realize you're going to be a millionaire?"

Snow gave an edgy laugh. "I can't take it in. I'm still trying to absorb the fact that there's ten thousand in my checking account. A million's beyond belief. I mean, a couple of times I've flashed on it and thought, wow, I could do anything, get a new place to live, buy a Hasselblad, go anywhere I want. Then I think, no way. It's not real."

"I think you'll make a very good rich person." Head to one side, Katie studied her friend. "Some people, money turns them into monsters. All of a sudden they're rude to everybody. They go out and buy big ugly houses and a load of tacky furniture. They start wearing hideola designer clothes they think look good just because they cost a lot. I can't see you doing any of that."

"Me, neither. I thought I'd give Rudy the Buick. You think he'd be offended?"

"I do not. That junker of his has to be thirty years old."

"Close. It's a '66 Fairlane. He lives on a pension and Social Security. I'd love to give him money, but that probably *would* offend him."

"Probably. He's a proud old dude. You're safer to go with the car."

"Yeah, that's what I thought."

"Listen," Katie said. "I've got a feeling you shouldn't tell the stockbroker about Anne. The more I think about it, the more antsy I get. You don't know the guy all that well. And he's got this fiduciary position. Maybe he'd have to report the situation or something. It's better not to take any unnecessary risks, and I think telling this guy falls into that category."

"So what do we tell him then, to get him to give us the information?"

"I don't know. Why not some spiel about how your mother had this falling-out with the family and now that she's died you want to get in touch and let them know. Stress the family angle. He'll buy it."

"I hate lying. I'm lousy at it."

"It's not totally lying," Katie argued. "The fact is, you *are* trying to find your family."

"Katie, what if I never find them? What if I never get answers to any of this? I can see me going batshit, spending the rest of my life wondering."

"You just can't dwell on the negative possibilities. It'll wreck the present for you. And the one thing you *do* have is your life. Whatever happens, you've got to live it the best way you can."

"Why did she have to confess? Why keep a secret for thirty years but be planning all along to confess in the end?"

"Who knows? Maybe she was trying to balance the books. I mean, it's obvious she always intended you to know. That letter was there, waiting for you."

"But that was written pretty recently."

"True. Maybe she never expected to live as long as she did, and was kind of borrowing you temporarily, with the idea that you'd be returned to your family."

"Unh-hunh. She was healthy as a horse."

Katie shrugged. "All we've got is guesswork. We should get going. I hate being late."

"We won't be late. I just have to get myself psyched for this. I'd kill for a cigarette."

"I'll kill you if you have one. Let's go."

"Nothing's worse than a reformed smoker," Snow declared. "I really need a smoke."

"Get through this interview and you can have a drink instead when we get back to the house."

"Alcohol's way worse than tobacco."

"Could we please just go?"

Snow gave in, grabbed her bag, and slid out of the booth.

Nick Cameron had acquired many fine lines around his pale blue eyes but otherwise looked much as Snow remembered him from half a dozen previous visits to his office over the years with her mother. Tall and blond, with aristocratic good looks, deep lines bracketing his mouth so that he appeared to be permanently displeased or bored, he stood, shot his cuffs, then came out from behind his desk to greet Snow, keeping hold of her hand with both of his as he said, "It was a terrible jolt, hearing about your mother. I'm very sorry."

"Thank you," she said, carefully freeing her hand. How could she have forgotten how unctuous Nick Cameron was? "This is my friend, Katie Shimura."

"A pleasure," he said, all but bowing over Katie's hand, clearly stricken by her beauty. "Please do sit down."

The office was chaotic, with papers and prospectuses piled high on every surface, a row of dusty sports trophies crammed together on the windowsill, and three walls covered in slightly crooked photographs.

"I've already spoken to Marty Kauffman," he said, moving to sit back down behind his crowded desk. "He probably told you."

"Yes, he did," Snow confirmed.

"So then you know we've begun getting everything ready for probate. It's going to be a decent-size estate, and I realize it's somewhat premature but I was wondering if you've given any thought to what you're going to do with your mother's holdings."

"I really haven't had a chance. For the time being, I'd like to leave them as they are."

He nodded, turned to his computer, punched in some numbers, and said, "I'm bringing the current figures up on the screen. I don't know if you've had a chance to look at the recent statements, but I thought you'd like a rough idea what we're talking about."

"Sure," she said, still uncomfortable discussing Anne's money, with the ongoing, pervasive sense that she had no legitimate claim to it.

Katie had leaned forward, trying to see the computer screen.

Nick smiled at her, and adjusted the monitor so she could see. "I'd have to go in and check today's buy and sell rates to be completely accurate, but conservatively speaking, we're looking at around eight hundred thousand, give or take. Your mother was using a percentage of the income to cover living expenses. The rest was being reinvested. Most of the holdings are in solid, income-producing funds. You might want to think about hanging on to those. The oil stocks you could dump now at a profit. I'll get you an up-to-date printout and you can consider your options. Personally, I'd advise you to hang on to the bulk of the investments."

"I'd like to wait and go over everything with my broker, see what he thinks. I'm not going to make any changes right now. Later, once things have settled down, then I'll see. Anyway, according to the lawyer, none of this'll actually be mine for a year or more."

"Partly true," he said. "As executor, you can restructure the holdings if you see opportunities for more growth. You can even liquidate the entire account and have the proceeds held in a money market account. Of course the earning potential would be considerably reduced. But discuss it with your broker, see what he says."

"I will. I'll do that." She paused, then said, "Nick, I've got a bit of a problem you might be able to help with."

He sat up taller, saying, "I'll certainly help in any way I can," and smiled again at Katie, as if they'd joined forces as allies of the grieving daughter.

Katie smiled back, finding him oily and pretentious.

"That's very kind of you. You see, my mother had a big falling-out with her family years ago, and now that she's died, I'd like to try to get in touch with them, let them know. The thing is, I haven't been able to find any information in her personal papers, and I won't get access to her safe deposit box for a few weeks. So I was wondering if, by any chance, you might still have the paperwork on file, transferring my mother's account here from her previous broker."

He stiffened, his expression suspicious. "How would that help?" he asked, as if she'd cast aspersions on his brokering skills.

"Well," Snow ad-libbed, "it's my understanding that the family trust was managed by that brokerage." She paused, wondering if it sounded plausible.

"The previous broker might still handle the investments of other family members," Katie jumped in. "It's worth a shot, and might save Snow some time."

"I just think they'd want to know," Snow added, feeling transparent.

Nick's features relaxed. "What year did she move up here, d'you remember?"

"Sixty-three."

"Okay. That'd be before the ACATS system was set up."

"The what?" Katie asked.

"Automatic Customer Account Transfer," he translated. "The old transfer records would be on microfiche. But that could take ages. I'm fairly sure we'd have kept a hard copy of the transfer form. It's standard operating procedure for this company," he said proudly. "Have you got a few minutes? I could run down the hall, take a look."

"Sure," Snow said at once. "That'd be great."

"Sit tight, the two of you, and I'll have a go at the filing cabinets up front."

He left the office, and Snow wiped her damp palms on her knees.

Katie was studying the figures on the computer screen. "Taxes are going to wipe out a good third of this money," she said, turning to look at Snow who'd gone pale. "You okay?"

"Just nervous. I feel like I'm scamming the man."

"D'you see his face when you asked about the paperwork? I'm telling you, babe, you can't mess around when it comes to money, especially not with a guy who's right out of a Dickens novel. Can you imagine the number he'd have done if you'd told him the truth? He'd probably have called the FBI. Where'd she *find* this guy? He gives me the creeps—those moist manicured hands and the hyperthyroid eyes." She shuddered theatrically.

"I swear to God, this business is going to wind up giving me an ulcer."

"You and me both."

Nick was back in less than ten minutes. "A miracle," he announced. "It was right where it was supposed to be. I made a copy for you." He handed it to her before returning behind his desk where he referred to his copy of the document. "It's a good solid company, medium size, been around a long time."

"If we wanted to find her broker specifically, how would we do that?" Katie asked.

"See that code above the brokerage stamp—two numbers, two letters, followed by seven digits?"

Katie and Snow both looked.

"The first pair of letters and numbers indicate the location of the office and the ID of the broker. I'm guessing, but I'd say the MA stands for Madison Avenue, and 35 is the broker's number. What you'll want to do is phone the office and read them the code. They'll say something like, 'That's Joe Smith,' and if he's still around they'll put you through to him. If he isn't, they might know where he's working. If he's gone, and they don't know where he went, you're probably out of luck, unless someone else in the firm took over handling the trust account."

"This is very helpful, Nick. Thank you so much."

Preening, he said, "No problem at all. I hope you manage to connect up with the family. Must've been quite some falling-out, to've lasted so many years. Now listen," he said, rooting around in the desk drawer, "let me give you the prospectuses on some of your mother's holdings, so you can make an informed decision when the time comes."

"Certainly," Snow said, knowing she couldn't possibly refuse.

Her bag heavy with reading matter, she thanked him again, waited while he bowed once more over Katie's hand, then she and Katie left the office.

Once in the elevator, Katie punched her lightly in the arm, grinning. "It was worth having him slobber over me. We've got a definite lead now."

Snow found herself smiling. "You are the biggest optimist who ever lived."

"That's fine, because you're the biggest pessimist. Makes us a perfect team." As the elevator doors opened, she said, "Lend me your AT&T card and give me the copy of the transfer. I'm going to call that brokerage right now. Here, hold my backpack."

Snow leaned against the wall to wait while her friend made the call. Finally, Katie hung up, returned Snow's card, and said, "I got nowhere. The woman I finally spoke to said she thought maybe the ID belonged to a guy named Daniel Ambrose who hasn't been there for years. There was some guy who might've known but nobody answered his extension. So I guess we'll have to pay him a visit when we get back to the city. You won't believe his name. Huffy Compton. *Huffy!* Could you die?" Laughing, she retrieved her backpack, saying, "All in all, my darling, I'd have to say it's been a productive day. We're making some genuine progress."

Snow draped an arm around Katie's waist as they made their way toward the parking lot where Snow had left the Volvo.

That night Snow slept badly, awakening several times and finally, just past five, after a dream where she screamed at her mother who made no attempt to defend herself, she gave up altogether. She showered, dressed, and crept downstairs with her camera bag. While the coffee was brewing, she sat at the kitchen table with a package of optical tissues and a blower brush and painstakingly cleaned her lenses—an activity she always found comforting.

She loved every single piece of her equipment—the bodies, lenses and flash, the filters and tripods, even the camera bag itself—and felt a greedy pleasure in handling it. For a long time now she had believed that the images she made with these items were all she was likely to create in her lifetime because of a secret and abiding fear of childbirth.

From the outset of her sexual life she'd been obsessively scrupulous about birth control. She took pills twenty-one nights a month, used contraceptive foam, and insisted her partners wear condoms. She tended to panic if her period was even a day late, and was only eased each month once the flow began.

Nothing her mother had ever actually said fostered this fear. It was a result of a combination of things: Anne's squeamishness about physical matters in general and sex in particular, her faintly disparaging attitude toward men, and her failure ever to make even the slightest reference to the details of Snow's birth. Snow was left with the disagreeable impression that childbirth was unspeakably tortuous, and through the years had a recurring nightmare of herself grotesquely bloated, strapped down on a cold metal table, her feet tied to wide-apart elevated stirrups. While pain stormed her senses, her body struggled to rid itself of its writhing burden. Finally, after a tormentingly protracted labor, she gave birth to something not even remotely human that white-gowned-and-masked attendants quickly whisked from her sight. They whispered together, looking back at her over their shoulders as they carried the creature away. She awoke from these dreams sweat-drenched and trembling, queasy with relief. Aware of the discrepancy between her dire fear of becoming pregnant and her innate fondness for children, she had resigned herself to playing out the role of auntie to the babies of her friends.

Now her views were altering, her fear perceptibly subsiding. She'd begun ruminating on what it might be like actually to be someone's mother. None of the several women she knew who'd given birth had apparently suffered any long-term ill effects. They'd joked about the labor, about the episiotomies, the hemorrhoids and engorged breasts. There was no aspect of the entire experience, from conception to delivery, that didn't get offered up humorously. To a one they made it clear that the physical discomfort was insignificant in the face of the achievement: They'd produced lusty, ever-hungry infants whose faintest cries were audible only to them, even from considerable distances, and the sight of whom effected startling alterations in their features. As mothers they'd become more expansive, delighting in newfound instincts they'd been unsure, in advance of the birth, they possessed. They glowed, these mothers; they radiated well-being and ferocious levels of protectiveness. Snow held their babies with a sense of awe, but was still fearful.

The truth had to be that the impression she'd garnered from Anne Cooke was utterly wrong. And this understanding led her into a completely unanticipated sympathy with a woman who must have suffered an all but crippling need, as well as untold fears, to have been driven to abduct someone else's child. She pitied Anne, and pitied herself, too, for having participated so fully in her mother's apprehensions that she had, ultimately, adopted them as her own.

The equipment returned to the bag, Snow carried a cup of coffee into the living room and looked at the things Anne had loved: her collections of music and films. She studied the videotapes, trying to see if they conformed to any particular pattern. They didn't.

The films ranged from *Some Like It Hot* to *Robocop,* which Anne had especially liked. Surprisingly, she'd enjoyed a certain type of violent movie—in which clever superheroes single-handedly decimated legions of lowlifes—while she'd gone thin-lipped with agitation at scenes of lovemaking that lasted longer than fifteen seconds. It was obvious the woman had suppressed a lot of anger, and had been seriously discomfited by sexual displays. But all in all that was fairly typical of her generation—a group that, for the most part, found change of any sort threatening.

Moving on, Snow saw there was no discernible pattern or consistent theme, either, to the cassettes and CDs, or the old record albums. It was simply an accumulation of wonderful music. And if she closed her eyes, she could see herself curled up on the sofa, and her mother in the Chinese Chippendale chair by the window. Carefully dressed and made-up, fingernails perfectly polished, legs crossed just so and a book in hand, Anne listened to the music, eyes rising slowly from the page to gaze beyond the window at the bay. Her blue eyes turning opaque, she went traveling, taken to unimaginable places by the music. And once again, Snow felt the pain of her absence.

The sky was beginning to lighten. She dashed off a note asking Katie to meet her at the café at eight if she was up in time, then gulped the last of the coffee and pulled on her jacket. With the camera looped around her neck, several rolls of film and lenses in both pockets, she slipped out of the house into the still-cold, salt-scented morning.

She had no specific destination. It simply felt important to get shots of the house on the point where she'd grown up, of Rudy's wonderful garden, and of Mrs. Hoover's historic dwelling with its graceful lines and widow's walk; of the Bull's-Eye riding at anchor, centered in the sun rising over the bay; of the several summer homes not yet opened for the season; of the tree-lined road leading into town; of the small white clapboard library and adjoining post office; of Lillian's Beauty Parlor, Mr. Willard's drugstore, and Abel's Amoco Station; and, at last, of the interior of the Stony Point Café, where a flushed and bustling Lucy was taking orders behind the long counter while the early birds read the morning papers and steam from their coffee cups curled into the warm air.

No one paid much attention. She'd been aiming her camera at the townspeople forever, even when she was only home for a weekend visit. And she was as much a part of the morning scene as Pete Briggs rolling through town in the cruiser, Jane Fergus sweeping the sidewalk out front of the boutique, or the brown UPS truck angle-parked outside the café while the driver, Buddy Bremer, ate his breakfast. Snow Devane had been clicking away at the town and its denizens since the Christmas she was twelve when she took herself into Providence—without her mother's knowledge or consent—to return the expensive, fussy royal blue velvet party dress her mother had bought her and used the refund money to buy a secondhand Nikon with two lenses and three rolls of film.

She'd discovered something very significant that year: Most people liked having their picture taken. They'd posed for her in front of their houses and stores, by their boats and cars, shoveling snow or weeding their flower beds. They'd paused, bloodied knives in hand, while cleaning fish at the marina, or scooted out, oil-smeared, from under their cars; they'd turned from their stoves, or their knitting, or their quilting, to smile for her camera. And she'd amassed thousands of prints, each one of which upon viewing brought back to her the precise circumstances that had existed at the moment she'd released the shutter. The photographs were not only a record of what she'd seen and done, and the people she'd known, they were potent evocations of her personal weather at any given time. She could examine, say, a shot of Wally Schaefer in his volunteer fireman's gear and remember that she'd taken the picture on a Saturday afternoon the second last weekend in August of 1978.

That morning she'd argued with her mother in Providence while shopping for school clothes. It had been a typically one-sided, whispered exchange that Anne, as always, had won because Snow hated arguing and wasn't very good at it. She invariably capitulated just to put an end to the grating sensation she got in her chest whenever she tried to stand up for her rights. Upon arriving home, she'd dumped the new clothes on her bed, pulled on cutoffs and a T-shirt, grabbed her camera and stormed out of the house.

In a foul mood, she'd kicked her way along the road, approaching the old firehouse where Mr. Schaefer was modeling his bright new yellow fire-fighting gear for his fellow volunteers. By the time she'd finished shooting him, she'd pretty much forgotten the argument. Taking pictures had a highly therapeutic effect that remained undiminished by time.

Pocketing the two exposed rolls of film, she slid into the booth opposite Rudy.

"Reminds me of old times," he said, "seeing you out at first light with the camera."

"Me, too."

"Planning on eating, Red?" Lucy asked, putting a cup of coffee down in front of her.

"I'll wait and see if Katie makes it."

"Toast in the meantime?"

"Yes, please."

Lucy patted her on the head and went off, and Rudy asked, "Making a memory book, Snow?"

"I think maybe I am. Half of me's dying to get back to the city and the other half of me doesn't want to leave."

"You'll be back."

"It won't ever be the same, though."

"Nope. But nothing stays the same. You know that."

"I have this feeling that if I do find my family, I'll have to start restructuring myself to accommodate that identity—as if the parts of me will still be the same but they'll get shuffled into a different arrangement."

He gave her a slow smile. "Don't go making yourself into a jig-saw puzzle. No matter what happens, you'll be who you are. When we climb into bed at night, we're always climbing in with ourselves, regardless of who might be hogging the blankets on the other side."

She laughed and reached across the Formica to take hold of his hand. "I love you, Rudy. And I'll miss you."

Twin patches of color blossomed on his cheeks. "I'll miss you, too. But it's not as if it's forever."

"No," she agreed. "It's not. It's definitely not forever."

Twelve

Nothing looked right. After her stay in Stony Point, the living area of the loft struck her as dismal: neglected, orderless and in need of a good cleaning. The window exteriors were grimy, the few pieces of furniture shabby, and the unmade bed was a nasty reminder that not long before Rudy's phone call she'd been making love with Mark. For almost a week she'd managed not to give him much thought. Now, briefly, she craved the sight and feel of him. But the craving quickly passed, and she was left disturbed by the graphic evidence of their primarily sexual involvement. Her reaction was all the proof she needed that the affair was over. If she couldn't bear looking at the stained sheets, she most certainly couldn't bear looking at the man responsible for their condition.

Hurriedly she stripped the bed, including the mattress cover. Everything went straight into the washing machine. She poured in detergent, slammed shut the lid, selected a cycle, waited to hear the first rush of water into the drum, then turned away, seeking comfort from Maria Callas singing Puccini and Bellini arias.

Not at all soothed by the music, she stood looking out the dirty window: cars double-parked as usual on the street below; people hurrying along the sidewalk; Irene, one of the local bag people, inspecting the contents of a trash can; sirens wailing in the distance. Noise, motion, overcrowding, despair. It wasn't just the windows that were grimy; the entire city seemed soiled, squalid. The surrounding buildings with their stained brick felt overly close, like too many sullen people crammed into a subway car, forced to breathe each other's odors and exhalations.

For the first time she saw with great clarity that the city was not beautiful. Fascinating, yes; in the way of certain reptiles whose sluggish movements lured you to come just a little too close, and who then displayed startling speed as their jaws opened to reveal rows of vicious teeth that could effortlessly sever limbs. Citizens were devoured by this city every day. It vibrated with an appealing boisterous vigor; its towering spires and tempting possibilities distracted you from its stealthy menace while purposeful strangers, intent on making off with your possessions, tracked your comings and goings, their unseen hands testing the vulnerability of your domain.

Shadow people shambled into alleys to buy, sell, or ingest drugs; or—mere feet from the passing traffic—they engaged in hasty, unpretty sexual acts with paying strangers while their narrowed attention was fixed on distant narcotized images. Homeless souls populated parks, huddled like windblown refuse in doorways, slept on gratings, begged listlessly with extended paper cups and dulled eyes. Angry swaggering teenagers toting immense boom boxes hiked up to maximum volume dared you to take offense at their roaring rap attack on your senses. Danger resided in the immediate periphery of your every action; ongoing caution had to be exercised if you were to survive relatively unscathed. Safety was an illusion, a lullaby sung to yourself from behind expensive Fox and Medeco locks and grating-shielded windows. In this city you fell asleep not to the sound of the surf but to the whine of sirens, and were sometimes abruptly wakened by a heart-gripping cry of terror from the street.

Turning, she surveyed the loft, asking herself what she was doing here, if this was really what she wanted.

She'd never consciously decided to make the city her home; it had merely happened. Her friends were here; her work was here; she'd long since accepted the local rules of survival—once beyond her initial forays into the early-morning streets, tempting fate and her mother's pain—and lived accordingly. She'd actually become accustomed to the sight of human misery, even fairly desensitized to it. And that wasn't right. She didn't want to think of herself as uncaring, but with her new finely tuned vision she could see that she'd been sliding in that direction. She'd grafted herself onto the city and become an offshoot of it, looking away from things that were too painful to see, and trying to grow in an absence of nourishing light.

Had she been in some kind of holding pattern for the past dozen years? Certainly nothing about the loft indicated permanence. Even the washer/dryer, the one major acquisition of her adult life, was a so-called portable unit. The furniture was all knockdown, short-term stuff—bookshelves and tables from Ikea she'd assembled herself or with Katie's help; a cheap bed that would probably destroy her spine if she didn't soon buy something better; hardware store utility lamps clamped to shelves; a mishmash of unmatched plates and cups, inexpensive stainless-steel cutlery; bottom-of-the-line white plastic verticals she'd cut to size and hung over the windows herself; unframed prints of her own work pushpinned here and there to the otherwise unadorned walls. The whole place had a temporary air, as if, unknowingly, she'd merely been biding time. Only the studio area had any feel of substantiality, of permanence. This was where her money had been spent, and it showed. But all this, too, was transportable, knockdown. The studio could be completely disassembled in a matter of hours and would fit easily into the back of a medium-size van.

What had she been waiting for? Where had she thought she'd go? Obviously she'd never intended to stay, otherwise she'd have acquired "real" furniture, comfortable furnishings. She'd have created a cozy nest and wouldn't still be living like a student on a strict budget. She definitely hadn't been counting on marrying her way into another existence. She'd never harbored the secret romantic notion that some man would come along to rescue her from the onerous responsibility of living her single life. She *liked* her single life—such as it was. So what had she been doing, beyond creating some fine portraits of some very lovable children? Getting by, going from day to day, her focus fixed exclusively on her career. Life was evidently something she'd been intending to get around to one day, when she had a moment.

It was frightening to think she'd wasted valuable time, and to concede that she'd had few enriching experiences—with either men or women. For the most part, since leaving school, she'd been an observer rather than a participant. And she'd preferred it that way; she'd felt comfortable watching, either from some sheltered corner, or on the streets late at night, or through the lenses of her camera. What did that say about her as a person? If she dared to look into a mirror now, would her own image be as disconcertingly unattractive as the view from the window? She actually had choices and, as well, she'd soon have the money to finance a move in any direction she chose. The problem was she had no idea where she wanted to go.

The telephone rang. She started guiltily, then went toward it, noting as she approached that the message light on the answering machine was blinking steadily. She really was off track. Usually the first thing she did upon returning home was check for messages.

"Does everything look as weird to you as it does to me?" Katie asked without preamble, an anxious edge to her voice. "I walked through the door and it was like I'd never been here before, and I'm not too thrilled about being here now. All of a sudden I understand why my mom refuses to come visit anymore. I thought it was just a mother thing, you know, because she's such a clean freak. But I came in and saw the place the way she probably does and realized it's a total shit heap."

Snow laughed softly. "I was just asking myself why I live here, and how come I don't have any furniture. It's as if I've been time-warped since graduation. I feel like a complete transient."

"Me, too! Is this amazing or what? I've been sitting in the kitchen staring at the floor, wondering if I've just been futzing around, deluding myself, while everything's been happening somewhere else, without me."

"Exactly!"

"I don't know about you, babe, but I'm on the verge of being majorly bummed. Young Dr. Kildare's on a three-day marathon gig at the hospital and I can barely remember what he looks like. Plus, he had the unbelievable chutzpah to leave me this snarky note saying the laundry needs to be done. I won't even go into *that*. There's not a goddamned thing to eat. I mean nothing, not even a cracker. All that's in the fridge is half a petrified lemon and a bottle of something that looks like a urine specimen."

Snow laughed.

"Hey! No kidding. I am *not* in the mood for a soul-searching session on what the hell I'm doing with my life. So what say we hit the library?"

Alarm like an electric shock sizzled through her, and Snow said, "Maybe we should wait."

"For what? Let's just do it, Snow. I'd like to nail down some facts, get moving. Wouldn't you?"

"Well, yes. But I thought maybe in a day or two. The place is a mess and I've got printing to do...."

"You're procrastinating because you're scared. I understand that. But the longer you put it off, the more scared you're going to get. Come on, babe. Meet me out front of the Forty-second Street library in forty minutes."

Frozen, Snow couldn't speak.

"Come on," Katie coaxed. "Now's not the time to hide out. This isn't going to go away, and crawling into a hole to brood about it is *not* going to help. You need some answers and, believe it or not, so do I. I'm right in this with you, Snow. I love you and I'm having trouble with this, too. I know I'm not going to be able to concentrate on anything else until we at least see the story in print, verify she wasn't just playing some bizarre mind game."

"Okay, you're right. It's *not* going to go away. And I probably wouldn't be able to concentrate, either. So, okay. Forty minutes."

Snow hung up and went for her jacket and bag. The messages could wait; unpacking could, too. A few more hours in the holding pattern wouldn't make any difference, because the simple fact was that, until she began unraveling the roots of her origins, she wasn't going to be able to change one damned thing in her life.

They made their way up to the newspaper division on the third floor, where they sought assistance from a most accommodating woman on the microform desk in the north reading room. Within half an hour they were seated side by side at reader/printers with film for every Manhattan newspaper that had been in print between the twenty-first of September to the end of October 1963: the *Post,* the *Daily News,* the *Daily Mirror,* the *New York Times,* the *Journal American,* the *Herald Tribune,* and the *World Telegram & Sun.*

Katie divided the spools of film between them. "I figure the *Times* and *Herald Tribune* probably won't have much, if anything, on the story, unless your parents happen to be high-profile types. So let's concentrate on the others first. Are you nervous? God, I am. My hands are all sweaty."

Snow nodded, unable to speak, and, following the instructions taped to the front of the machine, began threading the first spool of film under the lens and onto the pickup reel. Mouth dry, heart hammering, she advanced past the leader to the first pages of the *World Telegram & Sun.* In less than two minutes she'd found the story. Her fingers trembled as she adjusted the lens to pull the item into sharper focus. She was having such difficulty breathing she'd gone light-headed.

Beside her, Katie whispered, "Holy Hannah! I've got it!"

Snow nodded again, staring stricken at the photograph of a chubby baby grinning from the page. She felt ill. Her face was burning but her body was shivering as if from cold. She couldn't look away from the round-cheeked baby she'd been.

Katie was watching. "It'll be okay," she whispered, suddenly able to fit herself inside Snow's emotions, seeing the bleak landscape there. "D'you need a Kleenex? Here's one. It'll be okay, Snow. It will." Why am I telling her that? Katie wondered. Maybe it won't be. But what else could she say? It occurred to her that it was basic instinct to tell accident victims, bereaved people, banged-up kids everything would be okay. You had to keep assuring everyone the future would be better than this moment, even when so often you knew it probably wouldn't be. Because most people didn't have the heart, or the meanness, to say otherwise. What a goddamned world! she thought, studying Snow's shocked profile. What a lousy, fucking world! Why were people always messing with kids, one way or another? You were a freak these days if you had a reasonably happy childhood because all your friends had suffered some kind of abuse. And now this.

INFANT KIDNAPPED IN GROCERY

A seven-month-old girl was kidnapped this morning from a supermarket on mid-Manhattan's East Side. A 16-state alarm has been issued for the baby, identified as Victoria Mac-Kenzie, the daughter of Mr. and Mrs. William MacKenzie of East 68th Street.

According to officers from the 19th Precinct, the baby disappeared while her mother, Mrs. Patricia MacKenzie, twenty-two years old, was shopping in the Gristede's Market on Madison Avenue near 66th Street.

Mrs. MacKenzie told police she entered the supermarket with the infant at about 10:15 yesterday morning. She left the sleeping child in its infant seat in her shopping cart to go to another aisle for an item she'd forgotten, and when she returned the baby was gone.

Several customers in the market at the time recalled seeing a dark-haired, middle-aged woman of average height in a navy raincoat who apparently left the store without making any purchases. None of the cashiers remembered seeing the woman at their registers.

Police are continuing to question witnesses and a $10,000 reward has been offered for information on the kidnapping. Anyone with information is asked to call the police at the 19th Precinct.

Putting her head down on her arm, Snow cried with the abandon of a child, feeling everyone's pain: her own, her mother's, the MacKenzies'. *Why did you do it?* she asked the dead woman. *How could you do that to these poor people, a twenty-two-year-old mother, and to me?* In the space of time it had taken to read the article her grief had doubled, quadrupled. She remembered suddenly, arbitrarily, the afternoon she'd taken a spill on the front walk. Three or four, perhaps; she'd tripped, skinning both knees. In tears, she'd gone stiff-legged up the steps and into the house, calling for her mother who'd been on the telephone, talking and laughing. Her mother just hung up the phone without even saying good-bye. "Oh, poor you," she'd said. "You wait right here and I'll get the car keys."

She hardly ever saw her mother talking on the telephone, and never talking and laughing. It was different, funny. "I don't wanna go to the doctor!" Snow cried. "I want *you* to fix it." Taken aback, there'd been a long thoughtful pause while her mother had, with narrowed eyes, studied the injuries. "I want *you* to fix it!" Snow had insisted, feeling she had a power somehow because of catching her mother talking and laughing on the telephone; because it meant something.

"All right, dear," she capitulated, and carried the limpet-like Snow, clinging with tightly entwining arms and legs, upstairs to the bathroom.

"Don't use the stinging stuff!" Snow had half begged, half ordered, knowing just this once that she could make these rules because she'd got tears and blood all over her mom's blue dress, but her mom didn't get mad.

She just said, "Okay, dear. We won't use the stinging stuff." Instead she applied something that was wet and cool and didn't hurt at all. And Snow was so relieved at not having had to go to the doctor's office again, and not being scolded for messing Mommy's dress, she'd fallen asleep in her mother's lap, right there in the bathroom, wondering who Mom had been laughing with on the telephone. It had been the beginning of Snow's understanding that she had an emotional power over her mother. But only rarely was she able to use it because it was somehow too easy to hurt her. It was far simpler to hurt herself in the hope that the hurt might have a repercussive effect on her mother. In this oblique fashion, Snow had spent more than half her life trying to squirm free of her mother's overwhelming, yet too vulnerable, love. Now, she had a completely new perspective from which to view their entire relationship, and she suspected she'd probably spend the rest of her life randomly recalling incidents that would have utterly altered meanings. Her whole memory bank had just been stamped INVALID.

Katie was crouching beside her, stroking her back. "I'm really sorry. It was kind of like a game there for a while, but it's all for real now, isn't it?"

Snow nodded, marveling at Katie's insight and comprehension.

She handed Snow another Kleenex. "Just, bam! All of a sudden we're way beyond playing amateur sleuths, into real honest-to-God crime. You gonna be okay?"

"I don't know. But I want to keep going."

"Good for you. You're a gutsy woman."

"Yeah, well. I wouldn't go that far. I just have to follow the thing to the end." Snow wiped her face impatiently, took several deep breaths, and read on, moving from one day's reporting to the next.

The story was big news for several weeks. With almost nothing to go on, some of the papers created features out of interviews with the supermarket staff and customers who happened to be present in the store at the time of the kidnapping. Several people had noticed the mysterious dark-haired, middle-aged woman, and a police sketch (bearing no resemblance whatever to Anne Cooke) was carried for nearly a week in most of the dailies.

As sundry leads failed to turn up any trace of the baby, the items grew smaller in size and were relegated farther and farther back in the various papers until, finally, after about two months, the story disappeared altogether. A check of the newspaper indexes for the next ten years revealed no further follow-up. The MacKenzie baby had vanished off the face of the earth.

At last, drained, the two of them gathered up the copies they'd made of all the press items, and left the library.

"Where should we go?" Katie asked when they arrived back on Fifth Avenue.

Stunned, Snow couldn't think. She looked up the street, then down at the sidewalk, feeling completely disoriented and somewhat dozy. It was not dissimilar to how she'd felt as a child after attending a movie matinee with her mother, emerging from the theater into the glare of afternoon sunlight. It should have been dark, and close to bedtime. Her head, then and now, was so crowded with images and impressions that entertaining any new idea seemed like a physical impossibility.

"Let's go grab something to eat," Katie decided, looping her arm through Snow's, and directing her to the corner.

"Victoria MacKenzie," Snow said almost inaudibly, trying the name aloud for the first time. "William and Patricia MacKenzie. She was twenty-two, a kid, for God's sake. Did you notice none of the stories mentioned his age?"

"I noticed. I got the impression he was older. Junior partner in a law firm, it stands to reason he was at least in his early thirties."

"They lived on East 68th Street."

"And Anne Cooke lived two blocks away on East 66th. Maybe she stalked them."

"I don't think so," Snow disagreed, that dozy feeling starting to ebb. "She said something about how she almost took a boy by mistake, her first try. I think she just kept an eye on that Gristede's, probably went every day." Her knees threatening to unlock, she said, "This is starting to hit me hard. I could use a drink."

"Me, too. How does it feel," Katie asked quietly, "knowing your name?"

"It's just a name. It's strange to think that it's *my* name. I can't really connect with it. Oh, God, Katie! Reading about it made me so *sad.* I felt so sorry for that couple. She was so *young. Twenty-two!* A baby herself."

"It's a damned sad story," Katie said soberly. "Poor Patricia goes to do the grocery shopping for her family, and somebody steals her baby. She must've almost lost her mind."

"Maybe she did. Maybe she never recovered."

"Let's try to be positive, and work on the assumption that she did. Tomorrow, first thing, we should head up to the 19th Precinct, see if anyone'll talk to us."

"I've got to do up the Howland prints. And we've got sittings scheduled for this week."

"One Wednesday, two on Thursday. Tomorrow's only Tuesday."

"I need to get back to work. Maybe it'll help me get grounded." Stopping abruptly on the sidewalk, Snow gazed unseeing at the traffic. "Victoria MacKenzie. My mother and father are Patricia and William." She looked up at the overcast sky, feeling the lingering bite of winter in the air. "Is that who I am?"

"Yes, it is," Katie said firmly.

"How will we ever find them?"

"We'll find them."

Turning to look at her friend, she said, "Katie, she had to have reasons for doing it. She wasn't a bad person, or an unkind one. I never knew her to hurt anyone intentionally, so why did she do it?"

"We're going to try to find out. But," Katie said more gently, "you may never know why. The thing is, you're going to have to find some way to live with that."

"I know." Snow sighed.

"Is it okay with you if I tell Robbie what's going down?"

"I guess so. Why not?" Snow shivered and said, "I'm cold. And I need a drink."

"So, let's go." Katie tugged on her arm and they started walking again.

Thirteen

Back at the loft she transferred the load of wash to the dryer, then sat down on the floor and obsessively read every word of all the clippings, wishing there were photographs of William and Patricia. But there were none. As well, after the initial stories, the MacKenzies had stopped granting interviews. Their attorney spoke on their behalf, and Snow had the impression that the men in Patricia's life had taken charge and silenced her. They'd probably told her to be a good girl and keep quiet, let the men handle this. The imagined scenario infuriated her; it was so typical of the way men used to treat women and, if allowed, still did. She was deeply offended by the spurious notion that men were less emotional and therefore better able than women to handle difficult situations, as if the capacity to express one's emotions rendered one a less effective person.

Her emotions—those questionable attributes of the female psyche—were abraded, disordered, volatile. So shocking was the story to her now that she'd seen it in print that she kept wanting to pick up the telephone to call the MacKenzies and assure them of her well-being. A predominant streak of natural pragmatism kept her rooted in present-tense reality while a new and hungry part of herself anxiously urged her to set the record straight. Victoria MacKenzie, her identity now established, demanded an immediate reunion with her family. Snow Devane was willing to go so far as to get the white pages from the top of the refrigerator and look through the listings, finding that there weren't many MacKenzies, perhaps twenty. None was for a William or a Patricia, nor was there any listed on 68th Street.

Agitated, restless, she started tidying the place, dry-mopping the wood floors, then taking a feather duster to the surfaces. She kept going back to the stack of newspaper articles, pausing to reread some of them before heading into the bathroom to scour the toilet, and again before scrubbing the tub and basin. At last, having done as much housecleaning as she could tolerate, she paused on her way to the darkroom to play back her messages.

There were three hang-ups. Then, "This is Evelyn Miller. I phoned last week to make an appointment for a sitting. Please call me back when you get a chance." She gave her number, said, "Thank you," and hung up.

After the tone, Todd came on, saying, "Hi. Josie and I are getting kind of worried about you. Is everything okay? Give us a call, and let's get together. Talk to you later. Bye."

Two more hang-ups.

"I think I came on too strong the last couple of times I called," Mark said, atypically subdued. "Things have been going nuts at the office, and to tell the truth, life's generally been a bitch. I've got a lot to tell you. Call me, please. I miss you."

She felt a pang, suddenly missing him, too. Why had she been painting him in such unrelentingly dark colors? He wasn't a bad person, simply a married one.

Another hang-up.

"This is Lena Forstman. I'm calling on behalf of Joseph Broder to schedule a sitting for his daughter, Julia. Please call me to set up an appointment." She gave the number, and rang off.

"Uh, Snow, it's Rudy. Hope you and Katie made it back okay. I've been going through the old phone bills. I'm sorry to say so far I haven't come up with a thing. I'll be out tonight, going over to the Briggses' place to have supper 'n' watch the Red Sox game. It's awful quiet around here. Call me when you get a minute. Bye."

She reset the incoming tape, recorded a new message, and started toward the darkroom. But she just had to stop to take another look at the newspaper stories. Then, fueled by a steadily mounting anxiety, she got the Fantastik and began wiping down the kitchen counters and the appliances. After that, she got down on her hands and knees and scrubbed the linoleum, applied a coat of liquid wax, then retreated to the living area while the floor dried.

She stood at the window, gazing out again at the city as she had earlier in the day, feeling separated from it by far more than just a sheet of grubby glass. That sense she'd described to Rudy of being a correspondent in a war zone was back, stronger than ever. But foreign correspondents had homes they returned to eventually. Where was hers?

The intercom buzzed. Automatically she checked the time—7:15—as she went to the speaker on the wall beside the front door.

"It's Mark. I need to see you. We've got to talk. Will you buzz me in?"

"I don't think that's a good idea," she said, nevertheless grateful for the distraction he offered, and knowing she would see him.

"If you won't let me come up, could I buy you dinner, or a drink? I really think we should talk."

She hesitated for a moment, then said, "Okay. I'll be down in five minutes."

"Great! I'll be waiting."

She almost didn't recognize him. Leaning against a parked car, in jeans and a pink button-down shirt, with a gray Shetland sweater tied around his neck, he was tall, handsome and relaxed, very unlike the harried executive who usually rushed in and out of her bed as if he were in some kind of contest.

He smiled as she came through the door, saying, "I was afraid you'd say no," and moved to hug her, but fell back when he saw her expression.

"I would have," she confessed, "but I had a drink instead of lunch today and I'm hungry."

"Fair enough. Where would you like to go?"

"There's a coffee shop a couple of blocks over. All I want is a sandwich."

"Okay. We'll do that."

They started off, and Snow said, "Aren't you supposed to be home by now?"

"That's part of what I've been wanting to tell you." He seemed freer, more at ease than she'd ever known him to be. "What happened?" he asked. "Why were you 'unavailable' all week?"

"My mother died. I had to go home to Rhode Island."

"Oh! I see. That's a shame. I'm sorry." Effortlessly he kept up with her as she moved briskly along. "I thought maybe you were avoiding me."

"Not everything has to do with you, Mark," she said quietly.

"I know that."

"No, you don't," she said, amazed at herself. She had never spoken this way to any of her lovers. She'd always kept her thoughts, and her irritation, to herself. "All those offended messages you left were about you," she went on. "You never once asked if I was okay."

"I'm sorry. It's been a bad time."

"Not just for you," she said evenly, keeping her eyes forward, hands jammed into her jacket pockets.

"I moved out of the house," he announced with a certain pride.

She turned to look at him, taken aback. She had never for a moment believed he'd ever leave his family. "Why?" she asked, pulling open the door to the coffee shop and heading automatically for a table at the rear.

"I told you I would," he answered, sliding into the chair opposite. "I did it for you, for us."

She stared at him, absorbing the details of his dark good looks: well-set brown eyes, fine high forehead, strong nose and mobile mouth, a headful of thick dark hair. A truly handsome man, one a lot of women would do practically anything to win over. "You did it for you, Mark," she said, understanding all at once that the majority of things people did were done, one way or another, for their own benefit.

He stared back at her, noting a number of changes: a visible loss of weight that had turned her face more angular and made her eyes even larger; a more pronounced aura of melancholy, and a surprising new directness. "Okay," he conceded, "maybe it was. But I did it with you in mind. I've been telling you for a long time I intended to leave Caroline."

The waitress came over, pencil poised above her order pad.

Mark started to say he wasn't ready yet, hadn't even had a chance to consult the menu.

Snow said, "I'll have a BLT with well-done bacon on whole wheat, and a coffee, please."

Somewhat undermined by the way things were going and his inability to control the situation, he said, "I'll have the same."

The waitress nodded, turned, and went off.

"Mark, we don't know each other," Snow said tiredly.

"What're you talking about? We've been seeing each other for over a year. I've turned my life upside down..." He was going to say he'd done it for her, but he'd already admitted otherwise. "Your mother died. You're upset."

"My mother died. I'm upset. And we don't know each other. Could we be truthful for once? We've hardly ever talked. Most of our time together has been spent in bed. Which was all right. It was what I wanted, what we both wanted. The thing is, it's not what I want anymore. And you didn't leave your family because of me."

"But we talked about my leaving...."

"*You* talked about it. I listened. You've been wanting to do it. Maybe I was just a reason you used. It doesn't matter."

"It does," he disagreed.

"Could we *please* be truthful?" she asked, managing a smile because he was wonderful to look at, and more of a bright self-centered child than a grown man. "I really don't have the energy right now to play games."

He had the grace to smile, admitting, "Okay. You're right. I guess I did do it for myself." He paused, studied his hands for a moment, then looked over at her. "You're telling me it's over. We're finished. Right?"

"That's right," she confirmed, her heart suddenly pounding madly. What was she doing? She was throwing away a great-looking guy who'd left his wife and kids for her, who was good in bed, and no more selfish, really, than the majority of other men. Was she out of her mind, or finally in it? She was astonished by her assertiveness, by her newly formed conviction that it was better to be alone with one's integrity rather than involved in something illicit with someone who failed to merit her respect.

"Why? You know I'm crazy about you."

She sighed and looked around the near-empty coffee shop. Each day since her mother died had seemed longer than the one before. "I don't love you, Mark. And you don't love me. We were good in bed. That's physical therapy, not involvement."

He laughed, thrown. "Physical therapy? That's all it was to you?"

"Was it something more to you?" she asked, truly curious to learn if he was capable of introspection, of sincerity.

"No. Well, I don't know. Are we really going to be this honest?"

"Why not?"

"It's weird. I don't know."

"You might get to like it," she said with another smile. "We might even get to know each other and wind up friends."

"I do like you."

"Thank you. I like you, too—when you're wearing civvies and not looking at your watch every other minute."

"I do that, don't I? It's awful, a terrible habit. So you think we could be friends?"

"Why not? Or are you all booked up, with a waiting list?"

"That was harsh. I'm not that shallow."

"No," she allowed, "you're not. Sorry."

"You're taking it very hard," he observed, "your mother's death."

"Yes," she said, closing her eyes for a moment against that deathbed image, "I am."

"Is there anything I can do to help?"

A tear trickled itchily down the side of her nose and she thought she was probably a fool to be breaking up with this man, but there was no turning back. There was no room in her life anymore for deception. "No, there isn't, but it's sweet of you to offer." She grabbed a napkin from the dispenser and wiped her face.

"I do care about you, Snow."

I've put an end to us, she thought, feeling both sadness and relief, and wondering if she'd regret this later on.

The waitress came then with the food, and there seemed to be nothing more to say. They ate in silence.

On the way back to the loft, he told her he was staying at the Yale Club until he found an apartment. "You can reach me there, or at the office."

"Okay," she said, spotting Irene, whom she'd seen earlier that day going through a trash can, huddled now in a doorway. "Wait a minute, Mark." She went over to say, "Hi, Irene. How're you doing?"

Bothered, Mark kept his distance, watching with distaste as Snow dropped down on her haunches to talk with the woman. In his opinion it was a mistake to encourage these people. They had choices, just like everyone else, and it wasn't fair of them to blackmail passersby, cadging spare change. He resented the hell out of the way they did that, instead of pulling themselves together and getting jobs.

"I'm all right, dear. And how are you?" she asked, and Snow knew Irene had forgotten her again.

As a result of previous conversations, Snow had learned that Irene lived on the streets by choice. A fairly attractive, always clean Englishwoman in her late forties, Irene had, when asked, explained that she suffered from such acute claustrophobia that she had, in stages, given up her apartment, her job and most of her possessions, in order to live a life without walls. In the cold weather she often slept under the stairs in a nearby parking garage, and, in milder weather, in doorways on streets she considered reasonably safe. Sometimes she disappeared for weeks, and Snow would note her absence, hoping no harm had come to her. When she reappeared, a relieved Snow always stopped to ask how she was and to give her some money. Eventually, she had realized that, from one occasion to the next, Irene had absolutely no memory of having encountered Snow before. There were quantum holes in her awareness where things simply vanished.

Now, knowing a disapproving Mark was waiting impatiently, Snow asked the woman, "Is there anything I can do for you?"

"Oh, no, dear. Thank you. Now that the weather's warming up, I'm feeling much better. I don't care for the frightful fumes in the garage."

"There must be something you'd like, something I could do for you," Snow persisted.

"You're very nice," Irene said. "Are you a social worker?"

"No. I'm a photographer. Are you hungry? I could get you a coffee or a hamburger."

"Do you know what I'd really like?" Irene asked.

"What?"

"A lovely hot shower." Her face took on an expression of anticipation. "I would like that. It's very important to stay clean, you know. I'd saved almost enough for a night at a motel, but some nasty boys—little lads, mind, not even teenagers—knocked me down and nicked the bag with the money and my photograph album. I didn't mind so much about the money, but I do mind about the album. Now I haven't got a single picture of my boy."

"You have a son?"

"Oh, yes, dear, my boy Michael."

"Does he live here?"

"That's right. In Forest Hills." Irene frowned and looked away.

Sensing it would upset the woman if she pursued the matter, Snow got out her wallet and gave Irene five twenties and one of her cards.

"Oh, bless you!" Irene exclaimed. "That's very kind."

"Now you can have a room-service dinner and a shower," Snow told her. "And if there's ever anything else I can do for you, all you have to do is call or come ring my bell. My place is just down the street. Okay? Will you do that?"

"Snow," Mark said, his expression stern. "We really should be going."

"In a minute. Irene, this is my friend, Mark."

Irene smiled, showing a set of strong white teeth, and said hello.

Discomfited, Mark returned the greeting but continued to keep his distance as Snow stood up and waited while Irene struggled into her backpack before wheeling her shopping cart out of the doorway.

"Bless you, dear," Irene said, heading east. "Bless you."

"Did I actually see you give that woman a lot of money?" Mark asked as Snow rejoined him.

"Yes, you did." Angrily, she asked, "Do you have a problem with that, Mark?"

"Uh, no, of course not. Listen. I should probably be going. Why don't I call you tomorrow?" he suggested, wondering if her mother's death had unhinged her. Imagine giving the contents of your wallet to a street person! He couldn't get over it.

"Okay, do that," she said, unlocking the front door while he tried to think of what to say.

"Look, are you going to be all right?" he asked, concerned about the state of her mental health.

"I'll be fine. Thanks for dinner." She waved, then closed the front door.

He stood on the sidewalk, watching through the glass as she headed for the elevator. Crazy, he thought, glancing up the street to see if there were any cabs in sight. Talking to bums and giving her money away. A cab turned the corner. He stepped into the road and signaled. Maybe breaking up was the best thing that could've happened. He'd had no idea she was so...eccentric.

While she was reading the newspaper articles one last time before getting ready for bed, the telephone rang.

"I just realized something," Katie said. "You're only thirty, not thirty-one. In fact, you're almost a year and a half younger than me. You'll have to treat me with the respect I deserve as an older person."

"Of course. Absolutely."

"How're you doing? You okay?"

"For a while there after I got home, I really thought I was losing it. You won't believe it, but I actually tried to look up the Mac-Kenzies in the phone book."

"Sure I believe it. So did I."

"You didn't!"

"Hey! You've got to eliminate the obvious first. I mean, it'd be too embarrassing to chase all over looking for them only to find out they'd been in the phone book the whole time."

"I felt so idiotic."

"Well, you were just being practical. And by the way, have you heard from Wonder Dummy yet?"

Snow couldn't help smiling. "You really shouldn't call him that."

"Ex*cuse* me! Have you heard from *Mister* Wonder Dummy yet?"

Snow laughed. "He showed up at the door a couple of hours ago. We went out for something to eat and basically I told him it's over."

"Really?"

"Really. It was easier than I thought it'd be."

"And you even sound all right. *Are* you all right?"

"I'm okay. I'm not so sure it's the smartest thing I've ever done, throwing away the only man around who has any interest at all in me. But I did it."

"God! Listen to what you're saying! It's like criminal intent or something, the shameful way we feel about wanting and needing physical attention. Would you ever come right out and admit you like touching and displays of affection, that the whole thing's about that?"

"Maybe," Snow said cautiously, led by the question into another direction. "D'you ever find yourself doing something and think, Help! I'm turning into my mother?"

"Sure, sometimes. I never know if I'm psyched or freaked by it."

"I think I was getting to be a lot like Anne Cooke. I think Mark and all the others were part of that."

"Come *on!*"

"No, really. The whole time I was away, the only personal messages on the machine were from Todd and Josie. I hardly see my other friends anymore. I really was getting to be like her, Katie, narrowing my life down, reducing the number of people in it."

"You've been busy..."

"Not that busy. It was happening, I'm telling you. The past year or so I was staying home most nights, not having people over the way I used to, turning into a loner. I'd actually get resentful if I settled in for the evening and somebody phoned wanting to do something. I'm not saying it was conscious. But I can see now where it was going."

"Okay, you've seen it. You know it's not the way to go, so you'll get reconnected."

"I'm petrified," Snow admitted, looking at the clippings and feeling her heartbeat like the frantic wings of a small bird trapped in her chest. "The closer we get to this thing, the more I want to run, just take the ten thousand and get the hell as far away as I can. I mean, say I do manage to find William and Patricia. We don't know each other. We might not even *like* each other."

"So what? The point's not your liking each other. The *point* is letting them know you're alive, number one. Think what that has to mean to them, Snow! They lost their baby but she didn't die. Being reunited with you is going to be the most important thing that's ever happened to them. Man, I get all choked up just *thinking* about it.

"And number two, being reunited will be giving you back your history. Hell, half the people I know can't stand their parents. It's not even relevant. If you like each other, it'll be a bonus. If you don't, you'll just be running par for the course."

"That doesn't stop me wanting to take off. I can see myself grabbing the cameras, throwing some stuff in a bag, and just driving away."

"That *does* sound like Anne Cooke."

"See what I mean? Maybe all those years of subliminal messages took serious hold."

"Don't go trying to talk yourself into anything. You're no more like that woman than I am. You're worn out. Things are getting distorted."

"Could be."

"You need to get some sleep. I just wanted to check in, see how you're doing. Want me to come stay the night, keep you company?"

"No, but thanks for offering. I'll be okay."

"You sure? I could hop in a cab, be there in no time."

"Unh-hunh. It's not necessary. I'll see you tomorrow. Thanks for calling."

"Sleep tight."

After the call, Snow sat for a time staring into space, reviewing her encounter with Mark. It was as if, for that hour or so, she'd been someone else—someone more self-possessed than she'd ever known herself to be. Naturally, now that she'd ended the affair, she couldn't help wondering if she hadn't made a terrible mistake. Too late, she told herself, setting aside the clippings finally, and heading for the bathroom. No going back, no running away. But maybe she could slow things down a bit. The speed of events had her dizzy, the way childhood carousel rides once had.

Fourteen

Her sleep was taken up with maddening reenactments of the day's events that kept being rewritten over and over, so that the dialogue altered from one version to the next, as did the outcomes. She and Mark ended up making love like a pair of snarling dogs under the table in the coffee shop. Then they straightened their clothing, sat back down in their chairs and ate their sandwiches in angry bites while they argued savagely about Irene, who sat, dignified and quiet at an adjoining table, smoking a cigarette and offering Snow encouraging nods and intermittent smiles.

By five-thirty in the morning, hearing the chat and clatter of garbagemen emptying trash cans down on the street, she abandoned any hope of rest. After making the bed and taking a quick shower, she gathered up the clippings and read them again while consuming several cups of strong coffee. Then she sat for a time comparing the photograph in the long-outdated passport she and Katie had unearthed with the one in the newspapers. There was no question they were one and the same baby. She had accepted the facts of the matter, and yet couldn't stop searching for something that would prove it was all a crazy mistake. She didn't want to believe that her fastidious little mother had committed such an outrageous act. But the mounting evidence showed that she had.

Finding herself once more drawn to the window, she looked out at the predawn city, feeling as dark and empty as the street below—silent now that the garbage truck had moved on. No one out yet, a few lit windows, and a scrawny black-and-white cat slinking furtively from the opening of the alley. In the space of one week, her entire life had, like the reflected fragments of colored glass in a kaleidoscope, been shaken to form a completely new pattern. She felt as if she were clinging with greasy hands to a rope that was steadily slipping out of her grasp. And she was scared. So she turned for reassurance and comfort to the one thing that was undeniably hers—her work—and headed for the darkroom with the two rolls of black and white she'd shot in Stony Point.

At nine-thirty, when Katie let herself in, Snow was back at the kitchen table, examining the contact sheets. Katie got a cup of coffee from the fresh pot Snow had just made and said, "You must've been up early. Or did you develop the film after we talked?"

"I was up early. I had one of those nights." Her fears considerably reduced in the full light of day, she offered a self-deprecating smile.

"Too bad," Katie commiserated. "Mine wasn't all that great, either. Robbie decided to phone during his break, which just happened to be at two in the morning. After that, I kept thinking of more and more things we should do, like making a trip to the Social Security office in Providence, and trying to locate that C.P.A., May Connor. I also had a flash and got up to see if Daniel Ambrose was listed in the phone book. He wasn't. And of course neither was May Connor."

"Listen, Katie, I've been thinking, and I'd like to wait a while before we go talk to the police."

"But we agreed we'd go up to the 19th Precinct today. I thought it was all settled."

"I've changed my mind. The more I think about it, the more I realize I'm not ready."

"Are you being straight?" Katie asked, searching Snow's eyes. "Or are you trying to run away from this thing without actually moving?"

"Maybe a bit of both," Snow answered truthfully. "I need more time. Maybe it sounds melodramatic, but once we set things in motion, it'll be the end of my life as Snow Devane. I need time to get used to the idea of being Victoria MacKenzie, to get ready to be someone with a family. I do want to get to the bottom of it all—very badly. But it's only been a week, Katie. Do you *realize* how much has happened in just one week?"

"I do, but..."

Snow interrupted, saying, "I've started doing things that feel out of character—like the way I handled the situation with Mark. I was so cool, so remote. It was as if I was watching myself from over in the corner, and it was like seeing someone I didn't know."

"What's wrong with being cool and remote? You needed to get out of that relationship. He treated you like a bank, for God's sake. Like a place where he could whip in, make a deposit and whip out again."

Snow smiled grimly and shook her head, twisting a strand of hair around one finger. "It was what I wanted."

"Well, it was awful. Maybe now you'll stop wanting to be treated that way." Katie drank some of her coffee. "Okay," she said at length. "I can't argue with your timing. How long d'you think you're going to need?"

"A week or so, give or take a few days. It's been thirty years. One more week won't matter to anyone but me."

Belatedly, as if hearing an echo, Katie's gaze turned liquid and her lungs gave a preliminary heave in preparation for tears.

"What?" Snow asked with immediate concern.

"What you said just now about the end of your life. I hadn't thought of it that way, but it's true, isn't it? Once you start talking to the police things'll never be the same, regardless of the outcome. If I'm pushing too hard, tell me and I'll back off."

"If it wasn't for you, I'd probably have run away by now. So don't worry about pushing too hard."

"Okay, just so long as you're sure. What about the stockbroker? Are we still going to see him this morning?"

"Uh-hunh." Snow glanced at the clock and said, "I've got to call Rudy."

"Go ahead. And give him my love."

Rudy was glad to hear from her, eager to tell her about his attempt at playing detective. "I called up that hotel Anne always stayed at in New York," he began. "Managed to get hold of this young assistant manager, and said I was wondering if my wife didn't maybe get charged for somebody else's calls. He went into his computer and in about a minute said it didn't look like any mistake. The calls'd been billed to her room. I acted doubtful and asked if he could check to see what numbers were called. But no go. Once the bill's been paid, all they keep is the record of charges, not the details of the individual calls. So I guess we're out of luck in that department. I was hoping I'd have some clues for you, but it didn't pan out."

"Never mind. It was a nice try," Snow said, touched. "Katie and I did have some luck. We found the story. It was big news in all the papers for a couple of months back in '63. Everybody was looking for the MacKenzies' missing baby, Victoria. There was a picture of the baby...of me." She had to stop for a moment. Every time she thought about that photograph she wanted to go to pieces.

"Well, I'll be damned," Rudy said softly, awed. "The whole thing's true after all."

"Yes, it is."

"So where do you go from here?" he asked.

"Next week we'll try to talk to somebody at the precinct that handled the case."

"That makes sense. Next week, you say. Taking your time, hunh, Snow?"

"I have to, Rudy. It's a lot for me to deal with."

"That's sensible," he said. "No point in charging around every which way without thinking things through. How're you feeling about it all?"

"Up and down," she said inadequately. "But I'm okay."

"Glad to hear it. Well, I should let you go. You don't want to be spending all your money on long distance. Take it easy and keep me posted, will you?"

"I will. And thanks for trying with the hotel," Snow said. "Katie sends her love. Me, too."

"It was worth a shot," he said. "Love to the both of you. Just remember, I'm here if you need me. Okay?"

"Okay." Snow hung up and sat back down at the table. "I miss him, Katie," she said thickly. "And I miss my mother."

"Of course you do." Katie checked her watch. "I hate to be pushy again, but you should probably get changed if we're going. I told Compton's secretary we'd be there by eleven."

Snow wiped her face with the bottom of her T-shirt and said, "Right. I'll only be a couple of minutes." She started toward the living area of the loft, thinking about Irene, wondering if perhaps she'd gone to visit her son those times she'd disappeared. Maybe he didn't know his mother lived on the streets. Maybe, for those visits, she stored her bundles and folding shopping cart in a locker at the bus terminal where she got dressed in decent clothes a bit out of date but spotlessly clean, and emerged looking much like everyone else. Maybe, like Anne Cooke, Irene lived more than one life.

Huffy Compton was a tall, angular, slow-moving man who looked to be about seventy. With a singularly engaging smile and a glow in his intelligent gray eyes, he extended a big warm hand in welcome. His hair was an abundant pure white, and he wore a red hand-knitted sweater vest over a crisp white shirt and navy tie, gray flan-

nel trousers and a new-looking pair of Nikes that had to be at least
a size thirteen. "Please do come in," he invited, standing aside to
allow Katie and Snow to enter his large corner office that had one
vast window offering an uptown view and another, behind his desk,
facing west. The office was leathery, comfortably old-fashioned,
with a fine Persian carpet in deep reds and blues, and a vase of fresh
flowers centered atop a wood credenza. The only concession to
modernity was a computer terminal on a wheeled wooden stand to
the right of the desk.

"Most of my remaining clients are old poops like me," he said.
"It's not every day I have the pleasure of a visit from two lovely
young women with not a wrinkle between them."

Coming from anyone else, the comment might have been suspect, but this man was so open and charming it was impossible not
to like him. He sat beaming at them for several moments before
saying, with an almost disbelieving shake of his head, "I don't
think I've ever seen two more beautiful females. Please convey my
congratulations to your respective parents."

Katie chuckled. Snow smiled. He was courtly and charming, and
nicely off-the-wall.

"Would you care for some coffee?" he asked, a hand poised to
press the intercom button.

Both Katie and Snow declined.

"Tea, juice, a soft drink?"

"No, thank you," the two of them chorused.

"All right, then. How may I help you?" he asked, sweeping
imaginary dust from the polished surface of his uncluttered ma-
hogany desk with the flat of one hand.

"I'm trying to connect with relatives from my mother's side of
the family," Snow began.

"I see," Compton said, now paying close attention, both hands
fastened to the arms of his chair.

"There was a falling-out a long time ago, before I was born, so I
have no direct way of contacting them."

"I see," he said again, nodding.

"My mother died recently, and I'd like to let them know. I was
able to get a copy of your firm's transfer document from her present stockbroker—" she handed a Xerox of it over to him "—and
I'm hoping to get in touch with Daniel Ambrose who apparently
was her broker back in the sixties, when she lived here."

Huffy Compton put on a pair of gold, wire-rimmed spectacles and studied the document. "That's Danny's ID, all right," he said, looking at Snow over top of the glasses. "Unfortunately, he left us, oh, twenty-five years ago, at least. I have no idea where he might be now."

"I don't suppose the name Anne Cooke means anything to you?" Katie asked.

"I'm sorry to say it does not. This Anne Cooke was your mother, I take it?" he asked Snow.

"Yes." Snow took two photographs from her bag and passed them across the desk. "I don't suppose you recognize her by any chance?"

He looked first at the more recent picture, then at one Snow had taken better than fifteen years before. "A most attractive woman," he said. "She looks faintly familiar, but I can't place her. Of course, if she was Danny's client, it's unlikely I'd have come into more than passing contact with her. Still," he said, taking another look at the older photograph, "the face does seem to ring a bell." He studied it intently, then shook his head, removed his glasses and placed the photographs on the desktop. "I'm not being much help to you, am I?" he said sadly. "At eighty-six, my memory's not what it was."

"You're eighty-six?" Katie asked, staggered. "I don't believe it!"

Again he gave them a splendid smile that illuminated his entire face. "You don't believe I've attained such a great age? Or that I don't look a day over eighty?"

Katie and Snow both laughed.

"You don't look a day over seventy," Snow told him. "You still come to work every day?"

"Some people need to work," he said matter-of-factly. "I'm one of them. And I suspect," he directed himself to Snow, "you are, too. You have the look. I'd be bored witless inside a month without my work, and you would be, as well. Am I right?"

"Yes, you are," she responded, impressed by his powers of observation.

"Now your wonderfully exotic young friend handles leisure well," he said to Katie. "You're able to give yourself over to whatever takes your fancy. Flexible," he decided aloud. "And highly imaginative. I do admire your ensemble."

Snow turned to look at her friend, deciding the old man was right. Katie had on a long, intentionally wrinkled black cotton skirt, a figured silk vest over a man's white dress shirt with a pleated front buttoned to the neck, a black bowler hat positioned low on her forehead, and well-worn cowboy boots.

Katie, grinning, said, "Thank you. I like your Nikes and I love the sweater. Who knitted it for you?"

"I'll have to tell Cecilia you liked it. She'll be tickled. My wife," he explained, "is always knitting something. If it isn't baby clothes for the great-grandchildren, it's ski sweaters for the kids, or vests for me. She had to fight to get me into the sneakers, but now I won't wear anything else. When I think of all those years of my poor old clodhoppers crammed into tight leather shoes. But we're getting very far afield." He redirected his attention to Snow. "We were talking about Danny Ambrose."

"Would you have any idea at all where he went when he left your company?"

"He went over to Blandings, Montrose. But I very much doubt he'd still be there. Danny was aggressive and smart, a young man in a hurry to climb as high as possible as quickly as possible, make a lot of money and retire young. He might well have done it, too."

"You liked him," Katie observed, drawing his eyes and another appreciative smile.

"I was very fond of him," Compton confirmed. "I had a partnership planned for him. But he couldn't wait. They made him one of those infamous offers you can't refuse, and off he went. He did stay in touch for a time, but eventually we stopped hearing from him. Water under the bridge now. All I can suggest is that you check with Blandings, Montrose. Somebody there might know where he got to. They're downtown, near the Exchange. Let me write down the address." He took a piece of paper from a leather box, uncapped a gold fountain pen, and slowly wrote down the information. After blotting the page, he handed it to Snow.

She thanked him, admiring his flowing script, and said, "Okay, we'll contact them."

His brow furrowing, he retrieved the earlier photograph of Anne from the desk and studied it thoughtfully for a time. "She definitely does look familiar. Anne Cooke you say her name was?"

"She might have been calling herself something else back then."

"Oh? How so?"

"My mother changed her name. I don't know why."

"Did she change her hair color, too?" he asked with a bemused expression.

"It's possible. Why?"

"I'm not sure," Compton said, eyes on the photograph. "Something about her, but I can't get a grip on it." He gave the photographs and the copy of the transfer back to Snow saying, "Tell you what. Leave me your name and number. I'll make a few enquiries, see if I can't come up with something. No promises, you understand. But I'll call a couple of people. And in the meantime, you pay a visit to Blandings, Montrose and find out what you can."

"We will," Snow said, giving him one of her cards. "Thank you very much for your time."

"Thank you both for gracing my day." He opened his desk drawer, removed something, then lumbered to his feet, came around the desk, and presented each of them with a bar of Godiva chocolate, saying, "If you like chocolate, you'll love this."

On impulse, Katie kissed his cheek, and said, "Tell Cecilia, any time she wants to knit me a sweater, feel free."

He laughed and said, "She'd do it, too."

Snow shook his hand and thanked him again.

Back out on the street, Katie exclaimed, "What a wonderful man! Can you believe he's eighty-six?"

"I know. Amazing."

"Wasn't that strange, his asking if she'd dyed her hair?"

"Definitely. For a minute, I was positive he was going to say he knew her."

"I know! I had like this spasm, thinking, Oh my God! This is it! He's going to say, 'Oh, sure. That's Mamie Oglethorpe or whatever. I knew her.' Maybe he'll remember and call you."

"When he said that about the hair, I couldn't help thinking maybe Anne really was the woman in that police sketch. Ever notice how those things never seem to look like the actual people?"

"This is true," Katie agreed. "So now we've got another brokerage to see."

"Not today," Snow said in a tone that left no room for argument.

"Okay. Then let's head back to your place. I'm inviting myself for dinner."

"It's only two o'clock."

"I'll do the billings, call back some of those people who want appointments, get everything ready for tomorrow. And *then* I'll make dinner."

"What about Robbie?"

"Just to show what nice folks they are, they've added another twelve hours to his shift. By the time he gets home tomorrow morning, he'll be one of the walking dead. He'll sleep for at least ten hours. We'll maybe have time for a quick coffee together—and forget sex!—then he'll head back to the hospital. I think the deal is if they don't manage to kill you off during your internship, they'll let you practice medicine. Anyway, I've resigned myself to living with a zombie until the end of this year." Speaking of zombies, she thought, seeing Snow had tuned out again. Taking her by the arm, she directed her toward the bus stop.

Snow paused only long enough to change clothes, then, at Katie's urging, closed herself in the darkroom for the second time that day. She wanted to be alone, to concentrate on how many seconds' exposure she'd give the first negative, and which area of it she'd burn—exposing a part of the image to light by masking other parts—to heighten the impact of the resulting print. Just as she loved her equipment, she also loved the darkroom and printing. It was a form of magic that never failed to thrill her. She could lose herself to the arcane sorcery achieved through brief blasts of light through celluloid onto paper; get caught up in the mathematics of paper plus developer to create an image. In the darkroom she was powerful—potent and knowing.

Having set up the negative on the lens of the enlarger, she bent to fix the focus and thought of her mother, hearing her say it was important to finish one thing before starting something else. Her hands suddenly shaking, she sat down on the floor and stared into the darkness, surrendering again to grief and wondering how long it would take before she stopped plunging, without warning, into a dreadful sea of combined uncertainty and sorrow.

Fifteen

Snow opened the door and met the eyes of a very pretty woman as a thigh-high Superman whipped past her and Katie, and proceeded to fly through the studio, his cape fluttering from his shoulders, his curls bouncing like loosely coiled white-gold springs.

"That's Jonathan." His mother laughed, offering her hand. "And I'm Sam Daley."

"Come on in," Snow said, watching the pint-size dervish shoot into the living area of the loft. "You can sit on the stool there while we finish getting organized. There's coffee, if you want to help yourself. Or we can make you some tea."

"Thanks. I'll have coffee." Sam Daley put down a large leather carryall before reaching for one of the mugs Katie had set out earlier.

Jonathan's gleeful laughter decorated the atmosphere like airborne strands of tinsel as he paused to spin in a giddy, self-enchanted circle. Then, eyes locating something that attracted him, he flew off to examine his find—a bright orange, lacquered papier-mâché duck that Todd and Josie had given her years ago for Christmas. He opened the duck's back to discover the little egg inside and emitted a trill of elated laughter, then put the duck down, turned and continued his survey. He gave no more than a cursory glance at the box of somewhat shopworn toys Snow kept in the studio for her small clients. His interest was in Snow's personal possessions and in the equipment.

A tiny whirlwind of motion and inquisitiveness, he had, within minutes, been through the entire loft, including the kitchen and bathroom. From past experience, Snow had learned to keep the darkroom locked, and she observed, entertained, as Jonathan tested the doorknob, took his eyes up and down the length and width of the door, tried the knob again, then went to rest thoughtfully against his mother's knees. She reached into her carryall for a box drink, and while he drank the apple juice, one hand absently stroking the side of his cape, he tracked every move Katie and Snow made.

Beguiled, they allowed him to investigate at will while they decided on how best to light him, relieved that Sam Daley appeared content to sit on the sidelines, displaying none of the frequently encountered parental need to stage-manage the proceedings. A serene, smiling blonde in her late twenties, she visibly cherished her four-year-old's lively curiosity and eccentricity. Snow was impressed by her acceptance of the boy on his own terms. Too many of the adults she encountered in her work (not to mention her own mother) were determined to force their children to surrender their individuality and become miniature versions of themselves. Sam Daley was one of the rare people who not only liked her child, but had no desire to suppress his instincts. "He's passionate and obsessive," she told Katie and Snow. "He wanted to come today as Beethoven, but at the last minute changed his mind, and went back for the cape. We've got Beethoven in the bag, though, just in case."

"Beethoven?" Katie hooted with laughter.

"Some friends in Canada sent him this terrific video, *Beethoven Lives Upstairs,* and Jon's completely hooked on it. But that's pretty recent, and Superman's long-term, almost two years. He's only played Ludwig for a couple of months, and he likes either to have a keyboard he can work, or the Fifth Symphony going so he can conduct. He's also very into the *Eroica.*"

"It's too great," Katie declared, putting on a CD of the Ninth Symphony before offering the child an oatmeal cookie, which he accepted after gazing searchingly into her eyes for several seconds, as if deciding whether or not she was trustworthy. Then, cookie in hand, he danced off deliriously on tiptoe, head bobbing in happy recognition of the music, and furiously conducting between bites.

Snow couldn't take her eyes off him. He had a marvelously expressive face, with almost-white eyebrows, wide-set gray-blue eyes, a straight tidy nose and a broad, sometimes wicked smile that revealed an upper row of small gappy teeth. There was so much on show in his eyes, in his moments of quiet and in his sudden smiles, that she knew she'd have to shoot extra film in order to capture his essence. He was a quicksilver child, visibly sensitive, emotionally responsive, unexpectedly nontalkative. He seemed best able to express himself physically and would pause for a second or two—head cocked slightly to one side—to note what Katie or Snow or his mother were doing. Then, apparently satisfied, he'd catch up the sides of his cape, spread his arms outward, and take flight once more.

Sam Daley sat and observed, with a soft-spoken word now and then cautioning the boy against touching something. He'd look over at her each time, as if to gauge the depth and seriousness of the caution. Then, all the while keeping his eyes on her, he'd either go ahead and touch the tripod, or the cables taped to the floor, or the backdrop; or he'd obey and shift his attention elsewhere. He had his own agenda and only sometimes allowed his mother's influence and rules to impinge upon it. There was, however, nothing destructive about him. He handled everything that caught his interest with almost exaggerated care, intrigued by anything new and scarcely able to resist his need to put his hands on whatever he saw. He was, altogether, so unique, such an absolute original, that Snow wished she could sit and study him for days. She was irresistibly drawn to him.

The preparations completed, Snow surrendered to an unprecedented need and scooped the boy up to spin him around in circles, causing laughter to bubble from his chest in a long musical flow. All three women smiled automatically at the sound. It was delicious contagion. She held him, stunned by the realization that everything he was and would be was already within him—a small, compact package of endless potential. Once returned to his feet, he raced several times around Snow's legs, beaming up at her, before resuming his conducting. She'd only just set him down, yet she wanted to hold him again. She'd never responded in quite this way to one of her subjects, and, somewhat rattled, had to remind herself to get on with the job.

Actually shooting the boy was a considerable challenge. It wasn't in his nature to remain motionless for more than a minute or two, so Snow had to track him nonstop through the viewfinder, ready to release the shutter at any moment. And while she followed him, completely taken by his delicate features and alluring zest, she discovered that she *loved* this child. And, more than that, she *wanted* him. Had it been possible, she'd have snatched him up and run off with him, bent on keeping him forever. She wanted this boy for herself. *Just as Anne Cooke had wanted her!*

This was how it felt, she realized, her comprehension sudden, complete and frightful. It was a crazed, jittery need; a frantic longing to be forever close to a child, to be free through a lifetime of days and nights to witness and indulge its whims, its joys and disappointments, its progress and growth. This was what Anne Cooke had felt, what had driven her. It was a revelation. Snow knew without doubt that, despite her mother's disinterest in men, she'd have slept with any number of them if the act could have impregnated her. She'd stolen an infant and become a criminal *because she'd been physically unable to conceive.*

Overwhelmed by this new insight, Snow finished a second roll of film, then a third and a fourth until, finally, Jonathan grew wearied of the enterprise and went to lean against his mother's knees again, letting his head rest in her lap while his eyes fixed with mild recrimination upon Snow.

Setting down the camera, she went to crouch close to him, putting her hand on his silken, springy hair, saying, "I know you're fed up, and I'm sorry. But we're all finished now."

His head remained in his mother's lap and he tapped his fingers on her thigh, saying, "Goin' home now, 'kay?"

With a smile, practically strangling on her love for him, Snow said, "Thanks for letting me take your picture, Jonathan."

Giving her a sleepy, but forgiving, smile, he said, "Needa go home now, Snow."

She gave his curls one last caress and said, "Maybe you'll come see me again sometime. Okay?"

"Yeah, 'kay."

"Right in the middle of the shoot, I suddenly got a fix on why she did it, Katie."

"I'm lost. Why who did what?"

"My mother. I know why she did it." Snow was flushed, excited.

"Tell me!" Katie said, at once caught up in Snow's excitement.

"It's so obvious," Snow declared, suddenly brimming with a strange energy. "I *knew* that woman, Katie, and she always got what she wanted. If she wanted a black Buick with red upholstery, then the salesman had better be able to deliver, or she'd take her business somewhere else. If she wanted navy suede shoes with pointed toes and a three-inch heel, she wouldn't settle for anything else. Okay. So, somewhere along the line she found out she couldn't become pregnant, and wanting a baby turned into an obsession. Thirty years ago, no way could a single woman adopt a child, and unless she married a man who already had kids—which I categorically do not believe she could've carried off, given her aversion or whatever toward men—that left her two options. Either buy a baby or steal one. I'd be willing to bet any amount she tried first to buy one. And when that didn't work, she went out and stole one."

"It works for me," Katie said. "You seem really psyched."

"I am! I can deal with this, as long as I've got reasons. Maybe I'm conning myself, but I don't think so. The thing is, Katie, it makes sense. I know it's taken me a while to get to what's basically a pretty simple theory, but it all clicked into place for me shooting Jonathan. I suddenly understood how she felt."

"He was something, wasn't he? I'd be tempted to steal a kid like that myself."

"I actually thought about it for a minute or two," Snow confessed, then emitted a laugh. "Anyway, I'm dying to process the film, see if I managed to get him. You won't mind if I do this one myself, will you?"

"Of course not. Why would I mind? Tell you what. Why don't I go talk to people at Blandings, Montrose, and see if I can't get a lead on Daniel Ambrose?"

"Are you sure? I hate to think you're neglecting your own work because of this mess of mine."

"Get real, please. My work's going to wait for as long as it takes. I'm into this thing, and I want to find the guy. He's our best lead to find out who Anne Cooke really was. I will accept cab fare, if it'll ease your guilt. I'm getting kind of low."

"Absolutely." Snow went for her bag, came back and pressed a hundred-dollar bill into Katie's hand.

"Hey, wait a minute!"

"Take it! I owe you at least that, probably more."

"You don't owe me anywhere near this much."

"Katie, *take* the money! I'm not exactly short of cash, remember, and you've been running all over hell and gone for me."

Without further argument, Katie stuffed the bill into her pocket, looped an arm around Snow's neck and gave her a hug. "Don't spend the rest of the day in the black hole," she warned. "Take a little time out. Listen to your music, call some people. I'll check in with you later. Okay?"

"Okay."

* * *

While the negatives were drying, Snow fixed herself a piece of toast with peanut butter and went to eat it standing by the window where she watched the activity on the street, remembering the first time her mother had brought her to the city. She'd been six years old, and her mother had kept an almost painful grip on her hand as they'd hurried along the streets. When Snow complained—that they were going too fast, that she was hurting her hand—her mother had given her a distraught, garbled explanation about what a dangerous city it was, and how it was important, above all else, not to act like a tourist. It made no sense, and the net effect of her mother's words and actions was to convince Snow that her mother was afraid. Since she'd never known her mother to be afraid of anything—discounting her inability to deal with cuts and scrapes—she'd had to wonder why.

Well, now she had a pretty good idea why. More than five years after the fact, Anne Cooke had to have had a fairly compelling reason to risk appearing in Manhattan with her appropriated progeny. Very possibly that reason had had something to do with her finances. Snow could think of nothing else that would've prompted her mother to take that risk. And if that visit had indeed related to money, perhaps Daniel Ambrose had somehow been involved. She mentally crossed her fingers, hoping Katie had some luck with the downtown brokerage. The little luck they'd had at the outset seemed to have run out.

Finished eating, she got some grapefruit juice and returned to the darkroom to print the contact sheets. Examining them while they were still wet, she was very pleased. Jonathan Daley confronted the camera, one arm tentatively holding out his cape as if on the verge of flight; he peered questioningly over his shoulder at her; he showed his gappy teeth in a devilish little smile; he stood suspended in a thoughtful moment, fair brows slightly furrowed, one small hand pointing at something unseen; his face set with concentration, elbows elevated, he conducted an invisible orchestra. She had succeeded in capturing him. Gratified, she printed proofs of fourteen shots, and kept walking back and forth, looking at them, as they hung drying.

What her eyes saw was the child she'd fallen in love with that morning, but her mind's vision was traveling over images retrieved from her childhood: quick shots of her mother and herself, of their often conflicted exchanges, their interwoven emotions, their colliding intentions. When she examined her mother from this distance, she was able to recognize that what she'd viewed long ago as peculiar personality tics had in reality been building blocks of secrecy being steadily cemented into place. Once again, she found herself sympathizing with the woman, and it confounded her. She wanted to, but couldn't sustain her anger with Anne Cooke, especially not now, having gained a new understanding of how it felt to love a child and want to possess it.

Katie phoned just after six to say, "I'm beginning to learn the true meaning of frustration. Daniel Ambrose was with Blandings, Montrose until 1978. I talked to one of the brokers who'd known him, and he said Danny Boy left in '78 to go to Heston, Hughes and Finch. Name ring any bells?"

"No. Why?"

"They're the gang that got busted a few years ago for insider trading. They don't exist anymore. We've hit a dead end."

"Shit!"

"Exactly! Evidently Danny was raking in five, ten million a year. The guy I talked to said he thought he'd heard on the Street that Danny had retired two or three years before the whole thing went toes up. So, the bottom line is I have no clue where to go next. Unless dear old Huffy manages to have a flash or come up with a contact, we're out of luck. We really don't have much to go on now. Ambrose was our best bet. Have you tried that chocolate yet? I ate mine on the subway on the way downtown and practically slobbered all over myself." Katie laughed.

"It's in the refrigerator," Snow said distractedly, trying to think. "What about former employees of Heston and whatever? Maybe we could track them down, talk to some of them."

"Those people are gone with the wind, babe. Mind you, two of the top dudes are still in the slammer. I suppose we could always visit them in prison." Katie sounded thoroughly disgruntled.

"Mr. Compton might know somebody from the firm. I could ask him. He seemed anxious to help."

"Sure. Why not?"

"Maybe it's time to call Marty Kauffman's friend in security."

"Since we're taking it slow anyway, let's give it until next week. I'm not ready to quit yet. Unless you've changed your mind and decided to pull out all the stops."

"No, I haven't. I'm willing to wait."

"Okay, good. I haven't given up yet on May Connor. Sometime this week I want to check the records, see if she maybe belonged to an association of C.P.A.'s, or something like that. So what're you going to do tonight?"

Snow looked around the loft. "I don't know. Order a pizza and watch TV. I'm not up for much. What're you going to do?"

"Laundry. I get to sit guard over the machines for a couple of hours, to make sure nobody steals Robbie's boxers or my overalls. Is that a thrill, or what?"

Snow laughed and said, "I'll see you in the morning. Take care."

"You, too."

In the end, she didn't order a pizza or watch TV. She heated up some soup and ate it right from the pot. Then she sat on the floor surrounded by the proofs of Jonathan Daley, of pictures of her mother, and the clippings, going back and forth between the various photographs and the newspaper stories while on the stereo Renata Scotto and Carlo Bergonzi as Butterfly and Pinkerton sang of love and loss. And for the first time since the night of her mother's death, she actually felt recognizably herself.

Sixteen

Joanna Kingsley arrived precisely at nine-thirty, as scheduled. Grimly clutching her daughter, she was a small, tense woman of indeterminate age, clad in a long, shapeless navy corduroy pinafore over a light blue cotton turtleneck, heavy white socks and black Birkenstock sandals. Her light brown hair hung in a single skimpy braid that reached halfway down her back. She wore round wire-rimmed glasses, no jewelry but a plain gold wedding band, and not a speck of makeup. Her hello took the form of a wary nod as she looked at each of the women. She appeared to find Katie, in her usual all-black working outfit of overalls, shirt and army boots, with her hair haphazardly knotted atop her head, almost alarmingly outlandish, and chose to address herself to Snow who, with her mass of unfettered hair, was only somewhat less alarming in ancient torn jeans, a faded Johann Sebastian Bach T-shirt, and red high-tops. Ignoring Katie's invitation to help herself to coffee, she asked Snow in a rather shrill voice for herbal tea, if they had any.

Taking an instant dislike to the woman, Snow said, "Oh, sure we do. Katie'll get you some," and offered a smile, but failed to get one in return.

With a shrug and an Oh brother! grimace behind the woman's back, Katie said, "No problem," and went to the kitchen to put on the kettle.

While waiting for the tea, Joanna Kingsley stayed close to the door, holding on tightly to her twenty-month-old daughter, Hilary, and looked with anxious disapproval at the studio. Unlike her mother, Hilary burbled away, squirming to get free and explore this strange new place.

To the mother's discomfort, Snow stood close by, studying the child's features, deciding she liked the determined thrust of Hilary's rounded chin and her deep-set bright blue eyes. She wasn't one of those pretty children strangers clucked and cooed over. But she had energy and character and a tangible brightness.

"There's a whole box of toys," Snow pointed out, trying to imagine what sort of man could be married to this high-strung, bad-mannered young woman. "Maybe Hilary would like to play with some of them."

"I don't know," Joanna said doubtfully, as the child now fought to be released, kicking energetically at her mother and reaching toward Snow's outheld arms.

Feeling the child's agitation like sandpaper rubbing against her flesh, and irked by the woman's condescending humorlessness, Snow took charge. "Let's see if we can find something you'll like," she said, briskly lifting the girl from her startled mother's grip to carry her across the room.

With a happy, anticipatory chuckle, Hilary said, "Toys!" and waved her arms around.

Snow set her down in front of the battered wood chest, saying, "Wow! Look at all the neat stuff, Hil."

"Hilary," the mother corrected, wrinkling her nose at the well-used contents of the box, while the toddler peered with avid interest into it, reaching for the toys.

"How about this, Hil?" Snow asked, feeling Joanna's eyes drilling into the top of her head as she sat on the floor and held an old Cabbage Patch Kids doll next to her ear, pretending to listen. "She says she'd like to play with you."

"Yah!" Hilary crowed, chubby fingers reaching.

"Tea!" Without breaking stride, Katie plunked a mug into Joanna's hand, then went to pop a tape into the stereo.

As the first jolly notes of music emerged from the speakers, the toddler grinned, bobbed her head back and forth, and jiggled up and down in an uncoordinated effort to dance. Having a wonderful time, she got a firm grip on the doll, let herself drop bottom-first to the floor with a thump, and began trying to get the doll undressed. Her mother seemed frozen, watching the proceedings with a slightly open mouth, as if witnessing something on a par with devil worship.

Determined to establish control from the outset, Snow got to her feet, saying, "She'll be fine. Have a seat over there, please, while we get set up." She indicated the stool at the side of the studio. "Did you bring a change of clothes for Hilary?"

Reluctant to take her eyes off her child, as if expecting something disastrous to happen at any moment, Joanna stood holding the tea. "I wasn't told to."

"I'm sure you were, but never mind. She'll be *fine!*" Snow re-peated. This was going to be one of those dreadful shoots when the mother's ego and needs would interfere with the child's pleasure in the toys or the music, thereby forcing her and Katie to work like maniacs to keep the mood lighthearted. "Have a seat there, please," Snow directed the woman, taking her thin upper arm to get her to move. "Did one of your friends recommend me?" she asked, doubting this woman actually had any friends.

"My mother-in-law made the appointment," Joanna answered, watching with chagrin as Hilary zealously accepted a cookie from Katie. "Oh, no! We don't *allow* her to have sugar!" she com-plained too late, as Hilary took a big bite. "Hilary, don't eat that, please."

Hilary grinned and took another bite, her cheeks swelling like a hamster's.

"Nothing to worry about. They're soybeans and carob," Katie lied blithely, concealing the package as she carried it back to the kitchen.

"Please make yourself comfortable," Snow said. "It'll take us a while to get set up."

The disgruntled woman sat down. Her eyes briefly leaving her daughter, she discovered the mug in her hand and automatically began drinking the tea.

"It's not decaffeinated," Katie whispered to Snow. "Ten bucks says she asks for more."

"Con her into eating one of the cookies and I'll give you fifty."

"I'd like to sit on her and pour Hershey's syrup down her throat, then watch her jitterbug till she collapses!" Katie made a face, then grabbed a hairbrush and, ignoring the fairly malevolent look Joanna gave her, looped an arm around Hilary's waist and began brushing the girl's hair. "Gotta get you looking spiffy, Hil, so you'll look great in the pictures for Grandma."

"Piffy," Hilary repeated enthusiastically. "Gamma."

From across the room Joanna Kingsley glowered. "Please don't teach her slang."

Katie was thinking this was going to be a nightmare. She could see Snow was getting riled—something that almost never hap-pened during a shoot—and was tempted to warn the woman to keep quiet. But of course she wouldn't do that. Besides, she was curious to see how Snow would deal with this blatant little liar who'd been told not once but twice to bring a change of clothes for Hilary.

Halfway through the two-hour session, during which Joanna repeatedly distracted and worried the child by uttering some unwarranted caution precisely at the moment when Snow was about to release the shutter, Snow stepped back from the camera, drawing an exasperated breath.

Uh-oh, Katie thought, watching as Snow marched over to where Joanna Kingsley was sitting and began speaking to her in a furious undertone. Wishing she could hear what was being said, Katie played an impromptu game of "Itsy Bitsy Spider" with an enchanted Hilary.

Her voice husky and barely audible, Snow said, "Let me ask you something. Is Hilary your own child?"

"What?"

"Did you carry her for nine months, then give birth to her?"

"Well, natur..."

"Do you *love* her?"

"Just what are you trying...?"

"Do you love her? Yes or no?"

"Of course I do! What are you...?"

"If you love her, why are you doing your damnedest to make her unhappy?"

"I am not!"

"No? You haven't let up on her for a minute the entire time you've been here."

"You can't talk to me this way."

"Are you kidding? You're on my turf, and I can say any damned thing I want in here. And right now I'm saying you're needlessly upsetting a very good-natured child. She can't defend herself, but I sure as hell can and will. I want you to sit here and keep quiet! And while you're at it, think about the way you treat this child you claim to love."

Shocked and intimidated, the woman could do no more than stare unblinking at Snow's flushed face and sparking eyes.

"Maybe you don't even know how rude you are," Snow continued. "But let me tell you something. You're one of the most unpleasant people I've ever met. Is that how you *want* to come across?"

"Well, no," Joanna spluttered.

"Then shape up and start treating other people, especially Hilary, with some respect." With that, hands trembling, Snow got back to work.

Joanna Kingsley remained seated silently, hands knotted in her lap, her eyes glittery with incipient tears. She didn't speak or move until Snow indicated she could. Then, cowed, she walked across the studio to retrieve Hilary and, uncertain now, waited for some indication that it was all right to leave.

"I believe we have your mother-in-law's number," Snow said. "If you'd prefer it, we can contact her when the contacts and proofs are ready."

"No, that's okay," said Joanna Kingsley. "I'll come pick them up."

"As you like." Snow approached to say good-bye to Hilary.

Looking as if she were choking on a peach pit, Joanna said, "Sorry."

Snow smiled, and Joanna felt dazed.

"Don't be sorry," Snow said. "Just enjoy Hilary for who she is."

Katie was waving good-bye to Hilary who, red-faced and kicking, was angrily repeating, "No, no, *no!* No, no, *no!*" as her mother carried her away down the hall to the elevator.

"I think poor Hil was trying to say she'd rather stay here than go home," Katie said as she closed the door.

"Who could blame her? The woman was so *controlling!*" Snow ejected the kiddy music tape and sighed with relief in the ensuing silence. "I came this close to walloping her."

"I noticed!" Katie tossed toys back into the box, then retrieved several half-eaten cookies from the floor. "What did you say that shut her up and actually had her apologizing?"

Snow told her, and wound down saying, "Women like her should have to attend mandatory parenting classes. She has no clue."

"At the rate she's going," Katie said, "by the time Hil's twelve, she'll be eating red meat with a vengeance, drinking anything with caffeine, and carrying her cigarettes around in her backpack. She'll have purple hair, safety pins in her ears and a pierced nose."

"On top of that," Snow added, "she'll be angry all the time, and willing to do almost anything if she knows it'll give her mother fits."

"That about says it," Katie agreed. With a dustpan and brush she swept up the cookie crumbs, tossed the last of the toys back in the box and said, "That's it! Let's go eat, grab some fresh air before our two o'clock. Oh, yeah. I should tell you. Our original sitting had to cancel, so I booked in Joseph Broder for his daughter, Julia. How about Mexican? I could really go for some enchiladas."

"Okay, sure. Who's Joseph Broder?"

"His name was on your list of people who left messages while we were away, so I called and he was willing to take the cancellation. By the way, did you call Todd back?"

"Uh-hunh. I left a message on their machine, explaining some of what was going on. God, that woman was so rude, and had no idea. How can anyone be so oblivious?"

"She's also a liar. Of course I told her about the change of clothes."

"I know you did. It was so strange. I wasn't going to say anything. You know I never do. Then, all of a sudden I thought, I'm a millionaire. I don't have to take crap from anyone, ever again. I never realized money could free your mind that way. From that standpoint, I think I'm going to enjoy it." Thinking again about how she'd confronted Joanna Kingsley, she said, "God, I hope she listens and doesn't mess that child up."

"Hilary strikes me as a pretty strong kid. Maybe she'll be able to fight for herself."

"I hope so," Snow said fervently.

"Hey, *you* did," Katie reminded her.

"Yeah, I did, didn't I?"

"And she definitely heard what you were saying. Going out the door she was a whole other person than the one who came in."

"This voice in my brain kept going, Who the hell d'you think you are? But I just had to speak up."

"Hey, babe, if more people did that, there'd be a whole lot fewer screwed-up kids. D'you think we could we go eat now? I'm starving."

Arriving some fifteen minutes late, Joseph Broder came in smiling and apologetic. On the stocky side, about six feet tall, with thinning fair hair cut short and brushed straight back, he had very blue eyes and an engaging immediacy. He was well dressed in an Armani suit with a relaxed cut, an off-white, loose-fitting shirt and an elegant silk-screened tie. "Sorry to keep you waiting," he said, one hand on his daughter's shoulder, the other offered to Snow. "I'm Joseph, and this is Julia."

Snow shook his hand and smiled politely. Turning to greet Julia who, for an eight-year-old, had a solid grip, she had an overwhelming sense of recognition. She was a slight girl, with the large, aged eyes of a maverick, strong features she had yet to grow into and the telltale ramrod bearing of a ballet student. Her clothes might have been chosen by Katie: voluminous bright yellow overalls with at least a dozen pockets, an outsize yellow-and-white-striped shirt buttoned to the neck and at the wrists, heavy white socks and clunky black patent leather lace-up boots.

"You're very pretty," Snow said, feeling the girl's surprise as she kept hold of her hand and led her into the studio. "I like your outfit. Did you pick it yourself?"

She shook her head, regarding Snow uncertainly. "I know I'm not pretty," she said, looking around. "You like being a photographer?"

"A lot. And you are, very pretty. Someday, you're going to be beautiful."

"Not," Julia said flatly, but allowed Snow to go on holding her hand. "Can I see the rest of the place?"

"Sure." Snow let Julia lead the way to the living area.

"Someday I'd like to have a loft."

"And what will you do there?" Snow asked.

"You don't have much furniture, do you? I haven't decided yet. If I'm a famous ballet dancer, I'll have one area as my studio, like you do, but with mirrors and a barre. But if I decide to be a book writer, I'll have my desk and my books and everything. I might be a painter, though, and then I'll have an easel and a great big table for my paints and stuff."

"Katie's a painter."

"Is she any good?"

"Very."

"What's in here and how come there's a light outside the door?"

"That's the darkroom. When I'm working and I don't want anyone to come in, I turn on the light."

"I'd like to have a light I could turn on when I didn't want people bothering me," Julia said seriously. "It's a very good idea."

Having completed the tour, Julia finally freed her hand and crossed the studio to where her father was talking to Katie while helping himself to coffee.

"Want some juice?" Katie asked her. "Cool outfit."

"Yes, please. What kind do you have? Where'd you get your overalls? I'd like a pair just like that."

"Goodwill. We've got apple and orange."

"I guess apple, please. I never knew they had clothes like that at the Goodwill."

"They don't, usually. I got lucky."

"Yes, you did," Julia agreed, leaning against her father as if he were a piece of furniture, solid and dependable, and turning her intense gaze on Snow.

"Don't ask me to take you to the Goodwill, please, Jule," Joseph Broder said, anticipating what was coming. "I can't handle the idea of secondhand clothes. No offense intended, Katie."

"No problem."

Draping an arm across his daughter's shoulders, he said, "I know lots of people don't mind, Jule, but I do. Okay?"

"I guess."

Looking to help him out, Katie said, "Your dad's not alone, Jule. I know all kinds of people who get completely turned off at the idea of wearing somebody else's clothes." She went to get the juice as Snow headed for the stereo, asking Julia if she wanted to select the music.

"Okay." Puzzled by this strange woman, Julia went to look through the tapes and CDs.

Snow glanced over to see that Joseph Broder had slid onto the stool at the far side of the studio. He smiled at her over the top of his mug of coffee, and she smiled back, asking routinely, "How did you happen to pick me to take Julia's picture?"

"One of my clients, Susan Price, mentioned you'd done her kids. She was carrying some of the proofs. They blew me away. You do wonderful work."

Snow remembered the woman. She'd shot the Price kids a couple of years ago. There'd been three of them, all under five, and the sitting had been a circus; fun but exhausting. "She's still carrying around the proofs?"

"Yup."

"And she's one of your clients?"

"That's right. I arranged a trip for her and her husband."

"You're a travel agent?"

"Not exactly. I arrange special tours, primarily to the East. It's a bit complicated."

"I've never been outside the States."

"There are some astonishing things out there." He waved a hand at the window.

"Dad's been everywhere," Julia said. "Is it okay if I put on a disc?"

"If you know how, sure."

"She knows how," Joseph said. "Jule's had her own stereo system since she was five."

"That's impressive," Snow said, taken aback as Albinoni's "Adagio" began.

"She has very catholic taste," Joseph said with a telling show of pride.

"I did, too, when I was your age," Snow addressed herself to Julia. "My mother adored opera and classical music. Every Saturday afternoon we listened to the opera broadcast on the radio."

"We do that, too," Julia said with surprise.

"I think Jule was under the impression it's a punishment," Joseph Broder said, with a look at his daughter that had an I-told-you-so element that Snow recognized and found mildly disturbing.

Katie boogied over to Julia with a box of apple juice and some cookies. "Here you go, cupcake!"

Julia laughed and Snow knew all at once how she wanted to shoot the girl. Turning to look again at the father, she said, "I think I'd like to get a few shots of the two of you together."

He made a face. "I hate having my picture taken."

"But this'll be your picture with Julia. Not the same thing. And it'll be something nice for your wife and the grandparents."

"Maybe," he said. "I was planning to give my in-laws a framed print, but my parents might like one of the two of us. I'm a widower."

She felt an empathic pang of sadness, and understood why Julia had the eyes she did. Evidently, she thought, the territory of loss was immense, and heavily populated. "I promise it'll be painless," she told the man. "The kids usually enjoy themselves."

"I can see that." With a smile that showed his dimples, he asked, "Will I get a juice box and some cookies, too?"

"If you're good," she said, and he laughed.

She was for a moment discomfited by the echoes she seemed to hear of her mother and herself in this pair, then purposefully fixed her eyes on Julia. Temporarily ignoring the father, she headed across the studio to begin setting the lights on the daughter.

Usually she had to work to draw out her subjects, but as with Jonathan Daley the day before, Julia opened up from the instant

Snow began to shoot. Whether it was because she and the child had a rapport or because she had a performer's aplomb, Julia gave herself over to the camera, and thence to Snow. And what she revealed was a generous nature, agreeably coupled with a grace that was more than merely physical. She and Snow communicated with an intense silent complicity. For a second time in just two days, Snow had fallen in love on sight with a child.

Throughout the sitting, Joseph Broder merely observed and generally refrained from speaking. When Snow at last said, "Okay. Now I think I'd like to shoot the two of you," and turned to him, he frowned comically in a show of reluctance.

She crossed the studio and took him by the arm, saying, "Come on. This'll work. You'll see."

"Don't be chicken, Dad."

"I can't help it. I *am* a chicken."

Watching, Katie was intrigued and amused. Usually Snow retreated from men, unless they were married and sending out signals to say they weren't averse to playing around.

Making feeble clucking sounds that had them all smiling, Joseph allowed himself to be led into the lights.

"Let's put Julia on the stool," Katie suggested, "with Joseph standing in front of her. Jule can use him as a prop."

"Good call," Snow agreed, and encouraged Julia to drape herself over and around her father in whatever fashion took her fancy.

The two clearly adored each other, and once the lights had been readjusted, Snow immersed herself in the flow of energy between father and daughter, working to catch it on film.

When she took a break to reload, Katie led Julia off to help her change clothes, and Joseph said, "My camera, I drop the film in the back and it winds itself. Then I point it here and there, and press the button when I see something that looks as if it'll make a picture. When I'm finished, the camera rewinds itself, and I take the film to the drugstore."

Snow laughed, telling herself she was wrong about him. He wasn't a male version of her mother.

Julia came hurrying back in her pink practice clothes, and Snow turned to admire the child's carriage. "I bet you're a wonderful dancer," she said, touched by absolutely everything about this girl.

"I'm all right."

Snow dropped to her haunches and put her hands on Julia's waist, looking into her deep blue eyes. "Very pretty," she whispered.

Julia shook her head, but Snow could tell she was beginning to believe.

"What grade are you in?" Snow asked her.

"Third. I go to the Bailey School. Ever heard of it?"

"Yes, I have." It was a private school for artistically gifted children. "I knew you were good," Snow said, feeling for a few moments as if she'd time-traveled back to childhood; meeting someone new and wanting to be friends, observing the rituals that would facilitate it. After the initial exchange of names followed the invitation to come home and play. The new playmate's mother put out milk, or juice and cookies, welcoming her with politely probing questions about her mother, which she'd long since learned to answer with non sequiturs, while her recent friend reined in his or her impatience, eager to get on with displaying an accumulation of small treasures. She'd found it wonderful as a child, encountering someone she knew she was going to like. Of course by the time she was seven, she'd known all the kids in town, and the only newcomers she'd encountered were the children of people who sometimes rented the summer homes. But still this exchange with Julia had that feel to it.

"Maybe you could come to our house for dinner one night," Julia said carefully, turning to her dad. "Could she, Dad?"

The climate suddenly cooled perceptibly. "We'll see, Jule," he replied. "Things are a little crazy right now. But sure, sometime."

Julia knew he was saying no, and couldn't understand why. She climbed back onto the stool, sat on her knees, and folded her arms in front of her. Unaware of his child's hurt, Joseph smiled into the camera. Feeling a small, thin pain, knowing her initial assessment of their relationship had been right, Snow snapped off the shot even though all Julia's energy had evaporated.

Later, while Julia was changing back into her street clothes, and Snow and Katie were shutting down the lights, Joseph studied the prints tacked to the studio wall.

"Where is this place?" he asked.

"Stony Point, Rhode Island," she answered, wondering why he'd shut down so abruptly and had now decided to try to restore their former ease, "where I grew up."

"Wonderful pictures. They make me want to go there." He had no idea why he'd reacted as he had to Julia's enthusiasm for this woman, and was trying, indirectly, to get things back on a friendly footing. "Did your parents actually name you Snow? Do you have a sister named Rain and a brother Hail? Have you got a trunkful of mood rings and love beads, tie-dyes and headbands?"

Confused by his mood swings, distanced now, she said, "Not so far as I know."

Angry with himself, he turned to take another look at the shot of the boats in the marina. "This is wonderful."

"Have it," she offered. "I can see how much you like it."

"Are you serious?"

She walked over, popped the pushpin from the wall, and handed him the print. "It's yours. I'll get you an envelope." Her anger beginning to seep back, she went to the closet for a padded mailer, brought it back and handed that to him, too.

"Let me pay you for it."

"I wouldn't dream of it." She busied herself unloading the last roll of film from the camera, pointedly ignoring him.

Before they left, Snow again dropped down to put her hands on Julia's waist, saying, "When you see the proofs, you'll know I wasn't just being nice."

"D'you have a card or something?" Julia asked quietly when her father was out of earshot.

"Sure. Stand right here and I'll get you one."

Snow went to her desk and returned to give the girl her card.

"Maybe I'll call you sometime," Julia said.

"I would love that," Snow replied, one hand cupping Julia's chin.

Suddenly she wound her arms around Snow's middle and hugged her hard. Then she stepped away, and turned to look for her father.

As the two were leaving, Julia remembered, and turned to say good-bye to Katie.

"Bye, Jule." Katie waved, noting that Snow studiously avoided making eye contact with Joseph as he said good-bye.

"That was strange," Katie observed after they'd gone.

"What was?"

"Don't do that, please. The two of you were getting along great, and all of a sudden it turned to winter. I liked him up to that point."

"So did I," Snow admitted.

"Jule said she wanted you to come to dinner and the guy shut down."

"I kept telling myself I was wrong. But when he turned cold, I knew I wasn't. He's a male version of my mother: overprotective, doesn't want to risk having her form attachments to anyone else."

"You sure he's not just being careful? I mean, this is New York. Raising a kid here isn't easy."

"This is way more than that," Snow said firmly. "It was subtle, but he undermines her choices."

Katie was quiet for a moment, then said, "I didn't see that. But, then, I probably wouldn't. Too bad."

"Too bad for everybody. God, Katie! Why are men so weird?"

"If I had the answer to that, my darling, I'd write a book and get famous."

Seventeen

Katie was going home to make dinner for Robbie who was actually getting two days and nights off before having to return to the hospital. "This'll be different," Katie said, pulling on a crumpled black hat with a red silk rose pinned to one side. "The past couple of weeks was like being single again." She wrinkled her nose. "I think I liked it. But don't hold me to that. Call you tomorrow." She gave Snow a kiss, slung her backpack over one shoulder and left.

For a long time Snow just stood staring at the door, listening to the silence in the loft and the street noises rising from below. Then she stirred, and checked the time. Four-twenty. Too early for dinner, and, besides, she wasn't hungry. Reaching for the film in Katie's basket, she went to the darkroom.

By six-thirty, she was examining Julia's young-old features on the contact sheets, wanting to tuck the child into bed at night the way Anne always had, even when, as an adult, Snow was home for a weekend visit. She wanted to take this little girl shopping, and to brush her hair; she wanted to sit on the sidelines and watch her at ballet class, to hear her laugh again. A slight girl with wistful eyes and long, thick lashes, a nose too prominent for the small face, and a firm, cleft chin. A lonely child without a mother, and a father who appeared to get scared if he felt his daughter might be developing an attachment to someone else.

Snow printed a dozen proofs, then carried them to the kitchen to look at while the kettle was boiling for tea. Then, forgetting the tea bag slowly turning the water dark and bitter, she wept over a dramatically sidelit, three-quarters head shot that showed very clearly what a compellingly attractive woman this frail, determined sprite would one day be. Shadows minimized the strength of the nose, highlighted the length of the neck and the acuity of those remarkable eyes, conveyed the aspirations and diffidence of someone bound to the constricted realm of childhood primarily by her size.

This was ridiculous! Here she sat, mooning over Joseph Broder's motherless child while she herself had what might have been considered a surfeit of mothers—one recently deceased, whose identity was unknown, and one with a known identity who might be lost to her for all time.

Leaving the proofs on the table and the tea forgotten on the counter, she pulled on a sweater, got her bag, and went out. It was one of those mild spring evenings when the newly leafed trees and soft breeze robbed the city of much of its menace. But the pleasure she derived from the softened light and soothing flow of air on her overheated skin was, she well knew, only temporary. Once darkness fell, the menace would make itself felt again. Eyes taking in everything and nothing, she wondered once more why she lived in this city.

With no direction in mind, she started walking, scanning doorways and alleys for a glimpse of Irene, but didn't see her and was mildly disappointed. Surrendering to what had become an unavoidable craving, she bought a pack of cigarettes at the corner liquor store, pocketed the change, and continued walking. Only in Manhattan did she have the peculiar sense of being simultaneously visible and invisible. The majority of passersby assiduously avoided making eye contact, and so she was not seen. The shadow people, though, observed everyone and everything, looking for a mark, a score, anyone the least bit vulnerable. You might not see them, but they were there.

If you were foolish enough to park your car on the street and leave anything of value in it—whether locked in the car itself or in the trunk—it would most certainly be gone upon your return, even if you were away for no more than five minutes. If you were foolish enough to carry anything of value on your person—visible jewelry, cash, a Walkman—you risked, at the very least, having it simply whisked away by someone who would be half a block off before you'd even opened your mouth to protest, and at the very worst, being shot point-blank by a complete stranger who'd taken a fancy to your earrings/wristwatch/Sony/wallet/handbag/shoes. You could even be killed in plain view, simply stopping to use a public telephone. Everyone had weapons of one sort or another in the war zone, and had no compunctions about using them randomly, arbitrarily.

What the hell was she doing here? she wondered, sitting down on the steps of the nearest brownstone. Stripping the pack of its cellophane, she got out a cigarette. The feel of it between her fingers was at once familiar and oddly comforting, even after five years. One of her instructors in college had commented that his craving for cigarettes had finally disappeared after twenty-one years. A quickening of her heartbeat, she held the cigarette to her mouth, anticipating the first drag, and only then realized she had no matches.

Stupid. She laughed at herself, thought of Julia, gulped in prelude to more tears, and abruptly forced herself up and back onto the sidewalk. There was a lot she'd do, but she would not cry in public. Anne Cooke's daughter had been taught all her life to keep her miseries private.

Halfway home she stopped at a Blimpie Base to buy a tuna sub, and on her way out of the place dropped the cigarettes in the trash bin.

After another night of disturbed and restless sleep, she was up, showered and dressed by seven. But there was nothing to do. Until Sam Daley and Joseph Broder made their choices from the contacts and proofs, the only printing to be done was on the Kingsley shoot and she was holding off on that as her last legitimate excuse to close herself into the darkroom. Otherwise, she'd cleared the decks. Katie had even done the preliminary billings. The apartment was as clean as it was going to get; housekeeping had never been her strong suit. She wasn't hungry, had already had two cups of coffee and was feeling the buzz in her hands and feet, along with a restless anxiety that had her pacing back and forth the length of the loft, all but tearing at her hair. She thought of calling Rudy, but had nothing to say to him. And, besides, calling him would only exacerbate her longing to go back to Stony Point.

Pausing by the window, fists clenched and hips and knees aching from tension, she looked out at her slice of the city, gritty gray in a fuzzy rain, and felt like a prisoner. The view reminded her of Lou Stomen's striking 1940 photograph of Times Square in the rain, taken from the roof or window of a nearby building: the tops of the skyscrapers mist-shrouded, the streets shiny like the hair ribbons she'd had to wear as a child.

She shouldn't have thrown away the cigarettes. She wanted one now as she wondered why Joseph Broder had turned off and on with her like a jealous child. Didn't he realize his daughter needed female input? Why should he, or anyone, be threatened by a skinny redhead who'd taken a liking to his little girl? Not even twenty-four hours and she was an addict, needing her fix of the sight of that winsome child, or the adorable Jonathan Daley. Was she turning into her mother after all, hungering after other people's children? A terrifying thought! And she had to keep reminding herself that Anne Cooke was not her natural mother; a hard habit to break after thirty years. God! Her brain felt as if it had torn loose from its moorings and was floating in her skull like an astronaut on a space mission.

She had to get herself together. There were things to be done. She went to the desk, uncapped her pen, and began to make a list. Call Huffy Compton, number one. Call Benson in Providence, number two, to ask when she could get into that safe deposit box. Number three... What? Irma. Write a check to cover the next month, a note to go with it, address it to Irma. Good thing she'd remembered. Number four... four... She couldn't think of anything else. But now she had a legitimate errand to do. Jacket on, keys and bag in hand, she was on her way to mail the check to Irma. And just because it felt right, regardless of the risk, she grabbed the camera and a couple of rolls of black and white.

The letter safely dropped into a mailbox, she started walking uptown, considering that shot of Julia she found so moving, and decided it was because it had a feel similar to some of Julia Margaret Cameron's work: Pre-Raphaelite studies and dramatic images created by an English woman who'd died more than a hundred years before—mournful, contemplative, fanciful images, often on historical or romantic themes. There was nothing new. Everything had already been done: Henri Cartier-Bresson, Diane Arbus, Irving Penn. Anything different came down to a matter of the eye. Just as writers were thought to have "voices," photographers had to have a distinctive "eye." And she'd always known she had that; her teachers had confirmed her possession of this particularization of vision, this discernment that translated into representations—primarily of children—that could only have been hers.

Heading north on Hudson Street, she saw Irene emerging from a doorway where she'd obviously spent the night. Snow quickly caught up with the woman, and asked how she was.

"I'm fine, dear," Irene said. "The damp bothers me some, but there's not much to be done, is there?" With a shrug, she looked up at the uniformly gray sky. "It might as well be England."

"Could I buy you breakfast?" Snow offered.

"That's very kind." Irene smiled, showing her startlingly healthy teeth. "A coffee and a roll would be lovely."

"How about a real, sit-down breakfast?" Snow suggested, made aware by the polite but somehow empty quality of the woman's gaze that, once again, Irene had lost all memory of Snow.

"Really?" The woman stopped, one hand still on the shopping cart, and looked at Snow. "You *are* kind." She smiled suddenly and said, almost lovingly, "Bacon and eggs, toast and jam. Yes. I'd like that very much."

"Okay, great." Snow looked around. "There's a place open just up the street. Let's go there."

They started toward the restaurant with Irene still smiling. Snow held open the door while the older woman maneuvered the neatly loaded cart inside, the warmth of the place covering her in a steamy cloud redolent of bacon grease and hot coffee.

The restaurant was busy, filled with a mix of people; blue, white, and no collar, the majority of whom paused to look over with mildly vexed curiosity as one of the waitresses, menus in one hand, coffee pot in the other, angrily said to Irene, "You can't come in here!"

"Excuse me?" Snow said quietly, her temples suddenly throbbing. "What did you say?"

"She can't come in here!"

"Why not?"

"We're busy. We can't have these people sitting, taking up space for hours with one cup of coffee." Snow beckoned the waitress over with the forefinger of her left hand. Irritated, the woman said, "What? I'm in a hurry here. Okay? What?"

"'*These* people,'" Snow said very softly, "get hungry, too. And they *are* people. You're the second miserable woman I've run into since yesterday, and it's starting to get on my nerves. So lighten up, because I'm in the mood to make a major scene and I don't think you'd enjoy it. Irene is my guest, and we're going to sit at the table in the corner over there, where she'll have room for her cart. I'll just take these menus—" Snow pulled them from the woman's hand "—and why don't you bring us some coffee to start. Okay?" She smiled, wondering if the waitress could see the pulse beating in her temple.

To Irene who'd stood by, fully prepared to be turned away, Snow now said, "We'll sit back there, Irene," and followed her to the table in the corner. Then, while Irene was arranging her cart with care before removing her coat, Snow lifted the camera, adjusted the aperture for the low light level, and took several shots of the place and a few of Irene. The waitress responded to this with visible agitation and fear, and kept an eye on Snow until she flipped the shutter lock and put the lens cap back on.

Having studied the menu with intense interest for three or four minutes, Irene put it down and said, admiringly, "You're a very angry young woman."

Somewhat thrown, Snow acknowledged, "I guess I am."

"I find it quite appealing. I've always liked angry people. They're so energetic, for the most part."

"How was your night at the motel?" Snow asked in an attempt to determine if Irene actually had forgotten her again.

"It was very nice, thank you. I had a lovely long bath and watched television. Such a load of old rubbish. American television's frightful, don't you think?"

"A lot of it is," Snow agreed. "So you do remember me?"

"Of course I do."

The waitress came stalking over to the table and without a word stood with her eyes on the order pad, pen poised.

"What would you like, Irene?" Snow asked her.

"She's very angry, too," Irene observed. "But not in the way you are. Hers is an unhealthy anger. I'm quite an expert on the subject. You can't imagine how many angry people I encounter in the course of each day. I think everyone in this entire city is angry."

"You two gonna order sometime today?" the waitress asked Snow.

"Sorry, dear," said Irene placidly. She ordered the deluxe breakfast special—two eggs, pancakes, bacon, home fries, toast, orange juice and coffee.

Snow asked for a toasted bagel and coffee.

The waitress turned and left.

"I didn't think you remembered me, from one time to the next," Snow said.

"How many lovely red-haired young women d'you imagine stop to talk, or give me money? Of course I remember you."

"But it never seems as if you do."

"Yes, well. Sometimes people don't care to be reminded they once stopped to talk. They're embarrassed."

"I never thought of that."

"Well, you wouldn't, would you?" Irene said without rancor. "It's something I've discovered, living on the streets."

"We talked the first time a year or so ago. I asked how you came to be on the street, and you told me about your claustrophobia. Do you remember that?"

The waitress came, slid cups of coffee in front of each of the women, and flew off.

Irene said, "I remember," and concentrated on peeling the slippery little lid from a minute plastic container of half-and-half.

"I worry about you," Snow said. "Aren't you scared, being out there?"

"Sometimes, very." Irene lifted her cup and looked directly at Snow. "When I was growing up, there were Gypsy caravans in a nearby field. I always envied them so. I'd have loved to live in a painted wood caravan in a field of wildflowers." She smiled.

"In England, you mean?"

"Oh, yes. You couldn't possibly do that here. People in this country are so threatened by what they don't understand. The English tend to be somewhat more tolerant. Or perhaps just less violent. In any event, the Gypsies came and went, year after year. I've never forgotten them."

"Do you mind if I ask what sort of work did you used to do?"

"Executive secretary, believe it or not. I was quite the clever monkey before I went bonkers." She laughed merrily and, after a moment, Snow did, too.

"What about your son?" Snow asked.

"Michael." Irene frowned and looked into the depths of her cup.

"He lives in Long Island?" Snow prompted.

"In a manner of speaking." Irene sighed and folded her hands tightly together on the tabletop. "He's buried there."

Another citizen in the territory of loss. Snow reached across the table to place a hand over Irene's, and they sat silently for a minute or two until the waitress came with their food. Then Snow slowly sat back and watched Irene pull herself away from the never-distant sorrow and apply herself to the food. Her table manners were impeccable.

Eating the bagel she didn't really want, Snow sat thinking for a time, then said, "If it was possible, would you like to go back to England, Irene, and have that caravan in a field?"

"It's a fairy tale, dear." The woman regarded her with sympathy, as if she found Snow hopelessly naive or overly gullible.

"No, but would you, if you could?"

"I don't know that I could leave Michael. That would be very difficult."

"But you'd like to?"

"I suppose so."

"What about Michael's father?"

Irene raised her eyebrows and shook her head. "Long gone, dear. I scarcely remember him. A good-looking bugger, but utterly feckless. And what about you? How did you come to be so angry?"

Choosing to keep things simple, Snow said, "My mother died a week ago."

"Ah! That's very unfortunate."

"Yes."

"Sudden, was it?"

"Heart attack."

"That's a blessing."

"Irene, if you decide you'd like to go back to England and have that caravan, I'll give you the money to do it."

Irene regarded her with open skepticism. "Why would you want to do a thing like that?"

"Because I like you."

"You don't know me."

"It doesn't matter. Do you still have my card?"

"I do, actually."

"Hang on to it. If you decide you'd like to go back, I'll give you the money, Irene."

"That's very generous of you. Let me think about it, dear," she said as if humoring someone as bonkers as she claimed to be. "For now, this is a lovely treat." And she returned, with a formidable appetite, to her food.

Irene went off with her cart to see her social worker. Snow wandered across town in the rain, studying empty storefronts and the people on the streets, letting the camera hang untouched around her neck. She saw nothing she wanted to shoot. But she did see all kinds of things she'd have liked to buy for Julia and Jonathan and even for Hilary—toys and clothing, books and music. She lingered at the windows of a store catering exclusively to children, finding it ironic that in a matter of days she'd have more money than she'd ever imagined and yet any number of factors prohibited her from spending it in the way her instincts dictated. She couldn't buy anything for the children, and Irene had treated her as if they were fellow inmates of an open-air asylum.

Moving away from the window at last, she turned in the direction of the loft. Striding along the sidewalk at her usual vigorous pace, she asked herself what she wanted, aside from being reunited with her family and learning Anne Cooke's true identity. The answer seemed to be a child. And the implications of that were so alarming that she had to dismiss this answer and seek another.

What else did she want? She sorted through the ideas in her mind, automatically absorbing the visual details of all she saw in passing: a pair of underdressed teenage prostitutes standing in a doorway, their legs scrawny, their street-smart eyes squinting against the smoke from their cigarettes; a young woman aggressively pushing her child's stroller up the avenue, as if defying anyone to suggest she and her toddler shouldn't have the right of way; a well-dressed, elderly man muttering to himself as he shambled past her; a cabdriver leaning on his horn, head out the window, shouting at another driver, "What're you, fucking blind, asshole?"

Irene was right, she thought. Angry people did have a daunting energy. But unlike Irene, she didn't find it appealing.

It was almost eleven by the time she got back to the loft. Leaving the mail on the desk she went to listen to her messages.

Katie said, "It's just me, checking in. Robbie and I're going to catch a movie this afternoon. I thought maybe you'd like to come with us. It's now, uhm, twenty to ten. We're aiming for the one-thirty show. Talk to you later. Bye."

"Miss Devane, this is Hugh Compton. I've been making a few calls and I've had some luck finding Danny Ambrose. Unfortunately, he's out of town at the moment. I've left a message asking him to call me, and when I've heard from him, I'll let you know. Good day."

There was a hang-up, another hang-up, and then Mark saying, "Hi. Sorry I haven't been in touch for a few days, but I've been apartment hunting, among other things. How about dinner one night? I'll be in the office all day. Let me know."

Well, that was a surprise. She honestly hadn't expected to hear from Mark again. She had to give him points for determination, if nothing else.

After waiting for the tape to reset, she called Katie back.

"I'm not really up for a movie today," Snow told her. "How're things going?"

"Fine. I made a fabulous dinner, chicken and shallots in a brandy cream sauce. The poor baby ate three helpings then fell asleep while I was clearing the dishes. He slept for nine hours, got up at five to hit the books for a while, and brought me breakfast in bed. Blew my brain right out my ears." She laughed. "So, what're you going to do today?"

"I don't know," Snow answered, thinking about Julia and the Bailey School. "I had a call from Mr. Compton. He said he's tracked down Daniel Ambrose."

"Fantastic!"

"That's the good news. The bad news is he's out of town."

"Bummer!"

"Mr. Compton said he'd be in touch when he heard from Daniel."

"All right. That's good. You okay, babe? Why don't you come with us to the movies? You need distraction."

"I'm in a strange headspace. I'd be rotten company, Katie, really. And anyway, you hardly see Robbie these days. Spend the time with him. I'll hang out, probably print up Hilary's shoot and the stuff from this morning."

"What'd you do this morning?"

"Street people, this and that. I doubt it's any good. I wasn't really concentrating. But I'm happy with Julia's sitting. Some of the head shots are very strong. Anyway, look. Go enjoy yourself, and we'll talk tomorrow."

"You sound down. Maybe I should come over."

"Katie, don't. I need to be by myself. I've got to find some kind of mental position to take on everything."

"Okay. But if you change your mind, let me know."

"I will. Have fun."

She got out the phone book to look up the address of the Bailey School, told herself to forget about Julia Broder, and sat down to go through the newspaper clippings again.

Eighteen

Hoping to reestablish her self-control, she developed the Kingsley film and made up the contacts, thereby completing her current obligations. Of course, once the various parents made their selections, she'd have to do the printing, but for now she was free. To do what? She'd go see Julia. Bad idea. But she'd known all along she was going to go; she simply had to see the girl. And so, with the contacts and proofs from the sitting in hand, she went out into the now sunny afternoon to flag down a cab.

Leaning against a lamppost, she stood and waited, along with a dozen or so other women. She was reminded all at once of her kindergarten year when her mother had driven her to school each morning and had been there waiting outside when it was time to go home. She'd completely forgotten that, because once she'd started the first grade, she'd traveled with all the other kids on the school bus. It felt peculiar now to be waiting, as her mother once had, for the sight of a little girl who didn't belong to her. Had she, she wondered, evolved into the tainted fruit of a poisoned tree? No. Her intentions were entirely aboveboard.

Fifteen minutes later, she moved away from the lamppost to scan the faces of the children as they began pushing out through the doors, experiencing an elated inner leap of recognition at the sight of Julia emerging from the building, arm in arm with another girl.

Julia saw her and looked puzzled for a moment, then smiled brilliantly. Quickly saying good-bye to her friend, she approached Snow and said, "Hi. I'm so surprised to see you. How come you're here?"

"I wanted to see you, and to bring you the proofs." She handed Julia the envelope. "You don't mind, do you?"

"No. It's just a big surprise."

A small, wiry middle-aged woman came to stand next to Julia, taking hold of her hand in a manner that declared, I'm in charge of this child and you'd better have a good reason for talking to her.

She had a headful of wild, thick gray hair, narrow features and dramatic eye makeup that gave her a decidedly Middle Eastern look. She was, all in all, very attractive, in a rather forbidding fashion.

"Uhm, Clem, this is Snow," Julia explained to the woman. "The photographer from yesterday." To Snow, she said, "This is Clem, our housekeeper. She meets me every day after school."

Snow said hi, and the woman moved forward, her expression intensely suspicious. Daunted, Snow offered her hand. Clem smiled approvingly, and gave Snow's hand a short, hard shake, saying, "This girl, she's talking about you the whole time when she come home yesterday, eh? Me, I'm 'appy to meet you. My name is *Clemence,*" she enunciated carefully, casting a mock-evil glance at Julia, "*not* Clem. She calls me so because she likes to tease. In French, this name is mercy," she said, peering intently into Snow's eyes. "In French, you are called *neige.* Very unusual name. Such beautiful hair you have. I like very much."

"Thank you. I like your eye makeup. I've never been able to put it on right. You're from France?"

"Quebec." She pronounced it kay-beck. "I show you sometime. But I don't think you need it. Maybe a little mascara, *c'est tout.* Very fortunate not to need the *maquillage.* So you bring the pictures, eh?"

"Uh-hunh. I wanted Julia to see how very pretty she is." Snow's eyes moved to the child who, from habit, made a face at this remark.

"Don't make like that!" Clemence clucked and tugged fondly at Julia's hand, then said to Snow, "She don't like this face. Foolish girl." Gently chiding, she said, "I tell you you have a good face, eh? And now this Snow, she tells you, too."

"She's just being nice," Julia defended herself. "I know what I see in the mirror."

"No," Clemence disagreed. "You don't know this. *We* know, but not you. Is this not so?" she asked Snow.

"That's absolutely so. Look, I don't want to hold you up. I just wanted to say hi." She dropped down so that she and the girl were at eye level. "Maybe sometime, if it's all right with your dad, you could come out for lunch with me. Or to a concert, or matinee. If you'd like to, of course."

"Sure I would." Lowering her voice, not wanting Clemence to hear, she asked, "Why are you being so nice to me?"

"I like you, Julia."

"Is that because you don't have a little girl of your own?" she asked with an innocent directness that pierced Snow with an ice-pick pain.

"Partly," Snow admitted. "But mostly it's because I like you."

"I like you, too," Julia confessed, as if she had a pain of her own. "My pictures are in here?" She lifted the envelope.

"Just the contact sheets and some rough prints. You and your dad can look at the contacts and pick out what you want. I printed proofs of the ones I like best."

"Okay. You know what?"

"What?" Snow smiled, her hands on the girl's tiny waist.

"I made you something."

"You did? No way! What?"

Julia reached into her pocket and said playfully, "Hold out your hand." Snow did, and the girl placed a small origami bird on her palm.

"Julia, it's wonderful! Thank you."

"You really like it? It's kind of lopsided."

"I love it." Snow kissed the girl's cheek. "It's the nicest thing anybody ever gave me."

"Are you just being nice again?"

"No. Really, it's terrific. I'll put it someplace special." Reluctantly, she stood up, saying, "I'd better let you go. We're keeping Clemence waiting."

"I'll ask my dad about lunch," Julia told her. "Then I'll phone you. Okay?"

"Okay." Snow told Clemence it had been good to meet her, and headed off.

From behind her, Julia yelled, "Bye, Snow! I'm glad you came. I'll call you later."

Snow turned to wave and watched the girl go off—spine perfectly straight, her gait turned out—with the housekeeper. Then Snow continued on her way, the small paper bird cupped carefully in her hand.

At seven-thirty, inspired by an image of Rudy in his BarcaLounger watching a Red Sox game on TV while listening to the play-by-play on a small portable radio, she tuned in Channel 11 to catch the Yankees game. She had the TV sound off and the radio tuned to the broadcast just the way Rudy did, and felt closer to him as a result. Baseball was the only sport she'd ever enjoyed watching, and it was because Rudy had taught her to see the beauty and logic of the game. As a teenager she'd gone with him to Fenway Park in Boston half a dozen times to see games, and had loved all of it, from the hot dogs to the sudden eruption of cheers when somebody got on base.

The Yankees were ahead one to nothing going into the top of the third when her intercom sounded. Assuming it was Mark, she got up to answer.

"It's Joseph Broder. I'd like to talk to you, please."

Curious, she buzzed him in and went to open her door.

He came off the elevator, grim-faced and purposeful, as if marching into battle. "Why did you go to my daughter's school?" he asked, barely in control of his anger.

"Good evening, Mr. Broder. I'm fine, thank you. Nice of you to ask."

He stopped dead and stared at her, clearly questioning her sanity.

She stared at him for a long moment then slammed the door shut, turned the locks, and stood breathing hard through her open mouth.

He knocked on the door, saying, "I want to talk to you!"

"The hell you do! You want to play war games, and I'm not interested. Forget it! Hit the road!"

He was silent for so long she thought he might have gone. But then, in a calmer voice, he said, "I really would like to talk to you. Okay? Could you open the door, please?"

"I don't think so. Go away, Mr. Broder."

"Look, I'm sorry. Okay? Just put the chain on and open the door six inches, so we can talk face-to-face."

She did it, and peered out at him, saying, "What is the *matter* with you, Broder? Someone shows an interest in your little girl and you're so threatened you go berserk?"

"Hardly berserk." He managed a small smile.

"Hey! You're here knocking on my door. I'm not out wherever, knocking on yours."

"Okay, okay." He held both hands up, palms out. "I tend to be very protective of Julia. I'm sorry."

"Broder," she said tiredly, "there's protective, and then there's you and my mother. I'm something of an expert when it comes to protective parents. And I have to tell you, you're overboard. I saw it yesterday, and I knew I shouldn't go to the school this afternoon. But Julia's special, and I wanted to see her again, so I went. In your view, of course, that's a criminal offense."

"I don't think that at all." He rubbed his face with one hand, and backed up until he was leaning across the far wall.

"No?"

"You have to understand," he said. "She's all I've got."

"All *you've* got? What's Julia got, Broder? You have no clue, none, what it's like for her, the kind of damage you're doing. She'll grow up angry and alienated because you're not letting her *breathe!* Don't you realize she needs to pick her own friends, regardless of their age? Don't you see that by undermining her choices you're making her feel ugly?" Voice thick, eyes overflowing, she said, "Go away! I don't have time for this," and stepped back, ready to close the door.

Impressed by her impassioned defense of his child, and feeling guilty for handling the matter so badly, he said, "I'm being a real schmuck, aren't I? First I upset Jule. Now you. I'm sorry." He was quiet for a few moments, and the radio commentator's voice could be heard giving the pitch count. It threw him that she'd been sitting alone on a Friday night, listening to the ball game. He'd imagined such a good-looking woman would be out on a date.

No one had ever talked to him this way, especially not about Julia. And while a part of him wanted to reject what she was saying, another part was telling him to listen; he might learn something from this woman. "Have you eaten?" he asked. "Are you hungry? I am. Let me buy you something to eat, and let's talk about this."

Mopping her face on her sleeve, she took another look at him. "If you're willing to listen, and discuss things rationally, okay."

"I would like to discuss this. Julia's never had a mother. I've raised her on my own, and maybe I'm not doing the great job I thought I was. I get the feeling I should listen to you."

"Why?" she asked warily.

"Because you're making sense. It's never occurred to me that I might be the reason why Jule has some of the problems she does. It scares me to think that. But what you said hit a nerve. Obviously, you know something I don't. I may be a schmuck, but I'm not an arrogant schmuck."

"Okay." Amused, she shut the door, took the chain off, then opened it again, saying, "Come in, Broder. We'll order a pizza and talk. I'm not in the mood to go out."

"My father was at school in England when the war broke out. His older brother, my uncle George, was at Harvard, and their younger sister, Renata, was still at home in Berlin with my grandparents. To keep it short, my father and uncle never saw their parents or sister again. Relatives here in New York supported my father in England until they could get him out after the war.

"He arrived in '47, met my mother at Columbia where he was doing his master's in '48. They had my brother, Max, in '52 and me in '56. Max studied law. I majored in English, minored in economics, and did my master's in art history. Then, to the horror of the whole family, I went to work as a steward for TWA." He laughed and shook his head, then drank some more of the red wine Snow had opened. "I wanted to travel," he continued, "and I worked the international routes. That lasted four years. Then I quit, pulled a chunk of my savings and set off to spend six months on this idea I had to start up an exclusive travel service.

"Along the way I met Nicole. Within six months we were married, and we started the business together. We traveled, checking out the best hotels, the best things to see and do in Asia, the best places to shop, to eat, all of it. We were in the black by the end of the second year, getting a lot of word-of-mouth business.

"We'd been married three years when Nicole got pregnant. The pregnancy was fine—no problems. She went into labor right on time, and we grabbed a cab to the hospital. Things were fine. But then, all of a sudden, it turned sour in the delivery room. One minute everything was okay, the baby's head was just crowning. The next minute they were hustling me out of there, not telling me why or what was wrong." He sighed deeply, drank some more wine, then went on. "Her blood pressure bottomed out. They were able to save the baby, but Nicole's heart just quit. The autopsy revealed an aortic aneurysm. I couldn't get my mind around it. Just couldn't. I walked into that hospital with my wife, a happy man, a husband about to become a father. I walked out a widower, with an infant." His eyes filled with tears and he wiped them away impatiently.

"I couldn't manage, so I moved back home with the baby. My mother and the housekeeper took care of Julia while I was at work.

And eventually, when my parents retired to Florida, I bought the apartment from them, and hired Clemence, who thinks you're great, by the way, and called me all kinds of things in French for making such a stink."

"I liked her. And whatever she called you, she was right."

"I know, I know. But try to see things from my perspective."

"I do," Snow said. "It's a very sad story. But you're still a schmuck."

He laughed. "I deserve that, I guess."

"Well, you do listen. You get points for that."

"That's something. Want that last piece?"

"No, you have it."

He helped himself to the remaining slice of pizza and she got up to change the CD. Once past his snit, he'd turned out to be good company, relaxed and not without humility. It moved her that he still wept over his wife. "There's hope for you," she said, returning to the sofa. "You took that pretty well, my tirade."

"I know the truth when I hear it."

"Sometimes."

"Sometimes," he conceded, finding that her face was growing familiar, as was her habit of winding one strand of hair around and around her finger, and the way she chewed on the side of her finger when she was thinking. Her intensity was leavened by a good sense of humor, and he liked making her laugh; he enjoyed the unexpected heartiness of her laughter. She was also a fantastic photographer. The pictures of Julia were wonderful.

"So what's this travel thing you do?" she asked.

"Okay. Here's how it works. A couple, or two, maximum four, they come to me, they say how much time they've got, which part of Asia they're interested in, and I work up an itinerary and book everything from the air tickets to personal guides in each destination. I make sure they're met upon arrival, that their luggage is handled, there's a limo waiting, and their hotel rooms have an ironing board, or a fax, or a computer waiting for them. Whatever they want. I subcontract with local guides and half a dozen or so foreign travel agents I trust. Occasionally, I go along myself as a personal guide."

"Tell me about China," Snow invited, pushing away the terrible image of this man leaving a hospital with his newborn baby. She didn't want to become too sympathetic to him.

"I think it's your turn to tell me about you."

"I can't. I don't want to, not now. Tell me about China."

"Okay." He sipped some more wine. "It's incredible. Some aspects are positively Dickensian—the silk-weaving factories where there's almost no light and the workers go deaf in ten years from the noise of the looms. You can't speak because you can't be heard. My favorite city's Suzhou. They call it the Venice of China—all these canals. So beautiful. Then there's Shanghai, with the European-influenced housing and office buildings, remnants of the thirties when there was a large European community. Now most of those houses are ruined, crumbling from neglect, with maybe twelve families crammed into one, and laundry hanging from bamboo poles outside every window. It was a beautiful city once upon a time, with tree-lined boulevards. Now you turn a corner and there's a man squatting on the sidewalk, chopping firewood with a meat cleaver. There's the Great Wall outside Beijing, and the Forbidden City. And the terra cotta warriors in Xian. So many amazing things to see."

"I've always wanted to go to China," she said, thinking now she could go anywhere at all. "You said your brother's a lawyer?"

"Yup."

"I think I'm going to be needing a lawyer. Is he good?"

"The best. Let me know and I'll put you in touch with him."

"Thank you."

There followed the first uncomfortable silence that had fallen between them, and she thought she knew what he was working up to. "I only have affairs with married men," she said flatly, hoping to arrest any romantic ideas he might have.

He laughed and said, "Oh, very good."

"It happens to be true."

"You're serious?" He gazed at her quizzically. "You are serious. Why?"

"It's part of the history I don't want to go into right now." She looked over at the window. "I would like to spend some time with Julia."

"Sure. Why not, if it's what you both want?" Now that he'd spent some time with her, he was even more embarrassed by his behavior earlier. Because while she was less than forthcoming with personal details, it was very apparent that she had a unique insight into his daughter's problems and could only be a positive influence on Julia, and even on him, too. He'd never met anyone quite like her. And he enjoyed being with her.

"I'm crazy about your little girl, Broder. How do I know you can deal with this, that you're not going to start acting like a schmuck again?"

"You'll have to trust me when I say that I've listened to you and that I'm taking it seriously."

She studied him for a long moment, trying to detect any hint of insincerity. "Okay. I'll take your word. Go home now, would you, please? I'm tired. It's been a long, difficult week. Next week's probably going to be even longer and maybe more difficult."

"And you're not going to tell me why."

"Nope. Maybe some other time, but not now. I'll likely be in touch with Julia, because I want her to know I do genuinely care for her. And I might be calling you to get your brother's number. All right?"

"Sure."

"Good. I know you think I'm kind of a fruitcake, but one of these times I'll explain what's going on." She walked with him to the door. "Thanks for the pizza, Broder. And for telling me about your family."

"Maybe we'll do it again one evening."

"Maybe."

He said good-night, they shook hands, then he walked down the hall to the elevator. She waited in the doorway until it came. He looked back and smiled before stepping inside. Then she closed and locked the door, utterly drained but quite satisfied with the way things had gone. She left the dishes on the kitchen counter and went to get ready for bed, praying she'd be able to sleep through the night.

Nineteen

She woke up and looked at the clock. Twenty past seven; she'd slept for almost eight hours. About to get up, her eyes settled on the origami bird perched next to the telephone, and she began thinking about how she'd gone to see Julia even though she'd known it would cause what her mother would have called a ruckus.

As she got the coffee started, she thought about how in the last week she'd said and done things she'd never even contemplated before, culminating in her outburst at Joseph Broder. The impulses to which she'd surrendered in her teens had been primarily negative, usually premeditated ones that hadn't involved anyone else's vulnerabilities. Yesterday she had knowingly instigated a confrontation in the hope of sparing a little girl some of the anxiety that she knew only too well came as a result of being the sole child of a single parent with an attenuated focus.

While the price in terms of her own emotional wear and tear was fairly high, she was glad, even proud, of what she'd done. From the moment of their first meeting she'd committed to a moral contract with Julia. She knew, perhaps better than most people, how momentous it was to make declarations of caring to children, and how very seriously children took them, and she had never been one to take commitments lightly, regardless of how minimal.

So why had she taken the moral low ground on her own behalf? Why wasn't she out actively searching for her family instead of hiding in this dreary, underfurnished loft? She'd accepted the fact that she was Victoria MacKenzie that day at the library when she and Katie had found the newspaper stories. She believed she was the kidnapped daughter of William and Patricia. But so far she'd elected to concentrate on trying to uncover Anne Cooke's real identity rather than tracking down her parents, throwing out all kinds of excuses in an attempt to obscure her motives. Why?

As she drank several cups of coffee and ate a piece of toast with marmalade, she acknowledged her fear. It was reasonable, probably to be expected. But why was she able to put herself on the line for Julia, yet unable to stop procrastinating about going to the police? Surely it was time to honor some of the promises she'd made herself way back when she'd first escaped to New York. Those promises and her dreams of freedom had never been realized because, in a remote interior place, she'd never stopped feeling that she'd betrayed her mother by leaving home. It was insidiously subtle, but Anne had managed, in all manner of ways, to convey her pain at Snow's abandonment, thereby reinforcing the guilt. The phone calls and visits home, the remembered birthdays and holiday greetings were of no consequence. Snow had gone out into the world on her own and, in so doing, inflicted a massive psychic injury on the one person who—her mother always quietly reminded her—loved her more than life itself. Her hold, never clumsy, had nonetheless been unyielding. And even now was still keeping her captive. From beyond the grave, Anne Cooke continued to exert her considerable influence. "You must learn not to be so impulsive, dear. It's best to think before you go rushing into things."

Jolted, she reached for the phone.

Katie said, "Hey! I was just going to call you. How're you doing?"

"Okay. I had kind of an interesting drama here last night." She gave a brief synopsis of what had happened the previous afternoon and evening.

"And the two of you wound up eating pizza while he gave you his life history?" Katie sounded a little suspicious.

"Basically."

"And did you tell him yours?"

"He asked, but I didn't tell him diddly."

"Is this a romantic thing?"

"Definitely not!"

"Okay. Tell me this. Why did you go to the school if you felt it was a bad idea?"

"I had to. I needed to see her."

"You *needed* to? What does that mean exactly?"

"Please don't give me a hard time, Katie. I did the right thing. I know how that little girl feels. Maybe now Broder does, too."

"Let's hope." Katie sounded doubtful.

"Well, I gave it my best shot. So, how's it going with Robbie?"

"I knew we'd never get the full forty-eight hours. One of the interns came down sick, so naturally Robbie had to go back to fill in for him. He left about half an hour ago. But it was good, like a refresher course." She laughed, then asked, "What're you going to do today?"

"First I want to get the contacts to Sam Daley and Joanna Kingsley. Then, if you're up for it, I thought I'd head over to East 67th Street and try to talk to somebody at the 19th Precinct."

"For real?" Katie asked excitedly.

"I can't wait any longer. This morning I decided to stop procrastinating and start making a serious effort to find my parents."

"I'm going with you! Give me an hour or so to get myself together. Okay? Will you wait for me?"

"Definitely. I really don't want to go without you."

"Okay. I'll get there fast as I can."

Half a block from the station house, Snow pulled Katie to a halt.

"Hang on a minute," she said, and started bending forward as if she had stomach cramps.

"Are you okay, babe?" Katie automatically began stroking Snow's back.

Straightening, Snow looked ahead, and swallowed several times. "I thought I was going to throw up. I'm all right now."

"You sure? We could go somewhere and grab a coffee, take some time for you to psych yourself up."

"Forget that. Let's just do it." She reached for Katie's hand, her own cold, and forced a shaky smile. "If I get stuck, give me a poke."

"No problem."

The officer on desk duty was a tall man, forty or so, with the giveaway overdeveloped muscles of a bodybuilder filling his uniform shirt out to its seams. Bald, with a mustache, and oddly translucent gray eyes, he gave an impression of cold disinterest as he glanced up from some paperwork and asked, "Do something for you, ladies?"

Katie thought, Oh, shit, and studied the man's stolidly unrevealing features as Snow began trying to explain why they were there. It was obvious she, too, felt the negativity radiating from the guy.

"We were hoping to get some information about a kidnapping. It, uhm, took place in, ah, 1963. According to the, uhm, newspaper reports, officers from this precinct initially handled the case." Snow again swallowed hard.

"Nineteen *sixty-three?*" He leaned way back from the desk in an exaggerated pose of incredulity, his face a portrait of feigned puzzlement, the gray eyes icy, possibly contemptuous. "You're after information on a case more than thirty years old?" Shiny brow furrowing, eyes narrowing, he asked, "Why? What're you, journalism students, researchers or something?"

Katie wanted to wrap her hands around his neck—which appeared to be about the same diameter as his head—and choke him. He was the kind of guy she absolutely hated—a wiseass, macho bully. She wanted to scream at him. Couldn't he see how hard this was for Snow? Why did he have to make it even harder? Be decent, she told him mutely. For once in your rotten, chauvinistic life, be a mensch.

"Because," Snow said, sounding admirably calm, "I have reason to believe I was the kidnapped child." She hesitated. The man's resistance was so solid it seemed to have actual substance, like a wall of granite.

"And what might that reason be?" he asked with undisguised skepticism, his wintry eyes gazing straight into hers as if he were so accustomed to hearing fabrications and fantastic tales that he'd developed a special ability to see right through them.

She wanted to beg him to stop being so supercilious but sensed that any show of weakness would make him behave even worse. The only way to deal with him was to take a firm line and tough it out. "The woman I believed to be my mother died recently, and before she did, she told me she'd kidnapped me from a Manhattan supermarket on September the twenty-first, 1963."

"Your mother in her right mind when she passed?" he asked, with an expression that openly questioned whether Snow herself was completely sane.

"Yes, she was in her right mind," Snow replied evenly. "And I just told you she wasn't my mother. I *believed* her to be. She told me on her deathbed that she wasn't."

"People've been known to say all kinds of things when they're on the way out."

"Hardly something like that," Katie contributed, struggling to keep her temper.

"Hey! Who's to say?" He shrugged his massive shoulders, then ran a finger across his mustache as if reassuring himself it was still there.

"She was very specific," Snow persisted, "told me exactly how she'd done it."

"Okay, she told you all that. You have anything to support this story?"

"I have clippings, and a certain document," she said, hearing how flimsy and inadequate this sounded, but determined not to be bested by this man.

"Clippings and a document," he repeated, so unimpressed he was practically yawning. Snow was appalled by his rudeness; she couldn't believe how many ill-tempered people she'd encountered in only a few days. What was *wrong* with the people in this city? Was it the city that inspired the attitude, or did the people have it ready-built and move here so they could use it?

"You want to know about a thirty-year-old kidnapping because you've got some papers leading you to believe you were the victim of this crime. We'll let that ride for the moment. Just what're you looking to find out specifically?"

"I know it sounds like a wild story, but it happens to be the truth." Snow staunchly stood her ground. "I am trying to find my family."

Again he leaned way back, his eyes never leaving hers. Then he asked, "You have names and particulars, all that?"

"I have some, yes."

"So, okay. Correct me if I've got any of this wrong." He seemed to be working not to laugh out loud, and Katie wanted to walk behind the desk and kick him right in the nuts. "What I'm hearing is that your mother passed recently, but before she did she confessed to being a kidnapper. In 1963 this precinct fielded the case. You claim you've got reason to believe you were the victim of that kidnapping. Now you're trying to locate your parents. Have I got that right?"

"Yes," Snow answered. "Basically, you've got it right. My friend and I have done some digging, and we discovered that the woman who claimed to be my mother had in fact completely changed her identity and went to a lot of trouble to bury her past. She did leave a kind of paper trail, and Katie and I have been trying to follow it. We haven't had much luck so far, but we've got a couple of leads." His eyes were again boring into hers. It was making her sweat. Why was he giving her such *attitude?*

"Look," she said sharply. "I didn't wake up this morning and decide, what the hell, I'll just come uptown and make a complete fool of myself by trying to convince the first cop I can find of some bullshit story I concocted because I was bored. I came here hoping for some help. If you can help, tell me. If you can't, say so. But stop jerking me around and treating me like I'm some kind of mental defective." Looking past him, she said, "Maybe there's somebody else we could talk to who might remember the case, or at least be a little less hostile. I mean, Jesus! D'you give everyone who comes in here such a hard time? Or is today just my lucky day? It's not as if I'm asking for anything unreasonable. All I want is a little *help*. Aren't you guys supposed to be about protecting and serving?"

"There's no one in the One Nine's been on the job since '63," he said coolly. "And there's no need for you to go getting a mad on. Okay? I'm just trying to nail down some facts here so nobody goes wasting anybody's time. Okay? You seem rational, but I deal every day with rational-seeming people who do things you just wouldn't credit. Okay? Nobody's trying to make you feel foolish, but I'm here to tell you what's possible and what's just plain out of the question. *Okay?* Now. Mind if I see these so-called documents?"

"Could you please stop giving me attitude?" Snow said quietly.

"Lady, either show me what you've got or forget it! I don't *need* this grief."

"You're the one giving *us* grief," Katie declared. "I'd like to see your superior." Getting out a notebook and pen, she looked pointedly at his badge and noted the number. "I think we might want to file a complaint."

"Whoa! Wait a minute here." He held up a hand, looking from Snow to Katie then back to Snow. "You guys Internal Affairs? You yanking my chain here?" He started to smile.

"For God's sake!" Snow slapped the flat of her hand on the desk top. "Here are my goddamned documents. Look at them! Then either help, or get someone out here who will!"

"What're you getting so mad about?" he asked her, picking up the envelope.

"Would you just look at the stuff, or do you plan to keep stonewalling us?" Katie asked, taking hold of Snow's hand and giving it a squeeze.

"Okay, okay!"

While they stood by, he read Anne's letter and the clippings. Then he stared hard at Snow for a long moment before returning everything to the envelope and passing it back to her. Was there actually a slight softening of his features? No. He looked every bit as skeptical as he had at the outset.

"Okay," he said with less edge both to his voice and to his manner. "Lemme tell you how it goes. First off, the records for this case would've been sent downtown long since. We're talking *decades*. Okay? We wouldn't have one scrap of paper here, except maybe for the blotter covering that period, which would only show the case had been logged and who went out on the original call. And that would not do you one bit of good. Second, when it comes to something like this—kidnapping of a baby—it's probable the case is still open. I'm assuming you made sure this was the only case on record for that particular day."

"We checked the indexes and that's the only case on record in the city for three entire months," Katie told him.

"Fine. So you've got a reasonable certainty you're on the right track. Unless of course in the intervening years the real Victoria MacKenzie already turned up and got reunited with her family. But if she had, there would've been stories about that in the papers, and you'd've found them."

Katie and Snow exchanged a quick guilty look. They hadn't thought to search the newspaper indexes right to the present.

"Guess maybe you didn't think of that, huh?" he surmised with a hint of what might actually have been sympathy. "Never mind. Doesn't matter. It seems reasonable to assume it's still an open case. And that being the situation, it'd be on file with the Missing Persons Squad down at One Police Plaza. So that's where you'd want to go."

"All right. Thank you." Snow turned to Katie, ready to leave. She felt as if her nerves had just been rubbed raw with coarse sandpaper.

"Hold the phone there, ladies. Lemme make a call, see if we can't maybe save you some time and hassles."

Surprised, Snow turned back to look at him. His face hadn't altered a bit. Maybe, she thought, he had some bizarre kind of facial paralysis. "That's very nice of you," she said. "Mind if I ask what happened to your attitude?"

"Boy, you are some tough act. You know that? Believe it or not, I'm only trying to do a job here."

"Believe it or not," she said, "I'm trying to find my family."

"I believe you. And I'll tell you something. Okay? I've been on the job twenty-two years. I can guarantee you there's nobody on the force doesn't snap to attention when a kid goes missing, or gets killed. And every last one of us celebrates big-time when a missing kid turns up. Know why? Cause most of them never turn up. And that's a fact. I've never even *heard* of a case where a kid turns up thirty years later. That doesn't mean I don't believe it can't happen, doesn't mean I don't believe you. Okay? So you and your friend grab a seat there, lemme make this call, see if we can't open a couple doors.''

Katie and Snow sat down on a scarred wooden bench to wait.

"Why didn't we think of doing an index search right to the present?'' Katie berated herself in an undertone. "Dumb! Until he said that, it never even occurred to me that Victoria MacKenzie might've been located. It's like we fixed on the MacKenzies being your parents and never questioned it.''

"It didn't occur to me, either,'' Snow whispered back. "Maybe because I know there's no such story, because *I'm* Victoria. I know that, Katie, and so do you. You saw those baby pictures, the one in the papers and the one in that passport. They're the same baby. And that was me.''

"I go along with that. Man, I thought he was going to give us the hard time to end all hard times. Guy looks like Mr. Clean on steroids.''

Snow gave a low laugh and covered her mouth with her hand. "From the top, he was King of the Hard Guys. Now he's calling downtown, being helpful. I really don't get it. Are all men weird or is it just the ones I run into?''

"Trust me, they're mostly weird. I liked the way you handled him. The old you would never've done that.''

"Probably not, but I don't like the way it feels, this enraged adrenaline rush through my system, taking me out of control.''

"Control's okay. But sometimes it's good to get in people's faces, take a position. If nobody ever did, nothing would change.''

"I'd prefer to go for change by voting, if it's all the same to you.''

Katie laughed and slung an arm around her shoulders. "Sometimes,'' she said affectionately, "you're so droll.''

Snow raised her eyebrows.

"Droll, babe. Seriously.''

"God! I don't know if I like that.''

"You're in luck.'' The officer beckoned them over, and they watched as he wrote quickly on a piece of paper, then handed it across the desk to Snow. "You want the eleventh floor. Ask for Sergeant Ray Delgado. He's second in command of the squad, good guy, used to work out of this precinct. He's on lunch, but he'll be back by the time you get there. I left a message letting him know you're on the way down. Anybody can do for you, Ray's the one."

"I appreciate the help." Snow paused then offered her hand.

Thrown by the gesture, the man smiled for the first time, the gray eyes defrosting as he shook her hand and said approvingly, "You got some style. Good luck. Hope things work out."

Katie and Snow chorused, "Thank you," and left the station house.

"What turned him around?" Snow wondered aloud.

"You did," Katie said. "You wouldn't back down, so you got his respect."

"God, Katie. If that's what you have to do to get someone's respect, I'm not sure it's worth it."

"Can you *imagine* waking up and seeing that face first thing every morning?" She made a gagging sound.

"I hope this Delgado turns out to be human. I'm not up for any more hassles today."

"I've got a feeling this isn't going to be anywhere near as hard as we thought. Finding your family, I mean."

"Don't!" Snow said quietly. "I don't want to get my hopes up, the way I did with the lawyer and the rest of those guys in Rhode Island. It only makes everything harder. If I operate with the idea in mind that this whole thing is going to be one step forward and two steps back it's not quite so upsetting. You know?"

"Okay, I won't say another word. You want to grab something to eat before we hit the subway?"

"Maybe we should. Who knows how long this could take?"

"There's a great Italian place a couple of blocks over. Sound good?"

"Sure. I hope to hell they're a bit more accommodating downtown. I really couldn't handle any more flak today."

"It'll be fine," Katie said, and let it go at that.

Twenty

Ray Delgado was the antithesis of the bodybuilder they'd encountered uptown. A slim, dark-haired man, about five-ten, with his shirtsleeves rolled up and looking ready for business, he radiated energy. Greeting them with warmth, he invited them into the office he shared with two other men in the unit and, like the host of an impromptu party, asked, "How about coffee?"

Katie and Snow accepted.

"Great! Grab a seat. I'll be right back." He went off and returned faster than they'd have thought possible. "Here we go," he said, setting three mismatched mugs down on his desk. "Now we can talk." He slipped behind his desk and smiled over at them—the smile of a man with innate enthusiasm. "So. I got a message from the One Nine, but not much in the way of details. Why don't you fill me in, and we'll see if I can't be of some help to you."

He was a caring person. It showed in his every aspect, and Snow found this surprising, given the nature of his work. Whatever the reason, she was grateful. It made telling him her story far easier, especially since he listened avidly, never taking his eyes from hers. Winding down, she gave him the envelope containing her mother's letter, the passport for baby Snow Devane she and Katie had found, and the clippings, saying, "I know it's thirty years later, but if I am Victoria MacKenzie—and I believe that I am—I want to find my family."

"It doesn't matter that it's thirty years," Delgado said, growing excited as he studied everything, spending several long moments on the passport. "Our files don't get closed unless and until we find the missing person."

"You mean you'd have it here?" Katie asked, glad for Snow's sake that they'd found someone sympathetic to deal with. Delgado was a sweetheart, bright and open-minded and responsive. Noting the absence of a wedding ring, she couldn't help wondering if all those stories she'd read about the difficulties of police officers maintaining marriages were true.

"You bet," he told her as he got up from behind his desk. "We've got an office filled with 'em. In fact, I'm gonna go pull the file on this case right now, so we can go over a few things in more detail."

"Do you believe me?" Snow asked.

He stopped in the doorway and said, "I believe *you* believe it, and that's good enough for me, for openers. We'll check the file and see if it hangs together. Then we'll take it from there. Things add up, I'll run it by my commanding officer. You guys relax and take it easy for a few minutes, okay? With luck, I shouldn't be long." He gave them another of his winning smiles and went off almost at a run.

"Katie, he's taking me seriously. I can't believe it."

"I can." Katie took a sip of the murky coffee, made a face and put the cup back on the desk. "It's his job to find people. I doubt very many of them just walk in off the street, the way you did. It'd be interesting to know how many they actually do find. Based on what I've read, I doubt it's a lot. Did you know that something like a hundred thousand kids a year go missing in this country?"

"No way!"

"Scary, huh?"

"God, I'll say!" Snow tasted the coffee and said, "You're right. This is vile." Putting the cup down, she had the unpleasant sensation that ice water had just been flushed through her digestive tract. "I can't believe he's actually gone to get the file," she said, with that same fluttering in her chest she'd had the night Rudy had called to tell her about her mother's heart attack. "The information's right here. We're not going to have to go chasing all over, looking for it."

"It does seem as if it's going to be way easier than I thought. I guess Pete Briggs wasn't just being humble when he said he didn't know much about missing persons. I certainly didn't know they never close the files. I thought they sat gathering dust until somebody decided to give them the heave. Can you *imagine* how many they must have in this place?"

"All those missing children," Snow said sadly. "All those brokenhearted parents."

"And some not so brokenhearted. Plenty of people treat their kids like garbage, so the kids run."

"And plenty of people steal children," Snow reminded her.

"Yeah," Katie agreed solemnly, "and sell them or kill them. Sorry. But on the plus side," she said, striving to elevate the mood, "at least we won't have to spend days on end checking records."

Snow didn't hear. She was turned inward, astounded by the many different ways in which her body was reacting to the situation: heart flutters, cold rushing water in her bowels, a humming in her ears, a tremor in her hands. It was as if the parts of her had lost the ability to perform in concert and were all independently going berserk.

Once again, Katie automatically stroked her friend's back, hoping they weren't going to have to wait too long. She was afraid Snow might go to pieces. She looked dazed, and to distract her, Katie kept chattering away about whatever came to mind, aware Snow scarcely heard her.

Delgado was back inside ten minutes, carrying a thick file. "I just want to have a quick look-see," he said, "get up to speed on the ABCs of the case. Then we'll talk more."

Snow simply stared at the swollen file, trying to get her mind around the fact that all the papers in it pertained to her, and that she'd taken several giant steps closer to her family.

"Mind if I ask what's in there?" Katie sat forward as Delgado opened the file.

"All kinds of forms and statements," he answered, eyes on the documents he was perusing quickly, one at a time. "Everything from the initial report, to follow-ups with the family, interviews with anyone even remotely connected with the case. Statements from employees of the supermarket, customers who were in the store at the time of the incident. Pages and pages of telephone tips that were investigated, FBI input, anything relevant to the case. These appear to be letters from Mrs. MacKenzie over the years, asking is the case still open, and keeping us posted on her whereabouts."

At this, Snow's heart contracted painfully and she watched as he flipped through at least a dozen letters. From my mother, she thought, watching the pages turning from one side of the file to the other—flashes of large, looping script in black ink on several different shades of personalized stationery.

"Seems she moved a few times before settling in the Florida Keys back in '82. This last letter's dated June of '89."

"Does she say anything about my... about Mr. MacKenzie?" Snow asked, her pulse so rapid she was simultaneously sweating and chilled.

Delgado scanned the letters a second time, then looked over at her. "Doesn't seem to. But that might not mean a thing." He offered an encouraging smile.

It might mean all kinds of things, she thought, but refused to continue in that direction. The Florida Keys. She imagined intense heat and lazy palms, exotic flowers and a mother who, as of June 1989, was alive and residing at the very tip of Florida; a mother who had never given up hope and had stayed in touch with the police here, wanting them to know where she was in case her daughter one day showed up, looking for her. What extraordinary faith!

"Did somebody here answer her letters?" Katie asked.

"Believe it! We've got an entire file room—a *big* room—full of cases that're still open, even thirty, forty, fifty years later. Folks who've lost a child, they never give up. Never. And neither do we. We're in touch with a lot of people. Nobody forgets a missing kid," he assured them with formidable fervor. "I get calls every day on active cases dating back fifteen, twenty, years. People can't give up on their kids. They just can't. And neither can we."

Awed by his intensity, by the high degree of personal involvement he appeared to have with these people, Katie and Snow kept silent while Delgado spent the next twenty minutes examining the paperwork. Then, turning back to the beginning of the file, he said, "Okay. I know it's a headache, but I need you to tell me again everything this Anne Cooke told you about the kidnapping before she died. Just take your time, and tell me everything you can remember."

Snow closed her eyes and traveled back to the Intensive Care Unit, seeing that small pale woman connected by wires and tubes to the many machines and monitors. She saw herself pulling a chair close to the bed and sitting down, taking hold of her mother's smooth, manicured hand. She felt again the fierce grip, heard the deep raspy breathing, and felt her own lungs seize with renewed sorrow at the shock, the loss. She opened her eyes and wiped her face with the back of her hand. Katie handed her a tissue. Snow thanked her, and blew her nose. Then, taking a deep breath, she repeated, as accurately as possible, what her mother had told her. Getting to the end, she halted, scouring her memory, but there was nothing more, only the death, the sight of the tiny figure that had been left behind, the husk of Anne Cooke, the flesh residue of the woman who'd played out the role of mother to another woman's child.

"That's all," she said finally, grieving as before for both her mothers.

Katie gave her arm a pat. And Delgado looked as if he'd taken a blow to the midriff.

Snow gave a small shrug, attempting to indicate she was all right, but for a moment she wondered madly if this was hell, if, like some Sartre-like story, she'd died somewhere along the line and had descended not into the mythical fiery inferno but into a limbo of orphanhood where she would spend eternity seeking her parents.

"I buy it," Delgado announced gravely.

"You do?" Snow was taken aback. "You really do?"

"It works for me. Especially comparing this passport with the photo on file. That's the clincher, far as I'm concerned."

"My God!" Snow was so relieved she laughed aloud. "I can't believe it!"

"Hey!" Delgado smiled. "It's what you wanted, right?"

"Yes! I'm just so... God! How can it be this easy?"

"It's easy because you knew where and when, and you came to the right place. We've got all kinds of resources here that just didn't exist thirty years ago. Plus, if this hadn't been a kidnapping, it would've been a whole other thing, harder in lots of ways to verify. But there was a crime committed. You weren't *given* away. You were *taken*. And now you're found! Man, I'm very excited." He kept smiling at her and shaking his head in wonderment for a minute or more. Then he brought his excitement back into line and said, "So, okay. Let me go run this by my CO, get the lieutenant in here to hear your story, see the stuff you brought in. Then we'll go from there."

"Is there some kind of established protocol?" Katie asked.

Delgado came around and sat on the corner of his desk. "Getting ahead of myself," he apologized. "But this situation is a first for us, understand. So, no, there's no protocol, just chain of command. Right now, I'm going to my commanding officer. He listens, comes to talk to you, and if he buys it, he'll go to the Special Investigations Division and run it by those guys. If it flies for them, we've got an inspector involved. We'll keep going, right up the chain, probably all the way to the commissioner. If we can close a thirty-year-old case, it's not only great for you and your folks, it's great for the department. Great PR, and great for the morale of everybody in this building. Hell, everybody on the whole damned force. So, we're going to start up the chain now, and you'll tell your story a whole bunch more times today. If you've got a date for tonight, you should probably phone and cancel, 'cause this is going to take a while. Count on having dinner with a lot of very tickled cops who're all gonna want to meet you. Feel free to use my phone there. I'll try not to be too long. Okay?"

"What exactly is going to happen?" Snow asked before he could leave.

Displaying endless patience, he said, "We'll go over your story some more times. And then we're going to bust our butts to put you back together with your family. That's what's going to happen. If my CO agrees with my feeling on this case, and I know he will, we'll get somebody up here right away from the morgue to do a stick, take some blood for preliminary matching and DNA testing. If that's okay with you."

"It's okay with me," Snow said.

"The morgue?" Katie looked aghast.

"They handle all the DNA testing. Plus which we've actually got a satellite office there. Some of the detectives are licensed nurses. They'll send someone over to get the blood, and they'll test right away to see if the blood types match. We've got all the Mac-Kenzies' types on file. The DNA'll be the definitive test, but that'll take maybe four, five weeks. But we'll run your sample, compare it to the records and to what's on file." He looked at his watch. "By six-thirty or so, we'll know if all the blood types are a match." Seeing Snow's confused expression, he explained further. "If a mother is type O, for example, and the father is AB, the child could only be an A or B. A type O child couldn't be theirs. Okay?"

"I see," Snow said, vaguely remembering this information from one of her high school science classes.

"There won't be time to do more than a basic comparison, but when—not if, 'cause I know it's gonna be good—when we get the match," he said with ripening anticipation, "we'll get on the phone to your mother and arrange to get her up here right away."

"It's all happening so fast," Snow observed, feeling dizzy now.

Delgado came back, squatted in front of her and took hold of Snow's hand. "I know none of this is the way you thought it'd be. But it's definitely rolling, I definitely believe you, and you'll definitely be back with your family real soon. Okay, Victoria?"

She erupted into tears, then laughed at herself, apologizing. "I'm sorry. Yes, okay. Thank you, Sergeant Delgado. Thank you very much."

"Hey!" he said gently, smiling. "I knew it was for real when I looked at the picture in the file and compared it to the one in the passport. I got so worked up I thought I was gonna have a heart attack, if you want to know the truth. So thank *you*. This is probably gonna turn out to be my best day ever on the force. Sit tight now. Okay?"

In the course of the next few hours, she repeated her story for Delgado's CO, Lieutenant Baines, a thoughtful, soft-spoken black man with deep, sad eyes; and then for the chief of detectives, middle-aged and weary, who listened solemnly, head bowed, eyes on the floor, before graciously thanking her and stepping outside to confer with Delgado and Baines. The latter two remained in the office while the chief of detectives headed off to the SID. Officers came and went. She told her story again and again, answered batteries of questions, and lost track of the number of people who passed through the office—all of whom appeared astonished by the fact that she'd simply walked in off the street to solve one of their oldest open cases.

In the midst of this, a female detective arrived, pulled on a pair of disposable rubber gloves, swabbed the inside of Snow's left elbow and deftly plunged a needle into her vein. Watching, Snow was reminded of sundry childhood inoculations and injections, and of her mother's tearful countenance as she stood by, grimacing. How many times had Snow sought to comfort her, saying, "It's okay, Mom. It doesn't hurt," and smiling despite the needle's sting? So many lessons in learning not to show the pain, or the anger, or anything negative, in order to keep her mother happy. And it wasn't difficult, keeping her mother happy, because she saw every day what an effort the woman made to do what she thought would please her daughter. But the poor woman had been phobic about doctors and needles and blood, and about public displays of emotion. Why? Snow wondered anew, as the detective drew several test tubes of blood, tossed the gloves, wished Snow good luck and went on her way.

During a lull, Katie and Snow headed for the women's toilet.

"How're you doing?" Katie asked, studying her.

"I'm incredibly tired, as if I've been awake for days on end. Listen, this could go on forever. You don't have to hang around. If you feel like going home, I'll understand."

"Now I know you've finally lost it. No *way* am I going to leave you here alone. You actually think I could leave when the results of the blood test'll be in any minute? When there's a chance you might get to talk to your mother? Get real, please."

Snow nodded dumbly. "My eyes keep wanting to close."

"I'll run out and get us some decent coffee. And while I'm at it, I'm going to call home. With what's going on here, I kind of want to talk to my mom and dad." She clapped a hand over her mouth, eyes round, then said, "Was that insensitive? Maybe I'm losing it, too."

"No, you're not," Snow said, and hugged her. "Give them my love. I'm going to stick my head under the cold-water tap and try to wake up."

Just over ninety minutes later, after yet another trip to the women's room, with both of them fatigued from so many hours spent sitting in the unyielding institutional chairs, Delgado got on the speakerphone to talk to a sergeant in the Key West PD to confirm receipt of the material Delgado had faxed down.

The syrupy voice on the line said, "I've been on the horn to Miz MacKenzie, and she's expectin' your call. You really gone 'n' found her girl?"

"Yes, sir," Delgado said happily, beaming at Snow. "The lab just now called confirming the blood types all match. So I'd have to say it sure looks like we've found her."

A roaring in her ears, Snow reached for Katie's hand.

"Damn, but that's great!" the voice drawled. "Folks in the station here're real excited and we don't even know the woman. She lives way out to hell'n'gone the far end'a the Keys, but I sent one'a my men on down there, in case any help's needed."

"Good man," Delgado said. "I appreciate that."

"Good luck to y'all. You made my day, and that's the truth. Anythin' else we can do, just give a holler."

"Will do. Many thanks." Delgado switched off the phone, came forward folding his arms on the desk and, beaming, said, "What d'you think? Are you ready to talk to your mother, Victoria?"

Twenty-One

For a few moments, Snow was floundering, viewing a series of mental film clips. She saw herself on stage in the Thanksgiving pageant, a second-grade Pilgrim in a cardboard hat, searching the audience for her mother's smiling face, locating it and feeling a surge of satisfaction and pride. Next she saw herself packing to leave for New York, and her mother standing in the bedroom doorway looking stricken but trying not to reveal her distress. And then she saw herself on the train from New York as it pulled into the Providence station, and there was her mother on the platform, her dainty features radiant in anticipation of this, their first visit since Snow had left home.

She'd once had a mother, and that mother had died. Now she had another mother, alive in the Florida Keys, who was talking on the telephone to a remarkably compassionate New York police officer. It was preposterous, unthinkable. She didn't know how to feel, what to think. What was she supposed to do with thirty years of memories and their accompanying emotions? They were lodged in her brain for all time, ineradicable. But her life was about to be divided, half belonging to one mother, half to a second, someone she'd never known but who had an inalienable claim on her.

God! She wanted a cigarette, or a drink, or some potion she could quaff that would enable her to cope with the terrible blend of fear and elation that had her in a feverishly irrational state at one moment, and in something approximating composure in the next. Her mouth was so dry she had to keep swallowing as she watched and listened to Delgado.

He held the receiver to his ear rather than using the speaker-phone, a display of sensitivity that wasn't lost on either woman. Turning, Snow saw that Katie looked as overwhelmed as she imagined she did. And love for her friend dried her mouth even more, while her throat ached with the effort to contain all the churning emotions. She knew that the least little thing might set her off and have her howling like a five-year-old.

Feeling Snow's eyes, Katie turned and gazed at her, then shook her head to indicate the uselessness of the words that came to her mind. For close to two weeks, this quest had had many of the elements of an exotic game. Now there was nothing remotely entertaining about what was happening. The idea of the impending reunion and its implications simply left her speechless. She could only guess at what all this had to mean to Snow. Nothing in her life had equipped her to comprehend the situation. But then, she reasoned, nothing had equipped Snow either. Remember that! she told herself. It's as bizarre for her as it is for you. Reaching out, she took hold of Snow's cold, damp hand.

Delgado was saying, "That's right. It's about ninety percent certain we've got your daughter here. The preliminary tests match the blood types we have on file. There's always the remote possibility the match is a one-in-a-million fluke. Which is why we're having the DNA testing done." A pause while he listened. Then, with a smile, he said, "Would you like to talk to her?" Another pause and then, momentously, he held the receiver out to Snow.

Hands damp, heart racketing, Snow took the receiver, wet her lips, and said hello.

The woman on the other end had a young, pleasant voice that quivered with emotion. "I always believed one day you'd be found," she said, sounding stupefied, out of breath. "Some days it was easier to believe than others. But I couldn't give up hoping, and now you're on the phone, we're talking. I've imagined this so many times. I just wish your father were still alive so I could tell him. There's so much I want to say but I can't think rationally. I'm afraid I sound pretty incoherent."

"No, I understand. It's the same for me," Snow said, her hand slippery on the receiver. "I didn't know," she tried to explain. "I only just found out, not even two weeks ago."

"It's so incredible! I'm shaking from head to toe. I have to stop this. You don't need to hear me rambling." The woman caught her breath and said, "I'll get the first flight out of here in the morning. With luck, I should arrive there sometime in the early afternoon. I'll book a room at my favorite hotel." She named a small, elegant midtown establishment, and asked rather plaintively, "Could you meet me there? Would that be convenient?"

"Anywhere you like. Whatever's good for you. I could even meet you at the airport."

"No, let's make it the hotel. I'm going to need a little time to get myself together." She broke off for a moment. "How are you?" she asked anxiously. "Are you all right? Were they good to you?"

"I'm fine. She was... This is so strange.... Yes, she was good to me. Let me give you my number. Call when you're settled. I'll grab a cab and come right away. I'm so anxious to see you. I just can't believe this!"

The woman on the other end exhaled tremulously, gave a soft, bewildered little laugh, and said, "My photographs are all baby pictures. Years and years of looking at that baby face..." She laughed again, achieving a tone of wonder. "You're a grown woman, with her own telephone number. Sorry. I'm getting incoherent again. I can't find a pen. Wait a second. Okay. Give me the number." Snow recited it. Patricia MacKenzie said, "Okay, got it. I have to hang up now. I'm about to come unglued. I'll see you tomorrow." She said a strangled good-bye, and hung up.

Snow fumbled the receiver back into the cradle, looked at Delgado, then at Katie, and covered her mouth with both hands, attempting physically to hold back what felt like delirium. She laughed and wept simultaneously, embarrassed and crazed.

Katie handed her more tissues, keeping one for herself. She'd never witnessed such a display of raw emotion, and felt she could easily slide over the edge and become hysterical along with her friend. It took some effort, but she managed to keep a lid on her reactions.

Delgado gave Snow time to recover, then again came around to sit on the edge of his desk, and said, "There's a few things you should know, Victoria."

She nodded, thrown every time he used the name.

"First, the media are gonna be all over you. They'll be offering you and your mother the sun, moon and stars for exclusive interviews, for the movie rights, book rights. It'll be a regular feeding frenzy, I promise. We won't release information, but the press will insist on their right to print the story. And, frankly, as I told you before, we need all the good PR we can get. So what you want to do is talk to a lawyer soon as you can, let him deal with the media and the offers. That way, people are hounding you, you just say, 'Talk to my attorney,' and they'll get out of your face. At least for a minute or two.

"Second, if you think you'll need it, we'll supply manpower to keep people from hounding you tomorrow when you go to meet up with your mother. It probably sounds crazy but, trust me, you might be needing us. If you decide you do, call me any time—I'll give you my direct line and my home number—and we'll set something up.

"The last thing," he said, and gave her one of his lovely smiles. "The department would like it if we could arrange a press conference with you and your family. So we'd like to get you back here in the next couple of days to do that, give everybody a chance to meet you, say hi and how glad we are, give a statement to the press, and get some pictures. Okay?"

"We'll come back," Snow promised. "You've been..." Words were inadequate. In the course of the afternoon and evening she'd come to feel as if she'd known Ray Delgado most of her life. He'd shown himself to be a rare person, with a great sense of humor, tremendous pride in his work and an uncommon depth of caring. She got up and hugged him, tearfully whispering, "Thank you, Sergeant Delgado."

"Ray. It's Ray. And thank *you*," he said, hugging her back, then holding her at arm's length. "This has been an amazing day. I'll remember it for the rest of my life, probably bore the crap out of my future grandchildren, telling them over and over about the afternoon Victoria MacKenzie just walked in off the street after being missing for thirty years. You go on home and get some rest now, and we'll talk again tomorrow or the next day." Keeping hold of her a moment longer, he said, "I have to tell you, I think you've got real guts."

She shook her head. "Katie's the one. She's kept me going."

"She's got real guts," Katie disagreed. "She just doesn't know it."

Holding his hand out to Katie, Ray said, "You're both something else. It's been a pleasure. Any time you want a tour—any department, even the morgue—give me a call, and I'll arrange it."

"Homicide," Katie said promptly.

"You got it!" Delgado laughed. "Just say when. Enough advance notice, I throw in lunch, too."

They were approached by a reporter as they walked out of the elevator.

"I've been waiting all afternoon for a chance to talk to you," said the young man, offering his card and introducing himself. "Would you mind answering a few questions?"

"I really don't want to talk to anyone," Snow said, sidestepping him and heading toward the door.

"Take my card!" he begged, walking backward beside her. "Just tell me how you feel about being reunited with your family after so many years."

"It hasn't happened yet." Snow cast a please-help-me look at Katie who at once inserted herself between Snow and the reporter, blocking his way as Snow escaped through the door.

"She's going to have to talk to someone," the young man said, watching over Katie's shoulder as Snow hurried away from the building. "I'm from the *Times*. At least whatever I write will have syntax."

Katie laughed and took his card, saying, "I don't think she will. But nice try."

He gave up, saying, "I'm one of the good guys. I won't chase her. But stay tuned. It's going to get hairy. That's a guarantee. If she changes her mind, get her to call me. I'll do a first-class story, with no misquotes."

"I'll pass that on," Katie told him, and took off at a run. She caught up with Snow about a block away and fell into step beside her. After so long indoors, the cool evening air felt wonderful. "My mom and dad send you their love. They said to say *mazel tov*. They're very happy for you."

"That's sweet. I love your parents," she said, and burst into tears again.

"Let's grab a cab," Katie suggested, seeing how done in Snow was. "I'll drop you, then head on home. Unless you'd prefer not to spend the night alone."

"Actually, I would. But thank you, Katie. I'd never have been able to get through this without you." Snow mopped her face on her sleeve.

"Yeah, you would've. Ray's right, you know. You've got guts."

"If you knew how close I came to wetting myself when he handed me the phone, you wouldn't think that."

"But you didn't, did you? See! On top of everything else, you've got great bladder control."

Snow laughed and threw her arms around her friend.

When they were in the back of the cab, Katie asked, "Will you call me tomorrow, if you get a chance, and let me know how it goes? I'll be a wreck, waiting."

"I'll call." Snow was so drained she barely had the energy to process thoughts and respond with words. She stared out the window, then let her eyes close for a moment and the next thing she knew, Katie was patting her on the arm, saying, "You're home, babe."

Dragging herself awake, she embraced Katie again. "I love you, Katie. You're the best friend I'll ever have."

"I love you, too. Now get inside and go to bed." Katie reached across to open the door and gave Snow a gentle push. "Go on. We'll talk tomorrow. Have a good sleep."

Snow reeled from the cab, then turned back, pulling some money from her pocket and shoving it at Katie. "I almost forgot. Take this."

Katie took the money, blew her a kiss, and closed the door.

Riding the elevator up to her floor, Snow felt each little creak and shudder of the cage inside her bones. The indicator on the answering machine showed there had been seven calls, but she lacked the energy to play them back. Throwing off her clothes, she went into the bathroom for a quick shower, toweled dry, and dizzily made her way to bed.

Referring to the notepad beside the phone, she punched out the Broder's number.

Julia answered. "This is the Broder residence."

"Hi, Jule. It's Snow."

"Oh, hi! Hey! Guess what? Dad says I can go to lunch or a concert with you. He said he was sorry for being such a tool. We had a really good talk this morning. Really good."

"I'm glad. Listen, Jule, something's come up and it might be a week or two before we can do it, but I definitely plan to take you out. I just wanted you to know in case I don't get a chance to call you in the next little while."

"What's come up?"

"It's a family situation. Complicated. But you have my promise I'm not just saying that to get out of it. I like you a lot, and I do want to see you. Okay?"

"Okay."

"Jule, d'you think I could talk to your dad for a minute?"

"He's not here. He went to dinner with some clients."

"Oh!" Befuddled, Snow couldn't think for a moment. Then she said, "Could you do something for me?"

"Sure! What?"

"Your Uncle Max is a lawyer, right?"

"Right."

"I need a lawyer. D'you think you could get your uncle to call me? It's really important."

Sounding delighted to have been entrusted with this task, Julia said, "I can do that. If he's not home, I'll leave a message and tell him to call you right away."

"Thank you, Jule. You're terrific. I'll talk to you soon."

"Okay. Bye, Snow."

Just before she fell asleep she thought about the brief conversation with Patricia MacKenzie. She'd sounded so young. But then, thinking it through, she realized the woman was only fifty-two. Not old at all. Anne Cooke had been sixty-three, and she'd somehow expected her mother to sound like that. Ridiculous! Her mind was shutting down.

The ringing of the telephone startled her awake and she picked up the receiver, croaked out a hello, and heard, "Good morning. Miz Devane?"

"Yes?"

"Hi, there. Jack Murray from the *Post*. I was wondering if we could set up an appointment for an interview...."

"No. Sorry."

"Okay," he said quickly. "How about a statement? We'd ..."

"No, sorry." She hung up and looked at the clock. Ten past seven. Obviously the media liked to get a jump on the day.

As she was heading into the bathroom the phone rang again. She stopped, debating, and decided to let the machine pick up. Someone from *Newsday*.

While the coffee was brewing the phone rang again—a researcher from *Hard Copy*—and again—some woman from Channel Four—while she was eating a piece of toast with peanut butter and drinking her first decent cup of coffee since the previous morning. She wondered how Ray Delgado and the others could drink so much of that foul brown stuff they'd kept making.

Half an hour later she was about to play back all the messages when the phone rang, and she stood waiting to hear who was calling.

"Snow, this is Max Broder. I got a message from Julia asking me to call."

She picked up. "Hi. I'm here. The phone's been going nonstop, so I've been screening my calls. I think I'm going to need you."

"I'd say so. I guess you haven't seen the morning papers yet. It's pretty threadbare, but the story's front-page news."

"My God, so fast!"

"This is just the beginning. Tell me how you want to handle it, and it's done. If you want to sell your rights, we'll negotiate, get you serious six-figure money. If you don't, we tell them all to get lost. It's your call."

"Max, I don't want to wind up a movie of the week, or have books written about me. I hate the idea of people selling their lives, their privacy. I don't need the money and I want my privacy. I can't speak for my mother—" the word had an awkward new potency on her tongue "—but I'd imagine she's going to feel the same way, given that thirty years ago she refused to allow her photograph to be printed in the papers."

"Good for you! A woman with principles. I like you already. I know you're probably going bananas, but could you spare a little time this morning? I'd like to come by and introduce myself, work up our spiel for the media."

"I've got time. When could you come?"

"Why don't I hop in a cab and come now? It's not yet eight. I can probably be there inside half an hour. How's that?"

"Fine. I'll keep the coffee hot. Thank you, Max. I appreciate this."

"Keep screening your calls," he advised. "I'm on my way."

Max was a heftier version of his younger brother, with a short fringe of fair hair, the same clear blue eyes and the same immediacy. He arrived almost precisely half an hour after his call and greeted her with a hearty handshake and an eager smile.

"Boy, are you ever beautiful!" he exclaimed ingenuously with the delighted smile of the boy he'd once been and whose ebullience he still retained. "You're what my mother would call a real picture. Okay, I'd better explain," he said, setting a large briefcase down just inside the door, "Julia left me this excited message last night, raving away about her new friend, Snow, who needed a lawyer. I thought she was talking about some kid at school. I'm thinking, Great. Just what I need. Some eight-year-old who wants to divorce her parents. I need this like major surgery. Then I saw the morning papers and I realized she wasn't talking about a kid from school. So here I am."

"I appreciate your coming down here so early. Coffee? D'you mind sitting in the kitchen?"

"Love some. And I don't mind a bit. I'm a kitchen person. I don't know if you've seen the apartment, but all the years we were growing up there, Mom would give people the tour, show them the living room and whatever, then parade everybody into the kitchen. We lived in it—ate there, talked there, did our homework there, had visitors there. My place, we knocked out the wall and made the living room part of the kitchen. I brought fresh bagels." He bent to open the briefcase, removed a brown bag and held it out to her, saying, "Lead the way," and followed her to the kitchen. "Are you aware," he asked en route, "that there are reporters downstairs, waiting to pounce on you the moment you emerge?"

"You're joking!"

"No joke. Go look out the window."

She did, and was shocked to see two mobile TV units parked across the road and eight or ten people milling about on the sidewalk. "This is crazy," she said, returning to the kitchen to pour coffee for both of them. "If I give them a statement, will they go away?"

"Got a knife?" Max had removed his suit jacket and had a bagel poised on the cutting board.

"The drawer next to the sink. I've already eaten."

"I haven't. Hope you don't mind." He found a knife and looked questioningly over at her.

"No, please. Go ahead. I've got butter and some cream cheese."

"Cream cheese, thanks. They probably won't go away until we shout 'No!' very loudly in their faces. And even then they probably won't go. Media people tend to suffer generally from a rare form of hearing impairment combined with a high pain threshold that makes them less than susceptible to polite suggestions."

She smiled, finding him funny. "So I'm going to have to put up with this?"

"For a while. If you have somewhere else you could stay for a week or two, that might be a good idea. You could come stay with me and the dreaded Leo, the teenager from hell. We've got plenty of room."

"You have a son?"

"Sorry to say I do. I don't mean that. I adore him. I was granted custody when his mother and I divorced ten years ago. He's fifteen, built like a linebacker, and is currently going through another horrendous phase. I think they're seasonal. At the moment, he's demonstrating lip-curled contempt for everything I say, think, or do. Lawyers are the scum of the earth and he's been cursed with one for a father." He applied a liberal helping of cream cheese to his bagel and carried it over to the table. "To be honest," he said, sitting down, "he's a beautiful young man and on his good days a far nicer human being than I'll ever be. On his bad days, when he's performing psychological neurosurgery on my frontal lobes, I try to remember him as a baby and how I used to carry him around under my arm like a soggy little football."

She laughed appreciatively.

"So, are you going to keep calling yourself Snow, or do you plan to be Victoria?"

"I've been thinking about it. I think I'll go on using Snow as my professional name, and in the meantime try to get used to being Victoria MacKenzie."

"Makes sense. Well, there'll be some paperwork to do, getting you documented, but it shouldn't be too difficult. Lemme just grab something to write with and we'll work up a preliminary statement." He got up and went for his briefcase. "Some unbelievable story," he said, sliding back into his chair, "finding out you're not who you thought you were. How're you coping?" he asked with what appeared to be real concern. He was, she thought, what Katie would call a teddy bear, round and genial.

"I'm up and down," she answered truthfully. "The hardest part is thinking in terms of two mothers. It's insane, and I get stomach spasms every time I think about meeting Patricia this afternoon. I'm not really going to know how I feel until I do meet her. What kind of law do you practice anyhow, Max?"

"Didn't Joe tell you? I'm an entertainment lawyer."

"No wonder you know so much about all this."

"Well, sure. I'm surprised Joe didn't tell you."

"We were pretty busy arguing," she confessed.

"Yeah? What about?"

"Julia."

He gazed unblinking at her for several seconds, then said, "Tell me if I'm right. You and Jule hit it off and he freaked."

"Yup. He came over here practically foaming at the mouth, and I basically told him he was being an asshole and screwing her up. I've never talked to anyone that way before. But he just made me so mad."

"Wow! How'd he take that?"

"He took it. We wound up having a pizza, and talking. He told me about the family, and about how his wife died."

"Yeah," Max said with a sad shake of his head. "That was rough. She was a good kid, Nicole. He's had a hard time, raising Jule alone from scratch."

"That doesn't give him license to make her decisions for her, or to pick out who she can and can't like."

"Course not. We've all tried to talk to Joe, but could never get anywhere. He won't hear us. So good for you. I'm impressed."

"He made me mad, the way he was acting. It was too close to home. My mother...Anne Cooke was just like that. I grew up feeling as if I was suffocating. And I could see Julia felt the same way."

He nodded, took another bite of his bagel, then reached into the briefcase for a legal pad and his pen. "I'm glad you told him, and I'm even gladder he listened. Joe's not a bad guy, just kind of scared. And he probably didn't tell you about my practice because he's always thought I aimed too low, that I should've gone into criminal law. A sweet man, my brother, but he has no idea. You have to have a masochistic streak *and* a messiah complex to do criminal law. I have neither. Mostly, I do six- and seven-figure contracts for narcissists I rarely get to see. It's lawyers dealing with other lawyers, faxing contract memos here and there, making calls to the coast. High-level bullshit. But I don't have to go to court and I hardly ever have to leave my office. I just have to be conscientious and thorough, and I love it. So now, my dear. Let's figure out what we want to say to the folks hovering outside your door. This part of it's going to be fun."

Twenty-Two

Peeking out from between the vertical blinds, Snow watched Max read the statement they'd prepared to the now sizable crowd that had collected on the street below. Several news crews filmed him. He gave his card to a number of the more aggressive people, then hurried off up the street. At the corner he flagged down a cab, climbed into the back, and was gone. Within ten minutes half the people downstairs had also gone, but several remained, clearly determined to wait for Snow to appear.

Hoping the street would be clear by the time her mother called, Snow finally sat down to listen to the messages on the answering machine. They were almost all from the media, but there was one from Ruth Benson in the law office in Providence letting her know she would have access to her mother's safe deposit box by the end of the week.

Then there was Huffy Compton, saying, "Miss Devane, I've spoken to Daniel Ambrose, given him your number and asked him to give you a call. Hope he can help you out. Don't hesitate to let me know if there's anything else I can do to be of assistance. Good day."

Following calls from Channels Two, Seven and Eleven came Daniel Ambrose's deep, mellow voice. "According to Huffy Compton you'd like to talk to me about your mother. The name doesn't ring any bells, but Huffy says you've got photographs I might recognize. I'll be back in town tomorrow. Call me anytime after two and we'll set up an appointment to meet." He left his number, said good-bye, and hung up.

She reset the incoming tape and called Katie.

"You can't have seen her yet," Katie said at once.

"No. But I heard from Mrs. Benson. I can get into the safe deposit box by the end of the week. *And* I had a message from Daniel Ambrose. He'll be back in town this afternoon."

"Terrific! That means we'll be able to see him this week, depending, of course, on how things go with your mother. So, tell me! How does it feel to be a celebrity? Have you seen the papers yet?"

"I saw. Max brought them."

"Who's Max?"

"Broder's brother. He's a lawyer. An entertainment lawyer, as luck would have it. He's going to handle the media, try to keep people from hounding me. You should've *seen* them all, Katie! Some of them left after Max read them the statement we worked up, but there are still at least a dozen of them down there, waiting for me to show my face. It's very nervous-making. A little voice in my head keeps telling me to take off and head for the hills."

"Be cool. They don't know what you look like. Just sail out, and if anybody asks, you're Judy Pinkus."

"Who's Judy Pinkus?"

"Girl I knew in grade school."

Snow had to laugh. Somehow Katie always managed to inject a humorous note into the worst moments. "I think I'll climb down the back fire escape instead. I doubt anyone would buy me as Judy Pinkus."

"I'm afraid that's true. But if you're really scared, I could come over and act as a decoy, play at being you, while you slip out the back way."

"Too complicated. I'll just hang here until I hear from Patricia."

"Okay, but if there's anything you want me to do, just shout. And, *please* try to call me later to let me know how it goes."

"I will, first chance I get."

"Good luck, sweetie. I'm so excited for you."

After hanging up, Snow went to take another look out the window, dismayed to see one of the TV vans still remained, and a small group of people were leaning against parked cars, drinking take-out coffee and helping themselves to doughnuts from a large box someone had propped on the hood of a car. Each of them looked up at the building every so often. She stepped back and watched the verticals swing slowly back and forth. She'd only been joking about sneaking down the fire escape. Now she thought she probably would leave that way. She had no intention of trying to bluff her way through that pack of determined strangers. The thought of their collective appetite for the details of her life made her queasy.

She disliked daytime talk shows where people revealed far more than she'd ever want to know about their private lives. She disliked the fact that people who committed criminal acts often made substantial sums of money by selling the movie and book rights to the facts of their squalid lives. She wanted no part of any of it, and had to cling to the belief that Patricia MacKenzie would feel the same way.

While she waited, she called Joseph Broder at his office.

"Broder, I wanted to thank you for recommending your brother. And for fixing things with Julia."

"I told you I would. I'm a man of my word," he said with a smile in his voice. "How'd you make out with Max?"

"He's a sweet man. Is Leo really a monster?"

"Leo? We're talking about a kid who'll spend hours with Jule, playing with her Barbie dolls, or coloring. He's one of my favorite people. He likes to give Max a hard time, but that's what kids do." He paused then said, "I read about what's happening in the papers this morning. It explained a lot, and I have a pretty fair idea now why you went to bat for Jule the way you did. I'm really sorry about coming on like such a dork."

"Forget it. I already have."

"I'll try, but it'll take me a while to get my feet out of my mouth." She laughed, and encouraged, he asked, "When are you going to be meeting your folks?"

"Sometime today." Saying it caused her stomach to lurch.

"Unbelievable story," he said. "Listen, I'm glad you called. Maybe, when things have settled down, we could get together for dinner. With Jule," he added quickly.

"Maybe. Listen, Broder, I should get off the line. I'm waiting for my mother—" another lurch of her stomach "—to call. I'll be in touch soon and we'll make a date to get together."

"Okay. Good luck. If I can do anything to help, let me know."

"Thanks."

"I mean it. I can arrange limos, special services, all kinds of things. Something comes up, just call me. I'd like to make up for that scene."

"I told you it's forgotten. You don't have to make up for anything."

"You've got a good heart. You know that?"

"Don't go overboard on me now, Broder."

He laughed and said, "Okay. I hope everything works out. Talk to you soon. Take care."

"You, too." She hung up, smiling, and sat for a few minutes feeling pleased with the way things had gone. Then she picked up the phone to call Rudy and bring him up to date.

"Well, isn't that something?" he said when she'd finished. "Nothing in the papers here yet. But that's good news. You must be getting excited about meeting your mother."

"Logically, you know, I accept that she's my mother, Rudy. But I don't *feel* as if she is."

"No reason why you should. It's bound to be hard when you've never clapped eyes on the woman. You'll probably feel differently once the two of you are face-to-face. I'd imagine she's having the same kind of problems."

"She sounded as if she was. I'm so nervous about meeting her."

"It'll be fine, I'm sure. By the way, any news on when you'll be able to get into that safe deposit box?"

"I had a message saying probably by the end of this week. Once things settle down a bit, Katie and I will be coming up. How are you? It feels as if I've been gone for months."

"Oh, me, I'm right as rain."

"And how's Mrs. Hoover and Lucy and everybody?"

"Everybody's fine. Speaking of people here, you might want to think about what you'd like me to say when this story hits the papers. They'll be looking sideways at me if I go trying to pretend I didn't know about any of this. Everyone in town knows I think of you like my own child."

That got to her, and she had to take a moment to fight off the tears that seemed to come too readily of late. "I think of you like my own, too, Rudy. Just tell the truth. They'll understand, don't you think?"

"I won't go volunteering, but anybody asks, that's what I'll do. Take it easy now, Snow. And don't go trying to force the feelings. Meet the woman like a friend, see if the two of you have any common ground to stand on."

"I'll try. And I'll be in touch in the next day or two to let you know how things are going."

"I'll be here. And remember, Snow. Keep an open mind."

Her wardrobe depressed her. She wanted to wear something decent for this portentous meeting, but all her clothes were years old and entirely casual. That's what happened, she rebuked herself, when you only associated with married men. You never went out, so you didn't have to fret about how you looked. The men in question never noticed what you wore. Their primary objective was to get you out of your clothes and into bed as quickly as possible. What a pitiful commentary on the life she'd been leading! No doubt about it. She was going to have to make some changes and she'd start by getting Katie to go shopping and help her choose some new clothes.

When the phone rang for perhaps the twentieth time at eleven-thirty that morning, she was still confronting the scant collection of clothes that didn't even fill half the space in the closet. Turning away, she waited for the outgoing message to finish, then heard, "It's Patricia. I couldn't wait, so..."

Snow grabbed up the receiver. "Hi, I'm here!"

"Oh, good. It's earlier than you expected, I know. But I knew I wasn't going to be able to sleep last night, so I threw a few things in a bag, closed up the house, and got a flight out of Key West just after six this morning. I've been in the hotel for twenty minutes, walking back and forth, killing time, and all of a sudden I thought, this is nuts. I want so much to see you. If you're free, I was hoping maybe we could have lunch."

"I'd love to. What's the room number? I'll leave right now."

Patricia told her, then said, "Take your time. I'll be here."

"It shouldn't take me more than half an hour."

"I'm having trouble believing this. See you soon."

Thinking that she might not get back to the loft for a night or two, Snow shoved a change of clothes, clean underwear and some toilet articles into a carryall, then took another look out the window. The newspeople were still downstairs. She pulled on a jacket, looped the straps of the carryall and her purse over her shoulder, locked up the loft, then went to the rear of the building and let herself out the fire door.

With relief, she saw that the alley was deserted. The rusted iron stairs wobbled under her weight, and she kept a firm grip on the flaking handrail as she made her way down. She had to counter-balance the final length of the fire escape with her body's weight and for a moment as she hung on, waiting for the stairs to unfold and descend, she had a vision of herself dropping into space like a rock with the ancient metal disintegrating beneath her. But after a few suspenseful seconds—while she wondered if she wasn't going to have to turn around, go back into the building, and emerge through the front door after all—the staircase gave a loud, agonized groan and began to lower itself.

She'd just set foot in the alley when a couple of people she recognized from the crowd that had been hanging around out front of the building all morning appeared at the far end of the alley. Suddenly afraid they'd follow her and spoil everything with their invasive curiosity, she took off at a run in the opposite direction, feeling like a fugitive. Looking back over her shoulder, she saw they were gaining ground. This is crazy, crazy! she thought, looking ahead again as she arrived at the end of the block where a taxi was just approaching. Her hand flew up, the taxi screeched to a halt, she leapt into the back, announced her destination to the driver, and they were off, heading uptown.

Peering out the back window, she saw the two men emerge from the mouth of the alley to look up and down the street. Obviously they hadn't seen her get into the cab. Facing forward, she closed her eyes and tried to catch her breath, congratulating herself on her getaway.

By the time they were passing Fourteenth Street she was becoming afraid, her palms sweaty, breathing gone awry. She'd gone from feeling giddily pleased at having eluded the media, to feeling ill. Things were happening too fast; she needed more time to think. Maybe she'd stop, go have a coffee somewhere, phone Patricia and say she'd be a bit late. Her mouth was dry and she looked at the driver through the murky, scarred Plexiglas partition, wanting to tell him to pull over, but she couldn't speak.

By Twenty-third Street she had a stomach ache and was sitting bent forward, elbows on her knees as the cab bounced over potholes and lurched sickeningly in and out of the traffic. She reached over, opened the window, and gulped down mouthfuls of air, looking up at last to see they were already streaking through the intersection at Thirty-fourth Street.

She tried to conjure up comforting images, but they refused to come; her mental screen remained blank. She collapsed against the seat, sucking down the sooty air gusting in the window as the cab sat waiting for the lights to change at Forty-second Street. The reeking machine idled in a ragged, rocking fashion that brought to mind the heaving sides of some winded animal. Reluctance was like a block of ice at the base of her spine, making her back ache. She told herself she was being childish and stupid, an emotional Indian giver. You couldn't say you wanted something and then refuse it at the last minute. But she didn't want to go through with this.

The driver slammed on the brakes in front of the hotel and she paid him, got herself out of the cab and stood, shaky-kneed, on the sidewalk, pasting on a smile for the doorman who touched two fingers to his hat in salute before striding off toward a stretch limo pulling in at the curb.

Traversing the lobby, she was horribly self-conscious. In the end she'd gone running off without even thinking about changing her clothes. She was still wearing the navy turtleneck, jeans and ludicrous red high-top sneakers she'd put on that morning, with an old Harris tweed jacket she'd bought in a thrift shop maybe six years ago. Her hair was all over the place and she considered finding a women's room so she could at least put it into a ponytail, but she knew if she stopped she'd probably throw up. Her only hope of maintaining some semblance of self-control was to keep up her forward momentum. If she paused she thought she might, like some failed scientific experiment, topple off her axis and be unable to get up again. She could, all too easily, visualize it. So she went directly to the elevators, pressed the call button, then stood waiting, foot tap-tapping as she eyed the indicators to see which one would arrive first.

Halfway expecting someone from the hotel staff to approach, demanding to know what she—this distraught and lamentably disheveled creature—was doing and where she was going, she jabbed the call button several more times, and waited. Perspiring, hands clenched, foot tap-tapping manically on the dense, figured carpet, stomach cramping painfully, she kept her eyes moving back and forth between the indicators above the pair of elevators, wishing the damned things would hurry up.

Finally, when she'd begun looking around for the stairs, an elevator arrived. The doors parted and six or seven impossibly slow people took their time leaving. She stood breathing through her nose, grappling with admittedly irrational exasperation, then stepped inside, poked the floor number she wanted and tried to catch her breath. Just as the doors were closing, a trio of expensively dressed, heavily made-up, critically thin women came pushing in, causing the doors to jounce back open. Snow fought down a desire to scream. The three laughed shrilly, cast pleased looks at one another, as if proud of having defeated yet another mechanical contraption designed to make their lives difficult, and pressed the sixth floor button. After thirty seconds or so that felt like an age, the doors slowly closed and the cage began its ascent, with the middle-aged, anorectic trio chattering like grotesque windup toys.

Snow emerged on the ninth floor and stood, foot again tap-tapping, as she tried to make sense of the wall-mounted arrows that indicated which way the room numbers ran. She seemed to have lost some of her basic skills in her effort to get to this hotel and meet up with Patricia MacKenzie. Not only was her sense of time totally distorted, but her ability to comprehend simple graphics was fritzed. She looked at the number she'd written down, then again at the arrows. At last it registered and she turned to the left.

The corridor seemed miles long, and she still felt conspicuous even though there was no one around to see her. She walked, checking the room numbers, her breathing so shallow she was slightly light-headed from lack of oxygen. God oh God! What if they hated each other? What if they had nothing in common and couldn't talk to one another? The DNA test results wouldn't be back for weeks. It was possible she wasn't this woman's child, even though the initial workups showed that her blood matched that of Victoria MacKenzie and was a type compatible with that of William and Patricia. Type A blood was so common. Maybe it was pure coincidence that she and Victoria were both A's. What was it Ray Delgado had said? Something about quirks of fate and circumstances, and about how in a few extremely rare cases, preliminary matches were in later, more elaborate tests, disallowed. This could all be a dreadful mistake, with both her and Patricia MacKenzie sent aloft on a needless adrenaline high.

She arrived at the room and stood studying the door, wetting her lips and drying her hands on her jeans. Her underarms were soaked. A trickle of sweat ran down between her breasts. Had she remembered to put on deodorant? She sniffed at herself, hoping she didn't smell, then raised her hand to knock at the door, stopped, took a step back and looked around, grateful there was no one to see this dismal performance.

Go ahead and get it over with! Knock at the damned door! Her hand lifted a few inches, then fell. She took another step back and looked down at the carpet, dragging air into her lungs. She wanted to turn and run. She could hear Katie telling her it was time to confront what scared her and admit to it. This sure as hell scared her, and she could practically feel herself taking flight. Patricia Mac-Kenzie was a stranger. They didn't know each other, had no shared history. Why had she ever thought she wanted to meet the woman who'd given birth to her? That act didn't make Patricia her day-to-day, sickness-and-health mother. It only gave her a biological claim, nothing more. Only biological. For God's sake, it was everything. Be open-minded, Rudy had advised. Meet this woman like a friend.

She knew she wasn't going to run. She was no longer someone who did that. In the past week she'd acquired new skills, a certain proficiency at confrontation, and didn't wish to go back to being someone who regularly subsisted on a non-nourishing diet of un-diluted anger. So why couldn't she just knock at the goddamned door and get on with it? "Help," she whispered to the empty cor-ridor. "I need a little help here." Another step back, then another, and she was up against the opposite wall, feeling horrifyingly as if she might wet her pants—remembering from early childhood that awful, urgent, inner pressure. Snow closed her eyes and thought of Julia, knowing she was playing a mother's role with the girl, giving it her best effort because Julia deserved nothing less. She'd done battle for Julia with the girl's own father. And she'd won.

How could she be a grown-up for Julia and a child right here? It wouldn't fly. So what if she *was* scared? On the other side of that door was a woman who was probably even more scared, and with a whole lot more on the line. Put it in perspective! Do what has to be done!

Before she had a chance to lose her nerve again, she moved for-ward and knocked at the door, keenly aware of the blood surging through her veins, of the fretful cadence of her heartbeat, of the sea surf rushing in her ears. She was melting in her own body's heat.

The door opened, and she could only stare dumbly. On the other side of the threshold was a vision of herself, twenty-two years on. This vision had a mass of unruly fading red hair contained by a tortoiseshell clip; the same brown eyes and fair, freckled complex-ion, high cheekbones and wide mouth, the same short narrow nose. She was confronting a woman who was her height, who had the same lean body, and who was even wearing almost the same clothes: old worn jeans, a long-sleeved pale yellow silk shirt, white socks and loafers.

Patricia MacKenzie gasped, then laughed, and stood finally with one hand pressed to her breast, the other covering her mouth. For a few seconds both women remained frozen, each absorbing the unmistakable features one had inherited from the other. Then, a kind of joyful sob breaking from her, the older woman threw open her arms and closed them around Snow.

Snow gave herself up to the embrace knowing she'd very nearly made herself sick for no good reason. The two of them wouldn't have a shortage of things to talk about. This was her mother after all.

With a soft laugh, Patricia released her, then reached at once for Snow's hands and held them, gazing into her face. "You couldn't be anyone but Victoria," she said wonderingly. "Everyone kept wanting me to give it up, accept that you were dead, but I wouldn't. I couldn't. Right from the beginning I told myself that some poor woman who wanted a baby had taken you, that she loved you and was looking after you. As long as I thought of it that way I was able to keep going. I'd stop and think, today is Vickie's first day of kindergarten. Or today is Vickie's seventh birthday. Today she's a teenager. On and on. You were so real to me. I refused to let you die. I had to believe someone loved you and was taking care of you. And I was right, wasn't I? Someone did, didn't she?"

"Yes, she did. I brought along an old photograph album Anne kept until I was about eleven. I thought you might want to see it."

Patricia laughed. "I brought one, too! I thought you'd like to see your father, your baby pictures."

"I'd love to see them."

"God! What am I doing? Come sit down." Patricia led her by the hand into the living room of the suite where, unable to resist, she hugged Snow again. "I can't *believe* it!" she exclaimed, blotting her face on her sleeve. "I want you to know this is the second happiest day of my life."

"I'm glad," Snow said, humbled by the woman's extraordinary faith.

"The first," Patricia said, curving one hand over Snow's cheek, "was the day you were born."

Twenty-Three

"Everyone blamed me. Oh, they didn't come right out and actually accuse me of being neglectful or careless. It wasn't overt, but it was obvious nonetheless. My father wouldn't look directly at me. He'd half turn in my direction when I spoke, but he wouldn't meet my eyes. He seemed embarrassed, as if he'd have preferred to ignore me, but couldn't. And Bill." Patricia shook her head. Absently stroking Snow's hand, she looked off to one side, remembering. Another shake of her head and she turned back. "Once upon a time I adored him, thought he was the most wonderful creature on earth. We met just after I turned twenty-one. He was twenty-eight—by my sights a sophisticated, older man. He came after me with a vengeance and I ate it up and asked for more.

"My mother begged me to take my time. He was too old for me, too inflexible. I was too young for him, too impulsive. I just laughed and patronized her. I was so arrogant, so convinced she didn't understand, couldn't see that this was *different*. Why on earth should I listen to my mother telling me to go slow, get to know the man better before I committed myself? Bill's was the only voice I wanted to hear, and after eight weeks we were already making plans to get married. The only concession I was willing to make was to agree to wait until after I graduated—which meant another three months of furtive frenzy before we could go at it legally.

"Dad thought it was terrific. Bill was a great guy, on his way up in a major law firm, good-looking and smart. And from Dad's viewpoint I was one lucky girl. I'd picked myself a winner, and he would've been more than happy to dish out thousands for a big wedding. But I wanted city hall and a small party afterward, so he used the money as a down payment on an apartment Bill went ahead and picked out on East 68th Street, and told me about later. I'd have preferred the Village or Murray Hill, but if that was what Bill wanted, fine.

"Right up to the last minute, while I was getting dressed to go downtown, my mother was saying, 'You don't have to do this,

Paddy. It's not too late to call it off,' and I kept on laughing and patronizing her, saying, 'Mom, don't be *silly*. Of course I'm not going to call it off. I *love* Bill.' And, God help us, this woman I kept accusing of being silly said, 'You don't love Bill, Paddy. You love the sex.' Prig that I was, it actually shocked me that my mother, who'd nearly had apoplexy trying to tell me the facts of life ten years earlier, was standing there saying she knew what I was up to and it didn't matter just so long as I didn't allow it to cloud my judgment. Too funny and too sad. When did anyone ever listen to her mother?

"So we got married, and I got pregnant about five minutes into the marriage. Bill was not pleased. He made all the right noises to his parents and mine. But up until the end of my sixth month, when it was unsafe even to consider it, he kept asking me to get an abortion. The timing was all wrong, he insisted. It wasn't a matter of money. We could certainly afford a child. He was earning a very good salary, and we had our own home, courtesy of my father. No, it had to do with Bill's concept of marriage, and about a lack of complications. He'd found himself a playmate who had enough brains to keep herself amused during the day with her painting and her classes, and who was there every night to serve dinner, and to sleep with.

"It's not that he was a bad man, because he wasn't. He was just spoiled. We both were. Somewhat self-centered—children of privilege, that's what we were. He was old enough to be fairly well set in his ways, and I was young enough to be stubborn about my views. So the bloom was off the rose fairly early. By the eighth month I was thinking I'd probably be taking the baby from the hospital back to my parents' place. But, astonishingly, once you were born, Bill turned overnight into a father. He got his first look at you, and that was it, he was gone. It was touching and sweet, and just like that we were over the rough patch. He treated me with new respect, as if I'd done something positively miraculous. Which, of course, I had." Patricia smiled, squeezing Snow's hand. Snow was unable to smile back, or even to speak. She simply hung on to her mother's hand and listened, eager to hear everything.

"I kept you with me constantly, even had you sleeping in a basket in the studio while I worked. Sometimes, I'd put down my brushes, grab a sketch pad and draw you for hours. Or I'd get up in the middle of the night to watch you sleep. I'd have you with me in your infant carrier when I took a bath. I walked miles with you in your stroller, puffing up with pride whenever anyone stopped to admire you. And people did, all the time. You were the most adorable, good-natured baby, with all those red curls and a big toothless grin. I watched you change from day to day, fascinated by everything about you, discovering you loved applesauce but refused to swallow strained carrots, or that my singing made you laugh.

"Those six months after you were born were the best and happiest, most productive months of my life. I was painting up a storm, getting ready for a show I'd been promised in the spring. Knitting and sewing while you napped, making new clothes for you. Reading cookbooks and creating exotic dinners almost every night for Bill. I took life drawing classes two afternoons a week, had lunch with my mother every few days, and lunch with Bill's mother at least once a week, met up with friends when I could. I was Wonder Woman! The marriage was humming along, Bill was made a junior partner at his firm, and we were talking about having another child. We'd come past our differences, learned a bit about compromise, and the marriage was running like the proverbial well-oiled machine.

"Then, one Tuesday morning I went as usual to the supermarket. I looked at my list, saw I'd forgotten the oregano, and ran back to get it. Maybe forty-five seconds, maximum. I came back, and your infant seat was empty. I couldn't absorb it, that empty infant seat. I stared and stared at it. I even laughed, because it was just so ridiculous. It was a joke. Somebody was nearby, holding you and watching, having a good laugh at my expense. But there were only other mothers, other babies, and no sign of you. I ran up and down every aisle with this rising panic, this dread and disbelief, finding it harder and harder to breathe. You were gone. Vanished. It couldn't be, but it was true. Gone. One more time up and down the aisles, fighting the disbelief, wanting it to be a prank, but knowing it wasn't. And then I went berserk." Her eyes closed tightly and she exhaled very slowly. Snow consolingly squeezed the hand enclosing hers, wishing to ease the remembered anguish.

"So," Patricia sniffed and continued after a few seconds. "Once past their initial shock, everyone blamed me. Except my mother. She was practical and wise and kept telling me to get pregnant again right away. 'You'll never replace Vickie,' she said, 'but you'll have someone else to love. It'll make it hurt less.' I thought she might be right. God knows, I felt like someone who'd been left with a warehouse full of useless goods—all that love and nowhere to expend it. Bill wouldn't come near me, couldn't stand the sight of me. The moment you disappeared, I ceased to have any credibility, any viability as a person. I'd been irresponsible and stupid. I'd been negligent and self-involved. If I'd kept my mind on my *job,* which was looking after *his* baby, this would never have happened. If I hadn't been such a witless idiot, his daughter would be down the hall in her crib where she belonged. Oh, he blamed himself, too. He'd made a mistake, no doubt about it. He'd allowed himself to be dazzled by my wanton sexuality, and tricked into a marriage he'd never wanted. Overnight, he completely rewrote our history. I didn't care. It didn't matter. All that mattered was getting you back.

"After three months, when no phone call or ransom note came, and the story was out of the papers and pretty well forgotten, and neither the New York police nor the FBI had so much as a single lead, Bill moved out. I didn't try to stop him. By that point it was a relief to have him go. Within six months we were divorced. Less than a year after that he married an older woman from Tucson with two children, and he was gone—out of my life, out of the state, gone. He did stop by before he left, to give me a forwarding address, in case you turned up, and to say good-bye.

"He came to the apartment with a small bouquet of pink roses and stood in the living room staring at his feet, his mouth working. Then he looked at your picture on the mantel and started to cry. I felt this awful pity, and tried to console him because all at once I could see that he'd always been out of his depths with me. I was as intriguingly peculiar to him as a sideshow exhibit in a circus. He was always going to remain precisely who he'd been since about the age of sixteen, and I was always going to be trying to expand and become more. We'd never have lasted together. And at that moment, we both finally knew it.

"He said he was ashamed of every vicious thing he'd said to me, that he knew it really wasn't my fault but he'd been so devastated he'd just had to strike out to try to ease the hurt, and I was the only one he could blame. He said he'd managed to come to terms with the fact that our baby was probably dead and that he'd never see her again, and the best thing for me to do would be to accept that, too. I lied and told him I'd try, but only to humor him because he was being so painfully frank. I said I understood, and wished him happiness with his new family. We hugged each other for a long time, and then he left. I never saw him again." Eyes awash, she stopped and shook her head sadly. Then she looked penetratingly at Snow for a time without speaking. Snow looked back at her, allowing herself to be read. She had no inclination to withhold anything, and couldn't help thinking that, as she'd suspected, her life would very definitely be lived in two segments—the first portion spent feeling compelled to hide the majority of her emotions, and the second to be spent expressing them. This woman, this mother, was every bit as temperamental as she was, and there was something wonderfully luxurious in being allowed to let everything show.

At last, apparently gratified by what she saw, Patricia picked up the thread. "I stayed on in the apartment, afraid to leave. If I stayed there you'd somehow find your way home. So I sat, or paced, and waited. If I had to go out for any reason, I'd be a nervous wreck until I could get back, convinced that while I was out you were trying to contact me. I even got hooked up to a telephone answering service so the line would never go unanswered. It was crazy and, in my rational moments, I knew how crazy it was. You were a baby, with absolutely no identification. You couldn't say more than Mama and Dada, and you certainly weren't capable of using a telephone. It didn't matter. I had to get home in case you tried to call.

"My mother was wonderful. She came every day and cooked meals I rarely ate. She pushed me to get back to work until I gave in just to get her off my back. She played along with some of my nuttier notions—sitting in the apartment reading so there'd be someone there to answer the doorbell if someone dropped by to return you while I was at a life class, or at the deli buying food I didn't want and couldn't eat. I couldn't eat, most of the time, because, more than anybody else ever could or would, *I* blamed me. Everything Bill had said was true. I *was* irresponsible and stupid, negligent and self-involved. I was every last thing he'd accused me of being, and more. Anybody who left a six-month-old infant unattended—anywhere, but especially in Manhattan—even for one second was the utter living epitome of stupidity.

"For three years I was probably certifiable. The only thing that kept me going was the tale I'd concocted about a poor woman so desperate to have a baby that she'd stolen mine. I refused to hear about babies who'd been kidnapped and sold, who'd been taken for sexual purposes and killed. My daughter was with someone who loved her. She was being fed and sheltered and nurtured. I layered so many details onto that story day after day that, in time, it became real. And when I reached the point where I believed it was true, that you were safe somewhere, the stasis ended.

"I woke up one morning, looked around and thought, I've got to get out of here. I put the apartment up for sale, stored the furniture, went to a travel agent and bought myself a one-way ticket to Italy. I packed a couple of suitcases, kissed my parents good-bye, and left, thinking I'd come back in a month or two.

"I stayed for eleven years. And every time I moved, I wrote to let the police here know my new address. They always wrote back to say they appreciated being kept up to date, and that the case was still open. I can't tell you what that meant to me. It was like a very small, ongoing connection to you, and somehow they understood that. Anyway, one morning I woke up and knew I'd stayed away long enough. So I got in touch with a gallery owner I'd met in Florence who'd said she'd give me a show in New York any time I wanted. The paintings got crated up and shipped off, and back I came.

"But I just couldn't live here. Every day I spent in this city was a day I spent chasing after every young redheaded girl I saw, certain I was only steps away from finding you. The day after the show closed I was in a car I'd just bought, on my way west. I tried Utah and Montana, Oregon and Washington, Nevada, California, Arizona, Colorado, New Mexico, back to Montana a second time, in case I was wrong. I wasn't wrong. I couldn't settle. Places only *looked* right. Every few years I'd fly back into town for a show, visit my parents, spend a couple of weeks in this hotel because, for some reason, I've always felt safe here, then head back to wherever I happened to be living.

"I'd be okay for months at a stretch, then one morning it'd be time to go again. I met men I liked who liked me, but every time it threatened to get serious, I'd back off. I couldn't trust my judgment so it was better to keep things casual. My mother was right after all. I should've had another child immediately, but I didn't. And when the opportunities were there, later on, I was too afraid to risk it. If I had another one and something happened to it, I'd die. I didn't have the emotional wherewithal to survive any more losses. I wanted to stay alive for the one child I already had who was going to show up someday, looking for me. I had to be ready and waiting when she came back. When I turned fifty and it was far too late, I realized I'd been wrong. I should've taken the risk, had another child. It would've been all right." She shrugged and smiled.

Snow smiled back at her own softened and subtly altered mirror image, reluctant to speak and interrupt the flow of what her mother had to say. So, in silence, she absorbed through her skin the details of the hand enclosing hers, through her eyes each inherited characteristic, and through her mind the facts of this life she hadn't known of two weeks before, taking everything in as if auditing an odd postgraduate course that offered a rare and highly unusual form of accreditation.

"For years I was basically an upscale hobo," Patricia went on. "My parents had retired to Palm Beach and I thought it would be good to be close to them. Much as I loved them, though, I hated it there, and was getting ready to hit the road again when another gallery owner invited me down to Key West. At last, I found a place that appealed to something a little wild and very angry inside of me. I loved the Keys—the heat, the water, the tropical vegetation, the birds and bugs, the relative isolation. I rented for a couple of years and eventually bought the house on Candle Key in '82.

"Bill died in '81 of a coronary. Forty-eight years old. His wife phoned to tell me, and sent the obit. A decent woman. I think she put up with a lot. Bill wasn't an easy man to live with. He had so many preconceived notions about what a woman's role was supposed to be. Anyway, I will say this for him. He loved you with all his heart, and nothing would've made him happier than to know you're here. When I got that call yesterday afternoon from the local police telling me I'd be hearing from a Sergeant Delgado from the Missing Persons Squad in New York, my first thought was of your father, wishing I could call to tell him the great news. I wanted to tell everybody. But I'm the only one left. My father died six years ago, and Mother died last January. I think Bill's dad's in a nursing home somewhere. He has Alzheimer's, somebody told me."

"That's sad," Snow said softly.

"It is," Patricia agreed. "Bill's two sisters are still alive but I have no idea where they are. They never liked me, thought I was too artsy-fartsy for their family." She laughed again. "What a joke! In retrospect, I was so *tame*—innocent, programmed and obedient.

They thought I was daring because I wore black tights and black Capezio ballet shoes with a basic all-black wardrobe. Most of the girls at Parsons dressed pretty much the same way. That was our 'statement,' back in the early sixties. *I* thought I was daring because I was an art student and had a lover eight years older. But I was just a conceited puppy.

"It was a thousand years ago. Yet every time I look in the mirror, I'm shocked because I can still see myself heading down the street on my way to school, with a portfolio under one arm, and those paper-thin Capezios on my feet. I can still feel the eyes of the men in cars waiting at intersections, knowing they were admiring me, and reveling in it. Just before my mother died, I had this astonishing insight. We were having dinner in Palm Beach, and she laughed at something, and I suddenly realized that inside her head she was still eighteen. I saw the girl she'd once been laughing out at me, and all of a sudden I knew I'd been mistaken about a lot of things. It sounds simplistic, but I'd never thought the feeling was universal. My mother was a senior citizen. Therefore she had to think of herself as a senior citizen. But of course she didn't. When I asked her how old she felt, that fresh-faced young girl gave me a big smile and said, 'Eighteen.' And I realized at that moment that the truth is, we're all eighteen forever. The body slowly erodes, but, if we're lucky, the brain stays young."

"It is true," Snow concurred. "I think everything we experience collects, in a way, and sits to one side of that central fact. No matter what happens, we'll always be eighteen."

"Exactly!" Patricia said delightedly.

"D'you mind if I ask you something?"

"Sweetheart, you can ask me anything," she said with a laugh. "But, first, let me hug you again."

For a time, the two breathed in unison, arms around each other, absorbing their shared reality: two women meeting for the first time, yet profoundly connected.

"Okay." Holding Snow by the shoulders, drinking in the sight and feel of her, Patricia said, "Ask me."

"Were you very unhappy all those years? I can't stand to think your entire life was destroyed."

"Oh, my dear, no. It wasn't, not at all. You'd have to be...I don't know...fundamentally *defective,* I think, not to respond to Italy. It was the right choice, the perfect place to go. The remarkable light, the exquisite cities, the fantastic food, the people—so passionate and dramatic. I was happy there, often. I had wonderful chauvinistic lovers who cooked for me, and who threw spectacular but harmless tantrums when I refused to capitulate to their whims. I had friends and colleagues and students. I admit it was rough when I came back here and couldn't settle anywhere. But even then I wasn't unhappy so much as dislocated. I knew there was a place for me. I was simply having trouble finding it. It's not so far removed from how you've told me your life-style was dictated in many ways by Anne Cooke's influence. And speaking of her. Will you let me know what you find in that safe deposit box?"

"Sure," Snow replied, frowning slightly.

"What?"

"The way you said that, it sounds as if you're not going to stay in town for long. Will you be leaving right away?"

"Unfortunately, I have to, probably tomorrow evening. The thing is, aside from my professional commitments, I still can't take it here for long, especially nowadays. It's so dirty, so dangerous. It's not the city I grew up in. But you'll come to visit me, won't you? The house is huge, and you could bring anyone you like—your wonderful-sounding friend, Katie, or that dear man, Rudy. Anyone at all. I want to get to know the people who are important to you. And I want to know *everything* about you."

"I feel the same way, and I will come," Snow assured her. "Probably sooner than you think. I'd really like to see your studio. God, it's so ironic! I've always admired Paddy Gilbert. She was a huge influence on me at school. Back when I was still deciding between painting and photography, I thought if there was anyone I wanted to emulate it was her. Katie went to your last show and raved for days. She thinks you're a cross between Hopper and Wyeth, but more sensual."

"I have to meet this woman," Patricia declared, amused.

"What's really weird is, I was up in Stony Point for a week, or I'd have gone to the show with her." It gave her the shivers to think how close they'd been. If Anne hadn't, in her inimitable fashion, claimed she was feeling neglected, Snow wouldn't have closed up shop to go home for a week. She'd have gone, as planned, to the gallery with Katie. Instead, Katie had gone with Todd and Josie.

"It's a pity your loft is under siege. I'd love to see some of your portraits."

"I did bring one shot," Snow said, reaching into her bag. "It's only a proof but I wanted to show you Julia, the little girl I told you about."

Patricia looked at the photograph, then at Snow. "Such soulful eyes. I can see why you're so taken with her. It's an exquisite shot. I'm sliding toward the edge all of a sudden," she said, pulling a tissue out of her sleeve. She blotted her eyes and blew her nose, then sat back and again took hold of Snow's hand. "I like you more than I can say. You're honest and generous and not a bit judgmental, affectionate, too. Whoever she turns out to be, and regardless of her personal quirks, she raised you to be a good woman."

"I don't know how you can be so forgiving."

"Oh, my pet, I'll *never* forgive her," Patricia said calmly. "How could I? She shattered my life. Maybe the marriage wouldn't have lasted very long, but what she did killed it prematurely. She destroyed my ability to trust, and made me too frightened to have another child. But she kept you alive and didn't do you any serious harm. And who knows? Maybe her taking you forced me to become a better and stronger person than I might otherwise have been. God knows, I crashed onto the rocks those first three years, but I did survive. And my work got better and stronger, too. Who's to say adversity doesn't generate creativity? Pain has to go somewhere. Some of us channel it into our work. But getting back to what you said. No, I don't forgive her, and never will. I do accept that she played a very significant role in my life without our ever having met. And she did, regardless of how indirectly, send you back to me."

"I hadn't thought of it that way," Snow said. "But it's true, isn't it? She could've kept the secret, but she wanted me to know, maybe even wanted to set the record straight."

"Whatever her motives, she sent you back. And for that I will always be grateful." Patricia yawned, her eyes watering. "I think it's time we both got some sleep. It's almost eleven. I've been up for two days and nights, and I'm starting to get the shakes. But we'll have a late breakfast or early lunch together before we head downtown to the press conference. Okay?"

"Yes."

"How do you feel?" Patricia looked closely at her.

Snow considered it, then leaned forward to kiss her. "The same as you probably," she answered with a smile. "I feel fifty different things but they're all good. Primarily, I feel . . . integrated, finally. It's as if I've been looking for something all my life without knowing, and now I've found it."

Twenty-Four

Stepping out into the corridor with the door closing quietly behind her ended the spell. Walking soundlessly along the deserted, thickly carpeted hallway, she was assaulted by a sudden sadness. She'd been planning to book a room for the night at the hotel, but decided as she waited for the elevator to go back to the loft. She had a need to be surrounded by familiar things, and to talk to Katie. Too much had happened too quickly, creating a thick stew of emotions. Katie never failed to offer insightful feedback.

Funny, she thought, how feelings always seemed heightened by night; darkness somehow became a backdrop against which scenes were projected to far greater effect than in daylight. And traveling through the stillness of the elegant old hotel, she had the sense of being caught up in a dream where she was a ghostly figure, invisible to the skeleton night crew she passed on her way through the subtly lit lobby.

As the taxi raced downtown, she sat back heavily and gazed out the window at the unpopulated streets as if watching a documentary—one of those black-and-white, grainy films shot with a hand-held camera and full of jerky motions. Gratings over shop windows; sullen, soot-stained brick buildings; an open convenience store like a gaudy oasis in the night with its dusty windows almost concealed by advertising posters for the lottery, for beer, for soft drinks. Overflowing litter bins, trash in the gutters; here and there people sleeping in doorways, or in packing-case shelters. She looked for Irene, but didn't see her. Not that she'd have recognized her. If you didn't know, you might easily mistake the dark shapes for bags of refuse awaiting collection—a graveyard for those merely subsisting, with shopping carts for tombstones. God, but she was sad, and wished that she lived somewhere beautiful, in a place that didn't, by its dirt and menace, automatically compound any negative feelings she might have. She seemed to have reached the outside edge of her tolerance for life in the war zone, and had a craving for some place where it was possible to relax, where fear wasn't a full-time companion.

There were only a pair of determined reporters left waiting in front of her building, and they pulled themselves to attention when she climbed out of the cab. Both young, both women, they watched to see where she was going, and came on the run as Snow put her key into the lock, questions spilling from their mouths before they even reached her.

"Yes, I did meet my family today," Snow answered soberly, because it still struck her as so improbable. "I really don't want to discuss it right now. I'm sorry, but I'm too tired. My mother— " the word resounded inside her head like the deep clanging of an immense old bell " —and I will be answering questions at the press conference tomorrow. Okay?"

"Can I get a shot of you?" one of the women asked, hoisting her camera.

"Please, no." Snow got inside and hurried to the stairs, preferring not to offer herself as a target for the photographs they were trying to shoot through the door.

When she got the loft door open, Katie, in one of her oversize sleep shirts, came on the run. "I couldn't stand waiting. So I decided to camp out in case you came back. How was it?" she asked, able to see the upset shadowing Snow's features. "What's the matter? Didn't it go well?" She relieved Snow of her carryall, setting it down as she again asked, "What's wrong, babe?"

"I don't know. I just feel so sad."

"It was no good?"

"No. It was great. But when I left, I got bummed, for no reason."

"Maybe I should've waited at home," Katie said guiltily. "But I thought you might want to talk."

"I do. I'm glad you're here." Snow put her arms around her friend, feeling bereft, as she had in the immediate aftermath of Anne Cooke's death. Then as now, she was comforted by Katie's presence, and wondered how Katie managed to read her so accurately, so often. "I'm really glad you're here," she repeated, breathing in Katie's fragrance—an aromatic oil, exotic and lingering, she'd been wearing for years. "It's been . . ." She couldn't find words to describe quite how she felt.

Katie held her until some of the stiffness gradually drained from Snow's thin frame. She thought that what Delgado had said was

true: Snow really did have guts. The meeting had to have been har-
rowing for her and for her mother. "Are you going to be okay?"
she asked at last, scanning Snow's eyes and seeing fatigue, and the
familiar melancholy, but a definite resolve, as well. She was over the
hump, Katie thought. She wasn't going to retreat behind the bar-
ricades of diffidence as she had, so many times, over the years. As
Katie had hoped at the beginning, this experience was having a
painful but positive effect, and it showed.

"Yeah," Snow sighed. "I guess I'm just tired, coming down kind
of hard after such a major high."

"Tell you what. Why don't you get into your jammies while I put
on the kettle? We'll have a cup of tea, you'll tell me how it went,
then we'll put you to bed."

Snow agreed, and went off to change, noting en route that Katie
had cleared the answering machine and listed all the calls. The list
was a long one, and included Mark as well as Huffy Compton and
Julia. The sight of Julia's name gave her a little lift.

Settled in the kitchen with cups of Constant Comment, they sat
quietly for a time—Katie waiting patiently while Snow grappled
with her blue mood, trying to locate its origins.

Finally, she looked up, saying, "I guess part of how I feel has to
do with the fact that I never dreamed things would happen so
quickly. I didn't have a chance to get my head straight. You know?"
Katie indicated she understood. "It was all so fast, so absurdly easy.
Yesterday morning we went uptown to the police station, and
twenty-four hours later there I was meeting my mother. In the cab
on my way uptown, I was practically passing out from fear. Once I
saw her I was okay again, and while we were together it was almost
magical. We have so much in common, it was so easy to talk. But
the minute the door closed it was as if I'd dreamed the whole
thing."

"I think you're in shock," Katie said quietly. "I'm only on the
periphery, but I feel it, too. It *has* been fast, unbelievably fast. And
it's a hell of a lot to take in—losing one mother and getting another, all in the space of a couple of weeks. I don't think anyone
could handle a situation like this without experiencing some pretty
drastic highs and lows."

"You think? Maybe that's it. Maybe it is. I just don't know. I
loved Patricia on sight. But I loved my mother...Anne Cooke...
Jesus! See what I mean? This is so insane! How do I refer to them—

as Mother One and Mother Two? Which one's *really* my mother? Sure, I know Patricia is, biologically. But you were there, Katie. You know Anne was my mother. I can't write any of that off. Even being objective, admitting she messed me up in some ways, I *know* how much she loved me. Until two weeks ago, Anne Cooke was the only mother I had, and, in spite of everything, I'll always love her, regardless of what she did. Now there's Patricia and I've got this totally immediate, totally visceral love for her, too. It's so goddamned *complex,* it gives me a headache, trying to sort it all out."

"It's going to take some time to absorb everything, to compartmentalize your feelings somehow. I'm not sure. I don't have any answers. Nobody does—not for something like this. But I know you can deal with it. I definitely know that."

"Maybe." Snow's eyes drifted off, then returned to Katie. "God, I'm glad you decided to come wait for me. I needed so badly to talk to you."

"I was afraid you'd think I was acting like one of those media creeps downstairs, but I had this feeling that if you did come home, you'd be needing to talk."

"Well, you were right." Snow drank some of the tea, her mood slowly starting to lift. Managing a smile, she said, "You won't believe it when I tell you who Patricia MacKenzie is."

"What d'you mean, who she is? Who is she?"

"She's Paddy Gilbert."

"Get *outta* here! Are you kidding?"

"I am not. Paddy Gilbert is my mother."

"*No way!* You know how much I love that woman's work. I may faint. Oh my God! What was she like? Did the two of you go crazy over each other? I'll kill you if you don't tell me every last thing right now!" Katie leaned forward eagerly, mouth slightly opened, as if prepared to consume the slightest detail.

"We were together for—" Snow glanced at the clock "—eleven hours, and talked nonstop. Max came by in the afternoon to meet her and discuss the press conference tomorrow, and Ray Delgado stopped by on his way home from work. We never left the hotel, just ordered room service." She paused, then said wonderingly, "We look so alike, Katie. And we feel the same way about so many things. Even our energy is the same. It was wonderful, like a fairy tale. We're meeting for breakfast at ten-thirty, then there's the press conference, and after that, she has to leave. She's got a show opening in London in three days."

"So soon? That's such a downer."

"Definitely. But there's no way she could get out of it. And I'll be going to visit her in Florida. She said I could bring you along, if you wanted to come."

"If I *wanted* to? What time's the flight?" Katie laughed. "Oh, sweetie, I'm so happy for you."

"I'm happy, too. But now, more than ever, I want some answers about Anne. So on the way back here I was thinking we'd maybe try to see Daniel Ambrose the day after tomorrow. Then, depending on how things go with him, we could head up to Stony Point Friday, or next Monday, to check out what's in the safe deposit box."

"Sure. No problem. Tell you what. Why don't you give me his number, and tomorrow while you're doing the press conference and the rest of it, I'll try to set up an appointment with Ambrose."

"Okay, good idea." Snow took another swallow of the tea. "Why am I so wiped? I had a really good sleep last night, for a change. I shouldn't be this tired."

"It's shock, I'm telling you. I live with a doctor, don't forget. Listen, what time's your mother's flight tomorrow? If you're up for it, we could get together after."

"Four-forty. I ought to be back by five-thirty or six, depending on the incoming traffic. Let's have dinner."

"Perfect. I'll meet you here at six. We'll eat and you'll tell me what the mayor's really like. Okay?"

Snow laughed. "Okay."

"Now come on." Katie got up and took hold of Snow's arm. "Beddy-byes for you. Auntie Katie will tuck you in."

For a second time, Snow exited via the rear fire escape while Katie distracted the lingering media at the front of the building. The alley was clear, and Snow started toward the avenue, relieved not to be pursued.

It was a warm sunny morning, and the sadness she'd felt the night before was completely gone, in large measure as a result of Katie's having been there. Her mood was buoyant; she couldn't wait to see Patricia again.

In the lee of a Dumpster sat Irene, reading the previous day's *Times*. Snow said hello and Irene looked up at her over the top of the Metro Section, and smiled.

"Hello, dear. Lovely morning, isn't it?"

"Lovely. How are you?"

"Very well, thank you. Just catching up on the world, via yesterday's bin liner." She indicated the newspaper, which she now lowered to her lap. "And how are you? Don't you look well! You're ever such a pretty girl."

"Thank you. Irene, I've been hoping to run into you. I wanted to tell you I wasn't joking when I said I'd give you the money to go home. I really meant it."

"I'm sure you did, dear," she said, with the same smile she'd given Snow the last time they'd met—one touched with amused tolerance for a fellow nut case. "You're very kind."

"I'm about to inherit a lot of money, and I'd like to help you."

"If you go giving it to all and sundry, dear, it won't last long."

Squatting so she was at eye level with the woman, Snow said, "I *want* to do it for you, if you'd like to have that caravan. It's not safe out here, Irene." Snow glanced around. "It would make me happy to think of you warm and safe in your caravan in a field of wildflowers."

"What a kind girl you are! So few people are kind. Have you ever noticed that?"

"I've noticed."

Irene now looked up the length of the alley. "It would be very difficult to leave Michael."

"Michael is always going to be with you, wherever you are," Snow said softly.

Irene stared at her for a long moment. "I hadn't thought of that. I expect you're right. But even if I wanted to accept your offer, my dear, my passport's long since lost. And I don't even own a proper suitcase."

Thinking of Joseph, Snow said, "I know someone who could probably help you get a new passport. And, we'd go shopping, buy you everything you'd need. It'd be fun."

"Am I dreaming?" Irene asked. "Have I gone round the twist again?"

"No," Snow said firmly. "You know where I live, right?"

"I still have your card."

"Okay. I'll be free after today, so come by the loft any time. At the very least you can use my shower, have something to eat. And if you want to go back to England, I'll arrange it. Will you think about it, please?"

"Oh, I'll most certainly think about it. I must tell you, I'm terribly frightened of airplanes. I very much doubt I could set foot in one."

"No problem. We'll put you on a ship, send you first-class." Snow pulled a couple of bills from her pocket and handed them to the woman. "Come visit me. Okay?"

Irene accepted the money without taking her eyes from Snow's. "Bless you, dear. I'll certainly pop round sometime."

"Make it soon," Snow urged, standing upright.

"Yes," Irene said vaguely, her eyes drifting down to the newspaper in her lap. "I will."

Snow continued on her way. Stopping to look back from the top of the alley, she saw Irene trundling off with her shopping cart in the opposite direction. Let down, Snow thought Irene probably wouldn't come to see her, nor would she take Snow up on her offer. There was very little she could do to persuade the woman of her sincerity. Maybe in her lifetime Irene had been made a few too many promises that hadn't been kept.

Prior to the press conference, the reunited mother and daughter were photographed with Ray Delgado, with Ray and Lieutenant Baines, with the police commissioner and with the entire Missing Persons Squad.

Before, during and after the conference, they were photographed with the mayor, the commissioner and sundry other city VIPs. Throughout, expressing their mutual happiness while camera flashes sparked like outsized fireflies, they held hands. Frequently they smiled at each other, both of them, Snow now understood, in a state of shock.

Then, with police officers and Max shielding them from the more persistent reporters, they made it into a cab, and were on their way to the airport.

In their first telephone conversation, Patricia had said that there was so much she wanted to say that she couldn't think rationally. Now it was Snow's turn, and she couldn't speak at all. She sat trying to recover the conversational ease that seemed to have deserted her, and by the time she'd managed to arrange her thoughts in some semblance of order, the cab was pulling to a stop in front of the American Airlines curbside check-in. Their time together was suddenly close to an end, and she was getting panicky.

She stood by while, with practiced efficiency, Patricia disposed of her well-used suit bag, accepted her baggage claim check, and tipped the handler. Then she directed Snow inside to the Admirals Club where they settled in a quiet corner to spend a last half hour together.

"I can't believe you're leaving already," Snow said, unprepared for the abrupt, rending feel of this parting. "The time's gone too quickly."

"I know. But I keep reminding myself we'll be seeing each other again very soon. You'll have to do the same." Once again, they were holding hands. "When you want to come visit, call, and I'll be there to pick you up at the airport. It's that simple. Or I'll come here, or to Stony Point. I'd like to meet all the people I've been hearing about, especially Rudy. There must be a motel nearby where I could stay."

"Not really," Snow said, only belatedly realizing that Patricia would never set foot inside Anne's house, let alone stay there. She'd been imagining them sleeping across the hall from one another, having breakfast together in the kitchen. Cosy, impracticable images. How could she have been so harebrained? "A couple of places in town do bed and breakfast. We'd work something out."

"Of course we would." Patricia lifted Snow's chin with her fingertips. "Problem?" she asked, demonstrating yet again her acute awareness of even the slightest change in Snow's moods; an instinct that—much as Snow loathed making comparisons, she couldn't help but acknowledge this—Anne Cooke had never possessed.

"I didn't think this was going to be so hard." Fearful of breaking down, of creating a public spectacle, she looked around the half-empty club, trying to stay composed. The extent of her feelings for this woman was beyond anything she'd contemplated. Her newly found mother was tough, irreverent, funny, gentle and loving; she was truthful, cautious and wise. Snow loved her utterly, inexorably. She couldn't get enough of her, and wanted to hear every last detail of her experiences, wanted to learn her every gesture and mannerism. She'd barely acquainted herself with the essentials, and Patricia was leaving. It was altogether too soon.

"Things are always harder than we think they're going to be," Patricia said, her hand seeking Snow's once again. With a shake of her head, she fell silent, and examined Snow's hand, tracing its depth and breadth with the fingers of one hand while cradling it in the other. At last, she threaded her fingers so tightly through Snow's that each could feel the other's pulse. "They always are," she repeated. Then, mindful of their allotted time dwindling, she let go and reached to open her satchel-like shoulder bag. "I wanted to give you something to commemorate the occasion, something symbolic but not corny. This was the best I could do on short notice."

Snow sat, with unsteady hands receiving the first present she'd ever received from her mother. "I'm going to break down and embarrass both of us," she warned. "I thought I had more of a grip, but I was wrong."

"Me, too," Patricia confessed. "Ordinarily, I'd say what the hell, fire away. But this time let's agree to wait. You'll come unhinged in the cab on your way back to town, and I'll fall apart on the plane. Sound fair?"

"Sure," Snow said with a gulping laugh, and reached into her bag. "I brought something for you, too."

Patricia smiled. "Open yours first."

"Okay." Snow removed the top of the small jeweler's box to find an exquisitely simple gold key ring with a single shiny new key attached.

"It unlocks the door to your home in Florida," Patricia explained. "So you can let yourself in if you're going to be late, and I don't have to sit up half the night waiting and worrying."

Snow nodded, swallowing hard.

"It's just a bad mother joke, sweetheart."

"I know." Snow laughed, wiping her face with the back of her hand. "Sorry. I know. Thank you. I love it."

"Should I open this now?"

Snow nodded again and, watching, knew from Patricia's satisfied sigh that she'd made the right choice in giving her the self-portrait she'd done at the age of thirteen. Slightly out of focus, it was nevertheless a good shot, well composed and moody. She sat on the beach under an ominous sky pierced by arrowing shafts of sunlight, arms wrapped around her skinny, bent knees; in cutoffs and a white T-shirt, half-turned toward the camera, smiling, defiant; her still-round features on the verge of attaining adult definition, hair flying wildly in the wind.

Patricia bit her lip and put an arm around Snow's shoulders, drawing her in. "This'll go on my bedside table," she said, her voice gone thick. "I'll look at you first thing every morning and last thing each night, and feel very, very lucky. You have to know there was never a time when I didn't love you, and there never will be."

"I love you, too," Snow cried, scrambling around inside herself like a small house pet skidding across a freshly waxed floor, trying to keep from sliding over the edge into a gulf of distress. "I don't want you to go. Oh, God! I sound like such a baby. Sorry, sorry. Really, I'm sorry." Holding on hard, she said, "I *don't* want you to go. We need more time together. I need more time with you."

"I do, too. There's nothing I'd like more than to spend days on end with you. But I've got the opening in London. There's just enough time for me to get home, throw some things together, and fly out of Miami tomorrow night."

"Let's pretend I didn't say or do any of that," Snow said, reluctantly easing away. "I'm being ridiculous. Of course you have to go, and it doesn't do either of us any good to have me sitting here like a five-year-old begging you not to. I can't *believe* I'm acting this way."

"It actually makes me very happy that you're acting this way. Maybe it's selfish, but I want you to want me and need me and be greedy about your time with me. That way I don't have to feel guilty about wanting and needing you, and being greedy about our time together. I was so afraid you'd blame me, that you had thirty years of anger stored up just waiting to be vented. I saw myself opening the hotel room door and having you fly at me, ready to tear me to pieces."

"Why would I do that?"

"Because I was negligent. Because I left you unattended, because..."

"It wasn't your fault. How were you supposed to know you'd been selected, that you were being watched? You didn't do *anything* wrong. I'd *never* blame you."

"Thank you for that. Keep saying it, and maybe one day I'll begin to believe it. And thank you for this. It's a wonderful photograph." She cleared her throat, then said, "I *hate* good-byes."

"I'm hating this one," Snow agreed. All at once aware of being equally attuned to the nuances of this woman's moods, she knew she was being asked to go. "I thought it'd take us years to cover all the territory, to feel related, but it only took a few seconds. I'm going to act like a grown-up now, say good-bye, and go. We'll talk tonight. And when you get back from London, I'll come to Florida to see you. I've loved every minute with you. I like you and admire you, and I love you.''

They embraced and exchanged kisses, then Snow got up and hurried to the door of the lounge where she paused to look back. Patricia blew a kiss and waved. Snow opened her hand, made a show of catching the kiss, then left with her hand unthinkingly closed around something that had no substance.

Twenty-Five

"Hi, it's Mark. I just read the paper and I'm in a state of shock. God only knows how *you* must be feeling. The whole world's probably chasing after you, wanting interviews and all that. But if you find a minute I'd really like to talk. And, uh, I also wanted to apologize for behaving like such a dork the last time we got together. It's your right to give money to anybody you want, and I was way out of line. The good news is I found an apartment, the rent's not too outrageous and it's within walking distance of the office. The bad news is I'm sleeping on an air mattress and eating off paper plates, plus the phone won't be installed for another week, so call me at the office when you get a chance. I hope you're all right. Take care. Talk to you soon. Bye."

"Hi, Snow. This is Julia. Dad showed me the story in the newspaper with the picture of you as a little baby, and it made me very sad. But we saw you on TV today with your real mother and you looked happy so now I'm not sad anymore. You're the first person I ever knew on TV. And we saw Uncle Max, too. It was cool. Are we still gonna be friends and go to lunch? Dad says you're very busy, but will you phone me? Or maybe you could meet me after school again. I really liked that. Bye."

"Everybody in town's talking up the story, asking me all kinds of silly questions. It's very interesting how it turns out certain folks here claim they were suspicious of Anne Cooke all along, thought there was something just not right about the woman. Course it's all nonsense, but you know how it is here. I just wanted to let you know I'm thinking about you, and hoping things work out well with your mother. In the meantime, I'm stonewalling, not saying much of anything. You go easy, Snow, and don't ask too much of yourself. When you get a minute, maybe you could give me a call. I'm looking forward to seeing you, maybe on the weekend. Bye now, dear."

"Hi, it's Max. You would not *believe* the calls I'm getting! People in L.A. making offers that are just insane, faxing me deal memos when there's no deal. I've had four people offering book contracts, and calls from every TV show in the Western hemisphere. Let me read you some of them. *Today, Good Morning America, American Journal, Hard Copy, A Current Affair, Day One, Dateline NBC, Oprah, Donahue, Regis & Kathie Lee, Maury Povich, Charlie Rose*—a guy whose show I actually like—*Sally Jessy* and *Geraldo*. Feh. About the only shows that haven't called are *Sesame Street* and *Ren & Stimpy*—which just happens to be Leo's favorite show. Anyway, I'm saying no, but keeping notes on the offers, in case you change your mind. Hope your mother got off all right. Call me anytime. Bye for now."

"Snow, it's Josie. Todd and I just read the story in the papers. Man, you must be freaked! I can't get over it. It's too weird. I know you're up to your ears in it right now, so don't worry about calling back. We just wanted to let you know we're thinking about you, and we love you. When things quiet down, let's get together. Big hugs from both of us. Be strong. Bye."

Daniel Ambrose was a tall, solidly built man who looked to be in his late forties but had to be older, with movie-star good looks and an accompanying magnetism; thick silver hair expensively styled, startling green eyes, an easy smile, and the relaxed manner of a man in good health who'd made his fortune and was enjoying it thoroughly. He wore custom-made wing tips, a charcoal gray three-piece Savile Row suit and a pleasant cologne redolent of apples.

"I've been reading about you in the papers. Quite a story! A pleasure to meet you. And this has to be friend Katie with whom I spoke yesterday. Please come in."

His smile managed to be both welcoming and approving without being either predatory or lecherous. He seemed genuinely glad to meet them, and led the way into the ultramodern living room of his Gramercy Park penthouse. "I was about to have breakfast. There's fresh coffee and croissants," he said. "Would you care to join me?"

"Sure," said Katie.

"That'd be great," Snow said.

"Have a seat. I'll just tell the housekeeper."

He pushed through a door that opened far enough to reveal a large dining room furnished in the same style as the living room. Katie and Snow exchanged a smile.

Katie whispered, "He's gorgeous—reminds me of Stewart Granger."

"Exactly," Snow agreed.

"But the decorator deserves to be shot at dawn." Katie looked at all the glass, chrome and black leather, and made a face. "I call this style of decor early sadomasochism. Because only someone wanting to be punished would buy it. Sheesh. About all that's missing are the whips and chains. You think maybe Mr. Gorgeous is into boots and bondage?"

Snow laughed softly. "You're rotten."

"Remember what I said about people getting a ton of money and buying loads of ugly stuff just 'cause it was expensive?"

Snow nodded, her eyes traveling over the cold, stark room.

"Here you see proof of my thesis. Bet you anything he's got a den in the back somewhere with a big old comfy chair, a nice footstool and a forty-inch TV, and that's where he *really* lives. For sure he's not married. No self-respecting woman could live with so much *leather*. But he doesn't give off gay vibes."

"Not at all. I think he likes women. I'll bet they've been throwing themselves at him since he was about eight years old. No doubt he enjoys catching them, too."

"Probably has a busload of ex-wives and kids," Katie speculated. "He's definitely a breeder. Ten bucks says the family photos are in the den, on top of the forty-incher where he can admire them while he's watching Monday-night football."

"Stop!" Snow whispered, grinning.

He beckoned to them from the dining room. "We're all ready," he said, holding open the door to reveal the massive slab-glass table set for three, with a basket of warm croissants, butter and jam in crystal dishes, and a large pot of steaming coffee sitting atop a brass trivet.

Once they'd all served themselves, Ambrose said to Snow, "I'm indebted to you, you know. I'd lost contact with dear old Huffy. I hadn't realized until I spoke to him last week just how much time had gone by, and how much I missed him. Huffy was damned good to me when I was first starting out, took me into the firm fresh from college. We're having dinner tomorrow night, to do some catching up. However inadvertently, you've put us back in touch, and I thank you for that.''

"He's a wonderful person," Snow said.

Tearing apart a croissant, Ambrose said, "That he is. When we spoke initially, he told me you were tracking family members. But, having read the papers the past couple of days, I suspect you're really trying to find out who that woman you thought was your mother actually was. Am I right?''

Relieved to be able to tell the truth, Snow said, "Pretty much. Katie and I started tracking backward after my mother, after Anne Cooke died, and the trail led to you as her former broker. I've got a copy of the transfer and some photographs, if you wouldn't mind looking at them.''

"Not at all.''

She slid an envelope across the table to him.

Ambrose wiped his hands, then pulled a pair of reading glasses from his inside breast pocket and examined first the document. "No question, that was my ID number, and I definitely generated the transfer. Offhand, though, I can't for the life of me think who Anne Cooke could've been before she changed her name.'' Referring again to the page, he noted the date. "Twenty-nine years is a hell of a long time. But still I should be able to remember something. I don't know. There's not even the faintest of bells ringing.'' He let the glasses sit on the extreme end of his perfectly sculpted nose, took a sip of his coffee, then slipped the pair of photographs from the envelope.

He looked first at the more recent shot, slowly set it to one side, and sat staring at the earlier photograph.

Katie reached for a second croissant, tore it into three pieces and began applying liberal layers of butter and jam.

Snow sat holding her coffee cup, closely watching Daniel Ambrose's face, certain he recognized Anne Cooke. His demeanor had undergone a subtle change upon seeing the photograph; some of his jollity had evaporated.

After a while, his eyes still on the picture, he said, "Sorry to take so long. Seeing this brings back a lot of memories.''

"You recognize her?'' Snow asked, her heart rate quickening.

"Oh, sure.'' He looked at the more recent shot. "She was always a fine-looking woman. When did she die?''

"Two weeks ago,'' Snow confirmed, desperate to hear him say her name. Realizing she was clutching the cup too hard, she carefully set it down, then knitted her hands together in her lap. Suddenly she was sweating. Glancing sideways, she noted that Katie was staring unblinking at the man and chewing as if the croissant had turned to sawdust in her mouth.

With a sigh, he removed his glasses and set them down on the table. "You know you're getting old when hardly a week goes by that you don't hear about some old friend who's died. I was halfway in love with that woman years ago." He directed his now-saddened gaze to Snow. "She came to the firm in, I think, 1958. I was twenty-three, and she was one of my first major clients. Originally she was referred to Brad Chase, who took one look at Amy and turned into a performing seal."

Snow started. Amy. Her name was Amy.

"For some reason she took an immediate dislike to poor Brad. I always felt badly about that because he was a decent guy, but Amy didn't take to him. So I wound up handling her account. She never knew it, but I split the commissions with him. I felt it was only fair, under the circumstances, especially since he gave me a lot of good advice on managing the portfolio. And the fact of the matter was, I'd probably have behaved like a performing seal myself if I hadn't seen the kind of reaction Brad got. She made a very misleading first impression. It was completely at odds with the kind of woman she actually was. With that face and figure... Well, to be frank, her reaction to Brad threw a scare into me. She just turned very cold all of a sudden."

"I know," Snow said quietly. "She could do that. It *was* scary."

Ambrose nodded. "She wasn't easy to know, but I liked her. There was something about her that had me feeling sorry for her. Her ideas were so rigid, and you never knew when you were going to run smack into this wall of resistance she'd throw up. But there was a sweetness to her. She had this habit of covering her mouth when she laughed, like a kid. Then it was as if she'd remember she wasn't supposed to laugh or something, and she'd hurry back inside herself and shut the blinds. I used to wonder what had happened to turn her so wary."

It was so vividly accurate a picture of Anne Cooke that Snow was seized by an immediate, acute longing to see her again. She missed her badly, and felt the peculiar and contradictory aspects of her present life driving its sharp, ice-pick point once more into her belly. "I've wondered about that, too," she said. "Often."

His eyes took on a sad cast, and he shook his head slowly. "I thought she'd suffered some personal tragedy. But what she did to you and your family... You must hate her."

Snow realized all at once that beneath the charm was a caring, lonely man. She also understood that he'd been looking forward to this meeting—that he'd dressed especially for it, and that he'd probably sent the housekeeper out to buy the croissants just for her and Katie. "I can't hate her. She was my mother," she answered quietly, deciding she liked this man very much. The green eyes revealed a depth of concern that his very good looks hadn't primed her to anticipate. But perhaps after all he, like Anne Cooke, was a victim of the misleading impression his inherited handsomeness made upon people. "Do you have children, Mr. Ambrose?"

"Call me Dan, please." His eyes stayed fastened to hers as he shook his head. "My first wife died quite young. I rushed into a second marriage that was a disaster. It lasted not quite a year. I've stayed single ever since."

His skin looked soft and smooth, and Snow realized she was very attracted to him. So attracted, in fact, she'd go to bed with him in a minute, if he asked. "That's too bad," she said without thinking, causing him to smile.

"You think so?" he asked.

Katie watched the color rush into Snow's face, and thought this was all very interesting. "Do you like children, Dan?" she asked him.

"I don't honestly know," he answered, at last looking away from Snow and redirecting his attention to Katie. "I haven't been exposed to that many of them, aside, of course, from my own brothers and sisters. I have two of each, and grew up assuming I'd one day be a father. Funny to consider the expectations we have when we're young and then to look back and see that so many of those expectations were modified or abandoned altogether. I'll tell you something that might shock you," he said to Snow. "In retrospect, I don't find it hard to imagine Amy doing what she did."

"Why not?" Snow asked.

"There was something... *missing* in the woman. She was too perfect, too carefully assembled, as if she had no seams. D'you follow?" Snow nodded, and he went on. "It was as if every last thing about her, from the way she looked to the way she thought, had been carefully predetermined. I had the feeling that if something were to come at her from out in left field, she wouldn't have known how to handle it. She'd have fallen apart. Would you agree?"

Snow said, "Definitely." Not only was he exceedingly attractive, he was also very astute.

"In my opinion, Amy Linn Decker hid from the world behind an almost impenetrable, self-erected barricade. Fortunately for her, she had the money to do it."

There it was: Amy Linn Decker. Snow wanted to print the name in block letters on a large piece of paper, then touch it, examine it with a magnifying glass. In a near whisper, she said, "Amy Linn Decker," and felt Katie's hand on her arm. Snow turned to look at her, then turned back to Daniel Ambrose. "Dan," she said, liking the tidy feel of his name upon her tongue, "I need to know anything you can tell me about her, anything at all. I've got to know who she was."

"I'm not sure if I can help you there. I knew almost nothing about her personal life."

"Anything," Snow said, almost pleadingly. "We need some clue, something that'll give us a direction to go in."

"Let me think." He turned and looked off into space, presenting Snow with his aristocratic profile.

She inhaled his sweet-apple scent and imagined what it would be like to climb naked into his lap and kiss the corners of his eyes, to feel secure against the broad expanse of his chest. He was the single most attractive man, both physically and intellectually, she thought she'd ever met.

At length, he said, "All I can remember is that she said she was referred to the office by Betsy Sinclair."

"*The* Betsy Sinclair?" Katie asked. "The one with the hotels?"

"That's right," he confirmed. "According to Amy, they'd been friends since childhood."

"That's fantastic!" Katie exclaimed. "That's an honest-to-God lead! Dan, you're wonderful!"

"It's a lead," he said, "only if you can get to Betsy Sinclair. And that's a pretty big if. I'd imagine you'll have to get through her secretary first. But if it's a help—" his eyes again went to Snow "—I'm glad."

"It gives us something to go on," Snow told him. "Having her name makes all the difference. Until now, we've been spinning our wheels because she did such a good job of burying her identity."

"Did she have much of a portfolio when she came to you?" Katie asked.

His brows drew inward and he thought for a moment. "Seems to me it was fairly substantial."

"Did she happen to mention where she got it?"

"Inherited," he replied promptly. "That much I do remember. When I took over her portfolio it was full of acquisitions made way before the war. The account, as I recall, had been in the hands of executors for years. They hadn't done a thing with it, the result being the holdings weren't worth what they might have been. We had to liquidate most of it, reinvest in higher-yield assets."

"I don't suppose you know who she inherited from?" Snow asked.

"Oh, her father. She told me he died in the war."

"I'm confused," Snow said. "If he died sometime in the early forties, how come the portfolio wasn't touched until the late fifties when you became her broker?"

"You know something? I can't answer that. She never explained."

"That's so typical," Snow said, having to fight down an urge to reach out and touch him. "She wouldn't ever talk about the past. And beyond the fables she told me about my supposed father, Aidan Devane, she never spoke of anyone in her family. Not ever."

Regarding her now with great interest, Daniel sat with his elbow on the table, chin in hand, and said, "Forgive me if I'm out of line, but you don't seem particularly angry about what she did."

For a few seconds, as had happened during the press conference the day before, Snow felt somehow deficient, as if she were a failure in her role as the injured party. But then, seeing something in his eyes that she interpreted as reciprocal attraction, she moved away from the defensiveness inspired by the question and was able to answer openly. "I grew up as the child of the woman I knew as Anne Cooke and you knew as Amy Linn Decker. I'm accustomed to hiding my feelings."

"There's an understatement," Katie contributed with a laugh.

"Katie's put up with a lot the past two weeks," Snow said, looking at her friend, then turning back to Daniel Ambrose. "It's been one hell of a time, and it's turned me completely upside down. It'll take a while to get used to thinking of myself as Victoria MacKenzie. Just saying the name, I get this shock, as if I've touched a hot wire. The thing is, though, Anne...Amy was good to me. Yes, she was rigid, and there were quantum holes in her personal history. But she was my mother, and I loved her.''

"I think most people would be bitter," Ambrose said.

"You liked her, too," Snow pointed out. "You know she wasn't evil. My sense is she believed she had good reasons for what she did. So I'm trying to find out what those reasons were. There's a good chance I may never know, but whatever happens, I won't be able to hate her."

"Snow's not a hater," Katie told him. "She gives good anger, believe me. But she's not a hater."

Ambrose looked from Snow to Katie and back to Snow, then smiled. "You're very good friends, aren't you?" he observed.

"Frick and Frack without the ice," Katie quipped.

He laughed, a deep, delighted rumble, then pointed a finger at Katie, saying, "You're far too young to remember Frick and Frack."

"So're you," she shot back. "My grandfather told me about them."

"My father told me," he admitted, chuckling. Sobering, he turned his attention back to Snow. "I wish you all the luck in the world. You deserve some answers, and I hope you get them."

"I have a question," Katie said. "She must've changed her name shortly before she transferred her holdings to the broker in Providence. You obviously knew about it, because the transfer was in the name of Anne Cooke. Do you remember anything about that? Do you recall her giving any kind of explanation for why she'd done it?"

"Now that you mention it, I do remember. She came to see me once the name change had been effected legally. She wanted all her holdings to be registered in the new name. Naturally, I was curious, and she gave me a fairly convoluted explanation about having decided to adopt her mother's maiden name for sentimental reasons. It was such an obviously arrant cock-and-bull story that I assumed she was on the outs with some man and was going to extreme lengths to get away from him."

"Did you know for a fact that she was involved with someone?" Snow asked, studying the shape of his mouth.

"Actually, no. She said very little about her private life. But I was young, remember, and she was a most attractive woman, so I automatically applied my own, preferred, interpretation to what was, as I've said, a completely unbelievable story. People change their names for all kinds of reasons, and I had several other clients over the years who did it. But Amy was the first, and the reasons she gave were so absurd I just couldn't buy it. Now," he said sympathetically to Snow, "I finally know the true reason."

"She was clever and careful." Deciding they might have overstayed their welcome, she said, "We should be going. We've taken up a lot of your time."

"Oh, no. Not at all."

Did he look disappointed that they were going? Snow wondered.

At the door, he held her hand warmly in both of his, and said, "I wish you good luck. If you do learn who she was, would you let me know, satisfy an old man's curiosity?"

"You're not old," she said, looking into the clear green depths of his eyes. "I'll definitely let you know. Thank you for seeing us."

He shook hands with Katie, said good-bye, smiled a last time at Snow, then gently closed the door.

The elevator came. Katie stepped inside, and Snow said, "Wait for me. Hold the elevator," and ran back to Ambrose's door.

When he opened it, she broke into a sweat again, and in a low voice said, "Could I buy you dinner tonight?"

His luminous eyes fixed on hers for several seconds. "It's not necessary."

"I know that. But I'd like to. Unless you're busy."

"No, I'm not busy."

"Okay. Seven o'clock at Le Paradis?"

He tilted his head slightly to one side, and with a smile said, "You have good taste. Seven o'clock."

"Great! I'll make a reservation and see you there." She raced back to where Katie was holding the elevator and slid inside.

"What was that about?" Katie asked.

Dripping wet inside her clothes, Snow dropped her head and laughed breathlessly. "I can't believe I did that. I cannot *believe* I did that!"

"What'd you do?"

"I asked him out to dinner."

"No way!" Katie's eyes went wide.

"I did. I'm meeting him at Le Paradis at seven."

"Well, blow me down! Le Paradis. We're talking about a three-hundred-dollar dinner here. This is serious. We'd better go buy you something to wear." Katie stopped and gaped at her. "I could tell you liked him but, wow. This is major. It's not like a father thing or anything, is it?"

"Very definitely not." Snow raised her head, still very flushed. "He's so..." She rolled her eyes, unable to find appropriate words. "I know he's at least twenty years older than I am, but I don't care. He's so *lonely,* Katie. Could you feel it? I could. He was having a good time with us, and I got the feeling he doesn't have a good time very often. Lately, neither do I. And you said it yourself, he's gorgeous."

"Yes, he is. He's a nice man," she declared judiciously. "But what about Wonder Dummy, and Broder?"

"Katie, I'm not going to *marry* him. I just want to get to know him."

"Okay. But promise me you won't sleep with him on the first date."

Snow laughed. "I will *not* promise you that."

The elevator doors parted and they walked out through the lobby, past the concierge, without speaking. Once on the street, Katie grabbed her arm, and let out a wild laugh. "You are a very naughty girl. A *very* naughty girl."

"I'm afraid I am," Snow said, laughing with her.

"Too great." Katie looped her arm through Snow's. "Let's go get you something divine to wear." She giggled, squeezed Snow's arm against her side, and said delightedly, "You naughty, naughty girl."

Twenty-Six

The secretary had a voice that had been sculpted from ice, and an abruptness that was, Snow suspected, intentionally off-putting.

"Who are you with?" the woman asked.

"I'm not with anyone. My name is Snow Devane and I'd like to talk to Ms. Sinclair about a personal matter."

"In reference to what?"

"Look, it's complicated. Could you please tell her I want to talk to her about Amy Linn Decker?"

"Who?"

"Amy Linn Decker. I'm sure she'll want to talk to me. Would you please just tell her that?"

"Hold!" The line clicked abruptly into silence.

"Jesus!" Snow muttered.

"What?" Katie asked from across the room.

"The secretary's so rude. I'm on hold. Daniel wasn't kidding. Getting to this woman might turn out to be impossible."

She heard the distinctive sound of a receiver being picked up on the other end, and then, to her great surprise, a cautious voice said, "Betsy Sinclair here. Who did you say you are?"

"Ms. Sinclair, my name is Snow Devane. I'd like very much to talk to you about Amy Linn Decker. I understand you were childhood friends."

"What is your interest in Amy?" she asked suspiciously. "Tell me your name again!" she demanded in one of those old New York accents—all elongated vowels and crisp consonants—that sounded almost British.

"Snow Devane."

"Are you that unfortunate young woman who's been all over the media recently?"

"Yes, I am."

"A fascinating and terrible story. You have my sympathies. But why have you come to me about Amy Linn?" The suspicion was coupled now with confusion.

"I've been led to believe she was the woman I knew as my mother."

"And who, might I ask, has led you to believe that?"

"We managed to trace her back to the stockbroker here in the city who handled her investments back in the late fifties and early sixties."

"And he knew her as Amy Linn Decker."

"Yes."

"This is bewildering, to say the least."

"I know that. If you could spare a few minutes of your time I'd be able to explain more fully."

"Just a moment, please." The woman covered the receiver with her hand. It merely muffled her exchange with the frosty secretary. "What have I got down for tomorrow morning?" Snow heard her say. Whatever the secretary said was indecipherable. Betsy Sinclair uncovered the mouthpiece and said, "Tomorrow morning at nine forty-five. I can give you half an hour. Do you know the address?"

"Yes."

"Good. We'll talk then." The woman put down the phone.

"What?" Katie asked, seeing the look of near amazement on Snow's face.

"I'm still trying to get over her being listed in the phone book."

"This is New York, babe. *Everybody's* in the book. What did she *say?*"

"She'll see me at nine forty-five tomorrow morning."

"All *right!*" Katie jumped up and threw a fist into the air. "We're finally starting to cook here. Fantastic!"

"I'd like you to come with me, for moral support."

"Absolutely. We'll have to dress for this, you know. We can't go see Betsy Sinclair looking anything but establishment."

"I'll find something." Snow checked the time, and said, "If I hurry, I can meet Julia after school. You won't mind if I take off, will you?"

"Nope. I'll walk to the subway with you. Are you excited? I am. We're very close to getting some answers."

"I'm not so sure about that. She sounded very suspicious, almost spooked."

"But you got her on the phone, and she's agreed to see you. You're more than halfway there."

"I don't know." There'd been shock in the woman's voice, and something else Snow couldn't identify. It might have been horror. But surely it couldn't have been that. Why not, though? If a childhood friend turned out to be a kidnapper, wouldn't she sound horrified? "Maybe Betsy Sinclair was one of the people Anne... Amy... got in touch with whenever she came to New York. Maybe Betsy never knew her friend had changed her identity and was living a whole other life. If that was the case, she'd be shocked because she'd have had no way of knowing her friend had died."

"There's all kinds of possibilities," Katie said. "I happen to think we're going to get a bunch of answers from this woman."

"I hope you're right," Snow said guardedly. She'd been lucky once; it had been very easy to find her mother. But everything to do with Anne Cooke had dead-ended. There was no reason to believe this wouldn't be another dead end. Yet it was hard not to be infected by Katie's enthusiasm.

Since the press conference, people had been recognizing her—on the street, in the subway, in the corner deli, just about everywhere. Some had simply smiled; some had actually stopped to wish her well; and some had gawked, making her uncomfortable. She was anxious for the story to become old news, so she could return to traveling the city streets anonymously.

As before, a clutch of mothers was waiting outside the school. She spotted Clemence and went over to say hello. The woman took hold of her by the shoulders, kissed her on both cheeks, and said, "So much drama you are having. But you are happy, eh?"

"Yes, I am."

"Julia will be wild to see you are here. You stay, and I go home to make the dinner. Yes?"

"You don't mind?"

The woman smiled and said, "You stay to wait. And after your visit, you bring Julia home. You wish to dine with us?"

"I'm afraid I can't tonight. But thank you."

"Another time, eh?"

"Yes. I'd love it."

"Good. *Au 'voir, chère.*"

"Bye, Clemence."

After the housekeeper left, one of the mothers approached. With an uncertain smile, she said, "It is you, isn't it?" Snow nodded, and the woman said, "I thought so. I just want to tell you I watched the press conference on TV and cried my heart out. It was so good to see something upbeat for a change, instead of the usual film of carnage. I'm really happy for you and your mother."

"That's very kind. Thank you."

Just then the school bell rang. The woman said, "I'd better get back to my post. Good luck," and went to stand near the door to wait for the children to emerge.

Julia came through the doors, arm in arm and deep in conversation with a friend. Glancing up, she saw Snow, excitedly cried, "Hey, hi!" and, dragging her friend by the arm, came running over. She threw her arms around Snow's waist and hugged her, then giddily said, "This is my friend, Maddie. Maddie, this is Snow, I was telling you about."

Tall for her age, with a short boyish haircut and brown eyes owlish behind thick-lensed glasses, the girl was achingly shy. Looking indirectly at Snow, she murmured, "Hi," and then gazed at the ground, almost whispering as she told Julia, "I've gotta go. My mom's taking me shoe shopping."

"Okay," Julia said. "See ya later."

Keeping her head lowered, she said, "Bye," then turned and went off down the street.

"She's very shy," Julia said, watching her friend go.

"I could tell."

"Yeah?" Julia regarded her for a moment as if deliberating whether or not to pursue the subject, then said, "I'm so glad you came. I was hoping you would. Where's Clem?"

"She went home to start dinner. I promised to walk you home."

"Okay, great."

"Ever had a lime Coke?" Snow asked, taking the girl's delicate hand, touched by the eagerness with which it wrapped itself around hers.

"No. Sounds weird."

"It isn't. Want to try one?"

"You mean now?"

"Yup."

"Sure."

"Good. I think you'll like it."

"You gonna meet me after school from now on?"

"Sometimes, when I can," Snow said, and in answering realized she wasn't going to leave the city. She was unaware of having made the decision, but thought it was logical. After all, her career was here, and her friends. And it probably wasn't any better or worse than any other major city. Once she found somewhere nicer to live her take on urban life would probably improve.

"Did your mom go home?" Julia asked.

"Uh-hunh. Yesterday afternoon."

"Are you sad she went?"

"A little."

"Yeah, that's what I thought." She was quiet for a minute or so, then asked, "Am I still supposed to call you Snow?"

"Sure."

"But on TV everybody called you Victoria."

"I know. But my friends and all the people in the town where I grew up know me as Snow, so I guess from now on I'll be Victoria to some people, and Snow to others."

Julia nodded earnestly. "That makes sense." Again she fell quiet, and walked along at Snow's side, thinking. Then, she asked, "Are you gonna marry my dad?"

Thrown, for a moment Snow groped for an appropriate answer. Stopping, she dropped down to be at eye level with the girl, and said, "Your dad and I are just friends, Jule. We hardly know each other."

"Oh."

"My friendship with you is something separate from the one I have with your dad. Can you understand that?"

"I guess. But now I feel really dumb. I went and told the wrinklies you were gonna be my mom."

"Who are the *wrinklies?*" Snow asked, bemused.

"That's what me and Dad and Max and Leo call Papa and Nonno."

"They're your grandparents?"

"Yeah."

"Why d'you call them that?" Snow asked with a laugh.

"I don't know. We just do. They phoned from Florida last night and I told them all about you. They'll think I'm stupid."

"Don't worry about it. I'm sure they'll understand. And next time you talk to them, you can explain that we're friends."

"I guess. It's just that I wanted . . ."

"I know, sweetheart. I'd like to be your mom, too. Sometimes things just can't be the way we'd like them. So we have to be satisfied with the way they are. And I'm hoping you and I will be friends for a long, long time."

"Me, too."

"Would it be okay if I give you a hug and a kiss?" Julia indicated it was and Snow gathered the girl in her arms, held her close for a few seconds, then kissed her cheek and said, "It's good to see you."

"It's good to see you, too."

"I like you with your hair down. You look like a little princess."

"You always try to make me feel good," Julia said half-accusingly.

"You have a problem with that?"

"No. I guess not." They started walking again and Julia asked, "What's in a lime Coke anyway?"

Snow laughed and gave her hand a squeeze. "Lime syrup and Coca Cola. I guarantee you'll love it."

Julia looked up at Snow adoringly and said, "If you like it, I will, too."

It was as if the outer layer of her flesh had been peeled away, leaving her dangerously exposed. Her senses were in chaos. In the grip of an immense hunger, she was attempting to consume the tenderly ardent Daniel Ambrose, to swallow him whole. And if she opened just a bit farther, tightened her grip on him more, then more, she might actually manage to merge with him, becoming a single unit. Crazy. A panic in the exposed tissues. She was liquefying with the effort, yet possessed of superhuman strength. Fine steel cords had replaced her tendons and ligaments; her joints were composed of shiny polished bearings revolving smoothly in perfectly oiled housings. She felt a desperation of giving, a ravenous yielding. With a pinpoint focus on a driving rhythm in equatorial heat, she thought the soul could actually leave the body in circumstances like these. It might drift off and hover overhead, waiting either to be reclaimed or forgotten. The heart might simply give out and quit in such a climate. Hers felt as if it might, laboring so strenuously to send blood rocketing through her veins and arteries.

The air was too thin and her exhalations were short, jagged, galvanized sounds, unrecognizable to her but suggestive of some mythic bird that could soar but had no capacity for song. For the first time, as a direct result of her overpowering attraction to this

man and his affectionate responses, she felt that her body was a remarkable and perfect entity, lithe and adaptable and capable of
astonishing feats. It writhed, dancing in turbulent pleasure as her
soul made a final massive and savage effort to tear itself free, then
fell back, quivering, into its cage.

She rested inside the circle of Daniel's arm, her head on his
shoulder, her body turned inward alongside his; warm where they
touched and cool where they didn't, as if the world was temporarily at her back, safely distant. Contented, she listened to the night
sounds rising from the city streets below, thinned and tinny and
constant, and to the soft, even cadence of his breathing. The room
was dark except for a slant of light angling past the partly open
bathroom door, but her eyes had long since adjusted and she could
see to the far corners of the room.

She thought about the brief conversation she'd had with her
mother that morning. She very much liked Patricia MacKenzie.
Perhaps if they'd had thirty years together, she might not have
cherished each exchange of words and thoughts to the extent she
did. Familiarity would doubtless have layered a level of exasperation, however mild, atop their communications because, as Katie
had so rightly pointed out, it was the norm with parents and children. It came as a result of overexposure to the best and worst
qualities in everyone involved; but it had no place in her relationship with Patricia, and likely never would. They had come to one
another as adults and strangers, with a blood bond that now could
only be broken by death. And that was, with luck, a long ways off.

Daniel shifted slightly and she realized he'd fallen asleep. Taking
care not to disturb him, she sat up and fondly studied his well-
formed features in repose. During dinner he'd told her about his
first wife, a woman he'd loved, who'd died, after two anguished
years of suffering, at the age of forty; he'd told her about his second wife, a thin glittery creature, who'd had an interest primarily
in acquiring expensive things. Insensitive was what he'd called her,
with a fair degree of upset still. He'd leapt too quickly into the
marriage hoping to recreate some of the closeness that had existed
between himself and his first wife only to discover he'd exchanged
vows with someone who had no emotional depth. He'd actually
used those words during dinner. And that was when Snow had
reached over to take hold of his hand, unspeakably moved by him,
and by the understanding that everyone, except for the very young,
was a citizen of the territory of loss.

The illuminated face of the digital clock on the bedside table showed ten-fifty. She eased off the bed, picked up Dan's apple-fragrant shirt and put it on, gratified by the scent and feel of the fine cotton and the illusion of closeness to him it provided. Tiptoeing barefoot, she peered into darkened rooms until she found the right one, turned on the light, and stood smiling. Katie had been right. Here on his desk and on the wall above it were the framed diplomas and family photographs; here were the books and mementos, the stereo and a collection of primarily classical CDs; the Eames chair and ottoman; and a twenty-four-inch TV set on a sturdy oak stand with a VCR underneath. This room, perhaps fourteen by eighteen, was the real home of Daniel Ambrose. This was where, on a shelf in the bookcase, he kept a dozen or so tennis trophies, and, on another shelf, the books that reflected his interest in seashells and sailing and fiction. On the table beside the arm-chair were three recently published novels, a leather-bound book of Blake's poetry, a pipe rack and a canister of tobacco.

On impulse, she sat down in the chair—upholstered in a soft brown leather—picked up the canister and removed the lid to breathe in the aroma of a wonderfully fragrant tobacco. She had her eyes closed and her face almost submerged in the opening of the jar when, with a chuckle, Daniel said, "I take it you like the tobacco?"

"I love it," she admitted, returning the canister to the table. "And I love this room." He had on an egg-yolk yellow terry-cloth robe and was leaning in the doorway with his arms folded across his chest, looking as if it pleased him to see her ensconced in his chair, in his inner sanctum.

"It's the only room in the entire apartment I can stand. I think the decorator secretly despised me, and was challenging me to stop her. Of course I didn't. I've always been a little intimidated by women."

"Really?"

His smile widened. "Really. How about something to drink? We could investigate the mysteries of the kitchen. I'm also intimidated by gadgets and appliances. I use the microwave oven as a shelf."

"Okay." She laughed and climbed out of the chair, letting him lead her by the hand through the apartment.

He had no territorial imperatives and was happy to sit at the old pine table in the big kitchen while she plugged in the kettle and set about making tea. Waiting for the kettle to boil, she hoisted herself up onto the edge of the counter, asking, "What do you do with yourself now that you're retired?"

"I play tennis several times a week. I travel. I've got a boat at my place in Florida. This and that. I keep busy."

"My mother lives in Key West."

"Ah. My place is in Sarasota. Do you know Florida?"

"No."

"Sarasota's south of St. Petersburg, on the Gulf side. The house is nice, nothing like this place. I should never have let that woman get away with what she did. I keep promising myself I'll get rid of all that awful stuff and start again, but somehow I never get around to it. I don't spend that much time here anymore."

"It's a great apartment. Huge."

"It's definitely that. We bought it more than thirty years ago, when Joan and I thought we'd be having a bunch of kids." He looked over at the doorway as if expecting to see someone there. Returning his eyes to her after a moment, he said, "There's no future to this. I'm fifty-eight, you know."

"My concept of the future's undergone some radical changes in the past couple of weeks. I think now it's a mistake to worry about what might be instead of concentrating on right now. Let me ask you something. How old is your heart?"

"Oh, at least a hundred."

She smiled. "And how old is your brain?"

"Sixteen." He now smiled.

"And if you believe in something as nebulous as a soul, how old would you say yours is?"

"If learning through experience is your measure, I'd have to say five or six hundred years."

"See? It's an entirely elastic concept, age. I recently had a year taken off my age. I'm getting to be thirty twice. But it's only a number, isn't it? My brain is eighteen, which makes me older than you. Anyway, I'm not concerned with the future. I like you very much right now."

Leaning chin on hand, he said, "You're lovely. Do you know that? No, I don't think you do. It's probably better that way. People who think they're lovely have a terrible tendency to be vain, which ruins the loveliness. I like you very much, too, right now."

The kettle came to a boil and shut itself off. She slipped down from the counter, saying, "I could tell. You have a very nice way of showing how much you like someone. Do you see a lot of women?"

"Not a lot. I'm forever being introduced to winsome widows and charming divorcées, but I prefer to make my own choices."

"Me, too." She poured water into the teapot. "But you wouldn't have asked me to dinner, even though you wanted to. Would you? Because you've got this age hang-up."

"That's right."

"We'd have missed out on getting to know each other. And that would've been sad. Don't you think?"

"Yes, it would've been."

"So, now we will. Get to know each other. And the future will happen as it happens. In the meantime, maybe I could help you turn this apartment into someplace livable."

"Would you like to do that?"

"I'd love to."

"Don't you want to be married and have children?"

"I don't know, Daniel. Maybe. Right now it doesn't seem as important as just talking to you. I'll figure it out eventually." She poured the tea and brought the cups over to the table, set them down, then did what she'd wanted to do that morning at breakfast. She straddled his lap, wrapped her arms around him, and kissed him gently on the outer corner of each eye. "There's time for all kinds of things."

Twenty-Seven

She felt faintly debauched as she emerged from the cab in the clothes she'd worn the night before. Just past seven and she was clad in what Katie called "the basic little black dress" and low-heeled black patent shoes, both from their shopping expedition to Sak's. It was a relief to find that there was no one from the media waiting outside. She paid the driver and, after a quick look up and down the street to see if Irene might be in the vicinity, she hurried into the building.

The loft had a gauzy sort of atmosphere created by the pale early-morning light shining through a sea of suspended dust particles. The place had an empty, almost abandoned, feel to it, and she stood in the doorway for a time thinking, letting her eyes travel over the space as if she were studying an exhibit in a museum. It felt as if she'd been gone for years, and she was oddly averse to enter and thereby break the silence. But a need to shower and change prevailing, at last she did.

Standing naked on the bath mat, waiting for the water to run warm, she was actually reluctant to wash the residue of Daniel Ambrose from her skin. Unlike every other sexual encounter she'd ever had, this one had been unusually satisfying, both for her body and her brain. She had, for the first time, chosen to be with a man, not because of his ultimate unavailability or because, through him, she might inflict some degree of pain upon herself and, therefore, indirectly upon her mother, but because she truly cared for him. And she'd been truthful with him, and with herself—another first. The events of the past two weeks had proved to her the importance of living squarely in the present, finding what was best in each day's offering. She had discovered it was vital not to defer anything until a possibly more propitious time might present itself, because there was too real a probability that such a time might never come. As a result, she was responding to situations with more immediacy than ever before, and was finding that the barriers that had existed between herself and others had been, for the most part, erected by her. The majority came down with surprising ease once she could see why she'd put them up in the first place.

It took a while to assemble an outfit suitable for the meeting with Betsy Sinclair, but she managed to unearth a pair of charcoal gray slacks that required only a quick pressing, and a not-too-shabby pair of loafers. Hair neatly pulled back, with a white button-down shirt and her old tweed jacket, she would, she decided, look presentable.

After getting the coffee started, she went to check her messages.

"Hi, Snow, it's Joseph. We'd like you to come for dinner one night next week, if you've got an evening free. Call when you get a chance and let me know when would be good for you. Hope everything's going well and, by the way, Jule was thrilled you came to meet her after school yesterday. I think you know how much I love my girl, and you're working small miracles with her. So please understand that I mean it when I say thank you. Come to dinner and make both of us happy. Talk to you soon. Bye."

"Hi, it's Mark. I know you're probably run off your feet, but I'd really like to talk when you get a minute. I can't stop thinking about you, and I miss you—a lot. Could we maybe have dinner together one night this week? Please try to slot me in. Okay?"

"Hello, it's your mother. It feels so incredibly good to say that. It's your mother calling." She laughed and it echoed as if her voice were traveling through an actual underwater tunnel spanning the Atlantic. "I thought about you through the entire flight, and it was like a dream. From one minute to the next it's hard to believe it's all over, no more waiting and wondering. You're back, I'm a mother again. You have a life, and friends, and a home of your own. I must sound mentally defective but I find it all staggering. So. I just got up to my room and I'm going to take a bath, then grab a nap before I head over to the gallery. But I had to call to say I'm so happy and I hope you are, too. I love you and I'll talk to you in the next day or so. Take care of yourself, sweetheart. Bye for now."

"This is Dan. I just got back upstairs after seeing you into the cab, and I wanted to say two things. First, last night was delightful. It's the first time in a long, long while that I've enjoyed someone else's company quite so much. Thank you again for the dinner, and all the rest of it. Second, in the harsh light of morning, this place is even uglier than I thought, with all the warmth and charm of an abattoir." He chuckled. "So, if you were serious about helping me redo it, I'd like to take you up on that offer. I'm very attached to this apartment, and right now it's sort of like looking at a good friend who bought a bad toupee and I haven't had the heart or the guts to say so. I'm looking forward to seeing you again very soon, my dear."

A uniformed domestic came to the door, but before she had a chance to say a word, a woman in her early sixties and well over six feet tall appeared in the doorway of the room to the left of the foyer. "It's all right, Jean," she said in the gravelly voice Snow recognized from their brief telephone conversation. "I'm expecting the young lady." Her manner austere, she said, "You'd better come in," but made no move from the doorway.

"I appreciate your taking the time to see me," Snow said, looking into hazel eyes slightly narrowed with suspicion. "This is my friend, Katie Shimura. She's been helping me with the search."

Betsy Sinclair said, "Come along," and turned, expecting them to follow her into an exquisitely furnished sitting room. The walls were painted burnt orange and the wood trim a glossy white; chintz fabric on the overstuffed chairs and sofa, highly polished antique tables, the top of one bearing a collection of photographs in antique silver frames; a grouping of oil paintings on one wall, and a pair of immensely healthy Boston ferns on white-painted pedestals either side of the bay windows; an old silk-on-silk Chinese carpet, and porcelain lamps with white silk shades. Unlike its owner, the room was most welcoming, its furnishings chosen with love and superb taste.

Betsy Sinclair said, "Sit down," as she settled in the wing chair near the fireplace, took a cigarette from a crystal jar on the adjacent table, and lit up. "I smoke. If it bothers you, I really don't care. What I do in my own home, I do without apology."

"Good for you," Katie said automatically, wondering if the woman was this abrupt as a matter of course or whether she was pissed off with them specifically. And if she was pissed off, why had she asked Snow to come here in the first place?

"You're a smoker?" she asked Katie, making to offer the crystal jar to her.

"Former," Katie explained.

Snow was absorbing details, noting the somewhat masculine lines of Betsy Sinclair's profile, which was artfully softened by thick, steel gray hair shaped into a loose twist. She admired the woman's impeccably cut black suit, the slim length of her carefully crossed legs, the several lustrous strands of pearls around her neck and the diamond pin on the suit collar. She wore a pair of diamond eternity bands on the middle finger of her right hand and an impressive Art Deco platinum and diamond bracelet on her left wrist. Snow was fascinated by the woman's patrician bearing, and spent several moments considering how she'd light and pose her for a portrait. Then, realizing their time was strictly at a premium and that this woman was someone who, as Anne Cooke/Amy Linn Decker might have said, did not suffer fools gladly, she came quickly to the point.

"Daniel Ambrose, who was my mother's stockbroker at Compton Gale for a period of five years, told me the two of you were childhood friends, and that you had referred her to the brokerage. Since you've read about what happened, you'll realize that this was the woman I knew as my mother. I was hoping perhaps you could tell me about her."

"Let me be quite sure I've got this right. You say this Ambrose person claimed he knew this woman as Amy Linn Decker?" Betsy Sinclair's eyes once again narrowed.

"That's right," Snow answered, feeling cowed by the woman's coldness and obvious skepticism.

"And did he happen to say just when it was that she came to him as a client?"

"Nineteen fifty-eight, I think he said." Snow looked to Katie for confirmation and support.

"That's right," Katie agreed, puzzled by Betsy Sinclair's scathing tone and patent disbelief. "Fifty-eight."

"I find that nothing short of astonishing!" the woman declared, glowering now as twin streams of smoke snorted from her nostrils.

"Why?" Snow asked softly, having rarely felt more ill at ease.

"I'll tell you why!" she snapped, twisting in the chair to extinguish her cigarette in angry jabs. Turning to face them again, she sat up even straighter, squared her wide shoulders, and said, "This Mr. Ambrose was quite correct insofar as the fact that Amy Linn and I were indeed childhood friends. But not only have I never heard of Compton Gale and so could not have recommended anyone to their services, Amy Linn could not possibly have been his client in 1958 for the simple reason that Amy Linn was killed in an automobile accident in 1949."

In the shocked silence that followed this declaration, Snow understood why the woman had sounded the way she had on the telephone. Her childhood friend had been dead for years. Snow stared at the woman then lowered her eyes, feeling as if she'd stepped, all unknowing, into the elevator shaft of a high rise and was plummeting through a narrow black space with no hope of being rescued. Katie had been wrong: Anne Cooke had been very, *very* smart, and neither of them was going to be able to outwit her after the fact. Suddenly, she knew without doubt that they were never going to be able to unravel the past and pin an accurate identity on her mother.

Katie's mouth had fallen open and she sat gaping at Betsy Sinclair.

Seeing the effect her pronouncement had on these two young women bothered Betsy Sinclair. She disliked upsetting people, and had been in a state of acute apprehension since the telephone call the previous day, suspecting—incorrectly, it now appeared—that some sort of underhanded scheme lay behind this visit.

Taking advantage of the silence to study the young redhead, she felt increasingly guilty at having been so abrupt since their arrival, and at having stated the facts so baldly. The young woman was grieving. Betsy knew the signs all too well—the slightly glazed aspect to the eyes, as if the body had sustained a blow but the pain was taking a long time to make itself felt, and the subtle inward curve to the shoulders, as if in anticipation of additional blows. "It happened when the family was spending the summer at their home in Maine," she continued, her tone less biting. "I was visiting Amy Linn at the time, so there can't possibly be any mistake."

"I'm sorry," Snow said, believing she and Katie had reached only one more of many dead ends to come, and saddened that this woman had lost her friend. Everybody she encountered had suffered inestimable losses. She wiped her face with the back of her hand. Her mother would've been horrified at how frequently she was publicly revealing her miseries these days.

"Why on earth should you be sorry?" Betsy was feeling worse by the moment.

"Because you loved her, and you've had to live all these years without her. I just imagine something happening to Katie and I start to lose it, so I know it must've been awful for you." A tear trickled down the side of her nose and Snow impatiently rubbed it away.

Her voice and manner both softened now, Betsy said, "Amy Linn was only eighteen when she died. It was a terrible blow to everyone, but especially to me. She was my dearest friend, you see. We were as close as sisters." She paused and stared at the spot where Katie's hand had come to rest on Snow's arm, then sighed and lit another cigarette, sinking back into the chair. "I still think of her often. There are occasions when I actually go to pick up the telephone, thinking to call her. Nothing has ever had quite the impact Amy Linn's death had. Nothing." She paused again and drew hard on the cigarette. "It would appear that the woman masqueraded not only as your mother but also as Amy Linn. It's so monstrous I simply don't know how to react. Part of me is just furious at the cruelty of it, and another part is utterly mystified. When my secretary said you were calling about Amy Linn, I felt for a moment as if I were having some sort of seizure. There are very few people left, you see, who still remember her."

"I don't know how to react to it, either," Snow said, her chest aching as if she'd been kicked there.

Keeping her head in spite of a disappointment that was all the worse for having been so certain they were on the brink of uncovering Anne Cooke's true identity, Katie asked, "Would you mind looking at a couple of photographs, Ms. Sinclair? Maybe you'd recognize this woman."

"I wouldn't mind," Betsy said, regarding Snow a moment longer before turning to prop her cigarette on the lip of the ashtray.

Moving like an automaton, Snow got the envelope from her bag and crossed the room to give it to the woman, who put a hand on her wrist, keeping her in place as she said, "I found the story of your being reunited with your mother particularly touching, Miss Devane. I never knew my own mother, you see. She died when I was less than a year old, and I grew up alone in this house with my father, and the staff of course. He was a busy man who had no gift for dealing with children. So it was a very lonely existence until Amy Linn came into my life when we were both seven. Reading the story

I felt a certain . . . kinship, I suppose, with you. I hope you'll forgive my rudeness at the outset of this meeting, but I've always been what some would call 'a soft touch,' and experience has taught me the hard way to be cautious. I should have realized your intentions were strictly honorable.''

"It's all right, Ms. Sinclair. I understand." Unable to say more for the moment, Snow waited quietly until her wrist was released, then she sat down again, hoping against all odds that Betsy Sinclair would recognize the woman in the photographs, the mother without an identity whose loss she still felt so keenly.

Betsy Sinclair studied each photograph carefully for a time, then retrieved her cigarette and shook her head, saying, "It's ludicrous, but even though I was at my friend's funeral, I was actually hoping that somehow, miraculously, it would turn out that Amy Linn hadn't died. But of course she did. I have never seen this woman before in my life and have absolutely no idea who she might be. She most definitely is *not* Amy Linn." Reaching into the cluster of silver-framed photographs, she gazed at one for several moments with sad affection before picking it up and passing it over to Snow. "This was my darling Amy Linn."

With Katie leaning over to look, the two saw a dark-haired teenager in tennis whites grinning into the camera, her arm around the waist of her much taller friend who'd been caught looking off into the distance. The smaller girl was very beautiful, with dark glowing eyes, an aquiline nose, high slanting cheekbones and a full mouth. Along with having been at least six inches taller, she bore no resemblance whatever to Anne Cooke. "She was lovely," Snow said, hearing an echo of Daniel's voice as she returned the photograph to Betsy Sinclair who sat looking again at her lost best friend.

Katie cleared her throat and said, "It seems pretty obvious that Anne Cooke was in the habit of stealing the IDs of dead people."

"It would appear so," Betsy concurred, both of them turning to Snow who was staring fixedly at the carpet, deep in thought. "Miss Devane—" Snow looked up "—you've obviously had a very difficult time of it recently, and I know I haven't helped make it any easier."

Snow said, "No, you've been very fair. It's just that I want so badly to find out who that woman was, to understand why she did what she did."

"I'm sure you do. I would, too." Betsy Sinclair studied her large, square hands for a few seconds, as if debating with herself. Then she looked again at Snow and said, "I have a confession to make. Since you telephoned yesterday I had my secretary do some research on you. It seems you're a very gifted photographer. Now, I don't want you to think I'm attempting to offer you some sort of consolation prize, but I've been trying to find someone to photograph my grandchildren for quite some time, and I would like to commission you to do that. Would you be interested?"

Katie's heart jumped. An endorsement from this woman would bring Snow a whole parade of important clients. Say yes! she willed silently. She's doing something major for you, babe. Say yes!

Snow looked over at the wealthy and powerful woman seated opposite, seeing in the well-set hazel eyes kindness and a sincere desire to atone for her earlier incivility. "I'd be happy to," Snow said. "But on one condition."

"Oh, yes? And what might that be?" Betsy inquired. Her guard going up again, she took a hard drag on her cigarette.

Snow couldn't begin to imagine what kind of scams people had pulled on this woman over the years to turn her so guarded. But the fact that she was aroused Snow's sympathy. "I'll do it no charge, if you'll allow me to photograph you, as well. I know how busy you are, the kinds of demands that are made on your time. The thing is, you didn't have to see me but you did. I'd like to show my appreciation by doing portraits of you and your grandchildren."

Taken aback, Betsy Sinclair smiled for the first time and the person who was the "soft touch" was revealed. "I'm accustomed to people hounding me, wanting things—usually money. I rarely encounter people with generous natures, probably because they tend not to want or need anything from me. I accept your offer. But I, too, have one condition."

Snow smiled. "What?"

"I'd prefer to have you come here for the sitting, rather than the children and I coming to you. For reasons of security."

"It won't be a problem. Have your secretary call me at the beginning of the week and we'll set up an appointment for a time that's convenient for you. Now I think Katie and I should be going."

Snow left her card. Betsy shook hands with Katie. And Snow, acting on impulse for a second time in as many days, embraced the woman, gratified when she emphatically hugged her back, stating, "You're a woman after my own heart. I'll look forward to seeing you again soon."

* * *

"Well, shit!" Katie exclaimed as they headed back along East 62nd toward Madison. "I was so sure we had the whole thing nailed. What a downer!"

"We're at the end of the paper trail. All that's left is the safe deposit box."

"And the fake IDs. Don't forget those."

"I'm not, but I've got a hunch they're not going to lead anywhere, except to headstones in cemeteries."

"Maybe, and maybe not. One thing's for sure. We've gone about as far as we can go without some help. And you could hire an investigator, but what've you got for him to go on? *Nada.*"

"There might be something in the box, but I doubt it. If you're up for it, I thought we'd head up to Rhode Island tomorrow. Will you be able to come with me for the weekend?"

"I already told Robbie I'd be going."

"Okay." Snow linked arms with her. "I'll swing by and pick you up early, say eight?"

"Okay. So what'll we do now?"

"I've got a few calls to return, and then I'm not sure. Both Mark and Joseph Broder asked me out to dinner."

"What about the divine Daniel?"

"I told him I was tied up until after the weekend."

"Oh! And what's this with Wonder Dummy? I thought you told me you'd broken off with him."

"I did and I didn't." She shrugged. "We'll see. I'm not committing myself to anyone right now."

"So you're going to see all three of these guys at the same time?"

"Hardly at the same time."

"Come on. You know what I mean."

"Yes, I'm going to see all three of them. Right now there are only a few things I know for certain. I know I'm not going to move away even though I've been hating it here lately. I know I'm going to spend time with Daniel and help him do over that apartment. I know I'm going to see as much of Julia as I can. And I also know I'm going to take a week to go visit my mother in Key West when she gets back from London. You're invited to come with me, my treat. Other than that, I guess what I do will depend to some degree—probably a minor one—on what we find in that box."

"I'm so glad you're going to stay in town. I was scared you'd tell me you were leaving."

"I couldn't go off and leave you. It'd be like having an amputation or something."

"I feel the same way about you, babe. It's funny. When we first got there I thought she was going to chew our heads off. But she turned out to be an okay lady. And, thanks to her, you'll probably become *the* Manhattan society photographer."

Snow shrugged and said, "We'll see. I wouldn't get too worked up about it, if I were you. I don't think she's the kind of person who goes bragging about her latest finds."

"All that has to happen is one of her friends sees you took her picture and that'll be it, I'm telling you. These people run in packs."

"We'll see," Snow said again.

"Hi, Rudy. I just wanted to let you know Katie and I will be coming up tomorrow."

"Good. You planning to stop at the bank first?"

"Uh-hunh. I'm very anxious to see what's in that box."

"How'd you make out with the stockbroker?"

"Katie and I followed up on his lead but ended up hitting a brick wall. We'll fill you in when we see you. Everything okay, Rudy?"

"Everything's fine, Snow. It'll be good to see you. Mrs. Hoover's been wanting to know when you'd be coming, says you owe her a visit."

"She's right. I do. Tell her I promise to come over on Sunday."

"I'll do that. She'll probably bake you a couple of cakes."

Snow laughed. "Probably. See you tomorrow, Rudy. Lots of love."

"You, too, Snow."

"Hi, Broder. How're you doing?"

"Oh, hi. I'm great. How are you doing, Devane?"

"Pretty well."

"Listen, I understand Julia made you a proposal of marriage, and I want to apologize for that."

She laughed. "It's okay. I know it wasn't your idea."

"No. It's just that she's very smitten with you."

"I know, Broder. I'm smitten with her, too. She's only trying to make sure I'm going to stick around. And I am."

"That's good to know. So, how about dinner?"

"Could we make it next week? I have to go up to Stony Point in the morning for a couple of days. But next week is clear."

"Okay. How's Tuesday?"

"Fine. Why don't I meet Julia after school? I'll walk her home, and hang around for dinner."

"Great. I'll tell Jule. And we'll see you Tuesday."

"Hi, Mark. It's Snow. Sorry about not getting back to you sooner."

"That's okay. I know you've been busy. How are you?"

"Fine. How are you?"

"Better and better. Any chance of getting together?"

"Sure. Is next Thursday good for you?"

"Let me just check my diary. Yup. Thursday's good. Why don't I swing by around seven?"

"Good. See you then."

"I'll be looking forward to it."

"Me, too."

"Mr. Compton, it's Snow Devane. I wanted to thank you for putting me in touch with Daniel Ambrose."

"It's good of you to call. Cecilia and I are having dinner tonight with Danny, thanks to you."

"I know. He told me."

"Was he able to help you at all?"

"He identified my mother, but it turned out to be a false lead."

"That's a pity. I know you had your hopes pinned on him."

"It is a pity," she agreed. "There's one last thing to check out and then I may have to concede defeat."

"Will you be able to live with that?" he asked sagely.

"I'll have to, I guess. Anyway, thank you very much for your help."

"My pleasure. Stop in sometime to say hello if you're in the neighborhood."

"I will do that. Goodbye, Mr. Compton."

"Goodbye, Miss Devane."

"Josie, it's Snow."

"*Snow!* How *are* you? It's so great to hear from you. Todd and I have been reading all about it, seeing you on TV, the whole thing. It's unbelievable. You must've been going nuts."

"I was, kind of, which is why I haven't called . . ."

"Don't even *think* about it! It's great you're calling now. Tell me, was it fantastic, meeting your mother after all those years?"

"It really was. She's terrific. We hit it off right away."

"That is *so* cool!"

"I was wondering if you'd like to come for brunch next Sunday. I'm heading up to Stony Point this weekend to wrap up some legal stuff, but I'd really like to see you guys, if Sunday's okay."

"Definitely! Where?"

"Come to the loft. I'll see if Katie and Rob can make it, too."

Josie laughed. "If he makes it, he'll probably fall asleep in his chair."

"Probably, but I haven't seen anybody in forever. So let's say eleven, and I'll try to round up some of the crowd. Okay?"

"Perfect! See you then."

"Daniel, the flowers are fantastic. You didn't have to do that."

"Yes, I did. I'm not accustomed to having women buy me dinner."

"Maybe you'll have to become accustomed to it," she teased. "I definitely intend to take you out again."

"I definitely intend to make myself available. When do you leave for Rhode Island?"

"In the morning. Would you like the Stony Point number?"

"I would."

She gave it to him, then said, "I'll be back sometime Sunday. I'll let you know when. Okay?"

"Good. If it's early enough, we could get together, have dinner."

"I'd love that. Goodbye, Daniel."

The phone calls out of the way, she put on a CD of Tatiana Troyanos and Richard Stilwell singing the title roles in Purcell's *Dido and Aeneas,* then sat down with the *Times* to look through the real-estate listings.

Twenty-Eight

After clearing everything past its "Sell By" date from the refrigerator, she hefted the camera bag and the duffel, and headed downstairs, stopping along the way to dump the trash.

At the garage Mario said, "Hey, Snow. Haven't seen you in a while. How did things work out with your mother?"

For a moment she thought he was referring to Patricia. Then she remembered that the last time he'd seen her she was frantically rushing up to Rhode Island because her mother had suffered a heart attack. Obviously Mario was one of the few people unaware of the recent facts of her life. For some reason, she found this reassuring. "Thanks for asking, Mario. I'm afraid she died that same night."

"Aw, jeez. That's too bad. I'm real sorry. You hold on a minute, I'll bring your car right up." He patted her solicitously on the arm, then jogged off down the ramp.

When he delivered the car, he held open the driver's door for her, saying, "My mom died when I was eleven, so I know how rough it is. You take it easy and drive careful, okay?"

"Thanks, Mario. I will."

On her way to pick up Katie, she drove slowly, looking into doorways on the off chance of spotting Irene. She saw quite a number of homeless souls still asleep here and there, but not Irene.

Katie was waiting out front. She slung her backpack into the rear of the car, slid into the passenger seat, leaned across to give Snow a kiss, then buckled herself in, asking, "Are you nervous? For some reason, I am. Very."

"Yes and no. I think this is going to be our last chance to find out who Anne Cooke was."

"Don't be negative. All the answers could be right there in the box."

Snow chose not to say anything more, and pushed a cassette into the player. After a moment a lively fusion of jazz and chamber music began emerging from the speakers.

"I like this," Katie said. "Is it new?"

Snow shook her head, joining the cars queuing for the on-ramp to FDR Drive. "I've had it for years. It's Claude Bolling's *Suite for Chamber Orchestra and Jazz Piano Trio.* I know you think I'm rigid, but I do listen to other things besides opera."

"I never said you were rigid. Are we grumpy this morning?"

Snow glanced over and smiled. "No, we are not grumpy. I was merely stating a fact. I *was* rigid. But I don't intend to be that way anymore."

"Okay, don't be rigid," Katie said mildly. "Have you eaten?"

"You're hungry. You're always hungry. It's phenomenal. Can you wait a while? There's no place to stop along here."

"I'll tough it out."

They fell silent, listening to the music and watching the increasing flow of morning rush-hour traffic until Snow pulled off into the first rest stop on I-95. After filling the gas tank, Snow parked. They walked into the McDonald's and bought Egg McMuffins and coffee.

"The only time I'll eat these things is when I'm on the highway," Katie said, holding her McMuffin at eye level. "For some reason, they always taste great as road food. Ever notice that? Maybe I'll get a side of hash browns." She put her McMuffin down and dashed back to the counter.

Amused, Snow started eating, taking stock of the others in the restaurant—quite a number of truckers, and an equal number of seniors, a few kids who looked like college students who'd been up for days working on the last of the semester's papers. It was quiet, except for the inevitable Muzak offering a painfully strings-laden instrumental rendition of a k.d. lang song. Katie came hurrying back with the deep-fried wedge of quick-frozen potatoes, then took a big bite and smiled. "Junk is good," she said, her mouth full. "Junk is the soul food of a generation with no soul."

"God! That's profound."

"Grumpy. How are your six brothers?"

Snow laughed. "Can you and Rob come for brunch next Sunday? Josie and Todd are coming."

"Man, I haven't seen them in ages. I'll have to check with Robbie, see what his roster's like. But I'll come for sure. Starting up on your social life again, huh?"

"It's time, wouldn't you say?"

As they were leaving, Snow stopped to look at the "Have You Seen These Children?" poster—three small faces she remembered seeing the night her mother died. So many lost and stolen children.

Katie said, "Come on, babe," and took her arm.

After they'd driven some thirty or forty miles, Snow said, "Thanks for getting me moving back there. I have a lot of trouble with those posters."

"I know. I think most people do. It's kind of too close to home."

"Changing the subject, I spent a lot of time last night looking at real-estate ads and thinking, and I had an idea I'd like to run by you."

"Okay."

"I was thinking, since I plan to buy a decent apartment..."

"You *are?* Good!"

"Yeah. So, I thought the two of us could rework the loft space. If I'm not living there, I won't need the bedroom. The bed could stay, in case it got late and one of us wasn't up to trekking home. But most of the other stuff's only good for the garbage."

"This is true."

"So how would you feel about having a real studio to work in, instead of making do with that second bedroom you've been using at your place?"

"What, you mean share the loft with you?"

"Uh-hunh. We get rid of the junk and reduce the size of the living area, that would give us lots of room. We're talking about sixteen hundred square feet, you know And the light's very good in the part I've been using as a bedroom. The thing is, the lease has another three years to run, and the rent's not bad. The place needs work anyway, and I thought it might be fun to spend a little money and do it up right."

"The only problem is, it's tough coming up with my half of the rent on the apartment every month as it is."

"You wouldn't have to pay me," Snow said quickly. "You'd keep on helping me, so I'd still be paying *you.* Plus you'd finally have a real studio to work in, with room to spread out."

"You're serious?"

"Absolutely!"

"Snow, I would love it! And so would Robbie. He's been whining for three years about how he's got nowhere to work since I took over the second bedroom. He'd be able to move his textbooks and computer back in there, and get them out of the living room. Yes, yes! We could do amazing things with the space. When were you thinking of starting?"

"As soon as I find an apartment, which shouldn't take long, given all the listings that looked interesting in yesterday's paper. Of course I'll have to wait for the insurance money, but that ought to arrive in a matter of weeks. You could help me look."

"Definitely. You're not moving *anywhere* unless I check the place out first, and we'll get my dad to look it over, too. Oh, babe! It's going to be majorly great! I'm so psyched. What would you think about a real color statement, maybe going with a deep red for the walls with a high-gloss white trim? Or a hunter green, even charcoal gray..." Katie was overflowing with ideas.

Snow let her run on, preoccupied with other matters.

Bill Benson had already made arrangements with the bank for Snow to examine the contents of the safe deposit box.

The branch manager escorted Katie and Snow into the vault where he located the box and used both her key and the bank's to remove it from its locked chamber in the wall.

"I'm afraid I must remain with you while you go through the contents, in case there are items inside that could be construed as assets," he explained, directing them into a small room containing a table and two chairs. "For privacy," he said, indicating the two of them should take the chairs; he'd stand.

Perspiring, her hands unsteady, Snow lifted the lid. The box was packed full. Topmost was an envelope filled with cash. Wordlessly, she passed it across the table to the bank manager. Another envelope contained several certificates of deposit, which Katie took from Snow's hand.

"These are in Snow's name," she told the bank officer, "and they're all past their maturity dates, too." The CDs came to a total of two hundred thousand dollars.

"Ah, well, you'll want to hang on to those. Of course, if they were purchased through this bank, I'll be happy to arrange redemption and transfer the funds to your account."

"Thank you, but I'm not sure what I want to do with them," Snow said distractedly.

Where the *hell* had the woman got all her money? Katie wondered, looking over to see what else Snow was finding in the box. She saw a flicker of dismay crease Snow's features as she glanced into several envelopes, one after the other.

Keeping her expression bland, Snow said, "There doesn't seem to be anything more that should be turned over to you," and took a deep breath before pushing the box across the table so that he could see for himself.

The manager made a cursory inspection of the remaining contents, pausing for only a moment to exchange a meaningful look with Snow. "That would appear to be correct," he said, to her tremendous relief. "Did I mention that I saw you on television last week? Quite the story. Yes, well, I see no reason why you shouldn't clear the box. The cash will have to be held here until the estate has cleared probate, but we'll set up an interest-bearing account for you. It shouldn't take long, if you'd both care to wait in my office."

"What was that look you gave each other?" Katie asked in an undertone once they were alone in his office.

"I'll tell you when we get out of here."

After writing her name on signature cards as executor for the estate of Anne Cooke, Snow was given a savings passbook that showed a newly established balance of twenty-five thousand dollars. She thanked the man for his help; he wished her all the best. Then she and Katie walked out into the warm midday sunlight.

Once they were well away from the bank, Snow whispered, "My God, I'm shaking! I was so sure he'd say something. But then, when he said he'd seen me on TV, I knew it was going to be okay."

"Why? What's the matter?"

"Let's go somewhere and sit down and I'll show you. You're not going to like it. I don't, that's for sure, even though I was halfway expecting this."

In a nearby coffee shop, they ordered sandwiches and coffee, and after the waitress had gone, Snow opened her bag, withdrew the items she'd taken from the safe deposit box, and began tipping the contents of the envelopes out onto the tabletop.

Stunned, Katie watched until she stopped, setting the last and largest envelope aside. For a time they both sat staring. Finally, Katie picked up one of the rubber-banded stack of items. There was a passport, a Social Security card, a driver's license and a birth certificate. "These are all in the name of Georgeanne Lever, her date of birth is listed as January 1930, and her place of birth, Harrisburg, Pennsylvania." She reached for another. "This one's in the name of Ruth Olivia Squires, date of birth, April 1929, place of birth, Alamogordo, New Mexico."

Following Katie's lead, Snow slipped the rubber band off one of the packets. "Mary Edna Harding, date of birth, August 1930, place of birth, San Diego, California."

"Alexandra Jane Mortonson, February 1928, Billings, Montana," Katie recited.

"Jean Anne Booker, July 1929, Provo, Utah."

"Kathleen Curran Reed, April 1931, Greenville, South Carolina."

"Agnes Mary Riley, June 1930, St. Paul, Minnesota."

"Dorothy Miller, December 1931, Flagstaff, Arizona."

"Lillian Ruth Farrell, May 1931, Shreveport, Louisiana."

"Lavinia Kaye Brainard, August 1928, Mason City, Iowa."

"Jesus!" Snow let out a dismayed laugh. "It's impossible. There are, what?" She began counting. "Twenty-two different sets of IDs, plus three more, if we include Anne Cooke. Twenty-five identities. I was afraid of this. We are *never* going to find out who she really was."

"Every single one of these expired decades ago," Katie said, going through the passports and licenses. "And some of them date back to the forties. Which means she was collecting false IDs as a teenager. Man! This is unbelievable!"

The waitress arrived with their food. Snow opened her bag and swept the entire collection of IDs into it. Their sandwiches and coffees were placed before them, the waitress left, and Snow found herself staring at nothing, feeling a sick emptiness even though she'd been gearing up for this eventuality since their meeting with Betsy Sinclair.

"What's in that last envelope?" Katie asked.

"I'll look after we eat. I can't take any more for a while."

"Sure. I don't blame you." Katie busied herself adding cream and sugar to her coffee, then watched, nonplussed as Snow slid out of the booth, went to the rear of the restaurant and stopped to talk to the waitress. The waitress said something, ducked down under the counter, reappeared, handed Snow a single cigarette and a pack of matches. Snow thanked her then came striding back to the booth.

"Don't say a word!" she warned. "I don't plan to start smoking again, but right now I need one."

"I won't say a thing," Katie said, and began to eat.

The first inhalation made her so dizzy Snow thought she was going to pass out. Pushing her plate aside, she put her head down on her arms on the table until the dizziness passed.

Katie calmly reached over, plucked the cigarette from between her fingers and put it out, then continued eating. At last Snow sat up and drank some of her coffee. She managed to get down half of the BLT before she gave up and sat cradling her coffee cup in both hands.

"You okay?" Katie asked after the waitress had stopped by to refill their cups.

"I guess. I'll know for sure when I've seen what's in the last envelope."

"I'm ready if you are."

Reaching past the assortment of false documents in her bag, Snow fished out the envelope, opened the flap and peered inside. Feeling sickened, she saw that it contained newspaper clippings, stories about the kidnapping.

"That's all?" Katie asked as Snow set them on the table.

As an afterthought, Snow upended the envelope and gave it a shake. A tiny object fell to the tabletop, and both of them looked at it. Katie reached for it with thumb and forefinger.

"Did your mother say anything about this?" she asked.

Snow shook her head. "There was no mention of it anywhere."

With a fingertip Katie touched the tiny engraved gold identification bracelet sitting in her upheld palm. "It had to be one of those things the cops kept hush-hush because only the kidnapper would know about it and could therefore prove he or she actually had the baby. Except that the kidnapper never made any ransom demand."

"It's all over now," Snow said. "It doesn't matter."

"I don't know why, but seeing this really brings the whole thing home to me. You were a baby, and that crazy woman, whoever the hell she was, stole you from your family. I don't get it. How come you're not nuts? How come you haven't totally lost your mind over this?"

"I don't know," Snow answered. "Maybe I have."

"Excuse me, I think not," Katie argued. She looked again at the bracelet. "V.J.M."

"Victoria Jean MacKenzie," Snow translated.

"I was so sure we'd get some answers from that box," Katie said miserably.

"I knew yesterday that we wouldn't."

"Oh?"

"I just knew."

"You're giving up," Katie accused. "You're forgetting about the Social Security angle, and May Connor, the C.P.A., and maybe other hidey-holes she had Wally Schaefer build."

Snow shook her head. "No, I'm not, Katie. You're not seeing the bigger picture. Even if we got the Social Security records, they'd only show she'd once been Amy Linn Decker who changed her name to Anne Cooke. What neither one of us stopped to consider was the fact that she could just stop paying taxes under one name and start paying under another. I very much doubt there's any kind of mechanism built into the system that would allow the IRS or Social Security to track down people who stop paying and disappear into a new identity—at least not someone with the degree of skill my mother obviously had. I can practically guarantee that if we did find May Connor she'd tell us she knew the woman as Amy Linn Decker. And let's say for the sake of argument we got lucky and found someone who knew her before she became Amy Linn. Tracking backward we'd just find another alias and another and another. There's no way we'd ever get to the end of it. It goes back too far, and there are too many different names. We're going to have to accept that she was smarter than we thought."

"Seems to me, with all those fake IDs, she was some kind of career con artist. Which is probably how she got the money."

"Or maybe she came by the money honestly but just tried on a whole bunch of other people's lives. The only thing we know for sure is that every last one of those IDs belonged to someone who died. And there's no way anyone, not even the best investigator in the world, could possibly figure out her real identity. She didn't want anyone to know, and nobody ever will. It's over, Katie, finished, done."

"Yeah. I'd say you're right. This is yours." Katie took Snow's hand and placed the bracelet in it. "I love you very much, and I'm truly, deeply sorry about everything. Are you going to be able to deal with this?"

"I'm going to have to, aren't I?" Hearing how hard-edged that had sounded, she said, "I'm already dealing with it. I have been since we saw Betsy Sinclair. Come on. Let's get out of here and go see Rudy."

Everyone went quiet when they walked into the Stony Point Café that evening with Rudy. For what felt like an hour, but couldn't have been more than five seconds, all the townspeople present sat looking expectantly at Snow. Then Lucy yelled, "Hey, Red, you're home!" and came barreling out from behind the counter to give her a hearty hug before releasing her to enfold Katie in her embrace. "Grab a booth, you guys," Lucy told them, on her way back to the kitchen. "Be with you in just a sec."

The three of them started for the booth at the far end. But they hadn't gone two steps when Mr. Willard from the pharmacy got to his feet, extending his hand to Snow. "Just wanted to say how glad I am things're working out for you."

"Thank you, Mr. Willard. I appreciate that."

"Got just one question," he said, keeping his voice low. "What're we supposed to call you now?"

Snow looked at him, then surveyed the other familiar faces, all of which were turned toward her: Wally Schaefer and Pete Briggs, together at the counter; Jane Fergus from the boutique having a meal with Lillian, the hairdresser; Mrs. Menzies, the librarian, at a table for one with a book propped up against the sugar shaker; Matt from the marina at a center table with his teenage part-time assistant, Chuck, who was the son of Mr. Innes the bank manager. She knew everyone in the place; had known them all her life. These were her friends, her extended surrogate family. With a laugh, she said,

"To tell you the truth, I don't know what to call me, either. So let's keep it Snow, the same as always. Okay?"

Smiles all around, and a chorus of okays.

Katie and Snow stood barefoot on the beach under a hot August afternoon sun, watching Rudy fit a Mae West on Julia, then lift her into the Bull's-Eye.

"Now remember the rules, honey," Rudy was saying. "You sit nice and still till we're underway. And you don't ever stand up in a boat once it's out on the water. Okay?"

"Okay, Rudy," Julia answered soberly.

"You can turn and look around all you like. You just don't stand up."

"Okay," Julia said again.

He untied the mooring ropes and tossed them in, then stepped nimbly from the dock into the stern. "Got the perfect day for it," he observed to Julia, adjusting his peaked cap before putting a hand to the tiller.

"Perfect," Julia agreed.

The boat drifted away from the shore and Julia lifted a hand to wave, calling, "Bye, Katie. Bye, Snow. See you later!"

Katie and Snow waved, then turned and started back to the house.

"Have you noticed," Snow asked, "she hasn't once referred to Rudy as a wrinkly, even though she refers to every other senior as one?"

"That's because Rudy's position is way beyond that of a mere wrinkly," Katie said. "He's right up there with the Great and Wonderful Oz, and Obi-wan Kenobi. Jule's no dope. She knows the goods when she sees them."

"True. She's only been here three times and she already knows half the people in town by name. Lucy starts fixing a lime Coke the minute she sees Jule come through the café door. She's got Mrs. Hoover whipping up brownies in the dead of night. And Mrs. Menzies can't wait to recommend another book she just knows Jule will love."

Stopping to look around, Katie said, "Don't take this the wrong way, but I think you were lucky, growing up here."

"No, I know what you mean." Shading her eyes with her hand, Snow turned to check the progress of the small sailboat out on the bay. "I know exactly what you mean. And I think I was lucky, too."

Snow grabbed the mail from the box, shoved it directly into her bag, then hurried out into a lightly falling snow. After spending two weeks together over Christmas in the new apartment, she'd seen her mother off at the airport late the previous afternoon, then had driven back into town, turned the Cherokee over to Mario, and took a cab to meet Mark for an early dinner in the Village. After dinner, she'd taken another cab up to Gramercy Park to spend a couple of hours with Daniel, and didn't get home until almost one. She'd fallen into bed, completely forgetting to set the clock, and would've missed this morning's sitting altogether if Katie hadn't had a hinky feeling and called to wake her.

There wasn't a cab in sight, but the subway would be faster. Automatically, she looked at the street people in passing, pushing dollar bills into extended paper cups as she went, searching for Irene, worried. It'd been months since she'd seen her and she was beginning to fear something bad might have happened. Every time she came and went from the loft she took a few minutes to check the alley and nearby doorways, but the woman seemed to have vanished. It scared her; she couldn't stop thinking about her.

Katie had the coffee going and looked pointedly at her watch as Snow came through the door. "Your mad social life is going to do you in, if you don't watch out, kiddo."

"Oh, right!" Snow laughed, bending to remove her boots. "Get serious, please."

"It's a good thing I'm around to look out for you," Katie went on, leaning in the doorway, as Snow hung up her coat, bringing her bag with her to the kitchen. "I called and asked Mrs. Bassett if she'd mind coming half an hour later. So you can relax and have some coffee."

"You're a good girl, Katie Shimura." Snow gave her a kiss on the cheek, then began sorting the mail, stopping to examine an airmail letter with a British stamp.

"What's that?" Katie asked.

"Don't know. I'll save it for last."

Katie poured two cups of coffee and brought them to the table. "So what has the mailman brought? The usual tiresome invitations to charity balls, I suppose?"

"Would you give me a break, please? Betsy Sinclair has invited me to precisely one thing, which happened to be, as you very well know, a fund-raiser for a good cause. Don't try to make out like I'm some social butterfly."

"I saw the Divine Daniel in his tux, and you all tricked out in black velvet, remember. I know whereof I speak."

"Right."

Katie laughed. "So how was dinner with Wonder Dummy?"

"It was fine, thank you," Snow said, setting bills in one pile, junk mail and solicitations in another. "How was dinner with young Dr. Kildare?"

"It's weird living with a guy who has halfway normal office hours, after three years of part-timing it. He wants to get married."

"No way!"

"Yes, way."

"What did you say?"

"I said I'll see."

Snow drank some coffee, then asked, "What brought this on?"

"Oh, probably the death of Peter Rabbit."

Snow stared at her for a moment and then screamed. "*Katie! God!* You're going to be a *mother!* You're going to make me an aunt! I'll have to learn to knit! This is wonderful." She threw her arms around her friend, laughing, then held her away, asking, "Is it wonderful? Are you going to have it?"

"We told the parentals last night. They're all going batshit. Yeah, I'm having it. I'm really psyched."

"When? *When?*"

"The middle of August."

"Fantastic! I'm jealous."

"Nothing to stop you from doing it."

"Maybe someday."

"Sure. Just as soon as you figure out which one of these guys you'd like to settle on."

"Listen, I never pledged myself to serial monogamy. I like each of them for different reasons. Besides, I'm only sleeping with Daniel. And we're not talking about me here. We're talking about *you!* We'll have to go shopping. I'll buy everything you need. Will you let me?''

"You'll have to stand in line. Dad's already got the fetus signed up for St. Paul's. And my mother's applied for a Bloomingdale's charge card.''

"Will you stop, please?''

"You think I'm kidding? Phone them. You'll see. Grandma Shimura's been on the blower to Japan half the night, and Grandma Bloom probably called the entire Hadassah membership.''

Snow laughed just as the buzzer sounded. Katie automatically looked at the clock on the stove, and Snow at her watch. "Damn!'' Katie said. "They're early.''

"Never mind. We'll celebrate over lunch. I am so happy for you,'' Snow said, pinching Katie's cheek on her way to the intercom.

Snow didn't remember the airmail letter until she got home that evening. Pulling it from her bag she went to stand by the window for a few minutes, relishing the view from her tenth-floor windows. No warehouses converted to lofts, no industrial grime; just houses, brownstones and apartments, all beneath a camouflage blanket of snow that would, by morning, have turned to gray-brown slush but that was, for now, positively beautiful. She loved this apartment, with its old-fashioned high ceilings and ornamental moldings, its uneven floors and big windows.

At last she sat down in one of the commodious armchairs to read the letter.

Hollycote, Old Bodmin Way,
Bodmin, Cornwall

Dear Miss Devane:

I've thought of you often in the past months, having carried your card with me for quite some time, but this is the first opportunity I've had to sit down and write.

You may have wondered what became of me, and now that I am at last settled, I wanted to put your mind at ease, and also to thank you for inspiring me to do what I ought to have done far sooner.

Your enormously generous offer to pay my way home touched me deeply and started me asking myself why I was living as I was, in a city I disliked, in a country that had never felt welcoming to me. The answers that came were most unsettling and prompted me to contact my family after a very lengthy silence on my part. I enlisted their help in returning home and asked them to write to me in care of my social worker.

After posting the letter, I started back on my meds, which I'd been taking only intermittently up to that point, and waited quite anxiously for some reply. In the meantime, I came upon a piece about you in the newspaper and began to comprehend some of your anger, as well as your kindness. I think you are an exceptionally kind and courageous girl, and insightful, too. It was your comment that no matter where I went Michael would be with me that spurred me in the end to restore communication with my family.

My sister provided the British consulate in New York with the documentation I required to obtain a new passport, and she also arranged for my passage home by ship. I arrived back in England in early September to discover, happily, that I had, in my absence, come into a small inheritance, one sufficient to purchase a dilapidated little cottage I pretend is a caravan, situated near the moor, and to take care of my few needs. I recently befriended a rather scruffy mongrel who'd been abandoned. We have a great deal in common, said mongrel and I, and the two of us take long walks together and live quite amicably.

I am, of course, still bonkers, but, to be honest, I prefer madness. It has its comforts. And no one here has appeared to notice, which is so very British! I do like that about my fellow countrymen—they have such exquisite manners, for the most part.

If you ever come to England, I should very much like to see you again. I suspect you would enjoy Cornwall. Like you, it, too, has rather an angry nature, and refuses to be subdued. It would be lovely to hear from you, should you ever get a moment. For now, I send you my gratitude and my affection.

Your friend,
Irene Asher-Blaine

Acknowledgments

I am enormously indebted to Sergeant Frank Torres of the Missing Persons Squad (NYPD) for his time, his patience in giving me details of how his department operates, and his invaluable assistance in working out, step-by-step, the details of the reunion for this book.

I thank Cynthia and Michael Waldin for creating remarkable children and for allowing me to know, in particular, the peerless Sandy, and to use his Doppelganger as one of my characters.

I thank Jerry Davidoff of Davidoff & Saxl for his help regarding wills and probate; Frank O'Meara of Janney, Montgomery, Scott for his help with stockbroking information; Marc Silverman of Mann & Company for allowing me to "borrow" his accounting files system; Steve Davis (former Captain, NYPD) and Hank Flynn (former FBI agent) for their nuts and bolts assistance. I am also most grateful to everyone at Mira, especially Dianne Moggy and Amy Moore, for their faith in my work.

And, finally, my love and gratitude to Claire Smith for tolerance above and beyond the call for so many years, and to Dina Watson for the valuable brainstorming and for keeping my sense of humor alive.

TELL THE AUTHOR

Dear Charlotte Vale Allen,
I just finished reading Somebody's Baby *and wanted to tell you what I
thought of the book.*

_____

_____

_____

Sincerely,

name _____

address _____

city, state, zip code _____

(please print)

*If you are reading a library book, please copy this page and leave it for
the next reader.*

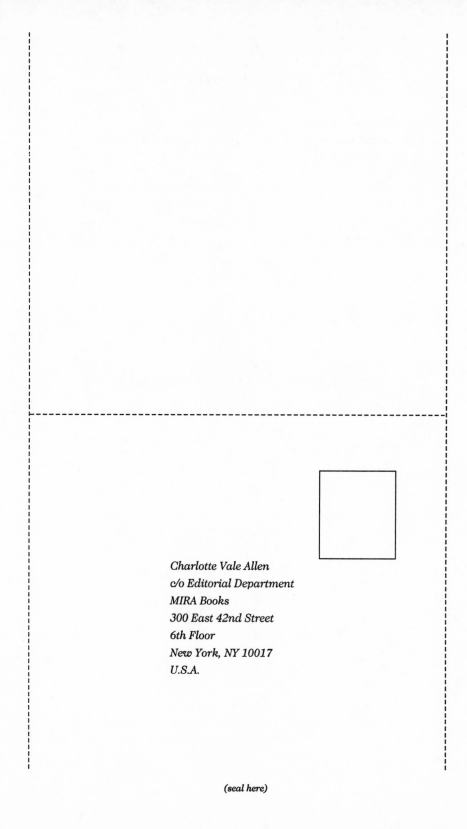

Charlotte Vale Allen
c/o Editorial Department
MIRA Books
300 East 42nd Street
6th Floor
New York, NY 10017
U.S.A.

(seal here)

TELL A FRIEND

Dear _____,

I just finished reading Somebody's Baby *by Charlotte Vale Allen and wanted to tell you about it because I think it's a book you will enjoy as much as I did.*

Sincerely,

_____

Somebody's Baby, *published by MIRA Books, is available wherever books are sold.*

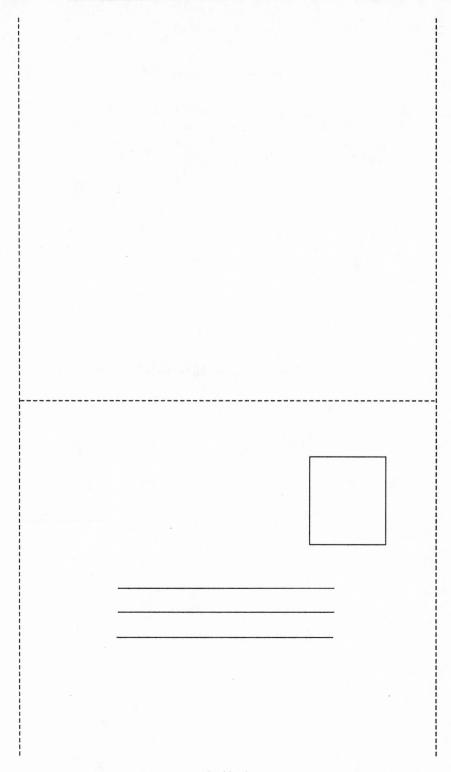

(seal here)